Praise for The Spy... Sing Until You Die

Whether reading sweet who-dun-its in fun rural settings, hard-hitting revenge, or behind-the-scenes of World War II with civilian spies or the harrowing aftermath of a soldier's experience, Carole Brown has a story for everyone. Clean, Christ-centered, and down to earth, Brown's multi-layered tales enrich all readers.

~**Lisa Lickel**, author
of **Understory** and **Undercut**

Excellent writer, excellent novel.

~**Donn Taylor, Retired Leutenant Colonel**
author of **The Lazarus File**
and **Lightning on a Quiet Night**

Sit on the edge of your seat for this roller-coaster ride of WW2 espionage. American spies with their French connections avoiding the dangers of the German Nazis, and juggling work with romantic capers...the only thing missing is James Bond himself!

~**Charles Seymour Sgt USAF**

*In **Sing Until You Die,** Carole Brown perfectly recreates the atmosphere and spirit of the American troops and those serving in other capacities during the depths of World War II. Claire Anne Rayner, beautiful and often considered to be spoiled, has the voice of an angel. She's selflessly devoting this talent to cheer the new troops who are being sent to fight in the war that raged across the seas. Wills Mason, an American civilian spy working with the Army, is a man Claire Anne has known all her life and despises. Could it be she is being used by nefarious forces to aid the enemy? Can Wills intervene and prove her innocence? This is a story that intrigues from the earliest chapters and would be a* compelling and engrossing read for historical romantic suspense fiction fans of all ages.

~**Nike N. Chillemi**, author
Acts of Malice, Courting Danger
and other mystery novels.

Nobody can write a scene like Carole Brown.

When you read her books you might want to grab something, like the back of a chair, least her writing knock your socks off.

~**Molly Noble Bull**,
Award winning author
Gatehaven

I, Steven Brown, as a proud veteran Marine Corps Corporal, have read this book and found it to be a really good read. Author Carole Brown wrote it so you wanted to finish the book to find out if who you thought was the villain was or someone else. She did a fantastic job with the time appropriate language. This book has a love story, a very good suspense plot...but what I liked the most, it had characters who loved this country the way I do and always will.

~ **Steven Brown, Marine Corps Corporal.**

Sing Until You Die

The Spies of World War II

Carole Brown

STORY AND LOGIC Media Group
Printed in the USA
For the discriminating reader...
Because we believe story *needs* logic

Sing Until You Die © 2020 by Carole Brown
Published by STORY AND LOGIC Media Group, New Carlisle, OH 45344
For the discriminating reader...
Because we believe story *needs* logic

Printed in the USA
Cover Design by SAL media

This is a work of fiction. Names, characters, places, and incidents are either a product of the author's imagination or are used fictitiously. Any resemblance to persons living or dead is purely coincidental.

ISBN-13: **978-1-941622-64-3**
ISBN-10: 1-941622-64-X

Library of Congress Cataloging-in-Publication Data

Brown, Carole
Sing Until You Die: a novel/Carole Brown
pbk) **978-1-941622-64-3**

1. World War Fiction 2. Military Spy Fiction 3. Historical Romance 4. Romantic Suspense 5. Inspirational Romance 6. War and Women.7. Woman Patriots Fiction I. Title.

Library of Congress Control Number: 2020945812

Any scripture quotations are from the King James Version of the Bible

WWII Expressions and Words

Ace: top notch expert

Cabbage: money
Corny: Hokey, tacky

Doll Dizzy: girl crazy
Dish: Good looking

Girly: affectionate term for a woman
Grandstanding: bragging/showing off

Killer-diller: the best

Lettuce: money
Lulu: excellent, outstanding

Mellow: attractive young man

Jerk: Less than desirable person

Stool Pigeon: an informer or tattletale

German Words:

Danke: thank you
Freund: friend
Ja: yes
Kaffee: coffee
Liebe: love
Schon: beautiful
Stark: strong

French Words:

Amour: love
Belle: beautiful
De Rien: you're welcome.
Fort: strong
Non: No
Oui: Yes

This book is dedicated to:

Tim, who's a faithful reader—always!

Meghan, who's promoted me and who loves my WWII books!

To all the **Fans/Readers** who enjoy my stories!

And to all **military individuals**
Who have served our country!

Acknowledgements:

Most of all to Danny, Dan and Amy
for listening as I read this book to them,
who offered suggestions and corrections,
and, as always, encouraged me.

To those who shared military information with me
so I can create realistic books.

And could I forget Sharon?
My encourager, my editor,
and my friend.

Carole Brown

Sing Until You Die

Did her promises mean anything when she couldn't even keep one?

The Spies of World War II

Chapter One

1944

Wills Mason stared at the stage. Or more specifically, the woman on the stage. Her voice was like the sweetest singing bird in the world, bringing tears to even the most hardened soul. And those who shied from showing such emotion, casually and furtively swiped at those traitor drops of moisture. Her voice rose to powerful, heart-stopping heights that boosted the most depressed individuals to levels of enthusiasm they'd never have dreamed they could achieve. The depths her voice sank to, crooned words of love, encouragement and hope to the most depressed.

Wills' own heart responded to that voice, the voice that belonged to the woman he'd loved all his life. Her blond hair with its touches of red gold shone like a crown on her shapely head. The white gardenia adorning her shoulder placed her in a different category than many of the singers who entertained the troops. She was confident and radiating love to the soldiers making each one of the men staring up at her feel she was their personal encourager. But more than that, in many a man there, memories of mothers praying and wives longing for their husband's returns, lingered as precious images in their minds.

The men adored her, and rightfully so. Not because of a romantic love, but because her voice evoked emotions some of them had not felt in a long, long time. Many of these men would go to sleep tonight dreaming, remembering the songbird who'd boosted their spirits as they prepared to leave on their tour of war

He hadn't seen her for over a year of the two years he'd been serving as a spy. She was still as small as he remembered her, but instead of remaining a young girl she'd bloomed into a woman.

The WAC who stepped up beside him didn't say a word until Wills glanced at her.

"He's ready for you, Sir."

Wills didn't speak, but turned again to stare at Claire Anne Rayner. He might never see her again, given what he was about to be asked to do next. His heart said *"stay,"* but his mind insisted he do his duty as he'd been trained.

"Lead the way, Owens."

The young woman, barely out of her teens, led the way, and Wills followed, not looking back at the woman who despised him and who would never forgive him for their past.

Chapter Two

The lights were bright, but not so much Claire Anne Rayner couldn't see the upturned faces of the men seated below the stage. Most times she avoided looking directly at them. She didn't want to see the expressions written across their faces. Too heartbreaking. Too emotional. It was better to focus on singing topnotch to give them the hope—and a bit of laughter and fun—they desperately needed before heading out to their war destinations.

She loved to sing. It'd been her passion forever—well, except for a brief period when she was rebelling a bit over her oldest sister's domineering ways. But Emma Jaine had been right, and Claire was glad she'd buckled down to do the study she'd longed for with the most prestigious voice teacher in the state.

She'd put all that on hold after a couple years of study. Singing for the service-men meant she was doing something good—giving a part of herself to help in this war that raged across the seas. Proving to her family and others she could do something beneficial. Maybe they wouldn't consider her so spoiled after this.

They loved her. Very much so. She missed them when she was away. All of them. From Papa Rayner to her sisters, Emma Jaine, her husband Tyrell Walker, and their adorable twins—Peter and Jaine Marie, to Josie, Jerry Patterson and their beautiful daughter, Josephine Elana. And could she forget Harriet and Jonah—their forever house-help?

Her gaze swept over the large group of soldiers and landed on the man and woman leaving the room. She could only see the back of them. Was that...Wills Mason, Harriet and Jonah's son? That straight back. That honey brown hair.

Turn around, you.

Of course, the man didn't turn around.

And why should she care anyway? She really, really didn't like him.

Chapter Three

"**S**he's an emotional singer. The men love her." The man spoke in a low voice to his companion, his feet shifting constantly as he waited on the desired approval he craved from his boss.

"Never mind that. All we care about is that the guy gets the message. That he knows the date and place."

"Yeah."

"Yeah?"

The snapped word, the sarcasm and anger coming from between the lips of the man's superior, caused the man to cringe. He hurried to correct his response. "You're right as always."

"You don't have to tell me something I already know."

The scorn in the voice didn't ease the man's concern any.

His superior went on talking as if not seeing—but probably gloating over his weakness. "I don't care how it happens, but it must be done. I want this more than I can express. You'd better be sure you don't mess it up for me, or I'll see that you disappear. No one will ever find your body."

With a cursory gleeful glance at the paleness of the man, his superior continued, "You keep your eyes peeled and report to me any sign of rebellion on her part. Are you listening?"

"I am." A vigorous nod of the head.

"She is not to get a hint that she's aiding us. Do you know what will happen if she starts sniffing around?

"I think I do."

"She'll not only get hurt, but you, being my right hand man, will suffer severely."

"You've made it very clear."

"I want to emphasize once again that this means more to me than anything. I will not hesitate taking down anyone who stands in my way. I will get what I

want."

The man nodded. "I understand. I won't fail you."

"Good. You do the job, and I'll make sure you're recompensed right along with me."

A lofty look and a smirk at the man was not much reassurance that his superior one could be trusted.

But the man decided he'd better take what he could get. Anything was better than an unknown grave.

Chapter Four

"There's been a new development in this case. Someone's reported a rumor of a special spying method going on. There are certain people being used to convey messages. I need to know if they know they're being used or are complicit. I want to know how this is working, who's doing the actual messaging and who's behind it all." Colonel Waverly sat back in his huge leather chair, hands folded over his stomach, the large window behind him allowing the sun to brighten his head of white hair.

Wills nodded. "I can work on that, Sir."

"There's been a name bandied about." Colonel Waverly eyed him. "It seems you know this person."

His white mustache bobbed every time he spoke, and Will forced himself not to smile. The colonel was a good enough man. Great even, but he was a serious-and-to-the-point type of leader who preferred nonsense be kept away from work. Wills had always understood that. In fact, he liked the man. Liked working under him. Respected him.

"I don't understand, Sir. I don't believe I associate with anyone who's possibly a spy."

"Are you sure about that?" The man lowered his head and gazed at him in an attempt, Wills figured, to make him squirm.

It didn't work. Colonel Waverly had tried that trick one too many times.

"I'm pretty sure, Sir."

"Pretty sure? That's not an answer."

"Who is the person you're talking about?"

"Claire Rayner. I think you've known her almost all your life?"

"Sir? Claire?" If the man had hit him with one of his big hands, Wills couldn't have been more surprised. "I can't believe that. I won't. This has to be bad information." He paced to the window then back again.

"Wills Mason?

"Yes, Sir?"

"It's up to you to prove she's innocent or bring her in. Find out what's going on. Keep track of her every move. Get close to her."

"That will be a little hard, Sir."

"Why is that?"

"She despises me."

Colonel Waverly stared at him, his eyes still as sharp as ever. "Then it's your job to change that situation."

When Wills looked doubtful, the colonel snapped at him. "Can you do the job, or do I need to assign someone else to it?"

"I can do it, Sir." He spoke the words with his mouth, but inside his heart he wasn't at all sure.

"Good. You're flying out tonight and your destination is France. Here's the file that we have on Claire Rayner. Not much in it yet." The colonel tapped the file. "This is top secret. You are not to speak to anyone about this newest duty. No one, Mason. Do you understand?"

"I do, Sir."

"Your plane is leaving at 2100 hours."

"You know I'm afraid to fly—unless it's that new fancy aircraft that was just tested. I really could go for that— you know, Sir, as a chance to experience flying in that."

"Are you finished?"

"Quite, Sir." Wills struggled to hide his grin.

"Then I suggest you stop wasting my time and get to work. You know I hate tomfoolery during work hours."

"Yes, Sir. I'll be ready." Wills snapped a salute and headed for the door. But as he shut it, he caught Colonel Waverly shaking his head, a grin on his lips. The old man was a good guy. A right down great guy, in his book.

All he needed to do now was pack a bag and wait till time to leave. On board, he'd settle into brushing up on his French and study the file he'd be carrying for part of the journey.

A file that contained all the information someone had found on Claire Anne Rayner: suspected spy.

Chapter Five

The taxi swerved in and out around the cars on the streets, speeding Claire toward the airport.

Normally she performed in the evenings after the soldiers had finished their daily routines. But today she'd sung to them earlier because of their upcoming flights to France tonight.

Claire blinked at the sudden tears that dampened her cheeks. She'd seen way more than she wanted. The suffering injured men this morning, the fear in the eyes of those being deployed tonight to France, that overcame all the pretense of bravado they might show, the desire in all their hearts to go home and forget this savage war that was devastating everyone.

Only none of it would stop. Not until peace was won. Claire swallowed back her tears. She would do her part, little as it was.

Minutes later, the taxi pulled into the parking area where an airplane waited and she saw the dark-haired man walking across the tarmac to her.

Norman Tyson. His stride was purposeful, the tilt of his head slightly arrogant and self-assured. He was a handsome man—a *wealthy*, handsome man—who made her heart beat a little faster every time she saw him. Which, if she told the truth, had happened quite often for awhile now.

She waited inside the taxicab and watched him come. And then he was there, tossing a bill through the window at the driver and opening her door, his moves smooth and calculated.

"Claire." He leaned down to kiss her cheek.

"Norman."

He tucked her arm under his after she stepped out of the taxi and picked up her bag. "Are you ready for this?"

"I am."

He gave her a glance of approval. "You're my type of

woman, you know."

She flicked him a smile. He was her type of man, too—at least the wealthy part, the good-looking part. Whether any of the rest of him figured into her plans was yet to be decided.

Claire started up the steps of the plane, Norman following. She walked straight to the front and the smaller, more private compartment. Two other people sat in seats across from each other. She had no clue who the one seriously-young woman was, but the other—

Was Wills Mason. Her sister's best friend. And the man she deeply despised.

~*~

Wills Mason saw her enter the cabin, and it startled him a little. Not enough to outwardly show it, but enough he felt it. The last time—not this evening at the hall where she'd sung to the troops, but at home in Cincinnati—she'd laid him out, but good. Let him know what she thought of him, and when she wanted to see him again.

Which was never.

Just because he'd finished up his last project of making sure Jerry Patterson was safe from an enemy and helping to bring that enemy down, he'd been in boisterous spirits looking forward to being with his doting parents and the Rayners again. Josie—and the others—had been overjoyed, but Claire?

Not so much. He'd whirled her around, hoping her attitude toward him had changed a little, but no. It definitely hadn't, and her scorching dressing-down had created shocked expressions on everyone's face but his.

He was used to it.

Or at least should have been.

That's what he got for dreaming and getting his hopes up.

Now, he watched her come down the plane aisle and saw the moment she recognized him. A flash of distaste ran across her face, followed by a definite look of annoyance, and then determination—probably to ignore him.

So be it.

~*~

The plane was a large military one, and the only reason Claire, her manager and their musicians had been able to hitch a ride was because of Norm's connections. When that man called in favors, they weren't usually ignored or refused.

It was already noisy. The back three-quarters of the craft was filled mostly with soldiers, laughing and hooting when she passed through them, but respectful enough. In the front of the plane the sergeants and Lieutenants had taken a few of the seats, her band members were slouching and preparing for a long nap, with only four seats still empty, and that was where she headed. Claire settled into her seat, across the aisle from Wills and the WAC, by the window, placing her bag at her feet, and a file and book to read on her lap, if she had a chance. Norman sat beside Claire, directing all his conversation at her.

She glanced out the window, but couldn't resist another quick glance at Wills, who was so much part of her family's life. She knew Josie and Wills had always been best friends, her father considered him like a son, offering to pay for any training he wanted, and Emma Jaine loved him like a brother. His parents had been with them forever, and she couldn't imagine the boarding house without them there.

So why did she dislike him so much? She wasn't jealous, not at all, that he was so well-liked in her home. She loved Harriet and Jonah, their employees, and like the rest of the Rayners, was close to them. She and her sisters had always felt comfortable talking with Harriet about anything in life that bothered them. And the woman had listened and cuddled them close when they needed some motherly loving.

"Have you had a chance to look over those new songs I gave you?" Norm cast a quick glance at her than returned to his study of the paper he was reading.

"A little."

"I really think you need to perform some of them in France. They were written for you to do that."

"I know, Norm. Stop pushing. I'm planning on working on them while we're flying. Looks like the crew is preparing to get some sleep."

"Yeah. Joey tried to whine his way out of coming, but I put the screws on him, and he saw the light."

"You're really mean, you know, when you want to be."

"Ah, girly, you know better than that. Ain't no one as soft as me." Norm reached over to pull her close.

Claire gave in to his hug which she was used to. But her gaze shifted across the aisle. Wills was staring at her, and was that a frown on his face?

Why should he be frowning at her? It was none of his business if a friend of hers gave her a hug. She frowned at him, but he didn't drop his gaze. Instead, it shifted to Norm...and was that hardness that filled his eyes?

She wanted to stomp her foot and scold him like she'd always done at home whenever he and Josie would be sliding down banisters screaming like banshees, laughing like hyenas, and getting on the nerves of everyone in the boarding house. But did they care?

Brash and annoying, there wasn't anything daring the two wouldn't try. And even today, even after Josie was married to Jerry and had borne an adorable baby girl, whenever the family was able to gather together, those two would behave like fat-heads.

She wanted to do a lot of things to show him her disdain, but she wouldn't. She, at least, was too well-bred for that.

Instead, she turned her head to stare out the minute window. Unwanted, the feeling of shame swept through her.

~*~

Wills couldn't take his eyes off of Claire. He knew it made her uncomfortable, but then she made him uncomfortable allowing that man to be as friendly as he was. Not that they'd been *too* friendly, but he wasn't keen on seeing her with...another man.

That was ridiculous. He had no hold on her. Not even a hope that he would ever have a reason to object. "Mr. Mason, do you need me to do anything for you?"

Wills glanced at the young woman. The WAC Colonel Waverly had ordered to be his attendant, his right-hand. She was attractive and seemed intelligent. Definitely young, eager and willing to help, so why not use her?

"You needing something to do, Owens?"

"Yes, Sir!"

Wills grinned as he held out the thickest file he held. "Then you can go through this and tell me what you think."

Owens stared down at the thick file, and just a touch of dismay quivered on her features, then was gone. She looked up at him, and they both laughed.

"Just read what you can. It'll be a big help."

Her smile widened her lips. "Will do, Sir."

"You don't have to call me sir, Owens."

"I think I do, Sir." Her gaze met his, an unspoken message blatant in her gaze.

Wills nodded then lifted his gaze to Claire sitting across the aisle.

Her gaze rested on him and his companion, and it wasn't goodwill he read in her eyes.

~*~

"Hey, look. There's that singer who entertained some of the troops in Cincinnati last week. Remember? We were there helping out at the center."

The voice was loud and caught Claire's attention. She looked up from studying the musical lines and notes of one of the songs in her file and cast a quick glance at the back of the plane. A man was standing, staring back at her, his excitement infectious. Other heads raised, gazes fastened on her.

"Hold on, guys. Miss Rayner has work to do. She needs to rest her voice." Norm had half risen, holding out a hand in protest.

Voices rose to argue with Norm.

"Sing to us, Songbird."

"We want to hear the songbird sing."

"Give us something to remember, Baby."

Claire touched Norm's arm as she stood. "I'll sing to them, Norm."

One of her musicians already had his guitar in his

hands, strumming.

Claire nodded at him, he played a short introduction, and she sang.

"*Soft as the summer breezes of home...high as the tallest church dome...my memories are played and replayed...of kisses from my soldier so brave.*"

She sang, and sang yet two more songs, before she held up a hand, and laughing, warned the crowd of attentive listeners, she'd be too hoarse to sing when they landed, if they didn't allow her to rest her voice.

They clapped then and cheered, and Claire tossed a kiss to the soldiers. It did her heart good to share a little sunshine to them before they headed to the battlefields, and many times, to death.

She sat as the applauding diminished.

"Well done, Girly, although I wish you'd listen to me. That's why you have a manager. You don't have to jump every time someone yells. You're a professional, on the road to success once this war is over..."

Claire tuned him out. She really wished he wouldn't go on and on about what he thought. What mattered was what she wanted, and neither Norm nor anyone else was going to stop her.

She gave another glance around the interior of the plane, but it ended on Wills Mason. He was staring at her, again, and the emotion in his eyes heated her face. It was so obvious, his honey brown eyes warm and endearing...

Endearing? Why would she think that?

Once again, Claire found herself turning her gaze to the window, where the night sky was dark, with no illuminating moon and no sparkling stars, and definitely no warmth like what she'd just seen in Wills' eyes.

Chapter Six

The spy—at least he loved calling himself that—read the letter again. They were always succinct and to the point. *We've got the girl on board. The one we talked about helping out? He's keeping her in line. Neither know the truth. We're good to go. Awaiting further orders.*

He wasn't supposed to read these messages. That was why they were stamped and sealed to be mailed. This letter should have already been in the mail, but he'd not had the chance to steam it open till now. So...tomorrow, for sure, he'd get it in the mail. He'd found a way to steam them open with little or no damage to the envelope. No one would ever know but him which made him much smarter than his unpleasant boss.

His boss was an idiot. That was a laugh. Could be, if he worked his cards right, he might advance higher than his superior. Wouldn't that be something? He could just see her face if—no, when—that happened.

His job was a fairly easy task—one of the easiest he'd ever done—given the subject bossy was talking about was easy to hoodwink. But then, he had to admit, when had he ever been known to fail in these assignments he was given? He wanted to yawn to show his boredom. He knew them by heart, but who would see—and understand—why he was bored?

The spy—it did sound good. As if he was dangerous and smart—looked across the street, thinking. How could he take his boss down? A stabbing would be quick, but too bloody for him. Hmmm. Shooting? He frowned. He'd never been much of a shot, and had had to bribe his way through basic training to pass. There had to be a way—an easier, unnoticeable way to kill his boss.

But why worry right now? Until he knew who was over his boss, then he could do nothing.

His mind moved on to much more pleasant thoughts.

He'd never been to France before, so while he was there, he planned on enjoying himself, as much as he could. Wine and women—that's if this insane war allowed for such frivolities. But there was more than one way to get what he wanted.

His boss had telephoned him earlier in the day and the cordiality had been a shock after their last meeting. "This is a big assignment. Bigger than what you realize. Bigger than any of us realized. But I want you to know, we've got your back, and when this job is completed, you've got a big raise coming. You get this done successfully, and you'll be in the right lane for more and better jobs." There was a brief pause. "I assume you like living the life of the successful?"

Oh, yeah. He'd work his tailbone off to get there. He could almost smell that luscious odor of success. The power. The riches. The parties. The prestige. The women.

But he was gonna do it his way. Right now, he'd keep her placated. "You betcha, I can do this. Just watch me."

His superior's tone turned serious. Deadly serious. "Don't get cocky. You know what happens to those who fail."

It wasn't a question, and it crash-landed him to earth fast. "That I do. That I do. Don't worry about me. I'm focused on making this happen. On seeing our side win. I'll do whatever it takes."

"Good. See that you don't forget that." And she hung up.

The subordinate looked down at the envelope again and re-read the name and address on the letter. He'd already memorized it from before. Now...well, now, he was growing tired of orders, orders, orders. It was time he had a talk with the real boss. The only one he wanted to answer to.

The real spy. This Albert Miller.

Chapter Seven

The aircraft was cruising to a stop when Wills stirred. He'd dozed off and on during the long flight, but none of it had been a comfortable sleep. Still, he was used to going without sleep, especially when on duty.

He glanced over at Owens, whose head lay on his shoulder. She was still asleep, so he nudged her arm. "Wake up, Sleepyhead. Time to rise and shine. We've got work to do."

She stirred, her eyes fluttered open, then as realization hit her, she sat up, her face rapidly turning a bright shade of red. "Sir, I'm sorry. I meant no disrespect."

"Don't let it happen again, Owens, or you'll be out on your ear. No cabbage for you."

She was floundering with an apology when he grinned. "Just joking around. Take it easy. No problem. Let's get our stuff together."

"Yes, Sir."

"I want you to get off here as soon as you can. Go straight to our hotel and make sure these telegrams are sent." He handed her a sheet of paper where he'd scribbled the information.

"Understood, Sir."

"Also be prepared to dress up in your fanciest clothes. I may need you to put on a good act tonight." He nodded and gathered up his files and jacket. He wanted to be one of the first off the plane. A walk to the hotel would clear his head and give time for certain other passengers to get there before he did.

He already had her schedule for her two weeks tour of singing. What he didn't know, and would have to be on the lookout for, was her daily activities. He knew she loved to swim, and like him—although he reckoned, if she had thought about it, she would have been irritated over the thought—enjoyed a good stroll every day.

But he wasn't kidding himself. It wasn't going to be easy to get close to her. Or if that failed, then to keep track of her and keep her from knowing about him following her. Still, he could always plead—well, whatever.

What would Josie have said, if she'd been in a similar situation?

Quit grandstanding. It's too bad if she suspects you. It just makes it all the more fun.

He missed Josie, missed their escapades, their comrademanship. She had been his best buddy, but now she was so wrapped up in her husband and little baby Fina she didn't have time to make mischief with him.

As it should be.

Besides, he was way too busy to have fun.

"I'm ready, Sir, whenever you are."

"Right. Let's go." Wills followed his companion down the aisle, purposely ignoring Claire and her friend. Better to play at disinterest than to force her into more negative reactions to his presence.

~*~

In spite of the war ravaging the world and part of France, it was still a beautiful country. Spring had pushed hard at old man winter, and now, everything was green with flowers everywhere. Well, almost. Men and women with worried, haggard faces waiting on what would happen in the next few months with the neighboring western part of France occupied with German forces.

But the Allied forces had landed in southern France, and troops roamed the streets. That was a measure of hope, although France and the good-ole-United States had never been friends, at least during the revolution, they'd been allies.

Wills had no doubt that the Germans would be defeated. His country's soldiers were too dedicated, too determined to succeed, even though the cost would be high.

He'd sent Owens on to the hotel with their luggage and the telegrams. Right now, all he could think about was breathing a spot of fresh air and taking in the sights. That, and the woman walking ahead of him

Claire didn't realize she was being followed, and how she managed to get rid of the leech that had sat beside her on the trip over here was beyond any guess he could come up with. Wills smiled. Let Claire Anne argue with him on their incompatibility again. She'd never convince him.

They were almost back to the hotel when a sleek, dark blue sedan passed him—slowly. The back window was down, and the man inside turned his head, the expression on his face frightening—if Wills had been the sort to be easily scared.

He wasn't, but that didn't mean he was careless or too comfortable not to pay attention to possible problems.

No, the guy's expression didn't bother him, but what did bother him was the car slowing even more to stay in step with Claire. He couldn't hear what was being said, but she didn't look too distressed.

Wills frowned. The guy in the car was holding out a piece of paper, and Claire walked over to the car, took it then walked away.

They had reached the hotel, and she was at the door, but before she entered, she tossed a laughing comment to the man then waved him away. The car sped up, and Claire entered the hotel. Safe. For now.

Wills heaved a breath of air, glad he hadn't had to intervene. That would have been disastrous, at least as far as the relationship between them went. If you could call what they had a relationship.

He followed Claire inside the hotel—the same one he was using—and watched as she crossed the lobby, never looking back. Just before she began climbing the stairs, she stopped, crunched the paper into a wad and tossed it into a trashcan, smiling.

When she'd disappeared, Wills hurried to the trashcan and pulled out the paper.

Meet me early, Girlie, and I'll take you to dinner. We've

got lots to talk about.

What was that about? He hadn't seen the man's face, just the ring on his finger. It wouldn't have been her manager who would have left a note at the front desk. One of her band members? Or something more sinister?

Had that car held someone besides her manager? And had she foolishly flirted with that person just because he'd offered some smiles and flattering words?

She was asking for trouble, if that was the case.

Chapter Eight

"**H**ow do I look?" Wills grinned at the brunette who answered her hotel door after he knocked that evening. "Wow, Owens. *You're* a dish tonight. Not sure I'll be able to keep those doll dizzies away from you."

She smiled up at him and tossed her hair off her shoulder. "You're pretty mellow yourself, Boss."

He gave her a mock scowl. "You remember that, will ya? I'm the boss, and that means you pay attention to me."

"Don't worry about me. I'm focused."

"You better be." Wills retrieved the crunched up paper Claire had tossed. "I want you later tonight or first thing tomorrow, depending on how late we are, to see if you can get a sample of Claire's manager's handwriting. See if it matches the writing on this paper. Can you do that?"

"I can, and I will. Let me lock it up in my room till we get back."

When she returned to the door, Wills instructed her on what he wanted. "We're in love, got that? I want to put on a convincing act to keep Claire from being paranoid at my presence or suspicious." He held out his arm then lowered his voice. "We can do this."

"You got it, Boss. I didn't lead in two of my high school plays for nothing. I'm good at pretending. I won't let you down." She picked up a tiny bag and a light-weight fur cape.

"Ooo la la. Where did you come across that?"

"My mother's. She loaned it to me on strict orders it wasn't to be returned damaged in any way."

"Then we'd better make sure of that, hadn't we?"

They headed down the wide, open, curving staircase, taking their time, pretending to ignore everyone else while murmuring comments that meant little, but keeping count of everyone lingering in the lobby.

It was only then that he caught a glimpse of the woman he was tailing, standing with that guy she'd flown here with, along with three other men and another woman.

He wanted to stare. He really, really did. She was a knockout tonight, in that metallic gold dress. She'd clipped her hair back on one side with a creamy-yellow gardenia—whether it was artificial or real, Wills couldn't tell, and didn't care.

She was stunning.

A nudge in his side drew his attention back to his companion.

"Hey, you. If you keep staring at that woman, people will wonder what's going on. Here I dress up for you, to help you, I mean, and you're all eyes for another woman. Should I pout?"

"Definitely not. You're pretty snazzy yourself." He tucked her arm a little closer to him. "Just remember, you keep those brown eyes of yours peeled on our target."

"Will do, Boss."

"Hey, none of that. While we're here, you'd better get used to calling me Wills."

She nodded. "I can do that, Wills Mason."

They loitered in the large entryway, strolling a bit but never stopping. Wills knew no one, but he nodded at several different people and kept an eye out for anything suspicious.

When they finally headed to the expansive—and expensive—looking restaurant, the maître de' nodded at them and escorted them to a table for two toward the stage area—but off to the side. Perfect. Just what he'd asked for.

They'd have a good seat tonight for the show. Wills didn't imagine Claire would be singing—at least, he hadn't seen the name of the hotel on her itinerary to do so, but he hoped she'd be dining here where he could keep an eye on her. If she and her crew had decided to head to a different restaurant, then this evening was a bust.

Wills had no more than thought that when Claire and

her crew entered the restaurant. They didn't have a front row table, but about midway back, they circled a larger table, laughing, and some of them—Wills frowned—seemed as if they were already wound up from too much to drink.

Claire. Claire. You know your father would be upset if he saw you around these people. You're too much of a lady to behave like them. Don't do it.

He'd been informed that the meals might not be quite what they should be with the war raging miles away, but he couldn't have asked for a better meal. He was used to home-cooked meals by his mother, and as long as it was tasty, he was satisfied.

Tonight, the Smoked Salmon with Herbed Crème that followed the appetizer was still the best he'd ever eaten. Only one other person he'd known had loved it as much as he, and that person sat at a table midway back. The singer on stage sang in French, for the most part, and his voice was good. Wills understood a good bit of it, thanks to his weeks of studying the language.

When the waiter brought a small selection of cheeses out, along with a couple different fruits, Wills looked up at the stage and saw Claire walking across it to the microphone. Her musicians had taken their places and were playing an introduction. Claire swayed with the music.

She sang each verse twice. First in French, then English.

"That ole man in the moon keeps watching me, smiling and making glee, 'cause my love's leaving me, and I'm lonesome tonight, while he's determined to win this fight. Oh, man in the moon, stop laughing at me, he's gone yeah, but he'll be back soon. I love him too much to ever let go, forever he'll be my beau."

Wills couldn't take his eyes off her. And though the only soldiers in this place tonight were colonels and such, from what he could see from their faces, few weren't thinking of home tonight. It might be glamourous to spend time in a swanky place like

France, but there wasn't anything that could take the place of home.

His own heart beat a little faster, and when once—only once—her gaze lit on him, that spark of hope that had almost died out, flickered a little steadier.

"William Mason. Is that you?"

Wills' mushy mood evaporated as quick as a fog did when a rising sun touched it. He looked up and took in the features of the man who'd been one of his instructors back when he'd been recruited for this work. Herman McCoy, better known by those who didn't care for him as Hermie.

The problem was, no one, except those closest to the cases he was assigned, was supposed to know where he was or what he was doing. For all the general military population knew, he was serving as a soldier wherever. For this man, whom he'd never seemed to be able to like, let alone respect, to see Wills here...

"What are you doing clear over here in France? Thought you had the ability to sneak out of dangerous jobs?" The man's smile was a fake one, his eyes cold and suspicious.

"Who, me?" Wills forced a laugh. "Not on your life. I was sent on an errand and then ordered to deliver a message tonight. I was the lucky one when I came across this dish."

Owens leaned on Wills, throwing an arm around his shoulders.

Wills heard the smacking of gum from his partner-in-crime and caught the glance from his past instructor as he studied Owens.

The man lowered his voice. "Big secret, was it? Anything to do with our next move?"

"No, Sir. It had to do with—" and for once in his life, Wills couldn't come up with a plausible reason.

It was then that Owens reached up, turned his head toward her, and planted a kiss on his lips. She'd barely pulled back when she murmured, "It had to do with a cancelled meeting. You don't know the details."

Wills pulled away from the girl. "As I was saying, it had something to do with a meeting my lieutenant had to miss. I don't know the details."

His instructor stared at him a long moment, not blinking, lips pursed. "Is that right?"

Wills couldn't resist. "Yep, it is."

The man finally swung around, shooting his parting words at him as he left. "I'll be seeing you."

"Let's hope not," Wills murmured then glanced at Owens. "That was some performance you put on there."

"As I said before, I wasn't lead in my school plays for nothing." She tossed that full head of hair off her shoulder.

He laughed and stood. "Let's get out of here."

Wills and Owens threaded their way through the loitering couples, but though he scanned the entire room as they left he didn't see a sign of Claire. He shrugged. Obviously she'd gone to bed, or...

Maybe she and her friends had slipped out to head to a little more rowdy place.

He and Owens were quiet as they climbed the stairs, but at the landing, he cast a glance down at the first floor.

Standing with the man she'd flown with, and two or three others, Claire was paying no attention to whatever was being discussed rather vigorously. Instead, her gaze was fixed on him, and instead of the usual irritation playing across her features, something else lay there.

Something he couldn't recognize at the moment.

Something very disturbing.

~*~

The arguments going on around Claire didn't penetrate her concentration on Wills and that woman walking slowly up the stairs, arm and arm. What did bother her was the continued closeness the two seemed to share. Wasn't she dressed as a WAC on the plane? What was she doing here, with Wills, dressed like the richest person in France with that mink stole over her shoulders?

Jealousy had never been a passion Claire had ever had to deal with. She was way too confident in her own abilities, her own looks and talents to award much attention to someone else's. But this...tonight had been a first, and Claire couldn't figure out why.

Why was she bothered with the picture of Wills and that woman together? And not even that. She figured he was a man and men usually enjoyed women's company, and *that* woman was a beauty with that luscious thick brown hair and eyes, that creamy skin with not a sign of a blemish. Who wouldn't be tempted?

But Wills? What made her think he wouldn't be interested?

Claire frowned.

"I'm going to my room. I'm tired and want to relax." Claire didn't look at Norm but spoke loud enough it got his attention.

"Now? It's early, and you don't have to sing again till tomorrow night. I thought we'd—"

"No. I'm not interested. Good night." And ignoring his continued argument, she headed up the stairs to the second floor. She started down the hall and caught a glimpse of a couple and knew in an instant who they were.

Wills and that woman. They seemed to be talking. Just talking. Until the woman threw her arms around Wills and pulled his face toward hers.

Claire wanted to look away. She really did, but transfixed by the disappointment she felt, she stood rooted in front of her door, key in hand.

And then they drew apart, and the woman tossed her a sheepish grin.

Shoving the key into the lock, Claire threw open her door, entered and didn't shut it any too quietly.

Wills Mason, I'm disappointed. Her words weren't spoken aloud, but deep inside her, she heard them and felt something strike her heart.

She leaned against the door, heat burning her cheeks. "What is wrong with you? Since when do you care what Wills does?"

The keys landed on a side table as she headed to the bathroom. She wanted to look over the words and music of that new song Norm had given her. He'd stated emphatically he wanted her to sing it tomorrow night, and when she'd questioned why, he'd made up some insane reason that was undeniably corny.

But she'd do it. When had she ever refused to do so? Never.

~*~

Claire woke with raindrops streaking down her window. That woke her up. Unlike most people, she loved a walk in the rain—as long as she had the proper gear to wear, which she didn't have. But that nice porter man who'd carried her luggage to her room yesterday might know where she could get some.

Claire stretched then rolled out of bed just as a knock on her door interrupted her thoughts. She grabbed her robe and wrapped it around her, tying the sash as she headed to the door.

"Who is it?"

"Milton, Ma'am. Your porter."

Claire unlocked and opened the door. "Good morning, Milton. I was thinking of you."

"Good morning, Miss Rayner. Surely a young lady like you has younger men to think of than an old man like me."

"Maybe, but sometimes the younger men don't measure up to my standards." She smiled at him He was such a dear. "Do you think you could find me some rain gear? I want to take a walk, but don't want to get all wet and cold. I can't afford to get a cold."

"I can do that for you. So you like to walk in the rain, do you?"

"I do. In fact, I love walking. Always something interesting to see, and besides, it gives me time to take in some fresh air, and I'm sure it's good for me, too."

"I do believe you're right about that." Milton handed her an elaborately decorated box. "I have a package for you."

"What is it?" Claire stared down at the small box tied with a purple ribbon.

"I have no idea, Miss." He tossed her another smile then turned and headed back down the hall.

Shutting the door, Claire moved to her bed and sat. She lifted the box and sniffed. Hmmm. Was that a faint smell of...

She hurried to untie the box, laid the ribbon on the nightstand, then lifted the lid. Inside, on delicate purple paper laid a single gardenia. Pure white with a faint purplish center. She stared down at the exquisite thing before lifting the box to her nose and breathing in deeply.

The smell of heaven, she was sure.

It was fresh and would be perfect with the outfit she'd picked out for tonight. Purple was her favorite color— that of the dress she intended to wear, and with the white gardenia on her wrist, white shoes and a feathery light scarf around her neck, she'd have the outstanding outfit she loved to wear.

There was a small bowl in the bathroom closet, and Claire filled it with water and tenderly placed her gardenia in it.

That Norm. After all this time, he still remembered gardenias were her chosen flowers for performances. Maybe he did care after all. She'd have to study on it some more.

~*~

"You know, don't you, that I need to figure this out, like yesterday, don't you?" Wills had his head in the files, trying to put together how the intelligence leaks were happening without any clues to who was behind it. Too many episodes of the enemy being ready when the troops supposed it would be a surprise attack. It couldn't be happenstance. There was a leak somewhere, and Wills prayed to God Claire wasn't involved.

"You'll do it, Sir. What can I do to help?"

Their connecting door stood open now, and though Wills had been awake since before five, he hadn't heard Owens stirring until six-thirty. He'd given her time to get ready for the day before hollering he needed her.

Last night had been disturbing for him. Though he'd been in some questionable circumstances—according to his own personal code of honor, because, after all, he didn't have a girlfriend, yet—none of the situations had been where he'd have to pretend a woman was his girl. Owens had kissed him as if she'd had a lot of practice. She was a looker, all right, but he hadn't ever wanted to kiss any girl but one. And that one had made it plain plenty of times she was not interested.

Yet their performance, hopefully, had been convincing to Claire, who might otherwise question if he was keeping tabs on her.

Wills lifted his head and stared at Owens. "What?"

"I asked what I could do for you."

"For starters, how about ordering some light breakfast and coffee?" Wills glanced at the rain-streaked window. "I'd like to go for a walk—"

"In this rain, Sir?" Owens stopped her march back to her room. "You'll get wet."

Wills laughed. "That's the point. It opens my brain. Helps me to think, especially once I get back home and am ready to settle down to work."

"I'll order that coffee then, Sir. At least you won't be alone in that drizzle. I saw that singer girl leaving the hotel, dressed in rainy-weather clothing. I reckon she must like the rain too."

Wills jumped to his feet. "Forget breakfast. Just have some hot coffee ready for me when I return. I'll need it." He grabbed his coat and hat and slid his feet into boots.

"But—"

Ignoring her protest, he grabbed his key and hurried to the door. "Go relax in the breakfast room, or order for yourself. I'll be back in an hour or so."

There was a chance he wouldn't find Claire, and she wouldn't want to be found by him anyway, but he was going. Whether he found her or not wasn't the point. He would be out strolling in the rain same time as she was. That was the point.

He almost ran down the hallway to the stairs, stopped and looked back down the hall, thinking, double checking that no one was watching. Could he? Should he? Would she ever forgive him if she caught him in her room?

Probably not, but that nagging order from Colonel Waverly pushed at him to do it. He had to do it, or said the nagging thought.

Wills retraced his steps, felt in his pocket for the set of tools he carried almost always, found the one he needed and inserted it. A few twists, and he heard the click. Giving a last glance around, Wills slipped into Claire's room and shut the door. The smell hit him immediately and he smiled. It was how her room back home smelled. Lady-like, sweet, strong and wonderful.

Stop it, he ordered himself. *You have no time to romanticize right now. She could be back at any time, and you sure don't want to try to explain why you're in her room, let alone try hiding in her room.*

Wills let his gaze wander around the room then moved. It wasn't his first time doing a furtive search, so he did it quickly but thoroughly.

In the bathroom, his gaze caught sight of the gardenia floating in the small but wide bowl, and he smiled. Claire and her gardenias.

It was time to go. He didn't want to get caught, and besides, if he didn't go soon, he'd miss out on that walk in the rain.

Wills left Claire's room after checking both directions, then headed down stairs. He shoved open the door before the doorman had a chance then studied each direction. Now where would she go? Not downtown where all the stores were. Not today, she wouldn't.

He'd seen the park when he and Owens had arrived yesterday. *That* was it. That was where Claire would go.

Turning right, he began walking, without an umbrella, but wrapped snuggly.

The rain had turned into a downpour. No lightning. No thunder, but quite a downpour. Wills didn't mind. It'd been too long since he'd enjoyed a rain like this. The park was around the corner, but Wills didn't hurry. As much as he hoped Claire was there, wandering around or sitting on a park bench with face toward the sky, allowing the rain to hit her cheeks and drip from her chin, if she wasn't, the time, as far as he was concerned, wasn't wasted. Already, he felt his mind expanding, thoughts and possibilities popping up...

There she was. Sitting in the very middle of the park, alone and quiet. Just as he pictured her. But then, unknown to her, he'd seen her many a time back home, when she'd slipped out after a row with one of her sisters. Trying to find her way as she grew into, and then out of, her teenage years.

Wills chose a bench farther away, one he hoped she wouldn't notice, but a good vantage spot where he could keep watch over her and still enjoy the rain.

It wasn't fifteen minutes later that a vehicle pulled up and a man exited. As tall as he was, as big-built as the man was, Wills was pretty sure it was Norman Tyson.

Was the man keeping tabs on Claire?

Right now though, he watched as the man—weather-proofed with boots, overcoat and umbrella sloshed his way to her. They talked not more than two minutes before she rose and followed him back to the vehicle.

He'd never known Claire to be so meek, but then she couldn't afford to catch a cold or worse. No doubt the man was just looking after her.

Wills watched as the car slowly crept down the street, wishing it was him and his car carrying her back to the hotel. It wasn't though.

He tried to be a good man. He was smart—or so those who ought to know had said—and if catching gals' attention was any indication, then he had to be decent-looking. And he sorely enjoyed a good joke or trick played on another person. That, and anything new and adventurous was up his alley. He couldn't deny it, with sisters—well, Claire, Emma Jaine and Josie—to verify it with differing enthusiasm.

Sighing, he realized that mooning over Claire was not clearing his head.

"What have we here? Why are you sitting here in the rain, dejected and all lonesome? Don't tell me you, of all people, aren't ready to spring another trick on an unsuspecting person?"

Applesauce. It was the jerk again. He'd trained under Hermie McCoy, along with a bunch of others, for the first few months, but then he'd been pulled aside for special training, and he hadn't seen the man for years...until last night.

He'd never liked the guy. Neither did anyone else, for that matter. Behind his back, most called him *Hermie Wormie* because of his constant striving to worm his way

into the higher-ups good graces. Always a stool pigeon, and if there was one thing Wills despised, it was a person always looking for something to push himself up the ladder a bit higher. And if that meant stepping on another soldier, then so be it.

"What are you doing out here in the rain, Hermie? Always thought you preferred your comforts, always sucking up to those in command." He really shouldn't call him out, but he'd wanted to for years. "Are you following me?"

The man smirked. "Why would I want to do that? What I want to know is why you're sitting out here in the pouring rain, doing nothing. Aren't you supposed to be working?"

Wills stood. "What I want to know is why you're not working. Or is bothering me called work nowadays?"

"I'm always working, Willie, and don't you forget it."

Ignoring Hermie's last taunt, Wills walked away, slid around a corner and hid long enough to make sure the man wasn't following him. For all the good that would do. If he'd appeared at the hotel restaurant last night, no doubt he had a room there. And if he had a room there, then he was on a mission. Otherwise, he'd be in the field.

It was time to get to work, and those files in his room wouldn't get studied and re-studied out here. Wills headed back to the hotel.

Chapter Nine

Claire stared down at the song—the second one now—Norm had just handed her. "You want me to have this learned by Friday night?"

"Come on, Baby, you can do this. You're a sweet little cookie, but you're also smart as a tack. Do it for me."

"And what if I say *no*? I mean, how many new songs do I have to learn on this tour? I seldom sing to the same soldiers. Why not repeat some of my oldies? I mean, listen to this:

"One o'clock, two o'clock, if you're not on time, then look out, Baby, you're gonna pay for the crime. I love you, Baby, but at 1620 Mossy Oak Street, You'd better be there, standing, on your feet. Wait for me, Baby, I'll be dressed in red, To you, tonight, I'm gonna wed.

"I don't like it. At all."

"So, you don't like it. Why does it matter?"

Norm eyed her, probably estimating how close he was to winning her over, but he kept on talking.

"And? When the top WAC-ers think they're songwriters, then what's a manager supposed to do? Defy, and lose my job? Then what are *you* gonna do, Girlie, if I go away?"

What had gotten into Norm? He'd never been like this before. She sighed. "All right. I'll sing it, but I've got to have some alone time, so that means get out of here. Send me up something for lunch—you know what I like—and don't let anyone bother me till this evening."

"Got it. Thanks." Norm leaned over and kissed the top of her head. "You're the killer—diller."

She waved a hand at him. "I know that, Norm."

Her day in the rain that had promised to be so restful and wonderful, had just turned sour.

~*~

43

That evening, Claire stared at herself in the full-length mirror. She had to admit—if there'd even been someone there to argue the point—she looked stunning tonight. But then the dress was a perfect fit, and purple always lifted her spirits. It was such a classy color.

She swiveled to glance at the gardenia from this morning. Milton had come through with finding someone who could turn the single blossom into a wrist corsage for her, and she'd been thrilled with the result. That man was well worth the substantial tip she'd given him. He was a gem.

A knock on her door, and Claire called out. "Come on in, Norm. It's open."

The door banged open, and the big man entered, all smiles. "You good?"

"I am, Norm." She accepted his peck on the cheek. "I'm rested and excited to sing tonight. I even memorized the song you gave me this morning. Now all I need to do is have my musicians practice tomorrow and Thursday to be ready for Friday night."

"Already set for tomorrow morning at ten. That work for you?"

Claire nodded. "Will you tie this corsage on my wrist, please? And thank you for it. It's gorgeous and perfect for tonight."

He glanced at her and shrugged. "No problem. Whatever makes you happy."

Twenty minutes later, as she was walking down the hallway, she caught a glimpse of the soldiers gathered in the room set aside for entertainment. They were in boisterous spirits if their laughter and jokes were any indication. Claire smiled. She was ready to give them a good time tonight and leave them with some musical memories to keep their hearts warm even in their toughest battles.

She stood at the sidelines, behind the curtain, listening to the guy out front passing out jokes faster than a racer could run. By the time he finished, the soldiers out front were ready and eager to hear her, and she was ready to sing her heart out for them.

There were a few seconds of silence as the evening

host introduced her. Then...

Claire tilted her head, hoping to better hear the whispered words somewhere near her, but out of sight. Words that were puzzling, but maybe not serious. Still...

"No problems on your part?"

"Not a thing...willing to do..."

Was that Norm? Who on earth was he talking to? He was a topnotch manager. Always on the ball where she was concerned, and probably anything else he dealt with.

"Boss is watching you closely. Careful..."

Claire moved toward the sound of the voices and peeked around the huge rolling platform used for microphones and cameras. Norm and someone else— someone she didn't recognize, a small runt of a man with a mustache and an attitude—stood there close together. She could hear them plainly.

"I'm doing this as a favor—"

"Yeah, yeah. Heard it before. You'll get your money." The man laughed as if he'd just told the biggest joke around.

The band was repeating her introduction, and she had no more time to wonder about Norm.

The men below the stage had quieted, and Claire turned and made her entrance, walking straight to the microphone and began singing a fast song that soon had the men nodding and clapping along with her. Their participation was just so much background noise, so focused she was on setting the atmosphere on fire with her voice.

After a half hour of singing, Claire took a break while a comedian came out to entertain the troops. That went on for forty-five minutes, and Claire took advantage of the time to get outside away from the cigarette smoke and noise. She loved these brave young men serving their country and helping keep America free, but she wasn't so crazy about some of their habits.

Claire strolled along the sidewalk, back and forth, not going far, but enough to stretch her muscles and relax a bit. She was almost ready to head back inside when she caught sight of a couple near one of the big trees in the yard. She walked closer. The woman was facing her, while the man had his back to her. She was the one doing most of the talking while the man sounded distracted and vaguely irritated.

"Are you sure you heard right?"

"I'm sure. I saw them talking, laughing and one time some pretty serious conversation...It *was* them. Tyson and..."

They were talking about Norm and that man, weren't they? Claire edged closer, hoping she wouldn't get caught. One more step to make sure she didn't miss any of the conversation.

"And, get this. He said *she* was willing. Willing to do what, and who else could it have been but C—?"

"Stop. Don't say names. You never know who's listening."

It was a man and a woman all right. The same one she'd seen last night locked in a serious kiss—Wills and whoever the brunette was. Tonight, though, it almost sounded as if they were arguing. Not quite, but on the verge. And they weren't only talking about Norm and stranger man any longer, but her. Or at least, Claire was pretty sure she was the one the woman was about to name.

"I don't have time right now. We'll talk later." Wills whirled and headed in Claire's direction.

No time to make it to the door. No time to pretend she was just passing. The only thing to do—there was Norm, almost on top of her. She did her own whirling and flew into his arms.

"Hold me, Norm. Quick."

He laughed. "What?"

"Do it!" She laid her head on his shoulder and locked arms with him, just as Wills and brunette-woman stepped into view. She ignored them, and pulled Norm on to the door.

Ten more steps. Claire counted them off, feeling Wills' gaze on her back, fearing lest he catch up with them any minute and demand an answer why she was outside, following him.

No. She wouldn't let that happen. Stepping it up a

notch, she paid no attention to Norm and his protesting. The door swung open as a young soldier hurried to open it for her, and Claire let go of Norm's arm and flew to the restroom.

Just long enough to steady her nerves and make sure she wasn't a mess.

~*~

There wasn't anyone in the public restroom when Claire ran into it. Good thing too because she was panting like she'd been chased by a wild dog. Only she hadn't been. It'd been Wills, and, as much as she disliked him, she knew he wouldn't harm a hair on her head.

Claire closed her eyes and moaned. Why was she letting the fact that he was here where she was, bother her so much? Why did it matter? He could go his way, do whatever he was here to do, and she could do the same.

She straightened and drew in a deep breath when the door swung open and Wills' cute brunette walked in. They recognized each other at the same moment, but Claire was the first to turn her attention back to her mirrored self.

The brunette stepped up to the second mirror and fluffed her curly hair. "You're a good singer."

Good? Claire glanced at her, unimpressed with what, she supposed, the woman considered a compliment. "Do you think so?"

Claire would have preferred not to have to speak to her, but even with all her faults, she wasn't mean-spirited. Spoiled, she might be. A snob, she was. Confident in her musical ability and person? Well, definitely. Why shouldn't she be? It was only natural for her to accept and acknowledge the truth.

"Thanks. I think."

The woman snickered. "You think? I just paid you a compliment."

"I see. Then thank you." Claire started to turn away.

"You're welcome." The brunette smoothed down her straight skirt, but glanced at her again. "You know, don't you, the Boss—Wills cares about you?"

Claire turned back to her. "I do know that."

"Then why do you..."

"Why do I what?"

"Why do you dislike him? Spurn him when he wants to be friends? He's a good man, smart, brave, lots of fun and...and loveable. Any woman should be happy to have his attention."

It had been a long time since anyone had criticized her so, subtle as it was. And why did she allow it to bother her now?

Wills had always been like family, a very annoying brother. He had been the worst—well, he and Josie— always loud and obnoxious and into everything daring and wild.

She'd always felt—what? Anger? No, it was deeper than that. Claire stared down at her clasped hands as she faced something she had never accepted before.

Jealousy?

But why jealousy? Because she'd never had anyone that close. Every last one of her family had loved her, but it wasn't as if...it was more as if she was a pet animal, someone to be petted and made over, but never anyone to share their closest secrets.

For a moment, Claire felt such a strange emotion roll over her, she wanted to reach out and hold onto something for support.

Instead, she turned and fled the room, wanting to clasp her ears shut as the brunette called after her. She didn't want to hear anymore. Nothing. The woman had said too much. She couldn't afford to be awakened into reality from the self-centered person she was.

Tears filled her eyes as she rushed toward the back of the stage, but she blinked them away.

Not tonight. Not tonight.

~*~

Her favorite songs to sing were the crooning ones, that left hearts warm and melancholy, and sometimes with tears in sad eyes, but hearts gladdened.

Tonight wasn't one of those nights.

"You ready to go, Girlie?" Norm stepped up in back of her and wrapped his arms around her as she stood on the sidelines ready for the next forty minutes or so.

She pulled away from him, suddenly irritated at him for taking it for granted she wanted his attention. "Stop calling me Girlie. I hate it."

He scowled. "Don't blow a fuse over a hug. I was just trying to give you some support."

Claire drew in a breath. He had, after all, been great in accompanying her, taking care of her in her travels and back home while doing these tours. "I'm sorry. I'm tense tonight for some reason."

"Ah, don't worry about it, G—Baby. You'll be fine. Here, I brought you something."

"What is it?" She didn't take the package he offered.

"Open it."

Slowly, she pulled the lid off the box. Inside laid a wrist corsage of at least three velvety white roses. She stared at them and ran a finger over one of the petals. "They're beautiful."

"I figured you needed something new for this last performance tonight. I sensed you were off kilter and wanted to give you something that would bring a smile to those lips of yours." He reached for the arm that still carried her gardenia from earlier. "Here, let me fasten this fresh corsage to your snazzy self."

He unfastened the beauty and tossed it aside then tied the roses onto her arm.

They were lovely and she appreciated his gesture, but it caused her heart to sink. He didn't remember she always sang with gardenias, if she could get them. Why, if he cared, if he knew her at all, did he not remember it? It was important to her and such a tiny detail about her.

Not that she didn't love other flowers, but the gardenias were special. They'd been her mother's favorite flower, and wearing them gave Claire a warmth and happiness that she carried with her in her finest hours. A bit of her mother.

She stared down at them, disappointed and sad. Which was crazy. *Just be glad he thought of you in such a lovely gesture.* Her admonishment to herself didn't help much, but she straightened her shoulders and smiled. "Thank you, Norm."

Her music cue began, and Claire started to turn and walk back to the stage. Then she looked at her manager. "Norm, I overheard you talking with that tiny man earlier. Who was he? Was he talking about me?"

The look on Norm's face was priceless. "You heard us?"

"I did. It sounded like you were talking about me."

"Now, Girlie, why would we do that? Anyhow, I have business dealings everywhere. That's why I have money, and that's why I'm a great manager. Now, you go and sing your heart out to those men out there."

He wasn't going to tell her anything. It was disappointing, but she had no more time to worry about it. She nodded at her musicians as she reached the microphone and began singing immediately.

She held the audience's attention, faces rapt with interest and personal memories. Song after song poured from her throat as she put all she had into each one, making the men, once again, love and adore her songs and ability.

On the very last song, one that Frank Sinatra sang, her eyes caught the image of Wills wandering around in the back of the room, not making eye contact, not giving any indication he heard her or knew she was on stage singing her heart out.

And that, perversely, irritated her.

~*~

What was The Dame doing here? When Owens had told him earlier this evening she'd seen the woman, whose real name was Matilda Nelson, it had unsettled him. She was in the WACs, and, though as far as he knew, had never met Hermie, The Dame could have been his twin, in so much as their determination to rise as high in position as possible.

Anyone around her for any length of time soon realized she was focused on what she considered her duty. She didn't seem to care what others thought, just plowed through her day with whatever her goal was for that day, ignoring what others said or insinuated about her.

So what was she doing here in France with Hermie Wormie—if they were indeed together?

The one thing that had her near Wills' good book— but not in it—was her closeness to Colonel Waverly. His wife had died several years ago, and though The Dame wasn't as old as the colonel, they had a close relationship.

Wills had never had much to do with her, only in passing, and she'd ignored him like he was an ant on the sidewalk. Didn't bother him any. She was just power hungry and he wouldn't help her there.

So why was she here? And why was she passing notes to people like Hermie? Probably an order or request for something she'd needed or wanted. Otherwise, she'd have nothing to do with the likes of Hermie. That was a given.

He really wished Owens wouldn't have brought it to his attention, now of all times. His job was to clear Claire. That's where he needed to keep his focus.

Claire walking arm-in-arm with her manager, all snuggly-like, had sent a rush of distaste and a bit of anger rushing through him.

Worse, had they heard Owens telling him her news?

Wills turned on his heel and marched out of the room, looking neither to the right nor the left.

~*~

He had to start somewhere. They'd been here almost a week. It was past time to do some digging.

Wills knew only one person in the France headquarters, and if he was working, maybe, just maybe he could slip inside without answering a bunch of questions. It was late, but not so much so that those out tonight would have returned yet. Or at least he hoped so.

Sure enough, when he arrived there, one of his best buddies from way back in basic training was on duty. He gladly pointed out where Hermie's bunk was along with where he stored his stuff. Wills walked straight there.

Two men were inside the bunker room. Wills waited outside until they left, then slipping inside he counted beds down till he came to the one his friend had said was Hermie's and searched it.

Nothing.

He turned to the square box beneath the bed and pulled it out part-way. Opening the lid, he sorted through various items.

No letters.

No notes.

A few pictures of people Wills had no knowledge of.

And a worn Nazi symbol, battered and rusty. Why would Hermie keep such a thing? The man surely wasn't smart enough to be a spy.

Unless his ignorant-act was just that. An act, and he was playing all of those around him for fools.

Wills replaced everything in the box and hightailed it out of the barracks.

~*~

Saturday morning, Wills was up early again. He'd gone for a walk at four-thirty and cleared his head. The sun was barely giving a hint of its rising when he returned to his room. He'd stopped at the diner and grabbed two cups of coffee and some kind of specialty sandwich which looked more like canned meat with an under-cooked egg on top, than anything else. It'd keep the hunger pain away at least.

When he heard Owens stirring in the next room, he called out. "Hurry it up in there. You've got work to do."

He heard her muttering but ten minutes later, the door clicked and swung open. "Sorry, Boss. Guess I was worn out. Didn't hear the alarm."

"No problem." He nodded at the rapidly cooling cup of coffee he'd bought for her. "Coffee there. Sit down. First thing, did you get anything off of the note Claire tossed that I gave you?"

"Yes, I heard back from our contact early this morning, but you were sleeping, so I figured I'd wait till you were awake. You need your rest, you know."

"Owens, don't tell me what I need. Just tell me about the note."

"It's confirmed its Norman Tyson's handwriting. The paper was his, and he is her manager."

Wills sat back in his seat, elated at the news, yet deflated too. If it was Tyson's handwriting, it wouldn't mean he was a spy. But who knew? Even spies fell in love. The thought made him feel a little sickish. "All right. Make sure that gets filed in my briefcase, just in case we need it. For what, I have no idea."

The WAC nodded.

"I've got a list of things I want you to do for me today. I'm going to be busy so I won't need you with me, but these things are priority."

"I'm supposed to stay with you, Sir." She gave him one of those who-am-I-supposed-to-obey looks.

"Colonel Waverly assigned you to help me. This..." He scowled and tapped the paper lying on the coffee table. "...is what I need you to do to help me. Now listen."

"Yes, Sir."

"Number one: Go to the local barracks and find out why Hermie is here. He's not known to travel. Hates it, the way I hear."

She nodded. "I can do that."

"Good. Next, I want you to do some discreet checking on The Dame. She's a strange one, and I can't wrap my head around what she's doing clear over here in France."

Owens nodded again.

"Just make sure you don't capture her attention. She has a mean personality if she thinks someone is questioning her moves. She's advanced fast up the WACs ranks, even if it's only in her head, so be careful."

"Don't worry about me. I'll be as discreet as a mouse."

He gave her a dry look. "That's not saying much, since most mice I've encountered weren't very discreet."

"I'll be careful, Sir."

"Drink your coffee, and for goodness sake, eat one of those luscious-looking breakfast sandwiches." Wills grinned.

Owens eyed the sandwich. "I'll drink the coffee, Sir, but think I'll pass on the sandwich."

He called out as she left. "Don't come back without some kind of good report. And if you have to, contact the States. I want answers. But be careful."

"I won't, and I will, Boss."

He shook his head as he heard her door shut and the lock click into place.

Now. For his own plans for the day.

First, he was going to see if he could track down any of Claire's musicians and find out what they thought about Claire, or even her manager. None of them were probably early risers, so he had some time to do a couple other things. And that included talking to some of the staff of the hotel. They always knew what was going on with their customers. He might glean a little information.

One more week, then Claire—and he and Owens— were headed home. If he didn't get some kind of clue whether she was up to her neck in sabotage or not, then Colonel Waverly would be giving him that special frown he reserved for those who disappointed him the most.

Or worse.

Wills stood, stretched and grabbed his wallet and key. Time to get to work.

~*~

"Milton, is it?"

It'd been easy enough to find out who the porter was, and all the young woman at the receptionist desk said about him was praise. Wills figured it was as good a place to start as any.

"Yes, Sir. What can I do for you?"

The man was stately, neat and friendly, and Wills liked him immediately.

"I wonder if you could tell me a little about this young woman?" Wills held out a photo of Claire. Granted it'd been taken a few years ago, but it still looked like her, only a little younger.

The man looked down at the picture then back at Wills. His smile had disappeared. "Are you a friend?"

Wills hesitated a split second. "I am. I think she might be in danger."

At least, he hoped so, and that was crazy, but what was worse? Being a spy, facing prison and worse if caught. No, if he had to choose, he'd choose the danger. At least, he'd do his best to protect her.

The man said nothing for the longest few seconds Wills had ever endured. Then, he nodded. "I'm got a break coming in a half hour. Meet me in the dining room then, and we'll see what we can do for you."

That would give him just enough time to talk to the maid who handled their floor. After a quick question at the receptionist desk about the whereabouts of the maid, Wills headed up the stairs again.

She was getting ready to clean Claire's room, but he stopped her. "Wonder if you could help me?"

"Not sure, but I'll try."

"I'm worried about this woman—Claire Rayner's her name. Have you noticed anything unusual taking place in her room? Any person who might look suspicious?"

"Can't say that I have. She's a pretty private person. The one time I was in her room while she was in there, she paid little attention to me other than to give me a nice tip. She had a paper in her hand, walking up and down the room, mumbling words. She didn't look happy, like you'd think a singer would be learning a new song."

Claire was unhappy? She was living her dream. "Why do you think she was unhappy?"

"I don't know why, she just appeared to be—maybe it was more sad than unhappy."

"Thanks." Wills started to walk away but swung back toward her. "What makes you think it was a song she was learning?"

"Because every once in a while she would hum, or kind of singsong the words." She gave him a crooked smile.

"Did you like her singsonging?"

"Oui, I did. She was nice and meant to be happy. I felt sorry for her, but I would never presume to tell her so."

"Thanks then. You've been helpful. Oh, wait. One last thing. Does she have many visitors?"

The woman shrugged. "Not that I know. That man—I think his name is Norman Tyson—was the only one I ever saw going into her room."

He waved then and took off downstairs again. Time to talk to Milton.

Chapter Ten

"**M**ilton, thanks for meeting with me." As he approached the table, Wills spoke to Milton and motioned to the server, standing close by, who poured Wills a cup of coffee.

The older man nodded and continued sipping his coffee, his gaze fixed on him. "De Rien."

You're welcome.

Wills opened his mouth to begin asking his questions, but Milton beat him to it.

"Tell me first of all, who you are, and why you're asking about that young woman." He set down his coffee, leaned into the back of the booth and continued his stare.

"I'm family—at least, almost family. We grew up together back in the States. I was asked to keep her safe—or words to that effect—and I'll do that or die trying. That's why I'm here."

Milton said nothing as he continued staring. At Wills, around the dining room, and out the window. Finally, he looked at Wills again. "My mother always said, a man with an honest face, a man who amours a woman deeply—that's a man you can trust."

"But how did you know—"

"Son, the passion in your voice told me all I need to know about you. No one amours—forgive me. I keep forgetting you're an American—loves a woman like you do and plans to hurt that woman." Milton nodded and a slow smile spread across his face. "Here's all I know about Claire Rayner."

Wills hadn't known he was so transparent.

"Claire is a belle—excuse me—beautiful soul, troubled, yes, and hasn't yet found her purpose in life."

"But, she's doing what she's planned and worked for all these years. Singing makes her happy."

Claire was unhappy? That made two people who'd

seen that in her, the maid and Milton. Why had he missed it? He'd always thought he was pretty perceptive, but, obviously, not so much.

"Working at what you love doesn't always make you happy. She's missing something vital in her life, and until she finds what that is, she'll never be truly happy."

Wills leaned forward. "What can I do to help her?"

"Since I sense you're not on the best of terms with her, I'd say nothing right now. If you're a praying man, then pray for her. Be there when she's ready to ask for help. And keep loving her. She'll feel that, all right."

"Really? You think she feels my love right now?"

"Sure, she does. It radiates through you, your voice, your words you choose to talk about her, your actions."

"I see." No wonder she hated him. "I'm not sure she sees me as someone she cares much about."

"Probably not. You come on fort, that is, strong even when you're not talking about her or to her. She's not ready for you. But don't give up. I predict when it happens, it will be sudden or furious."

"That's the craziest, and best, thing I've heard in years." Wills squinted at Milton. "How could you know all that anyway? Are you a psychic?"

Milton laughed. "Not hardly. I'm a preacher, lad. Just a plain preacher from the country. Don't do much preaching anymore. Moved into town after my wife passed away, then our only son got killed in this war..."

How sad. How horribly sad.

"But after all the years I've spent advising people over their problems and reading them, I guess I still have it in me."

"I guess you do. Since you trust me now, can you tell me if you've seen anything suspicious about Claire or the people around her? Anything that looks dangerous or unusual?"

"Didn't say I trust you." Milton lowered his head and frowned at Wills.

"But you said—"

"I know what I said. You love her, and it's written all over you. Bleeds from your pores, it does. Knowing that doesn't mean I trust you."

"So you're saying you won't help me?"

"Non. I will, just 'cause I don't trust you yet, doesn't mean I won't tell you a thing or two."

Applesauce. "Then...?"

"I'll tell you a couple of things."

Wills nodded.

"She had me do up a gardenia yesterday morning into a wrist corsage. But when I saw her late last night, she didn't have it on. Instead she was sporting a white, elaborate rose corsage, and as soon as she parted ways with that manager of hers, she tossed it into the trash. All happened in the lobby."

Wills' face suddenly felt hot, and why was that? He never blushed. "Doesn't sound like much, but it is strange. Claire loves flowers. And the second?"

"Claire seems affectionate toward that manager of hers, but I'm pretty sure she doesn't like him. Endures him is more like it."

"Really? Are you positive?"

"Non, I'm not positive, but I'm fairly sure those two things are strange behaviors for a woman like your Claire."

His Claire. Wills liked the sound of that.

~*~

Wills headed to the diner—two businesses down from the hotel—where Claire's band members hung around when not practicing with her. With it being four-ish, Wills figured he might catch a few of them and get them talking.

Sure enough, when he entered the room, at least three of the men and one woman sat at a table in the corner, drinking and eating peanuts, laughing and being too loud. He hesitated but approached them anyway.

He didn't speak when he walked up to them, but gave them a chance to make the first move.

The woman looked at him first. "Whatcha need, Good-looking?"

"Wanted to talk with you a bit about Claire Rayner."

Her brows lifted. "Pull up a chair. Why are you asking about Claire?"

"Heard she's pretty fabulous and going places.

Wanted to see what her band members think of her. Is she loyal? Temperamental? Hard to get along with? Whatever you can tell me."

A black-haired man, dressed in a satin blue shirt and the latest style of pants, leaning back in his chair, a cigarette dangling from his long fingers, spoke up almost before Wills finished. "I'll be glad to spill the beans on that gal. Thinks she's better than anyone else. Seldom talks to us and never goes out with us after a show. You ask me, she's a spoiled girl who doesn't realize she wouldn't be anyone if it wasn't for the rest of us."

Wills had asked their opinions but he hadn't expected to get quite the criticism of Claire he was hearing now. But before he could speak, the woman spoke again.

"Ah, Sully, you're just sulking 'cause she wouldn't have anything to do with you when you begged her to be your girl. As if she would." The woman turned to Wills. "She's a sweet woman who works hard to succeed. I'm proud to be her pianist."

That did Wills' heart good. Much better than Sully's comment.

But he needed to hear more. "So are you saying, there's no problems with her? Either from you all— except for Sully—or any of the other band members?"

They were quiet for moment. Thinking of how to say what they were thinking?

"There's only one more band member. He's feeling under the weather or he'd be here now." This from the woman.

"Well, there is that one issue—" The other man, who hadn't spoken yet, joined the conversation now.

"Benny..." The woman was cautioning yet another member.

Was she covering for Claire?

"Not meaning any harm to Miss Claire..."

The black man, older than the other band members, was soft spoken, his eyes open and honest, and Wills wanted to hear what he said.

"...I'm afraid Miss Claire's caught up in more than she can handle."

"Benny, that's nothing. You shouldn't be passing on

your feelings."

"Yes, I should, Millie. I can't help her, but, maybe you can, Mister."

"What do you mean, Benny? You can call me Wills."

The man nodded. "Wills. That manager of hers is constantly insisting on her learning new songs, which of itself is what all singers have to do. But they also have their signature songs and new ones to learn, but not at the rate she's learning them. And if she tries to slow him down or refuses, he orders, insists and coerces her until she gives in. The poor girl is worn out from all that memorizing."

"All the managers act that way." Millie was still defending the two.

"Yeah, some, but not like this. I've played with bands from all over, and I reckon I know whether things are good between a manager and his singer." Benny hesitated. "Something's wrong. Claire loses her spark sometimes, and that isn't a good thing. And I'm wondering if Tyson has her singing at heart or if he's pushing for something else."

"Would you happen to guess what that something is?"

Benny shook his head. "Have no idea."

Though no one said anything he could use as positive proof of anything to do with spying, after talking with Milton and now the band members, at least two members felt something was off about Claire's manager.

That ought to mean something.

When no one else offered any other helpful remarks, Wills stood and made his adieus. He'd gotten some information, but whether it would be a help or not was yet to be found out.

~*~

Claire's last week in France had flown by. She'd been so busy, with practicing every day and events at least two times a day, she was exhausted. Tonight was her last night, and tomorrow, she, her musicians and Norm would fly home.

Her mood had lightened from last week. Whatever had been the problem, she was over it now. And glad about that. Depression was not an emotion she enjoyed.

Claire stood on her room balcony, waiting till it was time to go down. She'd had an earlier show this afternoon, but the show tonight would be late, which meant only a few hours of sleep before they'd have to leave to board their plane. She shrugged. Wouldn't be the first time for her to lose a few hours sleep.

The sun hadn't set yet, but it was getting there. There wouldn't be many lights on due to the war, but she wouldn't be going far, and she trusted Norm to get her there safely.

Behind her, the door opened then shut softly, and Norm's loud voice preceded him onto the balcony. "How's my favorite girly doing tonight?"

His big arms slipped around her shoulder, and Claire leaned into him a little. She might get irritated at him occasionally, but he had a good heart. She was sure about that, the way he cared for her.

"I'm fine."

"Well, you certainly look fine enough." He gave her a big grin. "You look like a glitterati in that dress. I'm pretty sure red is your color."

Claire laughed, and slapped him lightly on the arm. "Silly creature. I look fantastic in any color. You should know that."

"I know you do."

His attention fastened on the street below them, and Claire turned to see what was so captivating, just in time to see a man's hand descending. Yet she still caught what seemed to be a signal. Two fingers were distinctly held apart and aloft, even as the person's hand descended.

The man was a sharp dresser and looked almost like one of the street painters that were usually so common in France. The flat painter's hat he wore was tilted so she couldn't see his face.

"Is that man signaling you?" Claire shot Norm a sharp glance. "Do you know him?"

Norm returned his gaze to her. "Of course not. Why would he be signaling me?"

Claire allowed him to guide her back inside, hold her

coat for her and escort her out the door. He was talking, as usual, so why did she get the distinct suspicion he seemed a little flustered?

That was ridiculous. Claire clasped his arm tighter. Totally ridiculous.

~*~

Wills paced up and down in his room. Not once, nor twice, but over and over again. He'd tried, but he couldn't shake the feeling that lurked in his mind. Of evil. Something—someone—was out to cause trouble tonight. That wasn't unusual, he told himself, not with a war going on miles—not a continent—away.

But what wasn't usual was the distinct feeling it would be happening tonight, and to Claire.

He stopped abruptly and pounded on his right-hand-man's door. "Owens, you in there? Wake up. I need you."

No response.

"Owens, get up or you're not gonna be flying home tonight."

A faint movement, then the door between their rooms flung open. Hair ruffled, eyes blurry with sleep. "Sorry, Sir. I dozed off. Didn't mean to, but you did have me out doing research since early this morning."

He flapped a hand at her and kept a straight face, though he wanted to grin at her underhanded criticism. She probably didn't even realize she had done it. "You'll see plenty more of those late, sleepless nights, if you work with me long enough."

"Yes, Sir!"

"Are you planning on sleeping all evening while I work tonight? If so, don't count on catching that flight with me. I'm not babysitting a lazy do-nothing." He peered at her to see how she was taking his imitation of Colonel Waverly.

Hmmm. Not so well, it seemed, if he could go by the look of distress on her face.

"I'm sorry, Sir. What do you want me to do?"

"First off, I want that report on why The Dame and Hermie are here in France. Find anything?"

"I did. The Dame requested Hermie come with her,

insisting for various reasons that he was the one she needed."

"And who gave her that permission?"

Owens lowered her head, but peered up at Wills. "Colonel Waverly, Sir."

"I see." Wills strode to his window and stared out it. "And why is The Dame here?"

"I don't know. I checked with all of our sources, the military and even with some nonmilitary contacts but couldn't find a thing. No one seemed to know how or why she is here in France."

"That's odd. Looks like that would have raised some eyebrows."

"You'd think so."

Wills turned from the window. "Can you get yourself ready to go to Claire Rayner's last sing tonight? You've got five minutes."

"I can, Sir."

"Then get to it."

She flew back into her room, and Wills could hear her shuffling and banging, trying to beat his deadline of five minutes.

She didn't have to worry. He wasn't heartless, although he sensed she needed a little more discipline. She'd gotten a little too cozy with him, and that wouldn't do.

Wills picked up and set his suitcase by the door. He'd stuffed papers and notes in his briefcase because, although Owens didn't know it yet, she would be in charge of that briefcase. He'd put together his thoughts on different people, including Claire, on anything and everything he could think of or had questions about. He meant to go over those on the flight home. And Owens keeping his briefcase, was of paramount importance to him. It held only a little bit of tangled thoughts and questions, but nevertheless, all he had. He wasn't about to lose it.

For himself, he was all set to hit the army field where Claire would be singing tonight. After that...then he'd have to figure out where to go from here.

~*~

"Come on, Girly, do it for me."

Claire stared up at Norm, wanting to be both defiant and willing.

Definitely not working. Defiant was winning.

"Why? Why this sudden change in my list of songs? Why do I need to sing this song? You know I don't care for these new songs that much. Whoever wrote them— well, let me say, they need to learn a few things."

"Really, Babe?"

"Really, Norm."

"What if I insist?"

"I might refuse."

"I wouldn't do that."

Claire stopped from whirling away from him. What was he saying?

"What do you mean by that? Are you *threatening* me?"

"Girly, why would I do that? I know you'll do what I want. It's important to me."

Claire cocked her head at him and gave him a sly smile. "And why do you think that's important to me?"

He laughed—although it did sound a little forced— and held her coat for her.

She looked up at him. "I'll sing the song, Norm. No worries."

He gave her shoulder a little pat as he helped her shrug into her coat. "You're the best, Girly."

"I know that."

~*~

Wills was determined to be early, in place where he could, hopefully, survey those attending, and observe any unusual actions. He succeeded in two of those goals, but surveying the attendees and the ones behind the scenes was a little more challenging than he'd reckoned.

Still, he'd keep his eyes peeled, and his attention focused. Most important right now, was watching those attending.

Wandering back and forth in the back of the group of soldiers, Wills caught sight of one of the people he had on his *watch* list. Hermie stood on the right side of the group of enthusiastic soldiers. He started to check out the stage, but instead was caught by an elegantly dressed man standing at the far end of the stage in the auditorium section. His pose suggested he was a confident man, one who knew his own value. He was in shadow so Wills couldn't make out his facial features, but his thumbs up was definitely noticeable. Then without Wills being able to identify him, he backed farther away and disappeared.

Claire was still singing, the same song he'd heard when she first arrived in France.

Nine o'clock, ten o'clock, if you're not on ti—, then look out, Baby, you're gonna pay for the crime. I love you, -- aby, but at 1840 Mossy Oak Street, You'd better be there, standing, on your feet. Wait for me, Baby, I'll be dressed in red, To you, tonight, I'm gonna w—.

Wills frowned. Was Claire fumbling over the words? He'd never—never ever—heard her fumble over any song. Strange.

Checking on Hermie again, he didn't see him. Where had he gone to? He should have kept Owens with him. No time to worry about ladder climbing Hermie now.

And it hit him. What if the man had been signaling to someone—someone like Hermie? Or The Dame?

Wills hurried after the man who'd raised his thumbs as if in a signal. He slammed through the door, taking care not to make too much noise, and rushed down the hallway.

He saw no one. Wills ran for the front door, and was just in time to see, in the distance, a man climbing into a taxi.

Too late.

Irritated at himself for his slowness and for not having enough foresight to keep Owens beside him where she could have followed the man, he returned to the auditorium.

Claire was winding down. She slipped into her last song, and Wills headed out. He was done here. She'd be on the same plane as him.

Headed home, like him.

And his premonition had been wrong. Claire had

made it through the evening safely.

~*~

Toward morning the airplane Wills and Owens were on, flew into turbulent winds. Contrary to the captain's forecast for clear skies, midway across the ocean, the worst storm Wills had ever experienced hit them. Hard. The plane bucked and rocked, shuddered and, once, even seemed to pause in the air before taking a heart-stopping drop.

Few seemed to be bothered. Wills glanced around the dimly lit cabin and caught Claire staring straight ahead. She was scared, Wills could tell, but no one who didn't know her well would ever have guessed.

He wanted to cuddle her close and assure her all would be fine, but he never had done that—not that she would have allowed it. He and Josie had been a bit of a trial to Claire. It wasn't until he allowed himself to examine his feelings for the most spoiled sister of the Rayner family and realized he was carrying a pretty big torch for the redhead that he knew she would always be the only one for him.

He couldn't do any cuddling, but he could pray. And pray he did. Closing his eyes, he beseeched his greatest friend for Claire's comfort and calmness. He didn't bother him for help with winning Claire's love. That was something, he figured, he needed to do on his own.

"Owens, you asleep?"

Owens stirred and opened one eye. "Yes, I mean, no, Sir."

"You better not be. We have work to do."

"In the middle of the night? Excuse me, Boss." She sat up straight and tried not to yawn. "What do you need me to do?"

"Listen."

"Listen?"

"Something's bothering me."

"There is?"

"Stop asking me questions. I'm the one to be asking questions."

"Of course, Sir." She yawned.

Wills gave her a look. "And stop that yawning. Are

you a soldier or not?"

"I am, Sir." She stiffened her back.

"Then listen while I go over a few things with you. Something feels off."

"It does?"

When Wills gave her another look, she hurried to correct her response. "Why would that be?

"I don't know why that would be. It just does."

"I see."

Wills was pretty sure Owens didn't see. "What I mean is, while we were in France, there were some things that bothered me."

"Like what, Sir?"

"Can I trust you?" Of course, he could trust her. For one thing, the colonel would never have assigned her to him, and for another, his gut told him he could.

But then, the colonel had also been the one to approve The Dame's request to have Hermie travel with her. What was that about?

She was protesting, but he waved a hand at her. "Nevermind. One thing was..."

"Yes?"

He kept silent, thinking. "I talked to Milton, the doorman, while there, about Claire Rayner."

Owens nodded. "Employees are always knowledgeable about people they serve."

"He was favorably impressed by her, but he felt she was..." How should he describe it? "...troubled."

"But, Sir, she seems so happy."

That she did. But what about that occasional look of melancholy? "Is she though? Is it a front for what she really feels? Is she worried? Upset over certain things—"

"What would those things be, Sir?"

Wills cast his WAC an irritated glance. "I have no idea."

"Is she more...more troubled than shows on the outside, normally? But over what?"

"Sir, could it be she feels guilty because she'd betrayed our country?"

Wills felt less and less favorable about talking over anything with Owens.

"Or maybe it's just plain ole homesickness."

"May I speak frankly, Sir?"

"When have I ever forbade you to do that?"

"Never. Well, Sir, I thank Claire may be innocent of any intentional spying. I think we need to focus on those surrounding her."

"You mean her manager?"

"Yes, but others too. We've been watching that Hermie guy and The Dame, I mean Lieutenant Nelson—"

"Why on earth is she referred to as 'Lieutenant?' WACs don't have ranks." Wills knew he was being a bit brusque, but it irritated him to hear the woman called a rank she didn't have.

Owens' lips tilted upward a little. "I wondered that too, Sir, and from what I can gather, she gave herself the title. If my source was correct, when she was over several of the other ladies, she insisted on being called Lieutenant. I think to lift herself higher than them. Maybe to instill within them a respect for her."

"It's still very irritating. But for now, we'll leave it. Now as to what you were saying before I interrupted you. I agree. Let's dig deeper on them."

"You're right, and we will as soon as we're back on U.S. soil."

Wills laid his head back thinking.

Claire had been beloved of everyone in the Rayner Boarding House, and the only one who kept a check on her rather spoiled ways was her oldest sister, Emma Jaine. Not that she didn't do any spoiling. But she'd seen Claire's unusual singing talent and had kept her toeing her practice and sought the best instructor she could for Claire.

"Milton said she wore a rose corsage when she sang tonight."

"I can see her doing that. Women like flowers, normally." Owens nodded.

"I can't."

"You can't see her wearing a corsage?"

"I can't see her wearing a rose corsage, seeing that gardenias are her favorite flower for her singing engagements."

"I beg your pardon, Sir, but that's kind of flimsy."

Wills glanced at the WAC who'd done above what he'd asked. "I suppose one could think that if you didn't know her."

"You know her well, Sir?"

"You could say that."

His gaze rested on Claire again. She had her eyes closed now, but her hands betrayed her. She wasn't sleeping. The way she gripped the armrests gave her away. She was awake, all right, and well aware of the battle the plane was in.

~*~

Their plane had landed safely, finally, and though Wills and Owens had done their best to find out Claire's and her companions means of transportation home, they'd not been quick enough or found enough information to follow them back to Cincinnati. There was nothing else to do but head there themselves and hope for the best.

Wills took a taxi back to the Rayner Boarding House where his parents worked and looked forward to a few hours of rest before tracking down Claire. He hadn't gotten nearly enough information about whether she was innocent or guilty of treason yet, and facing Colonel Waverly without that wasn't something he was particularly interested in doing. He'd never failed before in his spying activities and had no plans to begin.

It was early when Wills opened the back door of his home where he knew his mother would be preparing for a simple lunch for those who chose to eat. Harriet Mason had her back to him, humming, her body swaying a little to her music. He allowed the door to shut softly and crept across the room, wrapped his arms around her and whispered in a deep voice. "Give me a slice of that bread you're cutting or you'll be in serious danger."

The knife dropped to the tabletop and the woman gave out a little shriek before twisting in his arms. The tears that suddenly slid down her cheeks told him all he needed to know. She was overjoyed that her boy was home again.

"William Mason, will you never stop your pranks? I should box your ears as I've had to do all your life, but what good will that do? It's never stopped you before, and I reckon it's not about to cure you of those tricks now. Lean down here and let me look at you." She took his face between her hands and stared long and hard at him, the love and adoration shining brightly in eyes the same color as his.

"Now, Mother, you know you'd disown me if I did any different." He laughed. "Besides, it's your fault I'm this way. I inherited it from you, or so I hear from my father."

She gave him a mock frown. "Your father talks too much. Just because we grew up as friends, then sweethearts doesn't mean he has to tell everything he knows—or doesn't know."

"No, but it's sure helped me out of trouble many a time."

She did swat him on the arm then, but Wills barely felt the love tap. "I've missed you and our long talks."

His father had always been the gentle, polite and quiet one of them. Wills and his mother were more alike, but Jonah Mason was the one they both adored and relied on for the steadiness and guidance when needed. He was a strong man, both mentality and physically, but even more so spirituality. He was Wills' hero, and he loved the man as much as he did his outspoken mother.

She was still talking though she'd turned back to her bread slicing. "How long are you here for this time?"

He shrugged. "I think for several weeks. I wasn't able to finish up my assignment, so I've still got quite a bit to do, but I should be home most evenings. I can't wait to see the rest."

Her eyes twinkled at him. "I'm thinking they'll be just as excited to see their boy."

"You make it sound like—"

"Nonsense, you know they all think the world of you."

"Not quite all of them."

Harriet was silent for a few seconds, but slid a knowing glance at him. "She cares about you more than you realize. She's not ready to show her true emotions, but she will."

"How can you be sure? I just can't see it." He shook his head.

"Because I know Claire Anne. She's just about ready to grow out of that stage she's flaunting now. But it's fizzling. I saw that when she was last home. Don't you go doubting my words, Wills."

He heaved a huge breath of air, wishing he was as sure as she seemed to be. "I'm going to go rest for a bit then cleanup for supper to surprise everyone. Are Josie and her family eating here tonight?"

"I believe so. Go, now."

He leaned over to allow her to give him a peck on the cheek then headed toward their quarters in the basement. It was a nice sized apartment with two bedrooms, bathrooms, sitting room and a small private kitchen of their own. They'd always been happy here and felt as much a part of the Rayners as any of the actual family.

It was home.

Chapter Eleven

Wills opened his eyes and shifted his gaze to take in the large clock on his dresser. Six? He'd slept all day? But then he hadn't slept much the whole time he'd spent in France.

Supper was always promptly at six-thirty in this house, and if he didn't get a move on, he'd miss out on it and seeing everyone again. He'd been so busy, he hadn't seen any of them for several months. If he wanted to surprise them tonight, then he'd better change quickly and hightail it upstairs.

Promptly at six twenty-nine, he headed upstairs and glanced in the kitchen where his mother usually was making sure all the dishes of food were properly delivered to the residents, but she wasn't there. Turning, he headed down the long hallway to the dining room. He could hear sounds of muted laughter and low conversations, but not with the usual carefree joyfulness that came from a happy family.

He paused at the swinging doors, wondering at the sudden quietness. Maybe they were too busy dishing up his mother's excellent dishes of food—in spite of the rationing—to talk much. Whatever...

Wills stepped into room, opened his mouth to say, *Surprise!* when voices from around the room shouted at him. "Welcome home, Wills!"

His gaze flew from one face to another, resting finally on his parents standing in the back of the room.

Captain Ossie, motioned and bellowed, "Wills, come here, Son, and sit. We've arranged a special seat right here beside me. We're all thrilled you're home. For good, I hope?"

Wills didn't answer the question, but obeyed the command.

Josie's radiant face betrayed her excitement at his presence, and she gave him a fierce hug before resuming her seat beside him.

"Where's Fina?"

"She's with her nanny tonight. As soon as Harriet informed us you were home, Emma Jaine and Papa insisted on surprising you tonight. Everyone was glad to cancel plans to be here tonight."

Everyone but Claire, it seemed.

Dinner lasted over an hour, and by the end of it, Wills knew Claire wasn't about to show up. Perhaps she'd heard he was here, at home, where she'd seen him since they were youngsters. Still, he wasn't ready to give up. Yet.

He leaned toward Josie. "Have you heard from Claire?"

Josie sniffed. "No, but then I'd be the last person she'd fill in on her activities. She doesn't come home much anymore."

"I think she cares for you more than you realize," Wills argued.

"You think so?" Josie cast him a surprised glance. "Since when have you been her champion? If I remember correctly you were always the first to tease her."

Wills wanted to wince. Josie was right. No wonder Claire despised him. "Just would have liked to have seen all of you before I get busy again tomorrow. She's family too, in spite of her superior attitude."

"I suppose so." Josie shrugged. "She's a good enough sister, I reckon, but don't expect me to give her much attention. She manages to get that by herself."

"I'd say you're right. It's just that the longer I'm away, the more I realize how important family is, especially in these times. It's so easy to lose someone and you don't remember till then how much you do love them."

Josie's expression of shock was real. "Wow. You've turned into a sentimental person."

"Maybe it was there all along, but I was too busy getting into mischief." Wills leaned to one side as his father offered a refill on his drink.

"I'm impressed. After all, you were the ringleader of our—what shall I call them?—adventures."

Wills laughed with her, but it was forced.

He really did wish Claire was here, regardless of her opinion of him.

~*~

Twenty minutes later, the Rayner house people reassembled in the library. Emma Jaine sat at the piano, playing melodies they all loved, occasionally singing along, laughing and seeming to have a good time. Captain Ossie stood by a window, staring out into the darkness of the night, and as Wills passed, he raised a hand and motioned him closer.

"You doing all right, Son?"

Didn't matter he wasn't the man's birth son. He had always, especially as Wills grew older, called him son, not as a slight to Wills' own father, but as an affectionate term showing how much he cared for him.

"I am, Sir. Busy, but that's the way I like it."

The man's intense blue-eyed gaze studied him. "You've become a man, my boy, and I couldn't be prouder of you if you were my own son. I'd always hoped..."

What? What had the man left unsaid?

"Have you talked with Claire lately?" Wills broached the subject he was most reluctant to talk about. Yet the temptation was too great not to, regardless of his feelings.

"Early last month. I wish she wouldn't run around all over the country, although my sources say she's popular with the soldiers, and they love her singing. But why would they not?" The man's white mustache bobbed with every word.

"I believe you're right."

"Of course I am. Still, she's too young to be gallivanting around the country by herself."

"I believe she has a manager who goes with her."

Captain Ossie grunted. "That man. Don't care for him. Met him once, and once was enough."

Exactly. Wills couldn't stop his grin of agreement for the life of him. He liked Captain Ossie even better than before. If that was possible.

"Son." The man's eyes drilled into his. "Don't give up

on her. Do you hear me? Don't you even think of giving up on her. She'll come around when she gets this bee out of her bonnet."

Wills eyed the man. How on earth had he known that Wills loved his youngest daughter? Had always loved her?

"Don't look so surprised. Anyone with half a brain would know that." Captain Ossie slapped him on the shoulder. "And you have my full approval. You hear me? Full approval."

"Yes, Sir. I hear you loud and clear." What else was there to say? The woman he loved, the woman who disliked him intensely—he'd gained her father's approval of pursuing her without even asking.

A pretty good accomplishment.

~*~

Wills still stood at the window where he and Captain Ossie had talked earlier. Most of the boarding house residents had thinned out, choosing to leave the family alone for the rest of the evening. Shirley, Captain Ossie's close friend, stood near him and Emma Jaine, while Tyrell had left already to check on things at the church he pastored. Josie and Jerry were talking with his parents—at least Josie was. Jerry watched his rambunctious wife, who'd tamed down a mite but still showed that tendency to be high-strung and her own definitive person.

Only—

The front door opened, there was a brief silence as if someone was hesitating then quiet footsteps came down the hallway. All eyes turned toward the doorway...

Claire Anne Rayner stood in the doorway, still in her red coat and hat. Her gaze swung around the room, rested on him a moment—and he saw the sudden tense line on her lips—then swung back to her father.

"Claire, come, Child, to your father and let me feast my eyes on you." Captain Ossie held out a hand, and she hurried to him.

Clasping her tight in his big arms, the tears in the older man's eyes were plainly visible to anyone who happened to be close enough.

Holding her at arm's length, he scolded her even as one hand patted her shoulder. "You've stayed away far too long. Don't you know my heart can't stand that?"

Claire laughed, musical and soft. "Papa, your heart is as strong as mine, and I'm pretty sure mine's intact."

"Never mind that. Two special people have come home. This calls for a toast." He turned toward Jonah Mason. "Jonah, will you refill everyone's glass with their chosen drink, please?"

Wills' father nodded and turned to retrieve glasses. After he'd passed them to everyone, Captain Ossie held up his glass. "To my beautiful daughter, Claire Anne, who's come home to Papa—to stay, I hope!—and to a young man who is like a son to me, and maybe someday will be."

Claire didn't answer him with words, but her eyes spoke volumes to Wills when they flashed at him. He could probably have discerned her look in many different ways, but he supposed the contemptuous tilt of her lips told him best of all what her thoughts were to her father's none-to-subtle wish.

Over her dead body.

~*~

Claire wanted to grab her small luggage bag and flee the house. As much as she adored her father, he had made her a little angry tonight, and that seldom happened. She reckoned because he hardly ever embarrassed her like tonight and given her that smothering feeling she'd endured so many times when Emma Jaine had constantly insisted on her practicing. As much as she loved singing, as much as she adored Emma Jaine, it had been a bit too much. And as a teenager, she'd wanted to rebel many times. Only she hadn't.

But now she was an adult, and whether Papa liked it or not, she would not be pushed into marriage—if she married—to someone she couldn't stand.

She supposed Wills was all right. But she'd never liked Josie's tumultuous ways, and that went for Wills too, who'd always been in the thick of their pranks with Josie. Claire had been too focused on her music and what she wanted from life to even consider sliding down stairs, climbing on roofs and whatever else those two daredevils could think up.

Papa would just have to accept that she could and would make up her own mind about who she would have, if ever.

Claire felt an arm slip around her shoulders, and she looked up. Papa Ossie stared down at her.

"I'm sorry, Claire, if I embarrassed you earlier. You've been pretty quiet. Why don't you sing to us?"

She leaned her head on his arm. "I don't feel like it, Papa."

He pulled away from her. "Since when do you not feel like singing? You always liked *A Slow Boat to China.* Sing that for me. It will remind me of you as a young girl."

"I'm not a young girl anymore, Papa. I'm all grown up."

"I know you are, but you're still my little girl no matter how old or smart you get, and don't you forget it."

She giggled. "I won't, I promise."

"Then you'll sing for us?"

"I suppose. But just one." She gave her father a stern look, hoping he'd take the hint. "Emma Jaine, will you play for me?"

Emma Jaine smiled, nodded and hurried to the piano. "You know I will, Claire. Come, stand where I can see you. I've missed you so much."

"I've missed you too, Emma Jaine. More than you'll know."

Emma Jaine played the first notes of the song, and Claire began singing.

She'd barely finished the song when the hall phone rang. When Jonah reappeared in the library, he nodded at Claire. "Telephone call for you, Claire."

She hurried into the hall and picked up the receiver.

"Hi, Girlie. Wanted to make sure you'll be here in the morning to go over that new song I told you about."

"I thought I was getting a couple days off."

"Sorry. The soldiers really like you. Gotta keep it up.

All this work is gaining you some great attention. Once this war is over, you'll be getting calls from all over."

"You really think so, Norm?"

"I do. I've gotta go, but you be here. Ten sharp."

Before she could answer him, he'd hung up and Claire replaced the receiver, not moving but staring at the instrument.

She loved to sing, yes, but she'd been on a grueling schedule. It really would have been nice to have a few days to catch up on sleep and regain her strength. She took a deep breath and turned to rejoin her family.

"You all right, Claire?" Wills stood so close behind her, she jumped.

"Why wouldn't I be?" she snapped at him. "And why are you following me?"

"Why would you think that? I stepped out to check on something." Her, to be exact.

"Why were you in France anyway? And you stayed in the same hotel as I did. Did Papa ask you to follow me?"

Wills laughed. "What? That's crazy. I couldn't do that if he did ask. I have assignments myself, a very specific one this time in France."

"And I suppose that brunette was part of the assignment?"

He opened his mouth to clarify, when the thought hit him. Why tell her anything definite? Let her stew a little over his personal life. "She's very efficient, and being so good-looking doesn't hurt anything either."

If looks could kill...but there was something—something different in her eyes. He couldn't really read what it was, but it was hiding in the depths of those deep green eyes of hers.

"Claire, I can't ever talk about my work. Not just to you, but anyone. Not my parents. Or your family."

She tossed her head. "I really don't care. It makes no difference to me what you do."

"Of course, it doesn't." Then why had she asked? "You're so focused on one thing and one thing only, I seriously doubt you ever think of anyone else."

Her eyes darkened with—was it anger or doubt? "What do you mean by that comment?"

"I really shouldn't say."

"Afraid, Wills? You?"

Her taunt was enough to push him to say what he knew he shouldn't.

"Well, then, if you insist on hearing the truth, and since you're so all grown up, I'll tell you." Something inside him urged him to walk away. *Don't say it. You're going to regret this.* "You've always been spoiled to death in this household, and I suppose you still are. Perhaps you'll never outgrow that and realize that just because you are still the same spoiled child you've always been, that others *might* change, might have grown up, leaving you in the state you were in as a child."

It *was* anger in her eyes. They were flashing at him— or his words, and they foretold of an immediate reaction from her.

"*Me?* Spoiled? What about you? You've been idolized and raised on a platform, and everyone—I mean everyone in this household, thought you could do no wrong. No matter how annoying you were, no matter how hurtful you spoke to—to others, they overlooked it all. If anyone was spoiled, it was you, Wills Mason. And you can't deny it."

Wow. He'd touched a sore spot tonight. He shouldn't have said anything. But he'd allowed that little bit of condescension from her to goad him into saying something hurtful. And that was the last thing he wanted to do.

"So can we agree we were both spoiled by our family?" He gave her as meek of a look as he could manage, allowing a small smile to curve his lips. "And you're probably right. I dare say, I was the worst of the two. I'm sorry for bringing it up."

She must have been taken aback by his apology, and for a moment seemed loss of words. She stared at him, and if he hadn't been convinced she'd never care enough about what he said to shed tears over them, he'd insist he saw the faintest glimmer of them hovering behind her eyes.

She didn't speak, only stared, and Wills' heart melted by the second.

"Are you ready to go into the library? Ready to sing one more song?"

"No. I'm tired. I'm going to tell everyone goodnight and head to my room." She nodded, turned, and walked away.

~*~

She couldn't stay another minute in Wills' presence. His words had hurt her far more than she liked to admit. She knew she'd been spoiled, but to have him point it out so—so blatantly—she was pretty sure, she'd never been hurt any worse.

And for that reason, she'd had to leave him. If she hadn't, her tears would have rained down her cheeks, and that she couldn't abide. She never want him to see her so defenseless.

Why was she so despicable to Wills? Everyone loved him. Everyone but her, that is. He was good looking. Far better than Norman, although he wasn't anything to sneeze at. And Wills was smart. He'd been at the top of his classes, and look at him now, doing important—she was sure—work for the military.

He'd settled down some, but there still lurked that tendency to pull the next prank, to tease the life out of an unsuspecting target. He and Josie had been impossible. At least, Josie had a leash on herself now, with Jerry and her beautiful daughter, Fina, giving her something important to focus on.

What about Wills and that gorgeous brunette? Were they romantically involved or as Wills had implied, partners in work?

Claire shrugged. Why should she care?

She started to turn away from her room's window when the sight of Wills headed down the street caught her attention. At the corner someone—was it a woman?—met him, and they stood talking for several minutes before turning the corner and disappearing from her view.

Now where was Wills Mason headed?

~*~

The unexpected call from Owens irritated Wills for a minute. She said it was important. Vital that he knew about it right away. That was the only reason he'd snuck out of the boarding house this late. And was he glad he'd listened to her.

"That Hermie guy is right now sitting at that late night diner on Eighth Street talking with someone. We have no idea who he is." Owens spoke rapidly and succinctly. "I didn't want to leave but called in a fellow soldier I knew I could trust. I wanted to personally make sure you knew this. I didn't think it should wait till morning."

"You're an ace, Owens. But don't tell anyone I said that 'cause I'll deny it."

It wasn't far, so unless the two finished their meeting quickly, Wills was hoping they'd still be there. Owens couldn't go in wearing her WAC uniform, but Wills figured he could get a seat close enough to overhear the conversation. Otherwise, following them was the only other option. Which might end up being beneficial. Or not.

Ten minutes later, Wills and Owens approached the diner. The man Owens had stationed nodded at them, indicating the men were still there.

"You..." Wills nodded at the man. "...I want you to watch the back door. Follow him if he leaves, but don't get caught. Owens, you take the front door. Stay out of sight. Don't make me have to rescue either of you."

"Right, Boss."

Wills was surprised to see the place was as busy as it was. His second glance at the customers told him the story. Many down-and-outers, older men and a few women just off their shifts in the plants, and a few couples who were enjoying their last few moments together before heading toward homes. Fortunately, he was able to get a booth right behind Hermie and the other man.

He recognized Hermie, but the other man—as far as he remembered, he'd never seen the man before. His blond hair, slicked back with hair cream, shone like a beam of sunlight.

Their voices were low, but Wills was able to catch a few words.

"So you think you can do a better job, do you? I know her. I don't know you. Why should I believe you?

The man's voice was calm, almost lazy-sounding—or was it confident?—yet there was an underlying hint of something sinister. Was it contempt?

"...know it...thinks I'm an idiot, but let me tell you something. I've been reading your letters...and she doesn't even..."

There was silence. A long silence. "I'm hearing no reason to—to promote you."

That man was definitely getting tired of Hermie's bragging. Whatever Hermie was wanting, if he couldn't come up with better reasoning, he'd lost his case.

"How's this?..."

Wills leaned back in his seat, trying to hear what Hermie was saying. But the few words he caught meant nothing. He sensed the unknown man was getting restless and sure enough, he caught him scooting out of his seat. He straightened and stared down at Hermie.

"When you have proof you're the better choice, then, and only then, will I talk with you. Don't waste my time again." He moved as if leaving then spoke again. "I don't suffer fools lightly. I just might give your boss a heads up."

He walked away.

But just as he stepped out the door, he returned his gaze to the back of the diner, which grazed over Wills and seemed to settle on Hermie.

And then he did leave.

Wills sipped at his coffee, thinking of what he'd just heard. Nothing made any sense or seemed to pertain to what Wills was after. Whatever Hermie had wanted from the stranger, he hadn't gotten, and didn't seem to leave much of a favorable impression on the man.

There was something about the second man that caught Wills' attention, but he couldn't put his finger on what it was.

Wills didn't follow. He knew Owens, and probably the man she had helping out tonight, would be sure to follow the two. He could go home and get some rest.

Thankfully, he'd always been a light sleeper, one who

caught sleep when he could and existed on only a few hours if necessary.

Wills left the diner and headed home. Hopefully he'd be awake early enough to see Claire, whether he talked with her or not. He chuckled, although he had to admit it was a grim one. Either way, he'd be seeing more of Claire Rayner. He had his orders, and he'd follow them to the letter.

~*~

The light knock on Claire's door woke her, not that she'd gotten much sleep. The nightmare that had haunted her sleep had tortured her sleepless hours. She'd tried pacing, tried staring out into the dark night, tried praying, but nothing erased it.

Now she wanted to groan and pull the covers over her head.

"Claire, Sweetheart, it's Emma Jaine. May I come in? I have breakfast."

Claire rolled over, groaned, and called out, "Come in, Emma Jaine."

Emma Jaine shoved open the door and entered, placing the tray of food on a nearby stand and pulling it close to the bed. "Are you tired, Claire?"

"Yes, but I have to be at the studio by ten to go over yet another new, unpleasant song." Claire sat up and lifted the cup to sip. "Hmmm. This tea is heavenly."

"I figured you hadn't had any in ages, and persuaded Harriet to give up a little this morning for you." Emma Jaine settled at the bottom of the bed. "Maybe you should stay home today and rest."

"I wish. I had a nightmare last night that not only disturbed my sleep, but my waking hours too."

"You should have called me."

"You have enough to do with a busy husband, two darling children and a boarding house to run. You don't need to babysit me too."

"I know I don't have to, nor do you need me too, but I enjoy looking after my baby sister. I miss you."

Claire sighed. "I miss you too. Miss all of you. But I love singing, and for the troops. I just wish Norman wasn't always springing these new songs on me. I don't like them, but he insists, so I give in."

"Will you be home tonight?"

"I think so. The last I heard I didn't have to sing until this weekend."

"That's wonderful. Maybe you'll have time to see the twins."

"If not before." She nibbled at the toast and took one bite of the egg before shoving away the tray. "I have to get ready, but my head hurts so badly, I'm not sure I can."

Emma Jaine glanced at Claire's clock on her dresser. "I'll tell you what. Let me draw you some bath water. I have some bath salts saved back for a special time. I'll sprinkle a few of them in the water, you can soak for a bit, and when you're done, I'll brush your hair for you."

"Emma Jaine, that sounds marvelous. You always did have a gentle touch with a hairbrush. I'd love that. Thank you." Claire leaned forward to give her sister a hug. "You're the best sister ever."

"You're not so bad yourself." She stood. "Let me get that water running and the salts in it, then I'll take the tray to the kitchen while you're soaking. I'll be back then in about twenty minutes."

Forty-five minutes later, Claire sat in her dressing table chair while Emma Jaine ran a brush through her hair. "That feels so good."

"You used to love it when I combed your hair. I thought you were my very own baby doll Mama brought home to me. I adored you."

Claire could see her sister in the mirror, smiling, remembering. "I think you're the one who spoiled me the most."

"Maybe. But you were so tiny with that red tinting your blond hair. And those eyes of yours would fix on me when I talked to you. I thought you understood everything I said." Emma Jaine gave a pat to Claire's hair. "You know you can always come to me if you need to talk. Anytime."

"I know, Emma Jaine. I do get tired, but I also love to sing to the troops. They love it so much, and it's satisfying to know I'm doing something good for them.

You know? It's like I'm using my talent to help save the world."

"You are."

"I hope so." Claire rose and Emma Jaine laid down the brush. "I have to hurry, or I'll be late and my task-master doesn't like it when that happens."

"Why haven't we met this task-master?"

Claire shrugged as she pulled on her skirt and sweater. "The opportunity hasn't really presented itself."

"Why not bring him to dinner one night? You don't have to sing till when? Friday? Today's Tuesday. Bring him tonight. Or tomorrow. Just let me know so we can prepare something special."

"Meals here are always special. Harriet is the best cook ever." Claire grabbed her bag. "I'll think about it. Norman's helped me, but I'm not sure yet whether I want him to be a part of our family get togethers yet."

"I see. Well, do what you think best. I'll see you tonight."

Claire waved as she hurried out the door.

Chapter Twelve

When Wills woke early the next morning, everything about last night seemed clear as a bright day. He knew who the man was that had talked with Hermie last night at the diner—sort of. At least, he thought he knew.

He hadn't recognized him because of the thick glasses he wore. He had a thin mustache, and for the life of him, he wasn't sure the man he'd seen at the concert had one. Plus he didn't have a hat on at the table—not until he was leaving, and once outside the diner, the man had slipped his hat on, cocked just the way he'd worn it at the concert.

Wills would bet his life—if he was a betting man—on him being the same person.

He saw Owens waiting for him when he left his home the next morning. Her face was filled with excitement.

"Sir, I found evidence, I hope, of who that man was talking with Hermie last night."

He stopped walking and stared at her. "You did? Already?"

"Not exactly, but it's in the process. After you left, I went into the diner and got to the table where those two sat last night. I was able to get some fingerprints off of it and have sent it to forensics for testing. I'm hoping we'll identify him shortly."

"Owens. That's excellent. Very good work."

"Thank you, Sir. I hoped you'd be pleased."

"I am. I'm on my way to the colonel's office. He asked me to see him this morning. Make sure you let me know as soon as possible when you find out anything."

"Will do. Good day."

~*~

It took Wills only twenty minutes to reach the colonel's office. Now he sat outside Colonel Waverly's office waiting till the man could talk with him. He didn't have much yet to report, but he had something—more like a lot of questions—but better than nothing.

The colonel's door opened, and a young soldier spoke. "The colonel will see you now."

Wills stepped into the room and gave a second glance at the woman standing beside the seated Colonel. The Dame stood solemn-faced, and if Wills had been the nervous kind, he'd have been worried he'd angered someone in the room.

But the Colonel's cordial voice was anything but angry. "Sergeant Mason. It's about time you reported to me. Have you decided that you no longer have to do that?"

"Not at all, Sir. We landed early the day before yesterday, stopped in to see my parents and the next thing I knew I'd slept all day. Figured I wouldn't bother you till this morning."

Colonel Waverly said nothing for a moment then nodded. "Good thinking. Matilda here says she saw you in France."

Matilda? Were they that close to call each other by first name? "Yes, Sir."

"Have you learned anything about the Rayner girl? Spit it out, Mason."

"I have learned some, Sir. First of all, I didn't see anything suspicious from her. I did talk with some people who waited on her and were around enough to observe her actions. They all spoke favorably about her. I could find no one with negative thoughts."

"And?"

Wills hesitated. "I did sense tension in her. I also felt she and her manager—though on the outside seemed amenable enough together—were at odds. I can't pinpoint exactly why yet, but I have some ideas of where to go with that."

"That hardly seems reasonable. People who work together often have disagreements." The Dame's tight-lipped comment settled in a suddenly-icy room.

"True, Matilda, but you don't know the whole story."

The colonel was trying to placate her, but Wills saw the flash of anger in her eyes. She wasn't used to not being listened to.

"Sir, I think it does mean something."

"I see. Then you need more time."

"I do."

"Then I suggest you get to it. Matilda will be around about town in case you need extra help, you can call on her."

"Yes, Sir." His voice—he made sure—was agreeable enough, but his heart refused to echo his words. Not on his watch would he be calling The Dame for any kind of help.

He started to walk out then turned back. "Colonel Waverly?"

"Yes, Mason?"

"I've seen one man that Owens is trying to identify now. We don't know who he is, but he's shown up several times. He's a snazzy dresser, but elusive, and may or may not be involved in what we're interested in."

"What does that have to do with finding evidence of that Rayner girl being a spy? Ridiculous." Matilda snorted.

"It has everything to do with it." Irritation at her remarks crept up his spine. The woman was a nuisance. How could the colonel stand her? Better just to ignore her or he'd say something he shouldn't. "I'll let you know as soon as I found out anything.

"Very good. See that you do."

Wills exited the room and pulled on the door-knob to shut it, but Matilda's words managed to reach his ears whether he wanted them to or not.

"Really, Colonel? He's useless. All this time, and he knows nothing."

Her voice softened as if she was coaxing, but all it did to Wills' ears was make her sound false.

"Why don't you let me take over your investigation? I'll get an answer and quickly for you. What do you say?"

Wills didn't hear the answer because he shut the door—a little too hard, but right now, he didn't care that either one of them knew he'd eavesdropped. He hoped they did.

By the time Wills walked out of the building minutes later, he knew what his next task would be. He would make sure Owens had a list of items he wanted her to do today, then he wanted to check out what Claire's schedule was for today and the rest of the week. After that—well, after that, he might be able to sneak in another dinner with the Rayners tonight.

Wills headed for the next telephone box.

~*~

Something was wrong. It could be just her, but then when did an emotional feeling become wrong? No, it was something else.

Claire was almost certain she was being followed, being watched. But she couldn't put her finger on it. Who was following, and why on earth would anyone follow her? Then there was Norman. He'd always been different, and at first, she'd enjoyed different, but now? Now it was more annoying than anything else.

He persistently asked her to do things she was uncomfortable with or else she didn't care for. He seemed at times to be displeased with her, although that was another thing that she couldn't pinpoint. If she questioned him, he gave soothing or vague answers like, she was imagining it, or worse, she was allowing her emotions to get the best of her. He wanted the best for her, which was why she'd hired him, right? Worst of all, was his mushiness. It was the normal nowadays, but not for her. Papa and Emma Jaine had been strict with her about being careful, saving herself for her future husband, and more. Truth be told, she agreed wholeheartedly with them. The few times she'd tried to lighten up had given her nightmares.

She wasn't a fuddy-duddy by any means, but neither did she want some man she'd just met, or even Norm, thinking she was an easy-take.

As for Norm, she had no answers for his actions or questions.

And it had all started a couple months before her trip to France.

Claire flung open the door to the building where she did all her practices and where Norm waited. She glanced at the huge clock in the reception area. Right on time. He wouldn't be able to subtly complain about that...for once.

Norm was just inside the room where her band was making the usual musical sounds with their instruments. He held a notebook, staring down at it, his lips moving as he read.

He looked up as she approached him. "You're late. Here's your new songs. We'll be singing the first one tomorrow night. The others in the following weeks. We'll stagger them. The dates you'll perform them are listed at the top of each page, so you'll need to be ready to perform."

"But—"

"No time. Let's go. We've got a full day today of practicing to be ready for tomorrow. We'll be lucky to grab a sandwich." He started off, but when she didn't move, looked back at her. "What's wrong?"

"It's too much. I need a break—"

"Girly, I know you do." His voice softened. "I'm sorry. It's just that there's such a demand for your singing, it's hard to keep up. It's the biz."

She looked at him, but didn't speak.

"Remember what you told me when you asked me to be your manager?" He didn't give her a chance to answer this time. "You said, and I remember this distinctly because you were so sincere, you wanted to do something good for your country, you wanted to serve in the best way you could which was singing. That impressed me that you were a determined and soon-to-be successful singer. It was the one reason I agreed to be your manager."

Claire drew in a deep breath. His words made sense, and she was that person. But...

"What's it to be? Gonna be strong and give it all you got?"

"I am. Let's go." She led the way to the stage and climbed the steps, placed the music sheets on the podium and adjusted the microphone. She nodded at the musicians. "Guys, play it over a couple times while I get a sense of the music. I'll join in the third time around."

It was going to be a long day.

~*~

Wills' contact—a janitor—at the building where Claire was practicing had no trouble finding out her schedule for the rest of the month. He'd reported she'd shown up around ten and no one had seen her since. The contact had overheard her manager telling Claire she'd be practicing all day.

That was good, at least for Wills. He had a few more contacts around town to see if anything unusual was going on. Now was the time to locate their whereabouts.

His first stop was down by the docks of the Ohio River. He strolled among the dock workers, taking his time, greeting a few of the men he knew by sight or by name. After twenty minutes, he'd just about decided today wouldn't be the day he'd be able to talk with his main contact, E.I., when he caught sight of him lounging with two shady-looking men.

Wills paused across the street from him, caught the quick glance the other man gave him, then headed on down the street, finally stopping in front of what used to be a corner grocery, now closed down. When he saw the man in the distance, he headed to the back of the building and waited. Not five minutes later, the man who went by the initials E.I., came around the corner.

They didn't waste time on any elaborate salutations.

"News?"

"Maybe some that might interest you." E.I. leaned against the side of the building.

"Spill it."

"Heard some rumors there's some illegal shipping of weapons."

"Can't be. Cops are watching that."

"Not if they're disguised. Not if they're in bits and pieces, to be assembled here." E.I. gave him a sharp glance.

"Still hard to believe. Any proof?"

E.I. shook his head. "Not a thing. Just a rumor, and you know how that goes. Always rumors flying around. Most don't end up being anything important."

"Any way to find out? You got contacts we can use to get more details?"

"Doubt it. There was one guy, but I haven't seen him for a month or more." E.I. stared straight ahead.

Wills knew the man seldom made close friends. The only reason Wills was this close was because they'd been together at basic training and formed a friendship. But when he'd been targeted for special training as a spy, they'd lost contact, and only happenstance had reunited them. Now, the man, sent home from a severe injury, had chosen to serve the best he could as a homeless man seeking out foreign, dangerous information that could harm the United States.

"Anything else?"

"Maybe." The man hesitated. "Hate to speculate on this, but I hear there's some sabotage being planned here at home. Big wigs involved."

"More?"

"Nope, but if I hear anything, I'll get word to you." E.I. straightened. "Gotta go. Don't wanna get caught hanging around the likes of you."

Wills smothered a chuckle. "What's wrong with me?"

E.I. gave him a smirk, but it was a friendly one.

~*~

The next day, Claire stared from behind the curtain at the multitude of soldiers gathered in the stadium. They were wound up, giving their rambunctious shouts and laughter. She smiled, glad she'd be able to give them something to make them forget what they'd been through, what they had and were suffering now due to their service for their country.

"You ready?" Norm asked as he strolled up beside her.

He didn't look out at the soldiers, and Claire knew why. He neither cared about the soldiers nor why they were here—except as it concerned her performance and the popularity it gave her.

"I am."

"You've got ten minutes. Better get a drink or look over your list of songs instead of staring out at a bunch of hooligans."

Claire straightened. Hooligans? Since when did soldiers who'd done their duty and who'd come home injured become hooligans? She opened her mouth to scorch him with a rebuke, but he was walking away.

"Get that drink." His order came from over his shoulder.

If she'd been inclined to get a drink, she wouldn't now.

Her gaze swept over the group of soldiers on the other side of the curtain then shifted to the back of the stadium. It was still well-lit, and she could make out several men—workers, no doubt—walking around, and a few leaning against the back wall. Once she thought she saw Wills Mason, but after she pulled back, then relooked, she couldn't know for sure. Probably not. Why would he be here tonight? No reason.

The band was playing the opening song. It was time to go, but Claire took one last look out the curtain, and she lifted a hand to salute the soldiers. They would never know what she'd done, never realize her admiration for them. But it didn't matter. She knew, and it did her spirits good to know she recognized and saluted their tremendous sacrifice.

Claire squared her shoulders, brushed at the skirt of her lime green and navy dress, touched the white gardenia with its wreath of green shiny leaves in her hair and marched out onto the stage. She was gonna knock their eyes out, as the current slang went.

The soldiers yelled their pleasure at seeing her, and she nodded and gave them her usual beaming smile. But when the band began playing her first number, they quieted and fixed their gazes on her as she swayed to the music.

It was one of her favorites, *Shoo, Shoo, Baby*, and she gave it all she had. She finished and plunged straight into her second number. It was only when she began her third—one of the numbers written by some top WAC that seemed, to her, to have little talent and no imagination, that—the tune slowed.

"I'm crying my blue eyes out, Baby, reading each letter you write. You promised to be home by midsummer, but it's winter and so cold tonight. I'm missing you more every day that flies by, I'm as lonesome as lonesome can

get. Mr. Man in the Moon, tell my baby tonight, there'll never be another like him."

The guys swayed along with her, threw arms around each other's shoulders and joined in on the chorus, as she sang it not once, but three times. They must have liked this one pretty well, for them to be showing this kind of emotion. So much for her own dismissal of the newer songs.

When the song ended, Claire left the stage for a fifteen-minute break. She headed toward the room Norman always set aside for her for breaks, but stopped when she heard the voices coming from a room with a partially closed door.

"I was told to tell you, you've gotta...under control. Just till...job done. After that, we'll be on easy street."

"You sure about that?"

"...told you a million times...getting tired of your constant whining. You better do it. Your head's on the..."

"*My* head? Think again. I'm her cousin."

"Doesn't matter. Your cousin heard...our female deliverer was getting restless. Do better."

Who were they talking about? Her? Why would it be her? For that matter, who were they? It was hard to tell with their voices so low. Why not find out who was talking as if they had something to hide? It would be simple enough to pretend she'd entered the wrong room by mistake or that she was looking for something.

She touched the door, and it barely moved, but enough that the two persons stopped talking.

And she panicked. Turning she ran lightly down the hallway, turned a corner, and plowed into a tall man. She looked up, prepared to apologize and run on. But why run? Here was the perfect person to foil anyone's suspicions if they came looking for a reason why a door was moving.

She plastered a smile on her lips and started to speak as she looked up into the honey-brown eyes of Wills Mason.

He wasn't smiling.

"You."

"Yep. This *you* has a name, in case you forgot."

She jerked back. "I haven't forgotten."

"Is something wrong?"

"Why would anything be wrong? Did you hear the thunder of approval from the soldiers?"

"I did, and believe they loved your singing."

"Then...?"

"Your eyes are betraying you, as usual."

Claire frowned. "What do you mean?"

He took her chin and lifted her face. His gaze roved over it, but returned to her eyes. "There's pleasure at the soldiers' response to your performance. There's satisfaction that you, once again, wowed anyone in hearing distance—and you know that. But most of all, there's a trace of fear lurking deep inside those dark pupils of yours."

"Fear?" She didn't have to ask how he knew that. Faced with the truth, she acknowledged it. For some odd reason, she felt a fear inside her after hearing those two voices. She, they'd said. Claire reasoned it wasn't her. She argued, why would it be her when there were plenty of other *shes* in the world? But hidden inside of her was that fear that it could be her. That they would catch her for eavesdropping.

He hadn't said anything else, just seemed to be waiting on her. And she had no idea what to say. Five minutes had already been wasted on this nonsense. She had ten minutes to do whatever she was going to do.

She reached out and gripped his arm. "Come with me."

He didn't say a thing, but allowed her to pull him along until she came to a room that had a small sign on it that said, Claire Rayner. Shoving the door open, she entered, motioning for him to enter.

Wills shut the door, but didn't move away from it. His gaze drifted over the room then returned to her, and she almost—but not quite—wished she'd not been so hasty.

"I heard something."

"You heard something."

"Don't mock me."

"I wouldn't think of it. You're too..."

"Too what?" Her brow furrowed as she glared at him.

"Nothing. Go ahead."

"As I said, I was headed here when I heard something—"

Bang. Bang. Bang. "Claire, are you in there? It's time to begin again."

Norm. Claire sighed.

"Go. What time are you finished? Can you meet me afterward? At that corner diner before you turn onto our home street?"

She nodded as she turned to leave. "Ten sharp?"

"Good. I'll see you then."

Claire opened the door but looked back at Wills. He was watching her. There were no teasing lights in his eyes. No mischievous plots revealed themselves from his eyes. No doubts she was being paranoid.

Wills nodded and the slightest of smiles tilted his lips.

He'd be there, waiting.

~*~

Exactly at nine forty-nine, Wills entered the diner. Claire wouldn't be here yet, but just in case, he wasn't about to be late and have her leave before he arrived. There were only two other customers, and that suited Wills just fine. The fewer the better.

He chose a seat toward the back of the restaurant, with his back to the wall where he could see any coming and going and keep an eye out for any suspicious action. He didn't expect any, but one never knew. The door jingled as it opened, and Claire walked in.

She stood quietly glancing around the diner till she spotted Wills, then moved toward him. He stood as she approached.

"You made it."

"Why shouldn't I have?"

Hmmm. Not a good start. "You look like some megabucks in the green and blue dress."

"It's lime and navy, Wills, and you really should have spent more time on learning colors instead of making mischief growing up."

He cocked an eyebrow at her, but kept his smile. No need to ruffle her feathers too much. "Whatever the colors, they bring out the green in your eyes. Outstanding."

Was that a pink blush on her cheeks? She didn't lose her steady stare at him, but it sure did look like she was embarrassed...or was it pleased?

He could hope.

"Then, thank you, I guess. That was a very nice compliment." She nodded her thanks at the waitress who set down a glass of water then waved her away. "I'm not sure whether what happened today is anything to worry about, or if I'm allowing my imagination to run away from me. It's just that—"

"You can tell me, Claire. You know I would never betray your trust."

"It's not that. It's that now, after the fact, it seems silly and very unimportant. I don't know why I bothered you. Why I keep hearing whispering voices."

"You bothered me, as you call it, because I'm almost family. I'm your friend, Claire, whether you know it, or even like it." He touched her hand that lay on the table top then withdrew his. He didn't want to overdo the affection business. Not yet. "If it bothered you then it must be important. You don't jump at silliness or allow petty incidents to bother you. That's one thing I like about you. Now tell me what you wanted to say. What whispering voices are you hearing? "

She drew in a long breath, looked down at her hand then sighed. "I will share then, but please promise me you won't tease or laugh at me. I've always hated you and Josie doing that to me."

Her voice had descended into real hurt, and Wills realized that his and Josie's antics had hurt the one person he would ever love. Back then, he'd never had an idea that someday, Claire Anne Rayner would be the girl he'd fall in love with. Maybe he'd loved her all along but been distracted by her obvious dislike.

"I promise, Claire. I will never laugh at you again, unless you wish me to."

She studied him again, and he was pretty sure that blush deepened in color.

"All right, then I'll tell you. Over the past three weeks,

I've overheard conversations that seem to be...covert. Sometimes it seems it's about me, and other times I don't know. I know Norm was in some of them. It frightens me because I have no idea what's happening."

Wills frowned. "You have no idea who the other man was talking with Norm?"

"No."

"Can you describe him?"

"I can. He's a skinny, runt of a man with a weak mouth and a blotchy mustache to go along with it."

Hermie? Sure sounded like him.

"Very good, Claire. I think I know who you mean."

"Can you tell me who it is?"

"No, I can't. Not right now anyway. Tell me what you overheard today."

"When I was beginning a break, I came down the hallway and overheard voices in a room that's never—to my knowledge—ever been used by us at any time."

"Maybe they decided to use it again? Could it have been your manager or someone else who needed to have a private conversation?"

"Yes, it could have been, but..." She hesitated, a tiny frown between her brows forming. "...but it was what they said that troubled me."

"You're all right. I'm here. Go ahead and tell me."

She nodded. "Here's the conversation the best I can remember it:

"I was told to tell you, you've gotta...under control. Just till...job done. After that, we'll be on easy street."

"You sure about that?"

"...told you a million times...getting tired of your constant whining. You better do it. Your head's on the..."

"My head? Think again. I'm her cousin."

"Your cousin heard...our female deliverer was getting restless. Do better."

"Doesn't that sound like it could be me?"

Earlier he'd discerned fear in her eyes, and now, was it panic that seemed to be radiating off of her? Something wasn't adding up right. If, as Colonel Waverly insisted, Claire was involved in foreign spying, then she didn't seem to be doing a good job at it. But then, why would she? She'd do everything she could to convince him and anyone else that she was as innocent as a baby.

He wanted to believe in her innocence. How he did! But it was his duty to know for sure and not allow gut feelings to rule his judgement.

For now, he'd listen and watch and convince her he believed her.

He returned her worried look with one of his own. "It does sound suspicious."

"I started to shove open the door to look. I figured I could get them to believe I was looking for something."

Or not.

"It could be they weren't even talking about you. But it could easily have been one of your crew members or anyone."

"True, but what if they were? Why would they say what they did about me—or whoever—if I didn't suspect a thing and was innocent? Why, Wills, why?"

When Wills reached over for her hand this time, he didn't just touch it, he clasped it gently. Then he said with all the sincerity and promise he could convey, "I don't know the answers to those questions, Claire. But I do promise that I'm going to find out. I promise that, Claire. You can believe that with all your heart."

The tears in her eyes tugged at his heart, and he wanted to draw her to him, but he didn't.

Not tonight. She wasn't ready.

And he had to prove something else first.

Maybe, just maybe, God would see fit to allow all this to tie together, and he could wrap it up in one neat package.

Or not.

Chapter Thirteen

"Captain Ossie, may I ask a favor?" Wills sat in the man of the house's study the next morning.

Ossie Rayner was a big man, with a loud voice but a gentle heart. He had worked hard all his life as the owner and captain of a crew of cargo ships to provide for his family, and in return, no man could have asked more from his daughters than the love they showered on him.

"Of course, my boy, what is it?"

"I'd like to invite Colonel Waverly for dinner some evening. The sooner the better."

Ossie Rayner's eyebrow rose. "And I suppose this invitation has a reason behind it?"

"It does, Sir, but I can't reveal it. I do have a lot of admiration for the colonel."

Wills had no doubt the man understood more than Wills realized.

"Is that all?"

"One more thing. It's a little more tricky, but I think you could pull it off."

"Hmm. What am I getting into, Wills?"

"I don't believe it's dangerous, but it will take some care to carry this through without arousing suspicion from the wrong people."

"I don't want my girls in danger..."

"I would never purposely do that, Captain Ossie, but, if my suspicions are right, I'm afraid it's too late."

"Wills Mason, what are you saying?"

Wills chuckled. "I don't think you'll be in any danger at a dinner, but it may help me in my—uh, work."

"And you can't explain, I take it?"

"I can't. I wish I could share with you..."

"No worries. So what's this third thing?"

"I'd like the invitation to extend to Claire's manager, Norman Tyson."

The captain scowled. "I met him once when Claire first began touring. Didn't care for his lofty attitude then and doubt he's changed. Warned Claire about him, but she wouldn't listen."

"I do know that, but I think it's important."

"Then I'll do it." Captain Ossie sighed. "Don't worry any more about the details. I'll see that invitations go out to these two for the first night Claire has free."

Wills stood. "Thank you, Sir."

~*~

"Did you need me, Papa Ossie?" Claire peeked into her father's office.

"Come in, little girl. I want to talk with you."

"I have to be at practice at ten, Papa—"

Papa Ossie waved a hand. "Nevermind that. I need you."

"Is something wrong, Papa? Are you ill?"

"No. No, not at all. Never felt better. Come in. Come in and shut the door. Guess I can talk to my girl when I want. That hasn't changed, has it, Claire Anne?"

"You know it hasn't." She went to him and leaned down to kiss his cheek. "Let's talk."

"I'm inviting some people to dinner one night this week and need to know when's your first night off."

"Is that all? It's Friday, but why do I need to be here?"

"Because your manager is one of the ones getting an invitation."

"Norm?" Papa had never had any words of praise for the man, so why would he want to invite him to an intimate dinner party here in his home?

"Yes. Because it's time. Since the man is working with my daughter I need to get to know him better. Perhaps I misjudged him. I don't want just anyone hanging around my baby girl."

"Papa. I can take care of myself."

"I believe that, but it doesn't mean I don't worry." He stared at her. "Humor me. Let me have my way on this one."

"Papa, Papa. You always know how to work things to make us come around, don't you?" She raised a hand when he started to speak then. "But that's fine. We love you too much not to do as you ask. Do your invitations. I'll be here, I promise. Now I've got to go. Love you."

She fled the room afraid he'd ask even more from her. And as much as last night had gone well talking with Wills, she wasn't about to be roped into going beyond that.

~*~

Friday evening, Claire stood at one of her two bedroom windows watching as the visitors arrived. Norm by himself and two other people Claire didn't recognize. Norm looked snazzy as usual, his zoot suit fit well and was top of the fashion world. He was a big man, but thin enough he carried the look well.

Claire turned then when she could no longer see him and stared into the mirror. She'd chosen a sunshine yellow dress tonight. The scarf around her waist, her shoes and her hairclip that pinned one side of her hair back were all the medium brown color that toned down the brightness of her dress. She didn't wear a corsage tonight because it was the signature touch she usually only wore for performances or advertising interviews.

She looked good, she knew it. If only her spirits felt as good as her looks.

Heading toward the door, she shook her head. She was not looking forward to tonight, but she'd endure it for Papa's sake.

She took her time as she walked down the hallway, and at the door to the library, she paused. All of the Rayner Boarding House tenants were here, decked in their finest, along with a heavier man in a military uniform and a stiff-looking woman who'd tried to dress fashionably and only succeeded in looking ridiculous. The last two were standing close to Papa Ossie, the men laughing at something—probably at one of Papa's poor jokes—while the woman stood stiff and uncomfortable-looking. Claire almost felt sorry for her.

She headed their direction.

"Hey, good-looking. Don't you look spiffy tonight, but then when don't you?" Norm greeted her.

"Hello, Norm. I wondered if you'd come." Seeing as how Papa Ossie hadn't been any too polite to the man when Claire had introduced him as her manager several months ago.

"Why not when you're here? I pay little attention to what old people say or think."

He sounded brisk and on-top-of-the-world, albeit a little tipsy. Not too much though. He'd never been a heavy drinker and was always polite, although a mite pushy if needed. And she didn't care for the comment on old people.

Claire tucked her arm in his. "I'm glad you came. I'm headed over to speak with Papa a little. You coming?"

He pulled his arm away from her. "I think I'll skip that this time around. Maybe later."

Laughing, Claire said, "Don't get into any trouble then."

"You know I won't."

"Uh huh, right."

When Claire walked up to her father, both men and the woman stopped their talking and looked at her. "Papa Ossie."

"Claire, come and meet Lieutenant Nelson and Colonel Waverly."

Claire nodded at the woman and held out her hand to the colonel. "Colonel, do you and my father know each other?"

"Years ago, we met, but never got the opportunity to really know each other." The colonel's mustache wobbled as he talked. "I hear you're pretty famous. Soldiers love you, do they?"

"I don't know about being famous, per se, but the soldiers do seem to enjoy my singing. I'm sure they'd probably enjoy anyone's singing who could help them forget for awhile what they were facing."

"You're right about that." He nodded his head and seemed to be studying her. "Don't suppose I could persuade you to sing for us after dinner?"

"Oh, Sir, not tonight."

"Now, Claire, why not tonight?" her father urged. "There's no one here who doesn't love to hear you sing, and if there is someone, well, then they can get over it or leave. You know we all enjoy your singing. Be a good girl, Claire."

Claire frowned a tiny bit at her father but knew she'd give in. How could she tell him no? "We'll see, Papa, how the evening goes. Colonel, I'm going to get a drink. Would you like one?"

"I'll come with you. Give me time to find out a little more about the talented Miss Rayner."

"Well, I'd love to have you come, but not sure there's much to learn about me." She gave him her best smile. He was such a nice man.

"Oh, I'm sure there's more to you than meets the eye, and having said that, if I was younger, I'd be paying close attention to you. Where are all the young scoundrels that they're not flocking after you?"

"You're quite the flatterer, you know that, Colonel Waverly?"

He gave her his arm. "I've been known to flatter a woman or two in my day, Miss Claire."

She chuckled. She just bet he had.

~*~

Wills stood close to the fireplace. There was no fire inside it, but the candles' lighting gave off vibes of warmth and happiness. His gaze strayed from person to person, but mostly fixed on the ones he was most interested in.

Claire seemed to be in good spirits when she entered, paused long enough to speak briefly with her manager then moved on to her father, The Dame and the colonel. They must have gotten along well, because minutes later, the colonel and Claire headed to the table where a variety of drinks sat.

Good. Maybe the colonel would realize Claire was innocent. But just in case, he'd keep his guard up and his nose to the ground.

Time to mingle. Josie wasn't here yet, so Wills couldn't fall back on her if he needed someone to talk to. His father was refilling the drink table, so he ambled over to it. "Pops, everything looks killer-diller. You've done good."

"Thanks, Son, but you know Emma Jaine has a big hand in getting things ready. I just take directions."

His father was always quiet and entirely reluctant to accept praise, but Wills knew he was stronger than most people gave him credit for. Only a couple times had he seen his father stand up to unruly, pushy people. He hadn't backed down but stood his ground. He was a good man, and tops as far as Wills was concerned. "Love you, Pops. You know that, don't you?"

The man looked at him. "I do, Son. You make us proud, your mother and I, every day of our lives."

"Even when Josie and I were at our worst?"

"Well..." His father chuckled. "You go on now and talk to Claire while you have the chance."

"Pops!" Wills did as his father had suggested. Claire had strayed toward where Emma Jaine, Tyrell and Jerry stood talking, but before he could reach her, her manager walked up. Claire turned to him, touched his arm and appeared to be introducing him to the others.

Wills started to veer away, but Tyrell must have caught sight of him. He called out, "Wills, come join us."

Hesitating a second, he figured he might as well rather than cause a scene. "Some party, huh?"

Emma Jaine laughed. "I'd say it's similar to all the other get-togethers we have. Conversation, laughter, jokes and great food from your mother, Wills. We are a truly blest family to have so many people we love around us."

"I didn't know you had a brother, Girly." Norm looked down at Claire. "You never told me that. You didn't even speak of him on the plane."

"I don't have a brother, but Wills and his parents are family in our eyes. We've grown up together. The Masons are family."

"I see." Norm's eyes narrowed as he stared at Wills. "And where are his parents?"

"I'd say Harriet is putting the finishing touches on one of the great meals she prepares for us. His father—Jonah—is getting ready to announce that our dinner is served."

"Servants then?" Norm's lips wore a slight scornful twist.

"Family, Norm. Family."

Wills saw the tilt of Claire's head, the firmness in her words and tone. She was the Claire he'd known growing up, firmly placing another person where she wanted them to be.

"Whatever you want to call them, Girly, makes no difference to me as long as the food is good."

"There's none better anywhere. Harriet is very good."

"I guess we'll see, won't we?"

Claire opened her mouth to argue when Wills' father stepped into the room and announced dinner was served. The guests and family made their way toward the dining room, her father leading the way with The Dame.

The colonel headed toward Claire, and Wills stepped back to make room for him to approach her.

Colonel Waverly held out his arm to Claire. "May I?"

"Thank you, Colonel."

Wills saw Owens approaching him. "Where have you been? I didn't think you were coming."

"I was delayed, but I'm here now. Will you walk me into the dining room?"

"I will." Wills held out his arm. "You look ravishing in that rusty red dress. Careful or you'll catch everyone's attention and some of the hostesses might not care for that."

"Silly." She laughed. "Sir."

He patted her hand that rested on his arm. "I aim to please."

~*~

Where had that brunette come from? Claire hadn't seen her while mingling with the family and guests, and now here she was, holding onto Wills' arm as if for dear life and smiling up at him as if she adored him. Just fine and dandy.

She sat down a little too hard and realized she was angry. Norm had sullenly moved away to where he was to sit close to Josie and Jerry. She sat between the Colonel and Wills, with that ill-dressed woman on Papa's right-hand side. The rest of the assembly were scattered around the table.

Leaning closer to Wills, she whispered, "Did you ask

your mother to place us together?"

"I did not. Why would I do that? And what would it matter if I had?"

Claire didn't speak for a moment. "I'm sorry. I'm just on edge. It wouldn't matter. And believe it or not, I'd much prefer to sit by you as some people I won't name." She turned back to Colonel Waverly, who was speaking again.

"Do you know *Blue Birds Over the White Cliffs of Dover?*"

"I do."

"Then could I persuade you to sing it for me later in the evening?"

Claire laughed. He was so sweet. "I will do that for you."

His gaze rested on her face. "You seem to be such a good person in spite of all the popularity you have gained."

She thought about what he'd said. "I try to be. Papa and Emma Jaine did their best to make me a good person. I think I am."

"Emma Jaine, your sister?"

"Yes, she's been my rock as I've grown up."

"And your other sister?"

"Josie? She's exactly opposite of me. She and Wills were buddies growing up and are still quite close friends, but she's tamed down some since she married and has a baby girl now. That Fina is totally adorable, and I'm in love with her." She leaned closer and lowered her voice. "I try to stay close to the baby as much as I can, hoping I can be a good influence and keep her from being as wild as Josie was."

The colonel gave out a loud laugh. "You do, do you?"

"Definitely." Claire cocked her head in his direction and winked at him. "Josie's not a bad person. We're just so different, we kind of clash, but I do love her, as she does me, I'm sure."

"And all these people who aren't your family, they're boarders?"

"They are, and we're fond of them. Philip, who's becoming quite the popular artist, Miss Gertie—our decked out, all year, Christmas tree—but who's the smartest and nicest person alive. She's been here forever and keeps all of us accountable."

"And the older lady with the light brown hair?"

"Our retired librarian? Did Shirley catch your eye? Better not. Papa and she are pretty good friends."

"Has anyone ever told you you're sassy?"

"Me?" Claire widened her eyes at him. "Never."

Again, the colonel let out a roar of laughter, and Claire laughed with him, throwing her head back. Her gaze caught sight of Wills staring at her, a small smile on his lips as if he was pleased at her fun.

And Claire felt such a recklessness flood her being that she gave Wills the same wide-eyed look she'd just given the colonel and then laughed as shock and pleasure filled his eyes.

What on earth was she doing?

~*~

Colonel Waverly took that moment to speak to Claire, and Wills would have eavesdropped but Owens spoke to him. "You grew up here, in this house?"

"I did. Can't remember living any other place. It's home."

"And what a home. Don't you get homesick when you're away?"

He started to speak but Norm, sitting across the table close between Josie and Emma Jaine, spoke loudly. "She's my girl. I don't take kindly to anyone who tries to interfere between us."

He was talking about Claire for sure, and Wills was tempted to respond but let it pass. No need to create tension. Not tonight. He had more game to watch, and whether Norman Tyson knew it or not, Tyson was one of the ones he'd be watching.

He glanced at Owens who was staring at him. "Sorry. I got distracted. You were saying?"

"I asked if you got homesick when you were away?"

"I do. But my work is what I felt I should do for now. If all goes well, I'll be home when I'm finished. Then I can enjoy to the fullest being with family and doing something else I enjoy."

"What's that?"

Wills glanced at her again. "I'm going to college to study management and music."

"You?"

Owens lifted her glass and sipped, and Wills wondered if it was to hide her surprise at his revelation.

"Yes, me. I have several good reasons to, but one of the ones is, I feel it's what I should do."

"Meaning God?" Owens' eyes were wide. "You take this God-thing pretty seriously, don't you, Sir?"

"Yes, I do. It's vital to myself and what I'm striving for in life. And have you forgotten that we're supposed to be friends? None of this 'sir' business in front of others."

"Yes, S—I mean, Wills." She giggled.

A spoon clanked against a glass and all heads turned toward the end of the table. Papa Ossie stood holding his glass in hand. "I'd like to make a toast to two important people in my life."

"Here, here." Jerry, Tyrell, and several others called out an enthusiastic response.

"To a young lady—my youngest daughter, who's talented and beautiful, but who also knows her own mind and is working hard to keep the troops' spirits high and encouraged. She's worked tirelessly even when tired and needing a break. She doesn't realize others see it, but I do, and I'm sure many of her friends and other family members see and acknowledge her labor of love." He held up his glass as he spoke. "To Claire Anne Rayner, a beautiful singer and an even lovelier person."

Cheers resounded around the room as Claire sat, flushed and beaming at her father and the others who had risen as Captain Ossie led them in the toast.

In the spur of the moment, without a thought of what he was doing, Wills leaned down and gave her a hug. As soon as he did, he realized *what* he was doing and drew back. But shocker of all shocks, she didn't seem agitated at his move.

Wills didn't have time to think on that for long. Captain Ossie was speaking again as the laughter settled.

"I'd like us to give a toast to a young man who's more

like a son than a family friend. I've watched this man grow from a child, to a teen who—along with my spirited Josie—filled all our hearts with trepidation at what they'd get into next."

Laughter exploded at his somewhat dry explanation of their antics.

When it settled he spoke again. "But he moved on into adulthood, and became the man I'd hoped he would. Serious, sincere and steady. He didn't lose that interest into—let's call it adventure—but he's grown wiser and smarter in how he goes about it. He's become a man in every way, someone his parents and I—and well, all of us—have become so proud of. He works hard for our country and is loyal in his duties. William Mason, we all love you, support you and wish the very best for you in your future. To Wills!"

Amidst as much clamor as had praised Claire, Wills looked from face to face, but particularly to his family— his parents and the Rayners—and felt his heart warm at the love radiating from them. Who could ask for more?

It was close to nine when Claire went to the piano where Emma Jaine sat, and began singing. Once Tyrell joined her in a spiritual song, but the listeners seemed to enjoy all of them.

Wills circled the room casually, speaking occasionally, ignoring others. He'd just about decided to slip out to the kitchen where his parents would be resting and eating their own dinner before beginning the clearing up after everyone was gone.

He started to step into the hallway, glanced back to see if he was being noticed and caught sight of the two people standing across the room near the French doors. They were half-turned toward each other and appeared to be in serious conversation about something.

The Dame grabbed Tyson's arm, and he pulled away. By the look on his face, he wasn't happy at her action. They talked back and forth—appearing to be arguing— but then Tyson nodded as he accepted a small piece of paper from her and shoved it into his pocket. Without another word to him, The Dame walked away. Not to the colonel. That man's attention was fixed entirely on

Claire Rayner, who was singing her heart out.

When Wills glanced at the French doors again, Tyson was gone. A quick sweeping glance about the room didn't reveal his presence.

Had the man slipped out the doors while Wills was preoccupied in watching The Dame?

~*~

Wills headed for the front door to check to see where Tyson had gone, when he almost bumped into Jerry.

The usually quiet man grinned. "Just the person I was looking for."

"Me? What did you need, Jerry?"

"I don't need anything, but..." Jerry hesitated. "...but I know you were doing a bit of undercover work a few months ago. No one really knows what you do now, but I'm wondering if it's along the same lines as then. If so, you might be interested in hearing what I heard earlier."

He wasn't about to share his work with Jerry, even though he admired the man. He'd done similar work for awhile until Jerry had retired after a serious injury. But the man's strength in regaining his life after the depths of despair and the Combat Stress Reaction he'd battled through had given Wills an everlasting admiration for him.

"I'd certainly like to know that."

"I slipped outside on the side patio to get a breath of fresh air—even after all this time, I still feel a little smothered at times—and overheard a conversation."

This was interesting. "Go ahead."

"I couldn't see them, but I'm pretty sure it was that sour-faced woman and the big man who's Claire's manager. They were standing in front of the curtains, but the door was cracked open, so their voices were clear."

"You could hear over the conversations and Claire's singing?"

"I could. Claire's voice was coming from farther away, but these two, their words were low, but I was right by the door, almost close enough, if I'd wanted to, to touch them. They were talking about someone—a female because they said her."

"What did they say?"

"The woman—I assume it was the woman said, 'You know, if you can't keep her under check, we'll have to get rid of her.'"

"The man was really angry. 'She's done everything you've asked.'"

"'You think so?' The Nelson woman snapped back. 'She argues over everything being asked of her. You assured me you'd have no trouble with her. If you care about me and our country, then surely you can reason with her.'"

Wills' eyes had narrowed. What had The Dame meant by "get rid of her?" Let her go and not use her? Or something much worse?

Death?

~*~

Later in the evening as the clocks chimed eleven, Wills saw Owens into her taxi and walked slowly back to the house. Voices from the side of the house caught his attention and he paused. Sounded a little loud for this time of the night. He stepped closer and listened.

"Really, Claire? I thought we had something going between us."

"I don't see what the problem is. These people are my family, Norm. I do like you. I appreciate all you've done to help me. You've been fantastic. But all that doesn't mean I've quit caring about my family—"

"He's not your family. I saw the way he looked at you and that intimate hug. I don't like it."

"You're being silly. He's like a brother."

"That's the problem, Girly. He's not your brother. Not at all, and no matter how much you insist it's so, doesn't make it so."

"But—"

"I just want you to focus on your music. And if there's time after that, then focus on me. I have money, Girly, and I know people. You can go far if you stick with me."

Silence.

"We've got a good thing going, don't we? You love what you're doing. Don't let him come between your love of singing and me, who's your best bet at making it in this business. I wouldn't have to quit being your manager over something as silly as not focusing on what's important. When I ask you to sing a particular song, then it's your duty to do so. I have my reasons, and they are good ones. When I ask you to pay a little more attention to your music than your family, it's for a good cause."

Was that a warning?

Obviously, Claire was thinking on those lines too.

"Are you saying I have to choose between my family and my music and you? Is that what you're saying, Norm? Because you'd better mean what you say. I don't like threats."

Wills stepped closer, but hesitated in intruding. So far, Claire was handling this like a trooper.

More silence, then Tyson spoke again.

"Listen, Girly, I'm not trying to come across as bossy or unreasonable. Jealous? Maybe, a little, but I do care about you. I don't know what might happen in the future between us, but I'd like the path to stay clear of problems and interruptions. If things do advance, I want everything to move smoothly in that direction without any clouds of confusion. Understand what I mean?"

"Thank you for saying that, Norm. I do understand, and my regard for you is high. I suppose time will tell if we go further in our relationship." Claire paused. "What do you say, we try again. Let's not jump to conclusions and try to keep everything smooth sailing."

"I agree. I care too much about you to do less."

Wills stepped to the corner and peeked around it. Claire stood on tiptoe and pecked a kiss on the guy's cheek.

He frowned and wanted to stop her, but he didn't. He didn't have the right.

But he wanted that right oh-so-badly he could taste it.

Chapter Fourteen

After listening in on Claire and her manager's argument, Wills had headed back to the kitchen to help his parents clean up. Normally Emma Jaine pitched in, but he'd waved her away, insisting he wanted to talk with them while he had the chance.

Emma Jaine was a wonderful person, not just a friend to him. Her guidance and strictness had kept him in line, but he'd always admired her ability—as young as she was—to not only care for her father and sisters, but run a boarding house successfully.

She'd given him a hug and slipped out of the room back to her family's freshly remodeled apartment on the second floor.

"Are you staying safe, Son?"

"As safe as I can, Mother, at this time. I keep busy with assignments from Colonel Waverly."

"You have any thoughts on what you're going to do after the war?" Jonah entered the room and set down the last tray of glasses. "The library is in order, Harriet. All's left is cleaning up in here. Let me do those dishes. You sit down."

"I'm fine, Jonah. You sit there and talk to Wills."

"I think I can talk just fine while washing dishes, Mrs. Mason."

"Go on with you." Harriet laughed. "You didn't answer your father's question, Wills."

"I know it. If I could get a word in edgewise..."

Harriet slapped at him with a dishcloth, but he ducked the swat.

"I don't know for sure, Pops. I've thought about staying in the service to see how far I can advance, but there's a couple other options I'm considering too."

"Care to share?" His father's gentle eyes questioned him.

Wills hesitated. "I'm also thinking of going to college

114

and studying management and music."

His mother whirled from the sink, but his father's raised brows caused him the most embarrassment. "I shouldn't have said anything about that. It's so up in the air."

"You know we always want you to tell us anything that you want, Son." Harriet touched his shoulder then turned back to her dishwashing.

"Son, we're behind whatever you decide. Just make sure it's something *you* want to do—"

Wills started to protest, but his father kept talking.

"—because if things don't work out with Claire, you may find yourself educated in something you have no interest in. Do you understand what I'm saying, Son?"

"I do, Pops, but I won't jump into anything I'm not sure of. Especially to gain the attention or affection of someone else. I do think I'd be great at management, and I love music, so I'm thinking either or both could be something I'd stick with and like. Besides, you've raised me to pray over everything, and that's what I've been doing."

"Good. That's what I want to hear."

"And when I've decided, I'll let you know."

"Whatever you decide, you know we've got your back."

"I know that." Wills laid down the cloth he was using to dry dishes. "I think I'll take a walk. Looks like rain and I'd like to get out in it if it does."

"You'll catch a death cold." Harriet cautioned with a worried frown.

"When have you ever known me to get sick from playing in the rain?" Wills gave her cheek a kiss. "I'll be fine. Stop worrying about me and get to bed. You need that beauty sleep."

"Why you..."

She slung the towel at him again, but he dodged it and slipped out the door laughing.

Truth be told, it wasn't just the rain he was interested in. He needed to soak in and process the evening. He'd really gained very little from it, but there were miniature tidbits that had to mean something—if only he could figure out what.

The colonel and Claire had seemed to hit it off well. Colonel Waverly had even given Wills a subtle nod of approval when he was leaving, and the colonel and Claire had certainly seemed to get along very well.

But that didn't mean he hadn't sensed something wrong. If so, the colonel would let him know when they met tomorrow.

The Dame had been a bit of a surprise, but he assumed the colonel had gotten permission from Captain Ossie to bring the woman. For whatever reason, Wills had no idea. Surely the colonel didn't like the woman that much he'd bring her to every function he attended.

And there was that Tyson guy. He didn't like him at all, but he was smart enough to know the reason. Anyone close to Claire caught his attention and especially his disfavor if the person gave Claire the least bit of annoyance. And that man certainly had.

Besides that, Wills sensed something wrong about him. Whether it was his bold-faced flirting with her or his not-so-subtle pushing her to do what he wanted, Wills didn't like it. Not one little bit.

So what about this evening? Was anything helpful to be gleaned from it that might help him in clearing Claire?

First of all, the one thing that bothered him the most was Colonel Waverly's total ignoring of The Dame. He had watched her with others like the colonel and Tyson. But both had almost totally ignored her after a cursory greeting. It had been up to others—mostly Captain Ossie to entertain the woman. If she was so important to the colonel why had he left her alone all evening at a place where she practically knew no one? Was it important?

Secondly, the Colonel had seemed utterly taken with Claire. He'd spent most of the evening with her, laughing more than Wills had ever seen from him. To see them, one would never suspect the man had sent Wills on a chase to find out if Claire was a spy. He was a little irritated at that.

And lastly, that minute time when Tyson and The

Dame had talked at the French doors. They'd spoken only a few seconds, and she'd passed that paper to him. Why here at the Rayners? Was the conversation Jerry had overheard important or just a routine nothing? Maybe the colonel had asked her to speak with him or pass along something.

Wills laughed. Why not him, if that was so? And why would the colonel be passing along a note to Tyson?

He wouldn't.

Too many questions and not enough answers.

Worse than any of it, was the conversation Jerry had overheard. Jerry was a quiet man but smart. If he'd thought it important enough to share with Wills, then it must be. The remarks about getting rid of *her* bothered him. If it was Claire, she was in danger. But why would she be? Was there something she was doing for them, that they thought she wasn't doing well enough?

He was going to have to dig a little deeper to find the answers he wanted. Actually, all he cared about in this job was clearing Claire's name and—

At that moment, Wills felt pain in the back of his head and the world suddenly went dark—not nighttime darkness, but darkness that meant he was about to pass out.

No. He couldn't. Wills staggered and fell against a building, but had enough sense left to turn and see who'd just slammed his head with what felt like a mountain of a rock. Someone was leaning close to his face. A big someone. Someone who no one would ever guess would do something like attack a person.

Tyson?

Without thinking about it, he swung and connected with the man's cheek.

Eyes suddenly red with anger—glared at him. "Stay out of my business. Hear me? Stay away from Claire."

Wills didn't speak. He couldn't. He continued to stare at the man, his vision blurry, but his hearing just fine, as he slid down the wall of the building and sat on the cold sidewalk.

Then he watched as the man strode away.

~*~

Claire's sleep was restless after the dinner party with the colonel and the other guests. Colonel Waverly had been a fun guest, and she'd enjoyed getting to know him. He had seemed a little intense at times, but not negative. It was a good thing Papa Ossie had invited him.

She hadn't cared for that Nelson woman. At all. She'd seemed to be focused on one thing. Herself, or rather, how could she advance herself further in whatever it was she wanted.

And then there was Norm. Claire sighed. He'd been obnoxious to her and most of the other people here tonight. Whatever his problem had been, it'd been coming on for awhile now. Strange, when he'd always been so amenable and helpful. But he had sort of apologized, and they'd parted on good terms, so that was fine. She'd try to overlook his dinner disagreeableness.

Sitting up in bed, she thought for a minute. A nice cup of hot chocolate might soothe her restlessness and help her get a little more sleep tonight. Tomorrow promised another day of practice.

She scrambled out of bed, slipped into her robe and slid her feet into her slippers—her favorite that Emma Jaine had given her for her birthday. Then tiptoeing, she headed to the kitchen.

There she pulled out a pan, lit the stove, and poured a small portion of milk into the pan. Minutes later, she sat down and sniffed at the aroma of a bit of Harriet's guarded chocolate in her drink. Hmmm.

Lifting the cup, she pursed her lips preparatory to sipping it when—

She heard the noise from outside the back door. Claire froze, her cup still lifted, but her heart suddenly beating faster than it ever had. She set down the cup and stood. There was a minor crashing sound, a groan, then a fumble at the doorknob.

Claire opened her mouth to scream when the door slammed open and a soaking wet Wills stumbled into the room, bumping into a cabinet, then collapsing against the table.

"Wills? What's wrong?" Then she saw the bump on his head. "You're hurt. What happened?"

He stretched out a hand, and she took it and guided him to a chair.

Wills sagged into the chair and leaned against a fist. "I'll be all right. I just need to rest a minute, then I'll go to bed. Be fine as anything in the morning."

Claire crossed her arms. "You'll go nowhere once Harriet gets a sight of that bump on your head."

"I have a bump?" He lifted a hand, felt his head and winced. His eyes widened. "I do, don't I?"

"Have you been fighting, Wills Mason?" She ran cold water over one of Harriet's best towels and carried it to him.

"Me, fighting? Not on your life. Although I'd like to slug that manager of yours."

His attempt at being funny failed miserably.

"Tell me what happened before I wake up the whole household."

"You wouldn't—" He cast a quick glance her direction. "Yeah, I guess you would."

"You scared me to death."

"Didn't mean to. Just needed to get to bed to sleep and try to get rid of this headache."

"Tell me what happened. I mean it or I'm going to wake your parents."

"Did anyone ever tell you how bossy you are?"

"I'm not bossy, just determined. Are you going to spill all?"

"I went for a walk after helping my parents here in the kitchen a bit. Thought about the evening and the people and different things. My job, Emma Jaine and you."

"Me?" Was that her voice squeaking out the question?

"It started to rain—black as coal, it was—and all of sudden something hit me, and I almost lost consciousness. When I looked up, some man stood over me threatening me. It was too dark to see who it was."

"Someone attacked you?"

"I guess this bump is proof of that."

"But why, Wills, why would someone want to hurt

119

you?"

"Because of three reasons, I'd say."

"And they are?" She reapplied the wet towel after soaking it again in the cold water.

"Because they didn't like my looks, or they don't like my snooping."

"You're being ridiculous, and that's only two."

"Right. You might not want to hear the last one."

"Tell me now."

"Because I love you."

Claire opened her mouth to scold him, but it wouldn't have done any good.

Wills Mason had passed out.

~*~

Wills woke late the next morning with a throbbing headache. He groaned but sat up in bed—in bed? He glanced at his clock. How had he gotten to his room? Last night came rushing in, and he fell back against his pillows, wincing as his head hit the soft pillow. There was no way Claire had gotten him down the stairs and into bed. So it must have been…

His bedroom door opened, and a tray appeared and then his mother.

"Are you awake already, Son?"

"Mother, it's after ten. I was supposed to meet Colonel Waverly at eight-thirty."

"No worries. I had your father make a call to him." Harriet set the tray on a bed stool and placed it over his legs. "I don't want you to get up unless necessary until I'm sure you'll be all right. I might have to call the doctor later."

"I'm fine. A bit of a headache, but that's nothing."

His mother frowned at him. "You heard me. If your father comes down, you'll be in serious trouble. I don't care if you are a grown man. You listen to me."

She was as feisty as a woman her age could be. But he loved her all the more for it.

"I've brought your favorites, so I want you to eat it. You won't get strength until you do. Should I feed you?"

"Mother! Really?"

She pulled from her pocket a small bell. "I want you

to ring this if you need me. I'll drop everything and come running. Emma Jaine said she'd pitch in today, and Captain Ossie said he'd be down later today to check on you. So you behave."

"I promise I won't swing from the chandelier, and I won't bounce on the bed or—"

"Wills Mason. Respect your mother."

"I do, I do."

"See that you don't forget that," She snapped then bent down to kiss his forehead. "I'm not asking now what happened to you. I'm assuming it has something to do with your job, but you've got to be more careful. I love you."

"Love you, too."

When his mother left the room, Wills nibbled at the cinnamon toast she'd prepared, drank the coffee and juice, then shoved aside the tray. It was time to go see Colonel Waverly. He'd be late but at least he'd show up. He started to pull on his pants when the door swung open again, and the colonel stood there eyeing him.

"What do you think you're doing? Get back in that bed. That's an order, soldier."

Wills plopped back onto the bed. "Yes, Sir."

"How are you feeling?"

"Better. Head's still sore as blazes, and I'm not as lightheaded as last night, but—"

"Good. Now you listen to your mother and stay in bed as long as she thinks is necessary. Do you hear me, Mason?"

"Yes, Sir, but I don't want—"

"Don't care what you want. Do as I say or you'll answer to me." The colonel lowered his head and glared, much as a bull might do eyeing his target.

"Now, I want you to tell me if you learned anything last night."

"Actually, Sir, not much definite knowledge. I sensed some things, but that doesn't count in the overall scheme of things. I do think I have a better handle and am making progress, on proving whether Claire Rayner is a spy or not."

"Ah, Claire Rayner. That woman captured my heart

last night." Colonel Waverly smiled.

"She did?"

"Absolutely. She's a fantastic conversationalist, a wow of a singer that had this old heart weeping like an emotional woman, and kept me entertained all evening. I forgot Matilda was with me and hogged the girl so much no one else could talk with her."

"She didn't seem to mind much."

"You think she enjoyed my company?"

"She's a very unique and kind person, Sir. I don't doubt in the least that she was entertained as much as she entertained you."

The colonel harrumphed but Wills could tell he was pleased.

"That's not to say I'm suggesting you forget about investigating her. Don't you let up, Mason."

"I won't. As soon as I can I'm going to follow some new leads."

"Good. I'll expect to hear from you in a few days." Colonel Waverly stood and walked to the door but turned back. "Did you see who hit you?"

Wills hesitated. He was sure it had been Tyson, but what if he'd imagined seeing the man because of his dislike of him? "Sir, I'd rather not say right now. If I ever have definite proof it was who I think it was, then I won't mind revealing the name."

The colonel stared at him, measuring his words. Finally, he nodded. "Don't forget that, Mason."

"I won't Sir." If the truth needed to come out, then he'd be glad to share. But just because some jealous man took a swing at him...

Time would tell what should be done about it.

~*~

Two days after the dinner party, Claire happened to stop in at the practice building to pick up a song she'd left there the last time they'd practiced. She stared at her manager. Norm was slouched in a chair, almost as if a daze.

"Norm? Are you all right?"

He lifted his head, slowly, and stared at her a moment as if just waking up. Then he straightened.

"Nothing's wrong. Why would you ask that?"

"You were sitting as if you were carrying a burden so heavy it was weighing you down. I thought you might be asleep."

"At this time of the day?" Norm rose and walked over to her.

She stared at him, lifted a hand and touched his cheek. "Where did you get that bruise? Wow, it looks terrible."

He jerked away from her. "It's nothing. I ran into a board some idiot had laid across a table. Hurts like the dickens."

"It looks painful, too. Have you put anything on it? Seen a doctor?"

"It is. No, and no. Don't talk about it anymore. I'm headed home. Why are you here?"

"Forgot a song sheet. Thought I'd pick it up so I could run the words over in my—"

Claire gaped at Norm who was walking out the door as if he wasn't hearing her.

Something was wrong with her manager.

~*~

One week later, Claire stood on the stage in front of a group of men who'd been injured and were now recovering from those injuries. It was almost time for her mid-break. She crooned the last two measures of the song, the crowd of soldiers erupted into a roar of applause, and Claire smiled and waved over and over again to them. Slowly she moved off stage and headed toward the hall. She'd grab a few sips of water, sit and relax to steady herself for the final minutes of her presentation.

She was almost to her door when she heard voices coming once again from the same storage room as before. She paused. No one was supposed to be back here but the crew, Norm and her. She leaned close to the door and listened.

"Plans are in order and it's confirmed. He's to be in Cincinnati on the twenty-first. All items have been shipped except for..."

Someone spoke words in such a low, hoarse voice,

Claire couldn't understand them. Then...

"We'll need you to serve as head of security. That's a decision."

"Can do."

It was the hoarse voice, but Claire didn't recognize it.

"I'll be glad when he's dead."

"Heil..."

Who was that? She'd never liked cursing. Never. Papa had always taught her and her sisters not to use those words. It was low-brow, and, in her opinion, anyone who didn't have the words, besides curses to describe their feelings wasn't an articulate individual. So boring.

But worse than that, was someone planning a murder?

Footsteps sounded on the other side of the door, and Claire realized she was about to get caught eavesdropping. She ran, passed the first door, the second, and she heard the sound of a door opening. Her heart was racing, her hands sweating as she reached her own room and fumbled with the doorknob. Voices grew louder as the two people exited the storage room, and Claire slid into her own room.

She didn't slam the door, but shut it behind her without allowing it to latch. She stood near the crack, trying to get her breathing under control, trying to calm her nerves.

Footsteps grew louder as the couple neared her door, then paused.

"You sure no one could hear us? I don't hear that Rayner woman singing. Where would she be now?"

An undignified grunt from the hoarse voice, then the voice rasped out, "You don't have to worry. I've got this under control."

"You need to get some soup in you and get rid of that throat issue. I can't use you if you're only up to half-speed." Whoever it was sounded totally disgusted.

"Blame it on France. Crazy weather, but I'll be fine. Nothing a good dosage of my granny's awful tasting syrup won't fix."

"See that you do. And you keep an eye on those two. If you get the least suspicion they suspect anything—

you got that?—take care of it. I want no loose ends."

"And what about your new best friend?" If any coarse voice could smirk, this one did.

"Don't you worry about him. I've got him taken care of," The bossy one snapped.

That one was a tough cookie. Claire winced. She hoped she'd never have to deal with whoever it was.

The voices were fading. Should she take a quick peek?

And then she heard a voice that nearly gave her a heart attack.

"Claire, are you in here hiding? I need to talk with you."

Wills Mason. Why now, of all times, would he come looking for her? If those two co-conspirators were still in the hallway watching, or even listening, she was a goner for sure. And maybe Wills too.

She held her breath. Waiting...

A hand gripped the knob and opened the door. Feeling the panic spread through like a flooding river, she held up a finger to her mouth, shaking her head, and with the other hand motioned for him to leave.

For a split second—the longest in her life—she was sure he'd refuse and loudly enter the room, declaring defiantly he'd found her.

But he didn't. A second passed, two, as he stared at her in confusion, then swift comprehension crossed his face, and he backed from the room. The door shut quietly, and she heard his footsteps as he went further down the hall, opening and closing several doors as if still in search of her.

His voice echoed back to her. "Have either of you seen that singer? I need to talk with her."

The murmurs were so faint Claire couldn't make them out, then...

"She must have stepped outside. I've looked about everywhere. I'll check there for her."

Claire's heartbeats began slowing again, and she leaned against a wall, willing herself to stop shaking.

Whoever those two were, they probably weren't talking about her anyway.

Her behavior was silly, and now Wills would think she was the most nervous person in the world. Someone who went around thinking everyone was talking about her. Ugh.

No, reasoning wasn't working. Whether they were talking about her or not, their conversation definitely had implied death for someone. Probably someone important. But what could she do about it? She knew nothing about plots and such things and knew no one to confide in...

What about Wills?

The thought bothered her so much, she straightened and paced. She didn't like Wills, didn't want to talk to him, and definitely didn't want to confess her crazy suspicions to him. She could just see him laughing—like he and Josie used to do—at her notions, and maybe even share them with her sister making her, again, the brunt of a joke.

No, she wouldn't tell Wills anything, even if he asked. She'd just have to avoid him tonight and for several days.

Satisfied she'd made the right decision, she walked to the door and opened it.

There stood her childhood nemesis.

Chapter Fifteen

Wills had felt something was bothering Claire when he watched and listened to her singing tonight. If anyone had asked him why he felt that way, he'd never have been able to explain.

But he knew. So he'd sought her out during her break, to make sure she was fine. She probably wouldn't share, but he had to try.

Seeing that slender finger at her lips, her frightened eyes and motion to go away, he realized she was terrified. Of those two people—neither of whom he trusted—or someone else?

Didn't matter right now. The only thing important to him was to make sure she was safe. That meant he was going nowhere he couldn't keep his eye on Claire.

At the corner of the hallway, in the opposite direction where the other two were headed, Wills waited. He'd thought for a moment, those two wouldn't move, and he'd be forced to create a diversion so Claire could leave, but he hadn't had to. They sauntered away, and Wills headed to her door.

The tiniest of sounds came through the door as her footsteps came toward him, a pause, then the door creaked open, and Claire's green eyes stared at him.

"You."

"Did you think I'd leave when you were so afraid? Tell me what's wrong."

"I can't." She sounded panicked. "I'm late. The band and Norm must be wondering where on earth I am."

She half-ran down the hall, and Wills stared after her. But at the corner she turned back.

"Can you meet me after I'm finished?"

Wills nodded. "I can. I'll be waiting. Same place as before."

He was talking to the air as she fled the hall. In seconds, he heard the soldiers greeting her again with shouts of approval, and her beautiful voice filled his ears again.

Had she really just asked him to meet her?

He must be making progress.

Dream on, he scolded himself, as he walked to the back of the stage.

Listening to her singing never grew old with him, and the half hour of performance was over before he realized it. She was singing a new song again. Something about *I'd die for you...I'd take your place...*

Wills took his time, and kept his eyes open, as he walked through the building, along the back of the stadium. It was dark with only minimal lighting in the auditorium part, but he could clearly see Claire.

There was no sign of Tyson, so Wills took one more ramble behind the curtains. Nothing. Where had the man gotten to? You'd think he'd be close by in case there was an emergency, in case Claire needed him.

When at last she finished, Wills headed outside. He thought once about following her back to her room where she'd gather her things, then decided she'd be fine. It was only after a twenty-minute wait that he became alarmed and started to head back inside. But the outer door swung open and a disheveled Claire flew through it.

Wills reached out to grab her, and she swung her bag at him. "Claire, it's me, Wills."

She collapsed against him, and he could feel her body shaking. "What on earth is the matter? Did that manager..."

Claire pulled away, still half-sobbing. "No, it wasn't him."

He'd never seen Claire cry. Not like this. There'd been plenty of temper tantrums when she was a child or when hurt or afraid, but never this desperate, terrified reaction to whatever she'd just faced.

Pulling her to him, he cuddled her, not speaking but murmuring low sounds and stroking her back gently. He felt the minute she regained control of herself.

"I can't talk now, here. Can we go somewhere for a coffee?"

Wills raised a hand and hailed a late-night taxi. After they crawled in, he said, "The diner on ninth."

Then he spoke in a low voice. "Can you—"

"Wait." She glanced at him then switched her glance to the darkened buildings they were passing.

What was there to do but wait? She obviously didn't want to risk even the taxi driver overhearing what she had to say.

The taxi spun to a stop in front of the diner. Wills tossed a bill across the seat, and he and Claire exited the vehicle. When they entered the diner, there were more people than usual seated, but the atmosphere was quiet. Wills led Claire to the most secluded booth he could see.

They sat, accepted the coffee the waitress offered, but both shook their heads when tempted with a sweet.

Wills sat silent, sipping his drink, glancing at the girl across from him. When she didn't speak, he did. "You sang beautifully tonight, as always."

She nodded. "Thanks.

"Do you want to talk?"

"No, but..."

"But?"

"But I have to trust someone. I can't talk to Norm about this, and I don't want to trouble Papa Ossie or Emma Jaine."

"Claire, if you want to talk to me, I'll listen." He wanted to add, *I'll always listen* but thought better of it.

"Something happened tonight."

He waited.

"Two things actually."

"And they scared you."

"Yes, very much so. I suppose mostly because I don't know the answers to either." She lifted her troubled gaze to him.

"That's always the scariest part."

"I don't understand why I keep hearing people whispering, as if there are secrets floating around in the air. I know with the war, people have to be careful, but we're in the United States. We should be fairly safe, here on our own soil."

"Claire."

She looked at him.

"There's a war going on even on our country's soil. It's invisible in a way, but very real."

"Is that what you're fighting? An invisible foe?"

"I can't say what I do. You know that. But I will say, it's real. Very real. People here who want to bring down our country."

"I don't suppose you've ever been scared."

"Don't you believe it. I have many times. But I've learned that being scared doesn't matter as long as you're brave enough to do what you need to do."

"That makes sense even though I'm sure it's hard to follow through."

"Yes, it is, but a good man—or woman—does."

A small smile widened her lips. "Then I'd better get started. I went to my room at break time and must not have completely shut the door because I'd barely entered when I heard voices in the hallway coming toward me."

"Did you think they were after you?"

"No, not until..."

"Until what?"

"Promise you won't laugh?"

"I've already told you, you can trust me."

She studied him. "They didn't say my name, but it sounded as if some of what they said was about me."

Wills leaned forward. Could what she was about to tell him be important? "Can you tell me what they said?"

She shivered. "I won't forget it ever."

"We live in a scary time, but Claire, I've watched you for years. I've seen you tackle many things you thought you couldn't do. You've been brave when you didn't realize it. Just doing this service for the military men is a brave thing."

"It's what I felt I needed to do to help win this war. I'm not talented like Emma Jaine, but I can sing, and wanted to share a little bit of home and happiness with them."

"And you have."

"I hope so."

"What was the scary thing?"

"They were talking about someone being in Cincinnati on the twenty-first."

"This month?"

"I'm assuming so. They didn't name a month."

"What else?"

"The first person told the second person—who by the way, had a very hoarse throat and blamed it on France's weather—"

"Are you sure?" At her nod, Wills went on. "Then that can only mean he was in France. Hmm. I wonder if it was the same time as when we were."

"I have no idea. But the one who seemed to be the boss told him he was to be the head of security."

"Head of security. If these two are legit, then why the secret meeting in an entertainment building?"

"I have no idea. I was too busy listening at the d—"

Wills sent her a sharp glance. "What were you about to say?"

"It didn't happen exactly like I first said."

"What do you mean?"

Her sigh was not one of resignation, but of a woman suffering the whims of a man. "I didn't want to tell you, but when I heard the voices, I wasn't in my room. I was walking down the hallway and listened at their door."

"Claire Anne Rayner. You could have gotten in a lot of trouble. After doing that once already, what made you do such a crazy thing again?"

"I was being brave."

Her voice was low, but Wills heard the sassiness in it.

"I ought to tell your father."

"But you won't."

"No, I won't, but only because I don't want to drag him into this..."

"This what?"

"Nevermind. Can you tell me anything else?"

"The boss warned the second guy to take care of his throat. After that's when one of them said they'd be glad when he was dead and the other said a bad word."

"A bad word? Slang?"

"It wasn't a soldier's normal slang. It was..." She

131

described what she'd heard.

Could the man have been *saluting* Hitler? "Are you sure he wasn't saying a salute: h-e-i-l?"

"Wills. I don't know, but it could have been." She frowned as she concentrated. "One said they'd be glad when he was dead and the other followed right up with the h-e-i-l. I couldn't hear what else was said right then. He may have coughed or lowered his voice."

"I kind of figure that's what was going on. But if so, that means we have serious trouble."

"Why, Wills?"

"Because if my guess is correct, then we're dealing with Germans. Possibly German spies."

Her eyes widened and glittered like emeralds. "Really, Wills?"

"Really, Claire."

"What can I do to help?"

"Begin by telling me anything else you can remember."

"Is that all?"

Was that disappointment in her voice? After giving a convincing act of being so scared? "For now."

"One of them asked where I was. Said they couldn't hear me singing. The second person urged the first person to trust him, then emphasized that *he* had everything under control. That *he*—someone else, I assumed—thought he was helping out the country."

Were they talking about him? A jolt of shock ran through him, then his senses kicked in. Couldn't be. He hadn't been around Claire that much. No one would guess they were connected.

He hoped.

And then he remembered. The Dame had been at the Rayner House that night for dinner. Of course, she would know Claire and he were connected.

"You don't suppose they were talking about your manager, do you?"

"Norm?"

The surprise in her voice almost convinced him his suspicion couldn't be true. But then, who else could keep her under control?

"Who else keeps you under control?" He grinned when he asked it.

"No one." She was quick to set him straight. "I mean, I listen to Papa and Emma Jaine, but I try to stand on my own two feet. I listen, but I still make up my own mind about most everything."

"I see. That's a good thing. Makes you a strong woman."

"You think so?"

"I do." He grinned at her. "Well, I probably ought to see you home. It's getting late and the place is starting to clear out."

Claire didn't answer only stared down at her folded hands.

"What's wrong?"

"Since I'm sharing, I might as well tell you, there's one more thing."

Wills settled back into his seat.

"It happened after the show. That's why I came running out. It terrified me."

"Claire, you should have told me right then. Maybe I could have done something."

She was shaking her head. "I was starting to gather my things in my room when the lights went out. Next thing I know, someone grabbed me with a hand over my mouth and whispered in my ear."

Wills couldn't say a word. The terror that rushed through him held him silent.

"I think it was a man because of the strength in his grip."

Her eyes pleaded with him not to laugh, but there was no way he could laugh over this. The thought that someone had—could have hurt Claire—there were no words for the terror, then rage that flooded his being.

"He whispered, 'I know it was you listening at that door again. Little girls need to stay out of things they know nothing about. You get me? You do your singing and keep that pretty little nose from being too nosy or it won't be so pretty anymore. Believe me, it would give me great pleasure to hurt you—not because I want to hurt you but because I want to hurt someone who loves you.

I want that a lot.' He gave me a shake, let go, and before I could turn around to see who it was—it was dark—the door was shutting. I wanted to run to the door and check, but I felt my feet were encased in thick, sucking mud. I couldn't do it."

Wills grabbed her hand. "It's a good thing you didn't. Whoever it was meant business. You could have been killed. Thank God, you didn't move, you didn't see his face."

"I'm pretty sure I know who it was."

"Claire, don't tease."

"I'm not. It was the hoarse-throated man I heard earlier. He tried to disguise it by whispering, but I heard his rasping."

Wills wasn't about to tell her he knew the name of the hoarse-voiced man. Hermie McCoy had been in the hallway—although no one else was around—and though he'd sneered as he usually did when talking with Wills, his voice was as hoarse as any he'd ever heard try to talk. "I need to get you home—"

She started to protest, but he shook his head. "Not this time. This time, I'm seeing you home. If you're ready, let's go."

Claire didn't argue, and as they left, he glanced back at the almost-empty diner. A tall man, hunched over as if hiding his height, sat at a table two from where he and Claire had sat. His head was covered with a flat cap, his hand was up to his forehead as if he was leaning on it. His clothes were monochrome and no other identifying things stood out.

Except for a dark mark on his arm. Wills wouldn't have been able to notice it at all, if the man's sleeve hadn't fallen back, revealing the mark.

Wills hesitated, thinking, wondering if he should approach him. Claire spoke to him, and he answered, turned his back on the man and the diner.

If it was someone spying on Claire—and him—then they'd meet again.

He was sure of that.

~*~

Once they'd reached their home, Wills had gone on to

his rooms in the basement. Claire hadn't. She'd hesitated in front of her father's door, seeing a light from beneath it, knowing he was up at all hours, still dabbling in his previous business of shipping, reading and pondering on life. She wanted to talk to him—badly, but Wills' cautionary words reminded her not to tell anyone yet what she'd shared with him. And his last words particularly stayed with her.

What you've told me could have something to do with national security. Give me time to work on it. I'll let you know, if I can, what I find out. Claire, you could be in serious danger. Don't push any limits. Be careful. Don't take risks.

So she wouldn't share with Papa Ossie, but she would have liked to soak in his sturdy, enduring presence. He was a strength to be reckoned with, but also a bulwark that kept their family ship afloat.

Papa Ossie had always said she and Emma Jaine were like their mother. Strong, independent but gentle and kind. Everyone had loved her mother, Papa said, and everyone loved Claire.

It was nice of Papa to say that, but she wasn't so sure.

She touched his door then turned and moved on to the library. She'd grab a book to settle her mind and nerves for a bit. Hopefully it would help her sleep.

She knew what book she wanted and went straight to the bookshelf. Reaching up to get it, a movement—it wasn't light—caught her attention from the corner of her eyes. She tilted her head but saw nothing. Cradling the book against her chest, Claire headed to the door, she flipped the switch, and inside her, an instinct urged her to look back.

Her gaze roamed the room, flicked past the bookshelves, the grand piano, the glass French doors...and returned for another glance.

A face, pressed close to the glass door, stared into the room—at her.

Claire didn't run, didn't think, didn't put her courage into use. She screamed. Loud. Long. And terrifyingly real.

Doors slammed open. Voices called out, but it was Papa Ossie, then Wills who made it to her before the others. Wills flipped on the light, but by then her father had cuddled her in his big arms, soothing, rocking.

"What happened, Claire? Did someone frighten you?"

She didn't answer. Couldn't. Something was wrong. Very wrong, and she was afraid she was being pulled into whatever scheme it was. The problem was she couldn't share her fear with anyone.

Except for Wills. Because if it was a plot against the country, then she had to be quiet. Allow Wills to work, to find out what was going on. But her problem was, why her? Why was she being dragged into it?

She pulled away from her father, noted the residents and family who'd gathered around her, but ignored them all. She looked up into her father's face. "Papa Ossie, I need to talk with Wills by ourselves."

"Claire? Are you sure you don't want to talk to me?"

"I'm sure, Papa. I can't, I mean I have to talk with Wills. Please send everyone back to bed. I'm sorry for waking everyone."

"Don't you worry about anyone else. You know if you need me, I'll be there."

"I do. But right now, it's Wills I have to talk with."

"All right, Baby girl, if that's what you want." Captain Ossie flapped a hand at those standing in the room. "You heard her. She's fine. Go back to your rooms. She'll be fine."

Emma Jaine hugged her. "Are you sure? I can sleep in your room tonight if you want."

"Thank you, sweet sister, but I'm good. I have this to read if I have nightmares."

When everyone had returned to their rooms, Claire sank into one of the high-backed chairs. "Wills, he was here."

"Who?"

"I came in here to grab a book to read till I got sleepy. I started to leave and something urged me to look back into the room. I'd flipped the lights out, but I could still see a face at the doors. Startled me so much I screamed."

"That would be scary. I'm assuming you think the man has something to do with what happened earlier today—well, yesterday now?"

"I don't know, but I do wonder."

"Can you describe him?"

She shook her head. "Not much. His nose was large and I think he had dark hair. He didn't have a hat on, but his jacket was dark, maybe navy or black."

The man in the diner had worn a dark jacket.

"Listen, Claire, I don't want to scare you, but you need someone with you as you travel back and forth from your engagements. I'll do what I can, but please don't walk anywhere. Have Pops take you or one of the others when they can. I've asked you before, and you promised. Please do this for me. I can't do my work and worry about you too."

"I hate to give up my walking, but I'll do it for now. At least, unless it's raining." She grinned.

"Well, if it rains, I'll be here to walk with you."

He sent his grin straight to her, and she felt it warming her insides. Had he changed or was something else happening?

She'd figure that out later. Right now, she needed to head to her room or she'd never make it on time for practice tomorrow. Then a weekend to rest before beginning more practice and entertainment next week. Only two, so that meant she'd have time to relax a bit.

Wills stood when she did.

"You sure there wasn't anything else?"

"I'm sure. I think I may have scared him with my screaming as much as he did me."

"That's good. Maybe he'll stay away." Wills flipped off the switch as they left the room then waited as she walked toward her room. "I'm going to check around outside to make sure he's gone.

"Be careful, Wills."

He nodded.

When she turned to glance at him, she gave him a wave and shut the door behind her. Leaning against it, she breathed in and out slowly. It was only then she realized she'd forgotten the book on the table in the library, but she wasn't about to go after it.

Her fingers fumbled as she locked her door, then went to the window and pulled the curtains closed. As she did, she saw Wills' figure striding around the front yard, and a feeling of peace swamped her insides.

Claire stared at him as he disappeared around the corner of the house.

~*~

Wills grabbed a flashlight and headed outside. He seriously doubted he'd see anyone now on the property, but he needed to check. Unless the person was persistent and brave enough to face a household of men, he'd have hightailed it out of here by now.

Circling the house, he saw nothing. He expanded his search to the outer reaches of the property and close to the stream that ran along behind the Rayner House and Josie and Jerry Patterson's house next door. He paused beneath a weeping willow, thinking, studying the star-lit sky, wondering when the war would end, and life would get back to normal. Or if it would.

"Didn't mean to scare the lady."

Few things really frightened Wills that much, but this voice coming out of the darkness, unexpectedly like this, had him feeling his skin had come unglued from his body. He jerked around to face the voice behind him.

"Who are you? What do you think you're doing scaring the daylights out of women like that?"

The man shuffled his feet. "Sorry. Had a message to give you."

"Why would you have a message for me?"

"E.I. sent me."

"Well, for goodness sake, why didn't you say so?" A thought struck him. "He's okay, isn't he?"

"I guess. Said people were watchin' him, and he had to be careful."

"Then spit it out, man. Why are you standing here?"

"I was hoping I could get a sandwich and something to drink."

Wills huffed out a long breath of air. Really? But this house never turned anyone hungry away. His mother would have his hide if she ever found out he'd done so.

Late at night or not. "Come with me."

When they reached the back porch, Wills motioned to a rocking chair. "Sit. I'll bring you something to eat, then you can tell me the message. Agreed?"

The man nodded, and Wills went inside. As quietly as he could, he grabbed what leftovers he could find and piled them on a plate. Then filling a glass full of water, and a cup full of lukewarm leftover coffee, he placed everything on a tray, with utensils, and carried it outside.

He set it on the stand, but when the man moved to get it, Wills spoke. "No. You talk, then eat. Go ahead and drink the coffee though, if you want it now."

The man eagerly picked up the cup and drank half of it before setting it down again, and smacking his lips. "That was downright good coffee."

Wills nodded. "My mother can make the best coffee out of anything. Now talk."

"I.E. says, you watch out. They know who you are now, and are gonna take you down as soon as their big target is taken care of."

"Who's going to take me down?"

His gaze swept around the darkness, and his voice lowered to a whisper. "The spy."

"Who is this spy?"

"Mystery Man."

"Are you joking me?"

"No, siree. I'm not. E.I. was deadly serious, and he made me promise that I'd get this to you before I saw the light of day again."

"I see. Tell me more."

"He says he got it straight, that the guy who goes by Mystery Man—that's what he's called in the underworld—I reckon you know what I mean by that—"

Wills nodded, and the man kept talking.

"—He said to tell you that the man trusts few people and has only a very choice group helping him set this up. That's why, E.I. says, he's been able to keep from getting caught."

"Does he know his real name?"

"Nope. Nobody does. But he's real as us. He's a ghost,

but a flesh and blood ghost. And he's deadly. When he sets his aim on someone then he doesn't stop till he gets it done. E.I. hasn't heard a word on why he has his sights on this man."

"How did he find all this out?"

"Beats me. E.I. didn't say." The man shrugged and eyed the food on the tray. "Kin I eat now?"

"Just a couple more questions. Where is this event taking place and who is the big target?"

"Don't know the answers to those questions and don't know anything else."

Wills nodded at the man, and the guy reached for the tray. As Wills stared into the dark, and occasionally at the hungry man, he wondered about the state of the world and how it would all end. He had faith to believe his country would conquer and come out of the war stronger than ever, but what price would it pay?

And how could he stop this mess? At least now, he had accurate assurance that an event was taking place.

Chapter Sixteen

The next morning, Wills reported to the colonel's office. "I've watched her for several days now, Sir, and connected with her. I've seen nothing incriminating—"

"Mason, are you sure about that? We're still getting reports that messages are being passed along to suspicious characters. My source insists a woman is involved."

"If Claire is involved, it's unknowingly. I'm sure of that."

"I want to believe that. I really liked her at the dinner party. Quite the host, she was." Colonel Waverly gave a nod of approval, but his eyes were vacant as if thinking back on the Rayner house party.

Wills was in total agreement because, after all, he really, really liked the girl in question too.

"I still feel you need to stay on top of this. If Claire is unwillingly an accomplice, then you need to be there to make sure she's safe. These people don't care who they hurt as long as they get what they want."

"I understand."

"Mason, I'm serious. If Claire is guilty of the least bit of treason, then I expect you to do your duty. Do you understand that?"

"I do, Sir, and I will." Reluctantly, for sure, but he would do what he had to do. "I'd like to make a request, Colonel."

The colonel lowered his head and looked at Wills over his reading glasses. "What is it?"

"I'd like to have the services of Owens again. I could use her."

"You would, would you? Hmm. Not getting attached to her, are you?"

"No, Sir. My heart belongs to someone else."

"Care to tell me who?"

"I'd rather not, Colonel."

"Very well. I'll put in a request for her to report to you this afternoon for an indefinite period of time. Will that work?"

"It will. Thank you." Wills started to turn away, but spoke again. "Sir, I've heard through sources I'm confident of, that this event will take place this month on the twenty-first. No details of where or who the target is."

"Hmmm. I won't be of any help then, that night. I have a speech to make at the Center."

"I'm sure, if I have some backup, we'll be able to handle it, Sir."

"You sure about all of this?"

"Ninety-nine percent sure, Sir. My source has never failed me yet."

"Good. Keep me informed with new news. Otherwise, I want another report soon." The colonel stood. "Matilda and I are going to a private concert tonight. Can't be late. She's punctual and insists I do the same."

"I see."

The colonel glared at him. "What do you think you see? What are you waiting for? Go."

Wills went, chuckling to himself.

~*~

"Reporting for duty, Sir."

Owens, the brunette, appeared beside him that afternoon as he walked toward the park, the rain all but a storm, cooling down the late spring heat. Just the way he liked it. He sidestepped a puddle bigger than he usually waded through. "How did you find me?"

"A guess. I know you like walking in the rain, and what better place than this park?"

"Good deduction, soldier." He walked another twenty feet before speaking again. "I want you to run down all the events happening here in town on the twenty-first."

She started to speak, but he interrupted her. "Doesn't matter what kind of event. I want a list of all of them. Families. Churches. City. You name it, I want it. Got that, Owens?"

"I do, Sir. It might take me a few days—"

"I need it by no later than noon tomorrow. Can you

do that, or do I need to ask for someone else to accomplish this?"

"No, Sir. I'll get it done."

"Then why are you loitering here with me, disturbing my peace of mind?"

"Right." Owens did an about-face and headed the other direction.

Wills stopped walking and turned to stare after her. He'd definitely recommend advancement for that young lady when this was over.

He whirled again, caught a glimpse of a dim figure standing idly by a small grocery, a soggy newspaper in hand, and began walking again.

So...someone was keeping an eye on him. Good. But young as he was, there wasn't anyone as good as he at this spying business, playing this hide-and-seek game. Not with all the practice he'd had growing up with Josie as a best pal. He'd beaten her more than once at the game, and he'd beat this guy too.

He paused twice to get a look behind him, took a different path once, and popped into the diner near his home to grab a quick coffee, but the man had stuck to him like glue.

Well, if he couldn't lose him, then he'd catch him.

Wills walked steadily toward the corner, turned and then ran behind the building and around it, to circle back to the front, allowing him to follow his follower. When Wills peeked around the corner to see if he'd succeeded, the guy stood at the other end of the building, staring, probably wondering where he'd gone.

Time to let him know.

Walking quickly up the sidewalk, he tapped him on the shoulder, and when the guy turned, slugged him— not enough to hurt him, but just enough to cause him to lose his focus. The phone booth that stood close by proved to be handy. With an eye on the man propped up against the building, he made a call. Fifteen minutes later, an unmarked car pulled up and loaded the guy in the back seat.

"He was following me. Hold him till I get there later today to question him. If you have any trouble, call the colonel and he'll take care of it. Thanks, guys."

Wills watched as the car sped away. He wasn't one to go around slugging anyone he didn't care for, but he was pretty sure, this guy was here for a reason, and it wouldn't be a legit one.

The rain had slacked off, and it was time to move on to his next step in finding the spy. He knew only a few things, but he had a hunch those items would be beneficial as soon as he had a couple more details. Hopefully, Owens would come through with a thorough list of events that made the twenty-first important.

Those two in the room where Claire had eavesdropped wanted someone to die.

Claire had been warned by an unknown person, and she was under suspicion of being a spy. But the more he was around her, the less he believed she was guilty. He wasn't a patsy, easily fooled, and those clear eyes of hers, her actions, and reactions to the attack were pretty good indicators she was either innocent or an unsuspecting participant.

Time to do some digging. He wanted desperately to find out who those two people had been talking about Claire and someone they wanted dead. He had to start somewhere, and the best place was at the building where Claire practiced and sang so many times.

Pops had taken Claire to her practice this morning and was to pick her up tonight. If he could do that for a few days, then he planned to ask Owens to take over the job when he didn't need her.

Wills held up a hand, and a taxi pulled over. In minutes, they were speeding toward his destination. Hopefully, someone might have seen something last night...or heard...or even knew. He was counting on getting at least a nugget of useful information.

~*~

Wills swung open the heavy doors to the studio and stepped into the hallway. He saw no one, but the music came through the studio loud and clear. Claire must be on break because she wasn't singing. Maybe studying a new song.

He walked slowly down the long hallway, stopping at

each doorway and peering into those not locked. He was about midway when he came to double doors, closed, but clearly the music came from them. Wills tested them, and they opened easily. He slipped inside.

Claire saw him immediately, and she leaned over to whisper something to her manager then rose and headed toward him.

"How did you know I was trying to reach you?"

"I didn't. But thought I'd check out a few things."

"Did you think of something that would help you find out what's going on?"

"Not really, but I figured it wouldn't hurt to double check that room where you heard them talking."

"That's an idea. I'll go with you."

"What about your practice?"

"I'm sick of practice."

"I can't believe it." Wills leaned against the wall and pretended to fan himself. "Since when have you become sick of singing?

"Not singing. Never singing. Just the practice." She shoved open the doors and exited the room, motioning for him to follow. "I've never in my life had to learn so many new songs. What's wrong with the popular ones today?"

"Not a thing. And you sing them as well as the original singers. But whatever you sing, you'll always be my favorite."

Wills caught the quick glance she threw at him. Checking him out to see how sincere he was? Wondering if he meant what he'd said? It was the truth, and he wouldn't apologize for it.

"Been singing any at church?"

She shook her head and didn't look at him. "No, too busy."

"I imagine your family misses that."

"Maybe. They know how busy I am and don't say much."

"I might be able to attend Sunday. It's been way too many I've missed, except for a service now and then when I can get away from my duties. I've missed it."

Claire didn't say a word. Was she not interested? Had

she grown away from church, grown lukewarm to the meaning of being with other believers and fellowship? He hoped not.

"Here we are." Claire turned the corner of the hallway. "I could hear voices from here, but it was only when I got close to the door of this..." She walked several more steps and stopped. "...room that I could hear most of the words."

"Through the door?"

"The door wasn't latched, I couldn't see inside, but I could hear them talking."

"Shall we go in?"

Claire nodded and shoved at the door. "Let's see what we can find."

Wills touched her arm. "Maybe you shouldn't."

"Shouldn't?"

"Get involved."

"I was forced to be involved when I overheard that conversation. I was forced to be involved when someone threatened me. I didn't ask for this, Wills Mason. I'm terrified every day at some point or other. The man loitering not too far from my home. The person who gives me an evil eye when I stroll into a grocery. My team musicians who look at me like I'm privileged because I get here two minutes late. Whether I want to be or not, I am involved."

His tone was gentle at her agitated words. "You're right. Let's go."

"Before we do, I did my own investigating."

"You did?"

"I did. I talked with everyone here. The musicians, Norm, the sound people, the janitors. No one had a hoarse voice. So it couldn't have been any of them."

"Wow, that's great. Thanks, Claire. Now let's go in and check out this room." He still hadn't told her he already knew who the hoarse-throated individual was, and he wasn't about to. The less she knew the better off she was. But she was some little detective. He'd give her that.

Standing by the door, Wills allowed his gaze to first roam around the room, checking to see if anything seemed out of place, anything unusual caught his attention, or seemed off. Nothing. There wasn't a scrap of paper that looked as if it'd been dropped.

They prowled the room anyway. There wasn't a lot of furniture, but they explored every drawer, pulled out the drawers, searched under it, behind it, knelt down to look under each piece.

Nothing.

Wills checked the two windows, but there were no finger smudges on the dust, both locked securely. He climbed on top of the tallest cabinet and hoisted himself up to check the ceiling.

Jumping to the floor again, he slapped his hands together to rid them of the dirt. "We might as well give up. This place tells me nothing."

Claire didn't answer. She stood in the middle of the floor, a smudge of dirt on one cheek, hair disheveled, but a frown between her brows and a far-away look in her eyes.

"Something bothers me, but I can't put my finger on what it is."

"Are you sure? You're not imagining it?"

"Definitely not." She stood quietly another thirty seconds then shook her head. "I can't get it. Maybe I'll come back later after I think some more on it. If I'm by myself, I won't be distracted."

Was he distracting her? Wills didn't know whether to be upset or pleased.

"No, don't do that. Claire, you don't seem to realize that someone threatened you—"

"But I do. That's why I want to help you figure out who it was."

He heard her comment but kept going. "—and if they catch you alone, they might not be so kind next time."

She looked at him. "You mean don't show courage like you insisted I have several days ago?"

"You have plenty of courage, but you must also use reason. Think how your family would feel if something happened to you. They'd all be up in arms and may even blame me that I didn't stop you."

"I see. So it's not me you're worried about. You're

worried that my family will blame you if I end up dead or hurt."

"Claire..."

She grinned then. "I'm just teasing you, and I'll have to say, it feels—"

"Claire, where are you? Stop loafing and come practice."

It was her manager. Again. Was he following her? Maybe, to keep her away from him.

"Oh, dear. Now I've done it. He sounds upset."

"No worries. I'll explain I needed your help."

"Please don't. He's a little—"

The door slammed open, and Norm stood there, a worried look on his face that turned into shock, then anger. "I came looking for you because I thought you were upset over so much practicing. I wanted to soothe you, assure you all the practicing would soon be over, that we could get on with our lives, but obviously you don't need me. This is what you're doing when I can't find you?"

Claire laughed. "What do you think I'm doing, Norm?"

"It's pretty obvious. Sneaking away in a private room to be with—well, whoever he is."

Claire looked irritated, but she kept it hid fairly well. "I've told you before, Wills is part of my family, Norm. He needed to talk over some things, and I found a room that was private enough for that. Nothing more. He's like a brother."

Really? His imagination had deceived him in thinking her attitude was changing. A brother was all he was to her.

Claire walked over to Norm and thrust her arm through his, and although the man kept his stiff stance, she managed to accomplish the act.

"We're finished in here. Let's go practice some more. See you, Wills."

Her comment was casual enough, but the look she sent him and the wink was another deal. A very nice deal.

~*~

Claire figured she ought to give Norm some attention

seeing he'd been upset with her hiding away in a room with Wills. He had no need to be jealous. Wills, although she'd eased her feelings of distain toward him a little, could never be more than a passing friend. That said, she needed to soothe Norm's feelings. Right now, she didn't want to lose him. After the war, she'd see where she wanted to go.

Something bothered her about that room, but for the life of her, she couldn't think what it could be. They'd found nothing, absolutely nothing, that gave off any kind of clue-scent. So why would she be so insistent something was wrong?

She shrugged mentally. If she had a chance, she'd check it out again. Maybe stand for a few minutes by herself and see if it came to her.

That's what she'd do.

~*~

Later that day, Owens caught up with Wills at the door of the restaurant where they'd agreed to meet, in a private corner of the lobby, and handed over one sheet of paper about three quarters full of events happening in Cincinnati on the twenty-first. He scanned down through it, crossing off any that seemed too far-fetched to even be reasonable as a suspicious event. That left five.

He looked at her. "Did you have time to check these out? To see what was happening and who'd be there?"

"I did. Those five are the ones that seemed possible to me. None of the rest seemed even remotely suspicious. Here's the list broken down to those five of what's happening and who's to be there."

Wills took the second piece of paper and looked through it, more slowly this time, absorbing the names and the causes of the events.

He felt his breath catch as one name stood out. Claire Rayner.

"Claire is supposed to be there?"

"Yes."

He stared off in the distance, thinking. "Doesn't look good for her, does it?"

"No, Sir. But it could be happenstance."

"I hope you're right." He looked down at the sheet again. "I see Colonel Waverly's to be there, along with several others I've had my eye on."

"What should we do?"

"I was going to have you babysit Claire, see that she got to and from her musical practices and engagements, but right now, I think we need to do more research on these." He tapped the papers he held.

"I agree. Where would you like me to start?"

"There's only one with Claire's name on it. Start with it then work backwards on the others. Be thorough, Owens."

"I will, Sir."

"Check all the people who are attending, check their background, where they've been in the last few months. Check who their friends are, where they hang out, what their jobs are and who works there. That should give you enough to do till you report to me."

"And when should I report to you, Sir?"

"Let's say tomorrow evening, if all goes well right here."

"Sir? That's quite a bit to cover in twelve hours."

"Are you complaining, Owens? You have twenty-four hours to give me answers. If you need help, call on that young soldier who helped watch at the diner earlier."

Owens breathed a breath of relief. "That will work fine."

"The thing that bothers me, Owens, I'm pretty sure Claire is not a spy, but I have few suspects that could possibly be implicating her, and those who I'd like to point a finger at, but I have no proof."

"Yet, Sir."

He cast her an apologetic glance. "You're right, Owens. I can't give up yet."

She sat down on the edge of a chair. "Would you like to run all your thoughts by me?"

"There's not much to run by you."

"But remember, you've mentioned that sometimes the smallest thing will be the one that will lead to results."

"True. You're right again." He grinned. "First, Claire may be fooling me, but I can't see it. Unless she's changed a lot, and I'm too blind to see it, she's either not involved at all or she doesn't know she's involved—which is what I lean toward."

"Because of the warning to her?"

"Yes. Then there's the colonel. I know it's a long shot, but he's too smart to be fooled, too loyal—I thought—not to realize what The Dame is. Why is he hanging around her?"

"Have you considered he may be lonesome and want company, and sometimes a person accepts what is available?"

"Maybe. I still think he's too smart to be fooled by a person like her."

"Maybe he's not fooled."

"Meaning he's not fooled but just goes along with her greediness."

"Yes, that, and..."

"And what, Owens? You started this. Now say what you think."

"I don't want to upset you. I know how much you think of the colonel."

"Spit it out. I won't put you in jail for telling me your thoughts."

"Maybe he is involved, both with The Dame and with spying. Maybe he's sending you on a wild goose chase to throw you off, accusing Claire and even leaving rabbit trails to make it seem she's a spy. I mean, we have no definitive reasons yet to suspect anyone else."

"Owens, do you know what you are saying?"

"Yes, Sir, but hear me out. Who sent The Dame and that McCoy guy to France? Didn't their orders come from the colonel, seeing they're in our section?"

He stared at her. "Do you realize what you just said?"

"I'm afraid I do, Sir. I'm sorry if I spoke out of turn."

"No need to apologize. I asked you to tell me your thoughts." He rose and strode to the window and back. "But if that's true, then I need to be careful what I say to him. If I can't trust him, who can I trust?"

Owens was silent.

Chapter Seventeen

Betrayed. That was how Wills felt as he watched Owens leave the lobby, and it was ridiculous because nothing she'd said to him meant anything until proven. He would have given his life on the validity of Colonel Waverly's honor and loyalty. Now to suspect, to even think he might be behind these accusations—it was beyond his ability right now to process.

How could he, when the man had singled him out as a recruit for the undercover spy business? He'd been lead in training him, and only choosing the best men to help train Wills. Not only that, but the colonel had seemed to be fond of him, almost fatherly in his actions. Now, to find out he might be a weasel, corrupt?

Hold your horses, Wills cautioned himself. What he and Owens had talked about might be total nonsense, and he would not believe it till he found out for himself whether it was true or not.

And tonight might be a good place to start.

He knew on good authority that the colonel was attending the special concert tonight to raise funds for the military men who'd been injured in the war. Claire was to take part, and he was pretty sure the colonel had asked Matilda Nelson to go with him.

Colonel Waverly and The Dame, Claire and her manager, Norman Tyson, all would no doubt be in attendance tonight. Who else? He planned on being there even if he had to go as an employee. Could he, should he take Owens? She was pretty handy to have around, and good-looking enough to fit in anywhere. She sure dressed like a million bucks.

Whoa. How could a lowly WAC—or to be more specific, her family—who wasn't even a senior WAC, afford those mink stoles and swanky clothes? Hadn't she told him she came from a poor family?

Was she involved and pointing fingers at others to

keep him so busy with them, he'd never think about her and her possible involvement in spying?

Wills groaned. He couldn't trust anyone. His imagination was turning him into a Nervous Nelly. Great.

Straightening his shoulders, lips in a firm line, he reassured himself. *This is nonsense to go berserk on suspicions that are probably all wrong. Keep your head on straight and your thoughts on facts, not suspicions.*

Wills stood and strode toward the door of the hotel. It was time he talked to the man who'd followed him and who he'd slugged.

Twenty minutes later, Wills slipped into the barracks and headed to the section where they locked up troublemakers. When the soldier led him to the cell, Wills stared inside at the guy. He was sitting dejectedly, and didn't respond when Wills spoke to him.

"Can we go to a room so we can sit down?"

The soldier nodded. "You got it."

Once seated in a small room out of the cell block, Wills spoke again. "Why were you following me?"

The man didn't even lift his head, as if he couldn't hear a word Wills spoke.

"What's your name?"

Nothing.

"Did someone ask you to follow me?"

"He's not gonna talk. Hasn't spoken a word since he got in here. Ignored the lunch we brought him."

"He have any identification on him?"

"Nothing."

"That's strange." Wills sat back in his chair and stared at the window. "Hallo."

The man looked at him. "Hallo."

Wills turned to the soldier. "Bring coffee, please."

The soldier motioned to another one standing at the door, and in seconds, a pot of coffee and two cups were carried into the room.

Wills lifted the pot and poured coffee into the cups. He lifted one of them and held it out to the man. "Kaffee?"

The man's lips split a wide smile, and he spoke his

first word as he accepted the cup. "Danke."

They sat silent for several minutes as they drank their awful coffee and gave each other big smiles. Then Wills set his down on the table and pointed at himself. "Wills."

The man pointed at Wills too. "Wills?"

Wills nodded. "Wills."

The man gave Wills another big smile and pointed at himself. "Kurt."

Wills repeated the man's action. "Kurt?"

Nodding vigorously, Kurt laughed.

"Hat dich jemand geschickt?"

"Ja."

Hmmm. Wills' German was limited at best. How to convey his next question without the words to do so? He stood and pulled out his wallet, drew several bills from it, and tried to act out his question.

He walked away from the man, then abruptly returned, held out the money and pointed at the guy, then walked away, motioning on him to follow.

Kurt stared at him, confusion in his eyes, so Wills repeated the action, only reversed it by having the man give him the money. Then he motioned for him to walk away, and Wills followed. Kurt didn't take his eyes off of Wills as he did as Wills wanted. Then, of a sudden, as if a lightbulb had lit in his head, he nodded, laughed and slapped his leg.

"Ja. Ja."

"Hoo?"

Kurt shrugged and held out his hands, palms up. He then went into action mode by acting out what had happened. Wills gathered he was saying someone came up to him, offered money by pointing out Wills and asking him to follow him. He had no idea who it was but wanted the money.

Wills took his hand, shook it. "Danke. Danke. Freund?"

"Freund." Kurt nodded, laughed and shook Wills' hand.

Wills turned to the soldier. "Let him go. He's innocent and knows nothing."

After walking the man outside, and repeating over and over the word for good-bye, Wills watched him. He seemed a good person, and Wills was glad he had found out the truth.

One less person to suspect.

~*~

Time to go home, grab some lunch and spend time with his parents for an hour or two. If he could, he'd try to do some more intensive background checks on the five people who were at the top of his mental list of suspects. Surely he'd find something...or not.

Thirty minutes later, Wills entered his home. His mother wasn't in the kitchen, which was normal. She'd be taking a break before beginning the preparations for the evening meal. But he heard voices down the hall and headed that direction. As he neared the library, he heard a voice that was familiar.

Colonel Waverly's, and two others. Captain Ossie's and Claire's. Laughing. What was so funny? And what was his superior doing here in the daytime?

Time to find out.

He peeked around the doorway, and spoke. "Is this a private conversation or can a lowly sergeant enter?"

Three heads swiveled his direction. Silence, then Captain Ossie spoke. "Come in, my boy. Come. We've had a pleasant surprise this morning."

"I see." Wills walked on into the room and sat on the loveseat next to Claire. "Colonel Waverly, I didn't know you were visiting here today, or I would have stayed home."

"No, you wouldn't." Colonel Waverly gave him a look.

Wills turned to Claire. "I thought you had practice all day."

"I was supposed to, but Norman said one of the guys in my band had an unexpected emergency so I came home early. Met Papa and Colonel Waverly in here and have been chatting since then. Do you have the day off?"

"Taking a break. Have some other items to attend to a little later on."

"I see."

What did she see? "And you? Are you home for the

rest of the day?"

"No, I have an engagement tonight."

"I see."

Her quick glance at him told him she caught his repetitious words mocking her own. Time to have that visit with his parents. He stood. "I'm headed to visit with my parents for a bit. Have a good afternoon."

He didn't give them time to answer. His rapid departure was intentional. He knew when he wasn't wanted.

~*~

There were a sea of colorful evening dresses and white-coated tuxedos swarming in the concert room that evening when Wills entered the building. He'd asked Owens to meet him here, but in this crowded group, there was no way he'd see her from ground floor. His gaze swept upward and saw the balcony area, with a generous collection of individuals there, but not near as many as here on the ground floor.

It was a grand room, decorated in gold and red, and the colors must have increased the intensity of moods, because everyone seemed to be in high spirits.

He saw neither hide nor hair of the five people he wanted to keep tabs on tonight. Of course, Claire might not be here, right now. Not with singing later, but then why not? She had plenty of time to prepare...she was the final performer.

Wills strolled around the room, nodded to a very few he casually knew and ignored the rest. He had almost circled the room when he caught a glimpse of Claire, her head thrown back, laughing at something one of the two gentlemen with her had said. And those two were Colonel Waverly and Norman Tyson. What was so hilarious? He edged closer and joined a group of six or so other people—whom he didn't know—just to keep from being recognized by the three he was interested in. He was close enough to hear partials of their conversation.

"He thinks we don't know what he's up to. I snicker every time I hear his excuse. I guess I'm going to have to get rid of him, but I hate to. He's a nuisance but so talented in what he does."

Claire's clear voice reached him with no words missing. Wills paused in introducing himself to the group he stood with, frozen with what she'd said. Who was she talking about?

Him?

"He's...good...he does."

Colonel Waverly's usually boisterous voice had lowered to almost a murmur. Maddening.

"Well...all be over soon." Tyson added his thoughts or hopes, whatever they were.

"We hope." Claire's voice had turned solemn.

Wills moved just enough to catch their expressions, and all of them seemed to realize the severity of their statements. Whether they were good ones or not, Wills needed to know. But how? Bluntly ask the colonel? Coax Claire to talk?

He didn't think so. If either of them were involved, which it certainly looked like it now, they wouldn't be eager to share their plans with him.

"Sounds like someone is in trouble," A low feminine voice whispered beside him.

He turned his head just enough to see. Owens, and she hadn't disappointed. The navy blue dress with its row of gold buttons, her hair curled close to her shapely head, and her heels gave her a stately height she didn't normally attain to.

Time for some playacting. Wills refused to acknowledge his real reason as he moved to place her hand on his arm. But it wouldn't hurt to give Claire, even if neither of the other two cared a hoot, a double take.

"What say we wow certain people? Maybe even cause some to give us a look?"

"I don't know what your plan is, but I'm game if you are." She gazed up at him, all smiles.

Funny, he'd never noticed those twinkles in her eyes before. Was she a bit too overjoyed at his suggestion?

"Let's give it a shot then and see what happens." He grinned. "Maybe it'll work..."

"Or maybe it will bomb."

That serious expression in her eyes told him then she knew what he was doing. She was willing to help, but wasn't at all sure it was the right thing to do. Whether it was for work's sake or to make someone jealous—it could be profitable or it might end up disastrous.

He ignored it. If Claire was the least bit interested in him, then maybe it would give her the push she needed to get her act together. And if she didn't care about him—romantically—then it was time he accepted it and moved on.

His heart obviously didn't agree. It seemed to be pounding out the words—*don't be foolish.* But he ignored it and took the first step to pass by the threesome.

Claire saw them first, and Wills saw the expression on her face. It was so minute, a second later, he was convinced he'd imagined it. Then she nodded, and when she did, the colonel turned to see who was passing.

His brows rose, then he spoke. "Mason. You didn't mention you were coming."

"It was a last-minute thing, Sir. I had the opportunity and took it. Never miss a chance to enjoy some classy entertainment if I can help it." That was the truth. "Especially when Claire here is singing. She's always been my favorite singer of all time, you know."

"Is that so?" The colonel gave him a questioning glance. "I predict she'll go far."

Wills caught a glimpse of Tyson's mouth opening as if to speak, but he didn't give him a chance. "I have no doubts about that. I remember her singing as a child in her room after her sister and I had teased her to tears. Josie and I sat on the stairs many a night listening to her as she sang her anger at us and her tears away. Broke my childish heart that we'd done that to her."

"Really, Wills? You and Josie sat on the stairs and listened to me singing?"

"We did, and I'll confess what Josie would probably never tell you. I saw tears in her eyes—that she tried to hide—many a time. She might have been your constant tormenter, but she loved you dearly. In spite of your haughty manner."

"No. I was never—" Claire was laughing as she protested.

"Yes, you were. Very high-minded when it came to anyone who disagreed with what you wanted or thought." Wills held up a hand when she would have interrupted. "But you were adorable, and that's what I remember the most. You've grown up to be a lovely woman, sincere in what you believe, steadfast in what you want to attain, and loyal to your friends and family."

Could Claire's green eyes grow any larger? That was definite wonder in them.

"That is the nicest thing anyone has ever said about me, Wills Mason. I would never believe it would come from you."

"You're family. It came from my heart."

Wills had forgotten that others were listening, but a cleared throat gave him pause.

Tyson spoke in an overly loud, sulky voice. "I could have told you all that, Girly, if I'd known you wanted to be bragged on."

"No, you couldn't, Norm, because you didn't experience my growing up years. Only someone who was there would know that much about me and know just how to express it. I've told you before, Wills is family and..."

Her voice trailed off, and her glance flicked back to him, but she didn't finish her thought.

But it'd been enough. He'd seen her response, seen the emotion in her eyes, the minute tremble on her lips, the hint of a tear in her voice. His words had affected her, and maybe, just maybe, it had brought out the first of responses he'd been so desirous of.

If for no other reason, their conversation had shown everyone there was a tie between Claire and himself that others didn't have, and never would.

The mood was broken when Colonel Waverly spoke. "It's almost time to get to our seats. We'll be rooting for you, Claire Rayner."

Wills had forgotten Owens—still hanging onto his arm—as he watched Claire head backstage, and if he'd turned away, he would have missed her last action before disappearing there.

She looked back at him and smiled. And that smile did the trick. Now no one would ever convince him she was a spy.

No matter her words that condemned her earlier.

No matter who she hung around.

No matter what, his heart said she wasn't guilty.

And he'd prove it, if it took the rest of his life.

~*~

Claire sat on a stool, half-listening to the others who were singing and performing their acts, but nothing registered. Wills' words still resonated inside her, and she couldn't shake them off. She would have vowed over and over again that she despised Wills Mason, and though she wouldn't go so far as to say that about Josie, she hadn't liked her much, although in her heart she knew she loved her. So what did that make her? As despicable as she thought Wills had been.

Just a few words from him, spoken from the heart, and she'd felt her heart melting. Why? Because she had plenty of people who loved her, many who loved her just because of her voice, and those who liked her enough to put up with her because of the money she brought in when working.

But Wills...

She shook her head, and Norm spoke. "What's the matter, Girly? You feeling badly? You've got to get through this, and then you can take a break for a few days. We've got nothing else scheduled till Sunday night."

"I'm fine, Norm. Just thinking."

His glance was sharp and irritated. "Not about what that Mason guy was saying, I hope."

"Why would you think that?"

"Because you were fine till he showed up, sticking—"

"Norm." Right now, she was in no mood to listen him growling about Wills. She put a little extra oomph in her words. Anything to get him to leave. "I'm fine. Just let me have some quiet time to prepare for my part. I'm raring to go. Don't worry about me."

He took the hint, and Claire watched him go. What

was wrong with her? Only days ago, she'd thought Norm might possibly be her ticket to the life she wanted. Now?

She just didn't know. She felt she'd done a complete about-face. Lost. Confused. Worried that her life—the energy she'd always put into her singing career was waning away.

And most of all, she was afraid, very afraid her feelings about Wills was changing. Grown up, he seemed totally different than the youngster who'd tormented her childhood days. He'd always been cute as a child, and good-looking as a teen, but now. He was downright handsome.

And more important than that, he'd grown into his manhood. Mature, dedicated to his work, and always loyal and loving to his parents. That was a telling thing about any man—how they treated their parents.

Her cue that it was time came way too soon, but she was ready. Her mind had cleared, to a certain degree, and her spirits had revived. She headed toward the curtains, giving a small wave as her band prepared to give her a grandstanding introduction when the curtains opened.

Claire touched the gardenia in her hair then smiled that, at least, Norm had been good enough to remember her gardenia. The band did themselves proud as the curtains opened, and she walked to the microphone, a smile on her face, ready to sing.

When the band slipped into her first number, she sang with all the emotion in her, her training and natural talent serving her well. The overwhelming clapping didn't cease until she'd reached her second line, then rapt, upturned faces listened as she poured her heart out in song.

She sang three songs before taking a short break and prepared for her last number.

Norm was on the outskirts of the curtain, waiting. He grabbed her and swung her around. "Girly, you did us all proud. Did you see their faces? Their wallets will open wide tonight."

She laughed and slapped at him lightly. "Did anyone ever tell you you're money hungry?"

"No, most people like a focused man who can bring in the dough."

"Silly. Let me down. You'll muss my dress."

He settled her on her feet again. "Girly, when this war is over, you and I are going places. Together, who knows where we'll go?"

"I'd say you're right, Norman Tyson." The trouble was, a niggling doubt about that idea was beginning to fester into reluctance. Was it what she really wanted? The constant moving about from state to state, city to city in pursuit of money?

She shook her head slightly. Tonight wasn't the night to decide that.

Norm spoke again. "It's time for your final number. You go set them on fire."

She nodded and headed back out.

The last number was a new one again, but she actually liked this one quite a lot. The crowd hadn't grown tired of her, if the clapping was any indication, but she held up a hand to her band then to those congregated below her.

"Tonight, I want to dedicate this song to my very special friends who've chosen to come once again to support me. I couldn't do this without all of you and want you to know how much I appreciate your presence tonight."

She nodded to her musicians who played her introduction and she sang:

"The full moon is laughing at me tonight,
I think he knows my heart.
But on the twenty-first of the month,
I'll be swinging from a star.
Dropping notes of love to you,
From high up in the sky,
Watching over you that night,
With tears and a couple of sighs.

Stay with me to roam the hills,
Don't die, my love, it's my heartfelt sigh,
Walking sunlit valleys and hills so steep,

Carole Brown

The fields of flowers, through which we'll stroll
The flowers would weep, and I would cry,
if you don't come home to me tonight.

Claire sang her heart out, sang to the crowd below, to herself, and to someone who'd touched her heart tonight.

But when she'd finished and was acknowledging the approval from her crowd, she lifted her fingers to her lips and tossed out the kiss...

And her gaze flew straight to the boy—now a handsome man—she'd grown up with all her life. She saw his eyes in the lit room and knew he'd accepted the kiss when he lifted a hand, and his fingers closed on that air-borne kiss that had come from her heart.

That was the turning point for her, and she knew it.

Chapter Eighteen

Wills thought his eyes would pop out when he saw Claire's gesture on stage. His heart—well, it had taken wings, and though Claire probably hadn't sensed it, flown straight to her. No matter what happened in the future, he was hers, heart, body and soul. Whether she ever wanted him or not, he'd never find another woman like her, another woman who'd hold his heart in her hand to cherish or toss away on a whim. He was hers forever.

Whether she would ever be his was another story. He hoped so, wanted it, tried to have faith it would happen, but his faith, in spite of her action tonight, wasn't strong enough to overcome the lingering doubt.

And then there was the spying business.

"What next, Boss? I overheard that some are meeting at that bar downtown. Wanna go?"

Wills looked at the young lady beside him. "I don't think so, Owens. I try to stay away from those places. Besides, I have other plans for the rest of the evening. You should go back to your place too. We never know what tomorrow will bring. Besides, you've just wasted five hours here with me when you should have been getting answers for me from that list."

Owens' mouth opened then shut as she seemed to think better of saying anything. Wills hid his smile. She was taking his criticism like a trooper.

They threaded their way through the mingling mob of people and finally exited. Wills stepped into the street and hailed a taxi. "I'll see you tomorrow. Take care, and thanks for coming tonight as my escort."

"Anytime, Sir. I enjoyed it." She started to stoop into the taxi then turned and kissed him on the cheek. "Thanks for asking me."

Wills watched as the taxi left, rubbing his chin. Perhaps he was right, and Owens was getting ideas.

Better curb it before it went too far on her part.

"Saying good-night to your girlfriend, Wills?" Claire stood behind him, wrapped in a light, glittering shawl, plenty warm enough for tonight. "Not keeping track of me, are you?"

"She's not my girlfriend. Owens is a good woman. She's a big help in my work."

"Work? Is that all she is to you?"

"Why should she be more? The colonel assigned her to me to help with different duties I have."

"I see. She sure is pretty enough, and if I'm not mistaken, she's taken with you, if her breathless reaction to every word you speak is any indication."

"What on earth makes you think that? She's just being friendly—"

"I see." Claire repeated her words, but somehow they seemed a bit skeptical. "Is kissing in the class of job duties?"

She'd seen that. Of course, she had. "Meant nothing. Thanking me for inviting her when I didn't have to."

"Why did you?"

"Wasn't sure I'd know anyone—"

"You know me."

"That I do, and I know you well enough that I'm wondering if you're trying to pick a fight with me."

Claire sniffed and tossed her head. "That's not my tactic, like some people I know."

"I do have a question, if you wouldn't mind answering it for me."

"Will I regret saying 'go ahead'?"

"I don't know, but I'd appreciate you giving me an answer.

She studied him a minute. "Go ahead then, but I won't promise to answer, and if I don't like your question, I will walk away."

"Good enough." He drew in a deep breath. "Earlier tonight, before the program, I overheard you mention that someone was talented, but you thought his excuses were funny and you might have to get rid of him. Could you tell me who you were talking about?"

Claire chuckled. "That. It was nothing. One of my

band members was after me to date him for awhile. When I explained—pretty plainly—that I wasn't interested and our relationship would always be purely professional, he became a little sullen. From then on, he's been giving excuses to miss practices. If he doesn't change his attitude, I will have to look for someone to take his place."

Wills couldn't have explained the relief that flooded his body on hearing her explanation. "Perfect."

"I'm glad it's made you feel better."

Her amused look didn't bother him. She thought he was being silly, but the relief of knowing she wasn't plotting the demise of someone was well worth being laughed at. "Let's forget that. Want to stop at the diner and grab a coffee?"

"I have a better idea.

"What's that?"

"Let's go to the auditorium where I practice and let me check out that room that bothered me. I didn't get a chance to do it today. Too many people around. We could break in or we could…" she grinned and pulled out a key. "…use this."

"You sure no one will be around?"

"Positive. We haven't hired guards, and as late as it is, everyone will have gone home. My crew is looking forward to a few days of rest. As I am."

"Let's do it. Wanna walk?"

She cocked an eyebrow at him. "It's quite a few blocks. Sure you're up to it?"

"Ha. Watch me. I can out-walk you anytime."

"Says the man who's afraid I can beat him." Her laughter was like pure honey. "I might not be a runner, but I love to walk and do so every day. Brisk walks, leisurely walks, purposeful walks, and casual walks. I've done them all, and never fail to reach my goal."

"Which is?"

"I try to walk so many miles every day. I know sometimes I can't, depending on my schedule, but I do my best to get in a few miles. I love to walk. Gives me a sense of serenity and aloneness, which I don't get much of."

"I can just imagine. Are you getting tired of singing to the troops?"

"Not per se, but I do want the war over, and to be truthful, I'd love to take a couple more years of training. I was starting to get calls for engagements, but some of them weren't what I wanted to do."

"Not quite up to par?"

"Not up to Papa's standards for me, and, as much as I hate to admit it, I don't want to do things that will upset or disappoint him. His love and confidence that I will make the right choices mean a lot to me."

"Good for you, Claire. That not only makes sense, but shows your character at heart. I'm proud of you, what you've become."

"Even though I hardly ever get to church anymore?"

Was that wistfulness in her voice?

"You might do better in that area, if you really tried, but I think you haven't strayed too far from your father's training."

She was silent, her gaze straight ahead, her face a mask of confusion. "I don't know, Wills. I don't want to do wrong, but life keeps getting in the way."

"Well, I'm not a preacher, but I'd say follow your heart, remember your father's teachings and say your prayers. I do believe God will guide you in the path you should go if you're honest."

Claire looked at him then. "Do you believe, Wills?"

"I do. It took me awhile to realize I was hungry for something more than I had. Tyrell was a big influence on me, and of course, my parents, but I had to decide for myself what I was going to do with my life and my beliefs."

"Does it make you happier?"

"Happier? Not sure about that, but I always find peace when perplexed, guidance when confused, and hope that things will turn out all right."

"Are you saying God gives you everything you want?"

"Never. But I believe a sovereign God knows more than me, knows what's best for me, so I trust him to do so."

"Hmmm. I've never been in that place. Perhaps I

should check it out sometime. Do you think he would tell me what to do after the war?"

"Maybe."

"What do you mean by that?"

"His answers aren't always yes or no. Sometimes he says maybe and sometimes wait. But a believer always holds fast to the fact that God is omniscient, and when he deems it's right, he'll answer."

"I'm not sure I'm that patient."

"But it's not a matter of being patient. It's that belief that God loves us so much, he knows and wants what is best for us. We can always rest in that."

"You make a convincing argument. I think I need to figure out where to go from here."

"Sounds good. I'll be rooting for you." Wills studied the building they were walking toward. "Do you see what I see?"

"I do. Why are lights on this time of the night? It's late and no one should be here now. Who do you think it could be?"

"You should be able to answer that better than me. Does your band leave their equipment here?"

"Yes, we have extra equipment and a few other items we keep stored here. Do you think someone broke in to steal?"

"Maybe. Claire, I think it best if you wait out here while I check out the place. If you can find a spot to hide—what about that bench over by that tree? You'll be able to see and stay alert in case something happens—"

"Absolutely not. You're not going in there without backup. Meaning me."

Wills grinned at her. "You're forgetting I'm a trained soldier. I can take care of myself."

"And I'm not a helpless female. Papa trained all of us in the basics of protecting ourselves, not that he figured we'd ever need it. I couldn't forgive myself if anything happened to you..."

That sounded like she cared.

"...and what would I tell your parents?"

Or maybe she just didn't want to face his parents. Not so good.

"Then come on, if you insist. I could remind you that I'll have to face your father and sisters if anything happens to you." He slid her a doubtful glance.

"Nothing will."

Her chipper voice did nothing to reassure him, but he knew it was useless to argue. She was, after all, a Rayner woman.

They climbed the broad steps and paused at the entrance door. Claire whispered. "The door on the right creaks, so once we unlock them, use the left door."

Wills nodded and held out his hand for the key. The slight click sounded as loud as a firecracker, but there was no indication anyone had heard. He hesitated, then pulled gently at the left door. It opened without a sound, and he gave Claire a nod.

It was a one-story building, so once inside, they moved toward the rooms where the lights had been. Neither of them had a flashlight, so their movements were made with caution. Once Wills leaned toward her and muttered. "Any obstacles in the hall we might run into or trip over?"

"Nothing," she whispered back

They hadn't gone twenty more feet when the faint sound of a door opening behind them caught them unaware. The creaking right entrance door had just been opened by someone who hadn't known it would be so noisy.

Wills grabbed Claire's arm. "We've got to hide. Where to, Claire?"

She gripped his arm and pulled him behind one of the indoor posts that supported the hallway.

They squeezed together and Wills felt her body shaking. Not from fear, but laughter. Claire was laughing at their predicament.

He pressed his mouth close to her ear. "Really, Claire? Now, of all times?"

She giggled back at him. "Can't help it. So funny."

Wills was tempted to laugh with her, but he knew it wasn't funny. It was dangerous. She didn't know what he knew—or, at least, he hoped she didn't. And if she didn't, those men—if they were following Claire and him—would have no qualms about harming them.

The steps were getting closer. A flashlight shone in the pitch dark. Would this one post hide them well enough?

Wills spoke again in Claire's ear. "I'm going to try to distract them. If I get caught, and you can get outside, run for help. Call the cops. Do not follow me. Understand?"

"But, Wills, I want—"

"No! I can't do this unless I can rest easy you'll do as I say. Please, Claire."

He felt her nod, and her answer gave him the assurance she'd do as he said.

"I will. I promise."

He didn't speak again, only moved, running in a zigzag method. He didn't have a plan, except to keep Claire safe, and whatever happened to him, whether threats, a beating, or death, he could rest easy now.

~*~

Claire would have been filled with excitement if fear for Wills hadn't caused her heart to beat like a race car. She heard his running footsteps, heard the shouts from whoever had entered the building after them. She couldn't stand here and do nothing. Fortunately, she knew this building like the back of her hand, and in the corner behind this post stood two convenient boards she'd badgered Norm to have removed. Now she was glad he'd forgotten.

The men raced past her, their flashlights bouncing with their movements. Claire followed but much more cautiously. They had only a few more feet before they ran out of floor space, which meant Wills would have to hide in one of the rooms, and the men would be searching in each one.

Claire, from a short distance away, watched those bobbing lights move from one room to another, and waited.

It was only then she remembered about the lights in the rooms when she and Wills had first arrived. Where had the person in them gone?

Double trouble.

Wills was doomed. He'd never be able to fight off two of them, especially if they were heavy weights. Wills was strong, but he played fair, she was sure. These guys? If they were the crooks she figured they were, then they wouldn't care how they took him out.

She should have run for help. Too late now.

Claire approached the room she'd seen the men enter. She could hear their quiet murmurs and beneath the door, the flashes of light as they moved. One voice moved closer, just on the other side of the door, and the doorknob turned.

She knew because she had a hold on it. Letting it go, she gripped the board she held tighter.

The door opened.

The person spoke to the man still inside and stepped outside the room.

Claire swung with all her might, and without a word, he fell to the floor. He made no sound, so obviously, he was out, but the man inside the room had plenty to say as he rushed across the room.

Claire didn't wait. She turned and...hadn't gone five feet when she ran into a solid chest.

There was a grunt, and an irritated comment. Whoever it was shoved her aside, and as the second man exited the room, the man swung, and with one punch, the second guy was down.

Claire leaned against the hallway wall and gasped in her breaths. What was going on? That chest she'd plowed into was not Wills, although his was well-muscled. His, though, wasn't as heavy with years. Whoever it was, they'd seen plenty of life.

Lights flashed on, and Claire blinked at the sight of Colonel Waverly and The Dame standing over the two men on the floor. Had they been the two intruders whose light she and Wills had seen?

Chapter Nineteen

Wills had known that he'd eventually be caught if help didn't arrive in time. The room he'd chosen as a hiding place led to the stage with the auditorium below it. For them to find him there would take awhile. Besides that, where was the unknown person or persons who'd been in the lit room when they'd arrived?

He hoped Claire was all right. But when time passed and no searchers came looking for him, he figured it was time to see what was going on. Maybe they'd found Claire after all.

The moment he stepped into the hall, he realized something entirely different than he'd imagined had happened. Two unknown men lay on the floor. Claire stood leaning against a door. Most shocking of all, were the figures of Colonel Waverly with folded arms and The Dame, both looking hot and bothered. Their questions to Claire was not getting answered as she stood there gaping at the fallen men and ignoring both the colonel and the rather snappy Dame.

He stepped up to join them and got an angry glance from Colonel Waverly and The Dame. Claire's was full of relief. It was only then he realized she'd never left, never called for help, and hadn't kept her promise. He shot his own angry glance at her, but she ignored him as she was doing to the other two.

"What happened?"

He didn't expect to get a coherent answer right then, and didn't get one.

"The question is, what are you doing here in the middle of the night?"

Wills wanted to shoot the same question back at the colonel, but decided it wouldn't be the wisest thing to do. "Claire and I were walking. When we saw a light inside the building, we decided we'd better check it out. It's too late for her crew to be here."

The colonel had the decency to look embarrassed. "That would have been Matilda and me."

And why would they be here? Wills had barely processed the question when Claire spoke up again.

"*Why* were you here, Colonel Waverly, and *how* on earth did you get in?" Her voice was polite enough, but underlying it was a determination to get an answer.

"Matilda had a key. She wanted to show me something, but when we arrived, we got to talking, and, I guess we both forgot about what we'd originally planned."

Wills didn't say a word, but watched as Claire switched her gaze to the woman who seemed to be ignoring everyone.

"Miss Nelson?"

"It's Lieutenant to you." The Dame snapped her words.

Claire didn't raise her voice and neither did she back down. "And how did you get a key to this building, Lieutenant?"

Was the woman's face flushed?

"Not that it's any of your business—"

"That's the problem, Lieutenant, it is my business. I'm part owner of this building."

"You are?"

For once, Wills saw surprise register on the woman's face, but Claire wasn't done.

"And the key?"

"Norman Tyson gave it to me."

This time it was Claire's face that revealed her unexpected reaction.

"Norm? Why would he do that?"

The Dame shrugged. "You'll have to ask him. It was a private matter."

Claire was irritated. She held out a hand. "The key please."

The woman hesitated, but finally placed the key in Claire's outstretched palm.

"I will be talking to Norm. We don't pass out keys to friends, let alone acquaintances."

"You seem sure of yourself."

"I am."

"Just be careful you don't overstep your boundaries. People get hurt that way. This is a dangerous time we're living in."

This time it was Wills who saw red. "Is that a threat, Lieutenant Nelson?"

The woman shrugged. "Take it however you want. It's the truth, and that's what I deal in."

"Matilda, we'd better get out of Claire's hair." Colonel Waverly placed a hand on the woman's back before turning to Wills. "Can you make sure these men are taken to our headquarters for questioning?"

"I can, Sir, but did you knock both of them out?"

"You don't think I could?"

"I didn't say that, but..."

"Well, I didn't. Claire got the first swing in, and I came in to finish the job." He glanced at Claire. "She has a powerful swing. Take heed you don't get on her bad side."

Amidst Claire's and his laughter, Wills noticed The Dame didn't join in. Instead she was studying the two men still lying on the floor but beginning to stir.

~*~

It was close to one o'clock by the time the men arrived to escort the two intruders back to headquarters. Wills hoped he'd get a chance to talk to them again tomorrow—today. They'd not given him much, but he had gathered they'd been ordered to follow him and Claire. As to who'd done the ordering, they'd been mum, and nothing more had passed their lips.

He'd seen a flicker of fear in their eyes when he'd pressed them to reveal the person behind the ordering, but no manner of threatening had opened their lips.

Claire and he stood at the door of the building and watched as the military truck left with the captives. Then he looked over at her. "Hadn't we better head home? It's after one."

"And lose the chance to check out that room?"

"You sure you'll be able to make sense of anything after all this time?"

"We'll never know until we try."

"Then let's give it a shot."

Minutes later they entered the room. Claire went straight to the center of the room, shut her eyes and stood quietly. Wills didn't move, only watched as she stood like a statue. After five minutes, he was beginning to wonder if she'd fallen asleep on her feet.

She stirred, opened her eyes and smiled.

"You figured it out."

"No, I didn't."

"Then why are you smiling?"

"Because I saw the expression on your face."

"You really didn't figure it out?"

"I didn't. I still sense something I ought to recognize, but it won't come to me."

"Let's hope it does. Now, it is time to go. What will your family think of you coming home so late?"

"They'll all be sleeping. Besides they're used to me getting in late."

Wills shook his head at her. "Time to go, beautiful singer. No more delaying. Some of us have to work tomorrow."

"Spoil sport." She teased, but her eyes sparkled at him.

She was quiet on the way home, and Wills did the same. His thoughts were whirling with questions about tonight.

Why would Tyson give The Dame a key to Claire's building? For that matter, how did Tyson know The Dame? That was a crazy question. They'd talked together the night of the dinner when they'd both been there, so, obviously, they knew each other.

Why would The Dame take the colonel to *that* building to show him something? And why wouldn't they explain? Why wouldn't The Dame explain what was going on?

And worst of all, was Colonel Waverly involved someway? How, Wills had no idea, but he knew the man was smart. Unless he wanted it, he couldn't see him being fooled.

When they stepped out of their taxi and entered their home, Claire gave him a wave and whispered. "Thanks for the fun evening. It was just what I needed."

"Anytime. Good-night..." Wills lowered his voice and barely whispered. "...Gorgeous."

He watched as Claire tiptoed to her room then turned and headed to his own room downstairs. He'd barely reached his bedroom door when a soft voice stopped him.

"You all right, Son?"

Wills turned. His mother stood at her bedroom door in a dressing gown.

"I'm fine, Mother. Had a late night and escorted Claire home."

"I know you were the gentleman we taught you to be." His mother gazed intently at his face, studying his expression, no doubt.

"Always. You've taught me right. Good-night."

"Good-night, Son."

Wills shut his door and walked to his window. He couldn't see as much as he'd like with it being a basement window, but enough. There was no moon tonight, the sky overcast, but in his heart, stars were twinkling.

For the first time since he'd reached manhood, Claire had been civil with him the last few days. Not that it was her fault. Josie and he—best pals—had always given her a rough time of it, and laughed doing it.

But those days were past. All he wanted to do now was win her over and prove to her he'd love her the rest of his life the way she should be loved.

But as much as he wanted to shout his love to the world, it wouldn't work. She wasn't ready, and neither was he.

He had to prove she wasn't a spy.

Sometimes she seemed as innocent as a baby, but other times—like at that concert last night and her words—she'd looked as guilty as the worst criminal in the world. Thankfully, she'd explained her words.

One thing he'd put off doing in this case while trying to find out as much as he could about his suspects, was following each of them. Sometimes it helped and other times, it didn't. Either way, tomorrow was the day he'd begin. He'd like to start with Claire or the colonel, but he'd give them the benefit of the doubt for now.

He'd start with The Dame, and he had little time for sleep. Wills glanced at the clock on his bedside table. Three o'clock. He'd get no more than a couple hours sleep if he wanted to catch The Dame before she left her place. That meant he'd better hit the hay.

Wills set his alarm, grabbed his favorite cover and slouched in his big comfortable chair, ignoring his bed calling him.

The chair would do for tonight.

~*~

Wills was early when he arrived at The Dame's quarters. She had her own home, rather small and plain. No flowers gave the place any ray of sunshine. It was the drab and plain house of someone who really didn't care about looks.

The sun had just risen when he saw movement. The front door opened, and a figure emerged. It was a man, a man Wills knew well.

Herman McCoy. Hermie, the worm. What was he doing at The Dame's this time of the morning? A thought blazed in his mind. So these two unlikely people were a couple, were they? He'd have to keep an eye on Hermie if he was associating with The Dame that much. Who knew what those two were up to?

Forty-five minutes later, The Dame opened and exited the front door then locked it. After adjusting her hat, she marched down the street. No taxi for her. She strode with a steady tread, not looking to the left or right.

Half-way to the headquarters, she entered a restaurant, and Wills followed suit. While The Dame marched to the restroom, Wills took one of the two tables empty, hoping she'd sit behind him and not at the bar—that she planned on eating breakfast here.

Sure enough, five minutes later she slid into her seat, and to Wills surprise, another man joined her. It wasn't Hermie this time. It was Norman Tyson.

They ordered breakfast but said little until after they'd eaten. Then sipping their coffee—and with his back to them, he'd never have seen what they were doing, but when the waitress had poured them another cup, he heard their murmurs of approval. This restaurant must have laid back a reasonable amount of java before the war.

"What do you need this time, Matilda? I've done everything you've asked. She's getting restless. I don't understand why she can't be in on this. She's a good girl."

The Dame's voice was filled with tension and force when she spoke. "Absolutely not. She knows all I want her to know. We'll have one more message, but it will be a simple one. We have finalized that the first location is the one where the action will take place. Use the first song."

"Then it's still on? The ceremony?"

"Yeah, it is."

Why had her voice sounded funny with that short agreement? Almost as if she was hiding a chuckle. Maybe she was exactly on the up and up. Allowing certain ones to know only what she wanted them to know. Something important that only the higher-ups would know. Something she hoped would gain her another step higher in her climb to achievement.

Or was she the spy? The one he was looking for.

Who was the 'good girl' they'd mentioned? It had to be Claire, which sounded like she was innocent.

"You won't need to tell her until two days before the event—you did say she was a fast learner, amenable to changes—and if all goes as planned, we'll have succeeded."

The Dame again.

"And she'll get the recognition you promised?"

"No worries. She'll be famous."

"You'd better keep your promise. That's the only reason I agreed to your plans. That, and the money. You make sure everything goes as it should, Cuz. You hear me? I want no snags, no problems to upset her that I have to deal with."

"Settle down, Norm. You do your part, and we'll have no problems. Two weeks from today and victory is ours!"

The two behind him rose and headed out, passing

him, but paying no attention. Wills glanced behind him at the deserted table, saw the waitress coming to collect her tip, so he rose and glanced over it. On the floor, beneath the table, lay a crumpled wad of paper. He knelt on one knee and stretched for it. As the waitress reached him, he stood and thrust the paper in his pocket, nodded and left, leaving the money to pay for his coffee and a tip on his own table.

Outside, he saw The Dame striding on down the street, but there was no sign of Tyson. He turned to the left and followed The Dame. She took the next corner, and by the time he reached it, he was afraid she'd be gone.

But when he peeked around the corner, not twenty feet away, a sleek, dark green sedan had pulled up to the curb. One back window was down, and The Dame was standing close, stiff as a post, as if listening.

What he wouldn't give to hear what was being said. He flicked a glance around the area, but saw no way to get closer. He resolved to study her reaction, and that told him plenty. Whatever was being discussed wasn't complimentary, if her stance was anything to go by. Now and then, she nodded, tried to speak once, but was left with her mouth hanging open, when whoever was in the car must have snapped at her.

Her boss? But why chew her out in the middle of the street instead of in a closed door office? Wills was in a special service of the military—serving as a spy for the United States—but he knew enough to know that no knowledgeable and honorable officer would chide an underling on the side of a street. Either this was no officer of the military or there was something awfully wrong going on.

As much as he didn't care for the woman, he hated to see anyone—*anyone*—involved in undercover, crooked business, and with the war, although battles were being won by the Allies, no news of the end had been celebrated yet. Who knew when that would be?

A thought struck Wills. Could that be the colonel in the car? That settled it. The Dame was nodding almost continuously, and he decided. With a deep breath, he stepped out from around the corner, and headed their direction.

The Dame cast him a quick look and stepped back. He heard the engine in the car accelerate before he'd barely reached it, saw the window going up, and knew he'd missed the chance to see who was inside.

The Dame either was too distressed to pay attention to him or didn't care, because she about-faced and took off again. With the way she was going, she'd be at headquarters now in a matter of minutes.

Wills didn't hesitate. He strode after her, allowing her to gain a distance from him but not losing sight of her. It was only when she entered a building that he sped up and opened the door. And there he was confronted by two heavily armed soldiers.

Behind them stood The Dame, looking every bit as angry as a wet hen, as his mother always said.

~*~

Claire woke late the next morning, with the sun shining brightly. She stretched, smiling at being able to sleep in. First time in a long time. She had no agenda today, and that made her want to dance around her room in happiness. She needed this.

Throwing back her covers, she jumped out of bed, and grabbed her robe and toothbrush. Time for a long, hot bath. After that, who knew?

Thirty-five minutes later, she'd just re-entered her room when there was a knock on the door.

"Come in."

Harriet opened the door and entered carrying a tray. "Emma Jaine said to make sure not to wake you and to fill a tray with all your favorites once you were awake."

"Harriet, you angel. Oooo. That looks good." Claire snitched a bite of the light brown toast slathered with butter. "Thank you so much."

"You eat it all, Claire. You're thinner than a twig."

"I'll do my best, Harriet. I'm going to do nothing all day. Relax, eat, and laugh."

"You do that. You work too hard, and if you keep that up, you'll be old before your time."

"I wouldn't want to do that. Maybe I'll take more days

off once this war is over." Claire smiled at the woman who'd mothered her and her sisters. "I want to go see all the babies today. Haven't had play time with any of them in ages. They've probably forgotten me."

"I doubt that. They adore you."

"We'll see. But first, I'm going to devour this delicious breakfast. And if I eat all this, I won't want lunch."

Harriet shook her head and departed, but not before sending Claire another smile.

The food was as good as always. When was it never? When Claire finished, she dressed in a plum-colored skirt and white blouse with a tie. Slipping into casual shoes, she grabbed a sweater, thrust a little money and her keys in her pocket and headed out. First stop, Josie and Jerry's house next door.

They were the most unlikely couple Clair would have expected to succeed in marriage. Except for a brief few weeks after Jerry came back from Germany injured, they were inseparable. Their darling baby girl, Josephine Elana, named after her mother and paternal grandmother, was the most beautiful baby in the world. Or so Claire thought. She could see traces of Josie in her, but also a bit of babyish grown-up-ishness, that reminded Claire of herself, although she'd never say it aloud to anyone.

She didn't knock, but went straight up to the nursery, where she knew Josie would be with her daughter. She always spent several hours with Fina, as the baby girl was called, in the mornings, but a nanny came in at noon and cared for the child while Josie practiced her flute, worked on her chores, shopped and exercised by ice skating when in season.

Claire peeked into the room and saw Josie, hair mussed as usual, sitting on the floor, layering building blocks into a stack, only to have the baby knock them down. They did this several times before Claire laughed and Josie looked up and saw her.

"If it isn't my long-lost sister. Come on in, Fina's been asking about you."

"I doubt that, but I love that you said it." Claire reached for niece. "Hey, baby Fina. Auntie Claire is here to give you some much needed spoiling."

Josie snorted. "As if she doesn't get any. Everyone from Papa Ossie, to the boarding house residents and down to Peter and Jaine Marie, who think Fina belongs to them and spoil her so much I have to limit their being around her."

"And she does belong to the twins." Claire gave Josie a corner-eyed glance. "May I take her for a stroll in her carriage?"

"It's not too cold out this morning?"

Who would have thought Josie would turn out to be the worrying mother? Claire would have bet—if she was a betting woman—that Emma Jaine would claim that title.

"Not at all. We'll wrap her up in that darling purple coat and hat to match—"

"Sorry, Claire, she's already out grown that. She's now up-to-date in a yellow jacket and matching hat, courtesy of Jaine Marie, who wouldn't have it any other way but for Fina to have her own outgrown coat."

Claire listened to Josie's rambling on, but hugged the baby tighter in her arms and proceeded to put the coat and hat on the child. Done, she snuggled her to her shoulder and urged Fina to wave bye-bye to her mother. "Say bye-bye, Fina."

The child gave a vigorous wave but soon lost interest in favor of going outside.

Josie followed them downstairs and supervised the placing of her baby into the stroller, then waved and hollered last minute instructions.

Claire ignored her and kept walking slowly, talking to Fina, who seemed to be taking in all the sights with enthusiasm, if her cooing was anything to go on.

"What say we walk to that nice diner at the corner of our street and go inside for a few minutes to make sure you warm up before our trek back home? Look, Fina, at the red bird. Oh, look. There's a butterfly, yellow and black. Isn't it gorgeous?" She kept stopping and pointing out different items to the child. Whether she understood Claire or not, she certainly gave each thing an intense study.

Claire chose a window seat, ordered a fruit drink and gave Fina her bottle. They sat for thirty minutes before Fina began fussing.

She reached down to close the baby's wraps up again. "You ready to go bye-bye again? What do you think we'll see on the way home? Do you think a bunny rabbit or a plane? What about a neighbor's friendly dog or a little girl like you? Are you excited? I am. Let's go for an adventure."

Maneuvering the carriage out the door, Claire turned right and headed home. The sky was the bluest she'd seen in a long time. There was no wind, but none was needed.

"Look, baby, there's a woodpecker. See him up in the tree?"

Fina looked where Claire pointed, and Claire was sure the baby did her best to understand.

"Hear him pecking. Peck, peck, peck. Can you say 'peck'? Claire laughed when the baby made a sound not at all like peck then laughed. She leaned down to give her niece a hug, and that's when she saw him.

It was a man. He wasn't unkempt, but something about him spoke poor. Claire didn't consider herself to be unfair to anyone, so it wasn't his dress that upset her. More like his sudden stop and pretending—she assumed—to be studying a watch.

Claire stood and began pushing the carriage again, talking all the while to Fina. She managed to reach the Patterson's gate when the man caught up with her.

"Miss, could you tell me the time?"

What? Claire turned slowly and took in his clothes, his face, his demeanor. Seeing how she'd just seen him looking at a watch—or what she'd thought was a watch—he surely didn't need to know the time. She obliged him anyway. "It's almost noon, Sir. Now, I must get this baby inside."

She unlatched the gate, and he grabbed her arm. Looking down at his dirty-brown hand that clutched her wrist, she felt the tiniest bit of fear flutter inside her. "Let. Me. Go. Now."

He let go, but he didn't leave. Staring at her until she

looked at him again, he spoke. "Ma'am, you're in danger. I'd be awfully careful if I were you."

"Why am I in danger?"

The man stared at her with the most intent blue stare Claire believed she'd ever had. His eyes. It was almost as if there was some emotion behind them. As if he was laughing. As if he knew something she didn't know. Was he playing her for a fool? Was he someone more than he seemed?

Unable to speak, she stared after him as he leisurely turned and walked back the way he'd come. She wanted to throw a whole bunch of questions after him. Like:

Who do you think you are?

Who are you?

Who told you to try to scare me?

And the scariest one of all. What do you mean, I'm in danger?

But she didn't say a word. It was only when Josie's front door opened, that it hit her.

The man had looked like a poor person. Yet that smell. That cologne smell. It was the same one that was in the room at her entertainment building. Claire wanted to lean against something. Something strong enough to hold her suddenly weak knees and trembling body. That man—that poor person had been inside her building.

How could that be? Because his voice was definitely not one of the voices in the room that night. Then...

She needed to talk to Wills. Soon.

Josie was talking from the door of her home, and Claire walked toward her, pushing Fina's stroller.

Once Josie had gathered her child in her arms, she cooed at Fina. "Did you have a nice time with Auntie Claire?"

"We had a lovely time and saw all kinds of things, even a woodpecker."

"That's nice. Fina looks like she's ready for a nap. Thanks, Claire, for giving her an outing."

"I loved it too." She turned to leave.

"Want to stay for lunch?"

"I can't. I promised Peter and Jaine Marie I'd read to

them this afternoon."

"Oh, who was that man you were talking to outside?"

Claire shrugged. "Have no idea. He wanted to know the time."

"He didn't have a watch? That's odd."

"I thought so too, but he moved on, so I figure he must have left it at home." Or somewhere. Or was lying through his teeth.

Josie unexpectedly reached for Claire with her free arm and pulled her close. "Thanks, Claire Anne. You've grown into a beautiful woman. I'm glad you're my sister."

It was a nice gesture that warmed Claire's heart. Maybe she and Josie would be close someday. She hoped so.

Chapter Twenty

Ten minutes later, Claire had changed her shoes to house shoes and run to Emma Jaine and Tyrell's very nice apartment. It had been a big decision for the family to make, but none of them had wanted to have the couple move away, so they'd remodeled several of the upstairs rooms into a large apartment for the Walkers. There were fewer boarders, but that was all right. Tyrell made a nice salary from the church and there was a small income for them from the remaining boarders.

"Hey, kiddos. I'm here." Claire announced as she entered the apartment. The almost two-year-olds ran to her with hugs and kisses.

"Book. Book," they urged.

"I brought a book. Where shall we sit? Hi, Emma Jaine."

"I see they've stolen your attention for awhile, so I'm going to run down and talk with Harriet about supper tonight. You don't mind?"

Claire waved a hand at her. "Go! We've got this, haven't we, kiddos?"

The two bobbed their curly-haired heads and flopped to the floor, patting the area between them. "Sit, Auntie Claire. Sit."

She sat, opened a book called *Into the Forest,* about a boy taking a walk. The children's faces lit up as one by one different animals joined the walk. When they'd finished that one, Peter and Jaine Marie both shoved a book at her with demands of "Read." She obliged.

It was a full half hour before the two decided to move on to something different. An hour passed, then two, and Claire finally found them behind a chair, fast asleep on the floor. Lifting first one then the other, she placed them in their individual beds and smoothed their covers over them. Then bending over them, she gave them a kiss and smoothed their hair. "Have a good nappy, precious ones."

"They've been missing you, Claire." Emma Jaine stood behind her, smiling.

"And I've missed them. But you know I had to do what I do best for our troops."

"You've done well. We're all proud of you. I wish we were not so busy so Tyrell and I could take an occasional evening to attend one of your events."

"Couldn't you get Papa Ossie and Shirley to watch them now and then, so you can get out?"

"I could, but I adore being with my two rowdy children, and by the time Tyrell gets home, they have him locked in their clutches till their bedtime. Plus I have either our maid or laundry lady care for them once a week. They love our laundry lady—Tilly, so it's nice to have someone I can trust when we do go out."

"Are they single ladies?"

"One is single, but the laundry lady is widowed. Her husband was killed early on in the war. She has three children of her own, but they are old enough to stay by themselves when she cares for ours, and she needs the money, so it works out for both sides."

"You are such a good person, Emma Jaine. You've been a wonderful influence on me."

Emma Jaine chuckled. "Well, I did wonder at times whether I was making you a better person or ruining you."

"Never to the last. I wouldn't be where I am today if it wasn't for you. And Papa Ossie."

"I heard you came in late with Wills."

"Yes."

"Yes? Is that all you have to say when you've always vowed to hate him and Josie?"

Claire's cheeks heated. "They were awful to me."

"I know, Sweetheart. They were pretty mischievous, but they only teased you because of your reactions. I'm sure they loved you."

"Maybe, but I doubted that strongly at the time."

"And now?"

Claire didn't answer for a moment. "Now? I don't know. Wills and Josie both seemed changed. I always thought those two would get married."

"No. They're too similar. It would never have worked, all of us saw that. I believe they've grown up. Faced some hard places and realized life is more than fun and games. I see it in both of them."

"Well, I'm not relaxing my guard around them yet."

"So why is Wills bringing you home late at night?"

"Because we met at my entertainment business, and Wills insisted on seeing me home. Simple." Was her sister hinting at what it sounded like?

"And was it as simple as you say?"

"Meaning what, my loveable but nosy older sister?"

"I'm not that much older than you."

Emma Jaine sounded peeved.

"Meaning, is there something going on between you and Wills?"

"Do you mean interest? Love? No. Definitely not. I could never love him. Not in a million worlds." If that wasn't emphatic enough, then she'd never be able to convince Emma Jaine.

"Hmmm."

Impatience clawed its way through Claire's veins. "Hmmm what? Don't make something out of nothing. Wills and I might eventually come to terms with the past, but it can never go any further. Besides, I have my eye on someone else."

"Who is that?"

"My manager. Norman Tyson. He's rich, mannerly and an excellent manager."

"Perfect description for a manager, but I'm not sure it sounds like a perfect marriage partner."

Claire stood. Enough was enough. Next thing she knew, Emma Jaine would be choosing who she could marry. Which she wasn't at all sure she would. But if she did, it would be someone of her own choosing. She needed no help with that. "I've got to run. I want to enjoy my day and have a few things to do. Love you, Emma Jaine."

Emma Jaine gave her a warm hug as if to make up for her curiosity. "Do invite your manager in for dinner some night. Only let us know ahead of time so Harriet can prepare something extra special."

Claire nodded then cast a last glance at the twins before leaving the room. And, finally, she felt the tension flow from her body.

She hadn't lied to Emma Jaine. Her plans included reading the book Shirley had loaned her ages ago, having a talk with her father if he had time, and seeing about Harriet sending a tray with a few of her favorite treats—which she seldom ate—to her room. Some alone time at supper would be lulu, a favorite word of some of her band members.

Now to see if Papa Ossie had time for a nice long chat.

~*~

Wills studied The Dame standing before him—but behind the two sturdy, grim-faced soldiers—like an angry bull ready to charge. He wasn't afraid, but he did wonder what she thought she was doing. If she knew anything about him at all, she'd know he worked under Colonel Waverly. Upsetting Wills was nothing, but upsetting the colonel was another thing.

But then what made him think the colonel would be upset? Maybe he was in all this stuff, and being stopped by The Dame was in his scheme to slow him down.

"What do you want, Lieutenant Nelson?"

She glared at him before answering. "I want to know why you're following me."

"Am I?"

"You're here, aren't you? I saw you on the street."

"Yes. I didn't know we weren't allowed to be on the same street."

"You've got a smart mouth." Her scowl was the stuff that created nightmares.

"I'll agree that I'm pretty smart for a lowly soldier."

She snorted, actually snorted. "I have half a notion to ask these two soldiers to put you in solitary for a time. That might take some of that sass out of you."

"Just so long as I have a window."

The Dame actually stomped her foot. "That's it. Put him in a cell. Keep him overnight. Maybe that will make him show some decency."

As the two soldiers took hold of his arms and led him away, he called back to her, "Better make sure you let Colonel Waverly know you locked up his man."

He couldn't see her face since the soldiers continued to propel him along at a fast trot, but there was no answer from her. She wasn't afraid, he figured, but maybe—hopefully—was thinking over her action. Either way, it looked like he was in for the night, on a hard bed and awful food. He'd be lucky if there was a window and he had the cell to himself. But one night wouldn't kill him. It'd be a story to tell his children—if he ever had any.

The two soldiers gave him a shove as he entered the cell, but he turned immediately and gripped the bars. "Hey, don't suppose I could call Colonel Waverly?"

"You supposed right. No phone calls for you till the lieutenant says so." They left then and didn't look back when he continued to badger them.

Wills walked over to the bunk and tossed himself on it. The bed was as hard as he figured, but it'd do. He had no way to get ahold of anyone unless The Dame decided to be decent. Doubtful that was going to happen. She really didn't have anything on him to cast him in here, but she was showing her authority and never seemed to like him even when he was in training. She'd been one of the managers over the other secretaries and, even back then, had shown by her actions that she'd do anything to get as high in the WACS as possible—or anywhere else if necessary.

Why hadn't he just told her he'd seen her talking with a guy who looked dangerous? Why not tell her he'd been worried? Because he'd figured she was up to those skinny shoulders of hers in whatever was going on.

He'd told his parents he'd be home again tonight. They'd worry but think he'd had duties...

With little sleep last night, and for several nights before that, his eyes grew heavy. Drowsiness crept over him, and he gave into it and closed his eyes.

It was dark when he heard a voice, one that he'd never cared for.

"Fancy seeing you of all people in here. Brought you

something to eat. Hope you enjoy it." Hermie McCoy stood outside his cell holding a tin plate filled with a suspicious looking mound of something. His tone was such that no one who heard it would put any trust in his words.

Wills opened his eyes a slit, looked at the man outside his cell and closed his eyes again.

"Come on, don't you want it?"

"I'm not hungry. Anyway, I'll be out of here soon, and heading home to one of my mother's excellent meals. You can have it. I don't want it." Wills looked at the man again then sat up.

"I wouldn't bet on it." The man's face went livid with anger as he slid open the bottom small hatch in the door and shoved it inside, but not before he spat a gob of spit on it. "I fixed it special for you. You eat or I'll tell Lieutenant Nelson."

"Tattletale." Wills muttered it as if he didn't want Hermie to hear, but he knew he had when Hermie stomped off, muttering to himself. The man was disgusting.

But it wasn't a half hour later when he heard shoes clopping down the hallway, and in seconds, Colonel Waverly, The Dame and Hermie stood before his cell door.

"Open it." The colonel didn't look angry, but he sounded it.

The Dame fumbled with a big key and finally had it inserted, twisted and the door swung open.

"Come with me, Mason."

The colonel marched back down the hallway with Wills at his side and the other two following. Outside the cell section, Colonel Waverly turned to The Dame.

"I don't care where you see my man. He's on duty for me. I send him everywhere I think he needs to be. Don't—don't ever do this again." His voice softened, but just a mite. "Do you understand, Matilda? I believe you were upset and not thinking clearly, so let's let this go and all be friends."

The Dame's face was as stiff as a starched shirt. "Yes, I understand, Colonel. I misunderstood his intentions. It won't happen again."

She looked anything but certain about that last statement.

The colonel looked at Wills. "You can wait on me outside in the car. Hermie, get back to your duties."

Wills started to leave then turned back. "Oh, I didn't eat my dinner. Perhaps Hermie will want it?"

"You heard him, Herman. Go back and get the tin and eat it if you want."

Wills decided he'd pushed the boundaries far enough for one night and made tracks for the door.

Minutes later, Colonel Waverly joined him and motioned for his driver to go. They'd gone two blocks before he spoke. "What were you doing, Mason?"

"Could we speak privately, Sir?"

"Whatever you have to say, can be said in front of my driver. He's my most trusted employee. Been through war, and he's always had my back."

"Yes, Sir. I've been checking out everyone who's on my list of possible suspects. When I saw someone in a dark car arguing with Lieutenant Nelson, I figured I'd better follow her. Nowadays, you never know who's a friend and who's the enemy."

And that was the truth.

He eyed the colonel. "Sir, I might have to do some things that some people may not like, if I'm to get to the bottom of this spy thing. I don't have much time. I suspect whatever they're up to will happen soon. I don't have time to play games with people who don't understand."

The colonel ran a hand over his face. "You're right, of course, Mason. Matilda is touchy when she feels a man is undermining her or not taking her seriously. I'm sure she meant no harm."

Sure. He'd believe that as soon as a chicken ran into the middle of the road and cried, "the sky is falling." But he wouldn't tell that to the colonel. Until he knew without a doubt the man was as innocent as he seemed, he'd keep that suspicion under lock and key.

When they pulled up at the Rayner boarding house, Wills stepped out of the car and leaned back in.

"Thanks, Colonel. I knew when I didn't appear at one-thirty to talk with you, you'd be looking to see why not."

"Go on with you. And if what you've said tonight is true, then get busy and find the problem. I want answers. Today, not tomorrow."

"Yes, Sir." Wills watched as the car pulled from the curb and waited until it'd disappeared around the corner. He glanced at his watch. Just enough time to clean up, talk with his parents for awhile then enjoy dinner his mother had prepared for the house tonight. He glanced up as a movement caught his eye and spotted Captain Ossie and Claire at the window waving. He waved back and headed inside.

Claire and her father were waiting at the door of his study.

"Where have you been? You look worn out."

Was that a worried note in her voice?

"I've been busy dealing with difficult people."

"Will we see you at dinner tonight, Son?" Captain Ossie asked. His glance clearly showed he knew something more than dealing with people had gone on today.

"I plan on it if I'm not called out."

"Good. Good."

When Claire began to ask another question, the captain cut her off. "Let him go, child. He needs some alone time before dinner."

He thanked the captain with his glance but spoke the words. "Thanks, Sir. I'll see you both later."

Wills headed downstairs to his rooms where he hoped he could clean up and feel human again.

But not before he heard Claire's words to her father.

"I needed to talk to him, Papa."

~*~

Claire was singing, with Emma Jaine playing the piano, when Wills walked upstairs at six-thirty that night. He paused before entering the library, watching her from the shadows in the hallway. Almost everyone seemed entranced by her voice, or maybe it was the song.

Some of the boarding residents from when he was

younger were still here: Philip, the artist; Gertie Hanover, who'd been here from the first, a little more feeble but still as sharp as ever, sat close to the piano, listening and nodding, but not missing a thing in the room. Tom Akinson was still as laid back as ever, always quiet, but beneath that exterior lay feelings that ran deep. He'd gone through a lot with his wife in prison and losing his baby. But he never shirked his work in the plant where he served as a supervisor.

And there was Captain Ossie, his gaze riveted on his youngest daughter. Was he thinking about his first marriage and the death of his wife, or was he as happy with Shirley, the retired librarian? He laid a hand over hers just then, and Wills figured they were well suited. Her quiet dignified ways and his boisterous, loudness balanced each other. The man deserved happiness.

Tyrell was here tonight. Serving as a pastor kept him plenty busy, let alone all the volunteer work he did ministering to the injured soldiers who returned home. There was something steady and brave and wise about the man, in spite of being in his thirties. He was one to count on and, though he hadn't been around in Wills' childhood or even early teens, he had helped Wills, in the short time he'd known him, become the man he was today.

Emma Jaine looked lovely in her deep blue dress, her copper hair piled on her head in curls as she was wont to do for dinners. She was elegant without having any airs. She and Tyrell were a perfect, well-oiled couple.

Josie and Jerry sat in a corner snuggled together, listening, but consumed with their fiery love between them. They'd gone through a rough patch after Jerry had returned home from Germany, but Josie hadn't given up on him, and they'd come through with flying colors. Wills was happy his best pal and her husband were so in love.

And then there was Claire. He wanted to say *his Claire*, but that wouldn't be the truth. He knew his parents would be pleased if the two of them would fall in love, and he was pretty sure the Rayners would be too. But Claire. She was all lady, but she also had a mindset that, once made up, was hard to change.

She was like a luxurious queen tonight, in her silky gown—an old one for sure because of the war—but still lovely. Her raspberry blond hair fell in loose curls about her cheeks, partially hiding her face from his view, but that didn't matter. He had every inch of it memorized.

His peripheral vision caught sight of someone coming down the hall and he turned. Norman Tyson walked toward him, but didn't stop, didn't speak. He walked straight into the room, straight toward Claire and leaned on the piano, his gaze fastened on her.

The feeling that rushed over him was a new one, taking him by surprise, and it wasn't pleasant. He'd never been jealous of any man in his life. But this...this emotion was hot and unpleasant, making him feel that he wasn't in his usual control of situations.

He didn't like it and half turned to leave. Go anywhere until he could face the people in the room with a controlled countenance.

"Don't leave." It was Tyrell. How had he sneaked up on him? And how had he known what Wills was feeling? "Don't let that man win. You're stronger than that. Go in there and be the person you are, strong, confident and a man any woman would be proud to love."

"You know?"

"I know. I would have known even if I hadn't heard Emma Jaine worry so much about Claire and her love life and the perfect man right under our roof. I would have known just watching you, the adoration I saw in your gaze at her. Don't let fear stop you. God has this in control and will make you the victor in winning her hand. I believe that."

"I wish I did, Tyrell. You make me seem better than I feel."

Tyrell clapped a hand on Wills' shoulder and nodded at him.

Wills went. Amidst the voices of welcome, his father timed his announcement that dinner was served. Wills claimed Claire's arm before Tyson could reach her, and thankfully, Emma Jaine asked Tyson to see her to her seat.

"You look quite the hotshot tonight. I like that dusky gray jacket. It's a nice balance to your brown eyes." Claire's look was admiring, although she probably didn't realize it.

"I didn't think you'd notice."

"You didn't think I was smart enough or cared enough?" Her question was pert and inquisitive.

"Maybe both, but let's not talk about us when there's far nicer subjects to discuss."

He pulled out her chair, and as she sat, she looked up at him. "What would those be?"

Wills sat too. "For starters, how lovely you look tonight, but then you always do."

She gave out a small snicker. "You're still talking about us, but if you insist, I think I was born knowing how to dress, how to act."

"Maybe, but you've become..." He hesitated, not knowing if what he was about to say would offend her.

"I've become what?" she whispered as Tyrell was about to ask a blessing.

When the preacher had finished, Wills answered her. "In your younger years, although you were always beautiful, you hadn't grown into your manners in a way that you have now. You were doted on as the youngest child in the house, but now...now, you've grown up into a woman who's not afraid to be who she was meant to be. Confident, kind, loving to those less fortunate, passionate over your talents, caring about your family and friends. Far more so than when you were young."

"Are you trying to anger me?"

"Not at all. I'm trying to tell you what a wonderful person you've become." Wills gave her a smile.

"Then, I guess, I will accept that." She returned his smile.

It was then that he caught sight of Tyson glaring at them. He might seem to be a master at his trade, rich and snazzy, but there was something about the man Wills didn't trust.

And he'd find out what it was before he'd let Claire fall in love with him.

~*~

Carole Brown

Had she been wrong about Wills? Imagined him as some kind of rowdy boy who knew no manners and laughed at stupid jokes and capers that made Claire shiver with fear? He certainly was handsome enough, with that honey brown hair styled just right and his eyes that were clear and undefiled by anything bad. His parents thought the world of their son, and she knew Papa Ossie did too.

In fact, he'd given her a small nod of approval when Wills had taken her arm to lead her to the table. She'd known Norm would be unhappy about it, but Emma Jaine, as always, had come to the rescue, setting the man close to her and chatting with him to keep his attention from Claire.

But Claire had also caught his occasional glare at Wills, and that made her defensive of Wills. She wasn't Norm's property, not yet, and maybe never. Sometimes the thought of the money he had, the places he'd traveled—he was quite a bit older than her—it was tempting to accept his advances.

Always though, her father's eyes had stopped her. Like a warning flash they'd entreated her to go slow, be careful, think about what she was doing.

And she had.

She glanced at Wills again as she leaned toward him to allow Jonah to serve her.

"What are you thinking, Claire Anne? Did I ever tell you I really like your name? I believe it's my favorite name of all names."

"You're being silly again. And what am I thinking, you asked? Do you really want to know?" She gave him a smug glance. "You might wish I hadn't told you."

"I'm not afraid of anything you say."

"Bragging?"

"Hardly. Just sure."

"I was thinking about you and how *you've* changed. From a wild, undisciplined—or so it seemed to me— companion to my equally wild sister, you've become a responsible, intelligent adult who views the world with caution and wisdom before making your decisions."

"You really were thinking that?"

"Yes, since we're being honest tonight, I really was. You impress me."

"That's a good thing. I think." He motioned to his father for a refill on his glass, and when the man proceeded to pour it, Wills felt the pat of approval on his shoulder. Pops would be keeping his eye on the two of them, probably praying up a storm that it would work out like the whole household—it seemed—was wanting.

"It is, since you were definitely at the bottom of my list of least desirable people to spend time with, before you came home again."

"I've settled down, I know. I guess being the only male in a household of girls made me—erroneously, I know now—think I had to behave like I was the toughest and had to do daredevil stunts to impress all of you."

"Which it certainly did not do. At least for me."

"To change the subject. I like those gardenias you wear. They make you smell like a flower garden on a cool summer's night."

"That's nice. I didn't realize what a poet you'd become. Norm never forgets to get me one when I'm performing."

Should he? Would it cause trouble? He glanced first at the man, who appeared to be wrapped in Emma Jaine's tale, whatever that was, then back at Claire and decided.

He'd take the gamble.

"You never wear the ones I send you?"

If he'd wanted to shock her, he couldn't have done better. Her eyes widened as she stared at him in confusion. It was several seconds later, after she'd sipped her drink before she spoke softly to him.

"You send me flowers?"

"Gardenias, yes. Every time I know you're performing." He took another bite of his potato.

"But...I thought...I mean, it makes more sense. Why would you send me gardenias and not Norm? How did you know they're my favorites?"

"I've always known. That potted gardenia of your mother's you kept in your room for years until Josie and I destroyed it? How could I ever forget?"

Carole Brown

"Wills."

Just that one word. Her eyes had filled with tears, but she held them back, not allowing them to rain down her cheeks. Wills longed to wipe those tears from her eyes, but he refrained. Not yet, he cautioned himself. Not yet.

"It was the least I could do, and besides, you look so elegant with that creamy gardenia pinned in your hair or on your wrist."

Forty-five minutes later, Captain Ossie stood, signaling it was time to move back into the library, and Wills and Claire stood too.

She still stared at him, but when everyone had left the room, she whispered, "Wills, I think you...you...must be..."

But she didn't finish, and when Wills asked hastily, "I must be what, Claire?" she gave him a frightened, confused look again and fled the room.

Wills followed, wondering what Claire had wanted to say but fear had held her back. Something insulting?

No.

Something teasing?

Definitely not.

Something wonderful and magical that would make his heart sing?

He smiled. Maybe.

And that's as far as he'd allow his hope to go tonight. There would be tomorrow. He'd see what happened then, and the day after, and the day after that.

Chapter Twenty-One

Once dinner was over and after mingling a half hour or so with the boarding house people, Wills slipped outside. Tyson had taken Claire's attention once they'd gathered in the library, so Wills was free to visit with his friends.

Needing a fresh breath of air, he slipped out the library French doors and wandered around the darkened yard.

Time was passing fast, with little of it to discover a plot he still knew nothing about. The twenty-first—he was convinced—was the day that seemed to be important, the day that something was to happen.

The time limit set him on edge especially knowing he knew less than nothing. Suspicions of people meant nothing if he had nothing to prove them. And even if he knew who was behind the scheme, it would benefit no one unless he knew what it was and could stop it.

Colonel Waverly? He seriously doubted it. But sometimes the one who was less suspicious, was the problem.

The Dame? Possibly. She certainly was capable enough.

Hermie? Wills snickered. He wasn't intelligent enough.

Claire? His heart wrenched at the thought. He wanted to toss the idea of his love being involved in something so sinister, but he had a duty to prove it.

"Wills?"

Wills turned at the sound of the soft voice. Claire was heading toward him.

"I wanted to talk with you."

About them?

"Something strange happened today that bothered me, and I need to tell someone."

She'd chosen to tell him? Sounded like he was

gaining a little ground with her.

"May I?"

"You know you can talk with my anytime, Claire."

She nodded. "I took baby Fina for a walk in her stroller late this morning, and we stopped at the diner to grab a drink. When we started home, I noticed a man following us."

"How do you know he was following *you*?" Wills' heart beat faster. "Did he bother you?"

"I just knew he was. I could feel it. And, no, he didn't exactly bother me. When we arrived back at the house, he approached me before I could open the gate. He wanted to know the time."

"The time? That's weird."

"I thought so too, but worse than that, he grabbed my arm."

"Claire, did he hurt you? Scare you?"

"Hurt me, no. Scare me? A little. He said I was in danger."

"What? What kind of danger? I wish you'd told me earlier. I could have put out a lookout for him. Can you describe him?"

"He looked something like—don't laugh—like you."

Wills laughed. "You're joking. Paying me back for all the times—"

"I am. He had a big nose, like he'd drank a lot in his life time, but he was sort of pitiful too. He'd tried to spruce up a little, I think. He was wearing a suit jacket and his hair was slicked back, and he smelled—this is my second thing I wanted to tell you—he wore cologne. Good cologne. Like the room smells."

"The room?"

"You know, at my practicing building."

"You figured it out. Good work."

"He might have tried sprucing up, but he still seemed like a—a tramp."

"Claire." Wills spoke then hesitated. She didn't know about the man who'd approached him in this very garden days earlier. Could it be...was it the same person?

"Wills? What are you thinking?"

Wills felt a strong urge to confide in her. He wanted to. Badly. But caution warned him to wait.

"Seriously? I'm thinking about what a detective you've become. Wanna join forces?"

Claire laughed. "If I ever lose my voice, I might consider it."

He sobered. "I don't know what he meant by danger, but you can't be out and about by yourself anymore till we find out what's going on. You've already promised me you'd have Pops, Tyrell or even your father see you to and from your practices and events, or anywhere you want to go. You are doing that?"

"Yes, although it hurts me to bother—"

"Nonsense." Wills spoke sharper than he meant to, but his fright for her was ripping his insides like a sharp-bladed ax. "I cannot do what I have to do and worry about you at the same time. You must do as I asked. Please, this once I'm begging you."

"I think I like the thought of *you* begging *me* for something."

"Claire..."

"I'm sorry. If it will make you feel better, I'll do as you ask."

"Thank—"

"Miss..."

Claire and Wills whirled at the sound of a voice nearby. Wills moved to put Claire behind him. "Who's there? Show yourself."

"That's him. That's the man who stopped me when I was walking with Baby Fina today." Claire whispered the words from behind his back. "I recognize his voice."

"Are you sure, Claire? Positive?"

"I am."

The man stepped closer to them, and Wills had to admit, though he was unkempt, he didn't look the least bit dangerous. Still, he didn't much like the thought of him approaching Claire at any time. Or that Claire had compared this unkempt man to him.

"What do you want? Why are you bothering Claire?" Wills snapped at the man, which was mild, considering how he wanted to speak to him.

"I mean no harm, but I can't stand by and allow your woman to get hurt."

"I'm not his—"

Claire's objection was cut short by Wills' retort.

"What do you mean get hurt? Who's trying to hurt her?"

"I don't really know how, but she needs to be careful. Very—"

"Claire, what are you doing out here by yourself—oh."

Tyson was striding toward them, moving fast until he saw who she was with. "It's you, is it?"

"Yeah, it's me." Wills chuckled under his breath, although he wanted to say, *So? What of it?* Instead, he cast a look behind him. The guy who'd warned Claire was gone. He'd not found out who was trying to hurt Claire, nor why, nor how. It was beyond frustrating.

Wills' gaze swept the area in the darkness and saw no one.

Mr. Mystery Man had vanished.

Wills turned his attention back to the arrogant Tyson, who'd promptly taken Claire's arm and was escorting her back to the house.

She went but managed to cast an amused glance back at him, and Wills watched them go.

How could Claire endure such a pompous guy? Probably because he was a good manager. Or not. He didn't want Claire to like the man. That wouldn't keep her from doing so. It'd take much more than that.

How could he protect the love of his life if he didn't know what he was up against? Wills strode around the property, hoping he'd run into that strange, shabby man again, but no luck. He saw neither hide nor hair of him.

Another dead end.

~*~

Wills ignored the urge to stretch his tired muscles. He'd been up way too late last night with way too many things to think about after that guy had shown up to warn Claire again.

He glanced up. The bright sunlight shining through the diner's windows highlighted Owens' youthful features.

"What do you have for me?" Wills lifted his cup of coffee and sipped. Not nearly as good as his mother's, but it would do. Maybe keep him awake long enough to get things accomplished today.

"This is what I have for you." Owens pulled out a notebook and opened it. "Freddie—my friend, the soldier, helped me put this together. I did as you asked and started with the event Claire was attending. The others, we sorted into groups depending on several different categories."

"What were these categories?"

"We listed each event under any category we came up with such as people attending, location, speakers, singers, hosts, timing, the reason for the event, any out-of-state attendees, the importance of the people themselves, etc." She stopped talking and looked at him.

"What?"

"None of the events came under more than five categories...except one."

"The one Claire's attending."

"Right."

"And can you tell me—"

"Let me go through some of the things we found out about this one event."

She didn't notice—or was much too excited—that she'd interrupted him. But Wills didn't care. She had something interesting to share, and he was anxious to hear it.

"First, we checked to see how many people attending were from out of state. There were ten, so we checked these ten out thoroughly, even if they were well known with good reputations. Backgrounds, friends, jobs, family, etc. Nothing showed up on nine of them."

"And?"

"Albert Miller. Do you know him, Sir?"

"I don't think so. What about him?"

"He worked for six months with an ammunitions plant just across the river as a scientific specialist on loan from a state out west. He's a friend of the governor's, or so his application from the plant says. He has several high degrees, and his work history is outstanding."

"That all sounds good. What's the problem?"

"The problem, Sir, is my intuition."

Wills raised a brow. "You've been hanging around me too long."

Owens laughed. "Maybe. Anyhow, I tried to accept what I read, but one night I woke and realized what was nagging me."

When Wills didn't speak, she went on. "His name. I knew a person in school who was named Albert. He was standoffish, kind of timid, it seemed. But one day, I heard his father call him Ulbrecht, with a German accent."

"I see where you're going with this."

She nodded. "So...I did more digging. I really didn't think I could find anything. Spies know how to hide things, they're skilled at deceit, but I finally managed to find one little thing. That thing led me to more."

"What was that one little thing?"

"I went to a function where he was. I stood in hearing distance of him with my dressed-up soldier friend. I spoke the name loudly, saying it with the German pronunciation, laughing as if talking with Freddie. He turned—quickly and suddenly, and almost immediately recovered from that unconscious move. But he *had* turned, as if it was a natural habit from his youth. And, Sir, no one else did that."

"Owens, you amaze me. I'm impressed."

"Thank you, Sir, I hoped you would be pleased."

"Is there more?"

"Much more. Let me finish. Once I'd established that his real name was probably Ulbrecht, I thought about his last name. Checked German names and realized Muller was a common surname there. Get it? Muller. Miller?"

"I do. Very nicely done."

"I wasn't done. With Freddie's help, I moved on to research his past as much as I could. I couldn't find much, but I did discover that no one—and I mean, no one—even his so-called friends—knew much about his past."

"Even the governor?"

"Even the governor. Or should I say, one of his closest staffers."

"And how did you manage to speak to him?"

Owens grinned again. "Colonel Waverly."

"Of course. Go ahead."

"So I called the university where he supposedly taught, I spoke to the research laboratory where he supposedly worked for so many years. Both declared he'd been a valuable colleague, very intelligent."

Wills sat back in his seat, impressed as he seldom ever was. He thought over all Owens had relayed to him. "You know all this might mean nothing?"

"Yes, but—"

"But I'm inclined to believe you've latched onto information vitally important. Did you happen to obtain a photo of this man?"

"I did. It's not very good or clear, but it's all I could come up with so far." She pulled out a small picture of a well-dressed, slim man leaning against the trunk of a tree.

A spark of light had lit off a spot on one of his shoes, and Wills assumed it was because of the shine on them. He could almost smell the expensive cologne the man wore. A homburg was cocked on his head, but it was pulled low over his brow and shaded his eyes. But the mouth—his mouth was wide, but pinched as if the man had pressed his lips together in frustration or anger.

No one would have ever guessed, by looking at this picture, that the man was a scientist.

Wills studied the photo then tapped it. "He looks so familiar."

"Sir." Shock threaded its way through Owens' voice as she spoke the one word.

"I think I've met him. Or seen him." Wills closed his eyes, thinking, thinking. "But I just can't remember where."

"Where do you think you could have seen him?"

"If I did, I must have not given him a thought. Probably figured he was unimportant, and I'd never see him again. He couldn't have made much of an impression on me. I forgot about him. I suppose."

"Then do you think all this is helpful to you?"

"I do. We've not come up with much of anything else. Now to figure out how to tie this, this..." Wills tapped the picture. "...Muller to my suspects is another thing."

"How can I help?"

"First, I want you to go to Colonel Waverly. Tell him that I request this Freddie to be available to help you as necessary. Make sure you let the colonel know I need to talk with him privately soon, that I'll contact him and let him know what's happening, that we have a strong lead. Do not tell him anything else yet. And, by no means, speak with him if he has anyone in his office. Understand?

"I do."

"Then continue researching this..." Wills poked her notebook. "...see if anything else comes up. Dig deep, Owens. One other thing. Do you think you could talk with two men who were apprehended a couple days ago? I want to know why they came to Claire's entertainment/practicing building, who asked them to, and who they are. Find out anything you can, especially pertaining to our business at hand. Do you think you can do this for me?"

"Sir. I'm not a detective. Not even trained to do that. Do you think I can?"

There was doubt, but also hope in her voice, and Wills hastened to assure her. "I wouldn't have asked if I'd thought you couldn't do this. Wear simple, plain clothes and show them you're serious and strong. Don't let them frighten you or put you off. Demand answers and call for help if you need it. You can do it."

She straightened. "Then I will do it, Sir. Thank you."

"Good." Wills stood. "Can I take your notebook with me to study what you've gotten so far?"

"Sure." She handed it to him. "I made copies, so I have another one. Securely locked up, Sir."

"Then get with it. We only have a few more days, Owens. Let's get this lined up and ready for the twenty-first as soon as we can."

"I agree."

He started to turn away, to leave, when he swung back around. "Do you know what I was told everyone calls this guy, Owens? That's assuming this is our spy?"

"No, Sir."

"The Mystery Man."

"Really?"

"I'm pretty sure they are one and the same. Do you know why he goes by that name?"

"No.

"Because, they say he's like a ghost. No one has ever been close to figuring out who he is." Wills stared down at the brunette who'd been such a help to him. "That means we've got to be smarter than him. Be wiser and more cautious."

Without a word from Owens, Wills left the diner.

He had not a minute to spare.

~*~

It was five-thirty in the morning. It wasn't raining, but there was some fog from the Ohio River in the distance, trying to hide the rising sun. It was going to be a gorgeous day. Claire just knew it. Or at least she had for the first mile of vigorous walking. Now?

Now she wasn't so sure. This had been the third day in a row, she'd seen someone behind her, walking at her pace, never getting too close nor lingering too far behind her. Never passing her, never veering from the same direction she went. If it was the same man, he'd worn different clothing each day so she'd never be able to identify him if it came to that.

She was starting to get spooked. Especially since she'd promised Wills she'd not be out by herself. But, she'd argued, she couldn't give up her walking. It was good exercise and good for her lungs. Neither Pops Mason nor Papa Ossie could have kept up with her.

At least, that was what she assured herself.

She'd thought about confronting the man, but that might be awkward. She'd also thought about trying to elude him, but he'd just come back tomorrow if he was really following her. She'd given about ten seconds of thought to telling Wills, but it'd taken less than that to realize he'd put a stop to her walking if she did.

Stuck with the man, she reckoned, was the only solution. At least, he'd never tried to catch up with her or approach her. That was a good thing, wasn't it? Could be a guardian angel, but probably not.

It was almost time for her to head home. She always circled the park, enjoying the trees and lush bushes that were beginning to leaf.

She walked through the entrance to the park and began the circling part of her walk. She followed the paths, mostly, which were elaborate. Just walking through the park gave her another mile of walking to add to her daily exercise. When she was almost half way through it, she sensed something was wrong.

Footsteps. Footsteps louder than hers were slapping on the path.

For the first time, real fear flooded her being. She picked up her pace, almost running now. And then she smelled the cologne...

Hands grabbed her shoulders, and she glanced down at one gripping her right shoulder. Soft, clean, and strong, manly hands. An arm reached around her, closing tightly and pulling her back against a man's chest, even as they slowed to a trot. She started to scream, but a hand slapped across her mouth, bruising her lips. Struggling, kicking and floundering against the greater strength, fierce desperation gave her the strength to kick backward, as hard as she could, and she felt the man let go.

She didn't wait to see what he would do next. With the sound of his groans in her ears, Claire fled the park. It wasn't a walk home, it was a race.

A race, her terrified self insisted, to save her life.

~*~

Wills barely caught the train. He boarded just as it was pulling out and held out his pass to the ticket master. It would be a four-hour trip, but he was determined to find out more about the spy. He'd begged his father and Papa Ossie to keep an eye on Claire.

Meanwhile, he hoped the time would go fast, seeing how he planned to look through all the notes Owens had made.

Owens had telephoned him early this morning before he'd left the house with a report after talking with the two intruders last night.

According to her, the two men were local brothers, heavy-weights, who'd been hired—for some serious money, their words—by some stranger to follow Wills. They had no idea who'd done the hiring, and she was inclined to believe them.

Another dead end. But at least, they'd eliminated them.

Two hours later, Wills closed the notebook. He'd gone through, in his mind, every name he'd had contact with ever since Colonel Waverly had asked him to investigate Claire.

He lifted the sheet of paper where he'd written two thoughts.

Claire seemed so very innocent, but was she? Was she playing on Wills' emotions, knowing full well he'd fall right in line with the way she wanted him to? Perhaps even guessing he had strong feelings for her?

What about those strange words she spouted at that one event when he and Owens pretended to be close? What about her closeness to Tyson whom Wills was certain had been the one who'd hit him that night?

But—and there was that little word that always preceded the doubt he carried when it came to Claire and her innocence. Claire's training in a home filled with people who adored her, from his parents, to the residents, to her family. How could she have strayed so far as to become a spy when she had such a legacy?

But—another one—he loved her. He'd known her all his life. He'd watched her for weeks now. He'd seen terror in her eyes when she'd heard conversations she wasn't supposed to hear. No one—at least, not Claire— could have faked those emotions.

No, she wasn't a spy. Wills felt a sigh escape from his body. Now that that was settled, again, he could get on to the business at hand. Like, why he was traveling to the governor's house to talk with a man who didn't know he was coming.

~*~

Claire was still trembling when she re-entered her home. She wanted to run to Papa Ossie, as she'd always done when needed. But today—well, today she couldn't do that. For one thing, it would upset her father terribly, and she didn't want that. Not only because of him, but because of the restrictions he'd force upon her in taking care of her. Then there was the other matter in which she wished she'd kept her promise. Wills had asked her not to go anywhere without an escort, and she'd promised.

And what had she done the minute he wasn't around? Because she thought she was safe, could handle any problem?

Claire groaned, although quietly, as she headed to her room. She heard Emma Jaine's voice, talking with Harriet in the kitchen area, and Claire hurried so she wouldn't have to talk with her. Shutting her door, she leaned back against it and breathed in and out, staring out her window on the other side of the room.

She realized one thing. She couldn't tell anyone what had happened on her walk today. If a word of it got back to Wills...

A knock on her door had her jumping farther into her room, her heart pounding again. Reality hit her, and she breathed out an answer.

"Yes? Who is it?"

"It's Jonah, Miss Claire. Telephone call for you."

"I can't answer it right now, Jonah. Would you please tell them I'm not available?"

"I will. Are you all right, Claire?"

"I'm fine, Jonah. Thanks."

When he didn't give another reply, Claire whirled and gathered her things. Another soothing bath, a cup of tea and some cinnamon toast would be warm and soothing this morning—not only to her body, but her soul too.

Claire gave herself time to relax in the bath and allow the tension to let go of her body. After twenty minutes, she headed back to her room and dressed in a full rusty-red skirt and matching sweater, and tied her hair back with a satin ribbon. Then she headed to the kitchen where she found Harriet busy cleaning the kitchen.

"Hi, Harriet, could I grab a cup of tea before I head out?"

"Of course, Claire. Sit while I get it for you? Would you like some toast?"

"I would. One slice with a dab of cinnamon on it? You still have cinnamon?"

"I do, hoarded for sure, but I have a secret hiding place for certain things." Harriet grinned then frowned. "I hope you're having Jonah drive you? I remember distinctly Wills asking his father to be available when you needed transportation."

"I haven't asked him, but I intend to." She lifted the cup Harriet set down before her and sipped. "Hmmm. Delicious, Harriet. Thanks."

"You're welcome. And here's your toast, laden just the way you like it."

"You're the best, Harriet. I don't know what we'd do without you and Jonah."

"I don't know either." Harriet's cheeky answer had Claire laughing.

She was a wonderful person who helped keep an even keel in the Rayner household. She was a loving, encouraging mentor to the Rayner sisters, but when they needed a "talking to" she'd stepped right up and helped them to see the right. And they'd loved her for it.

When Claire rose to leave the kitchen ten minutes later, Harriet's words stopped her.

"Claire, I don't know where you're going or what you'll be doing, but I want you to know that Wills is really worried about you. He didn't say much, but I could hear it in his voice and see it in his troubled eyes. Don't you be doing anything foolish that hurts my boy."

Claire went to the woman. "I won't, Harriet. I promise."

But did her promises mean anything when she couldn't even keep one?

~*~

When Jonah dropped her off at Norm's apartment building, Claire stood on the sidewalk studying the building. It was a nice one, just like she knew he'd have.

If he'd kept to his schedule that he'd given her, he was out of town for the next two days on unknown business. He'd not volunteered the whereabouts he was going, and she'd not asked.

She drew her gloves from her purse and pulled them on then walked up to the doors where the doorman opened them before she had a chance to do so. Claire nodded to him but moved on inside and stood taking in the huge lobby area. She walked straight up to the desk, and when the young girl asked how she could she help her, Claire stated concisely what she wanted and then turned a little away as if there was no question that she'd get what she wanted.

The girl started to stumble a confused reply, but when Claire gave her a haughty glance, the clerk reached for the extra key and handed it over.

"Who shall I put down as borrowing it, Miss?

Claire hesitated as if pondering the question. "Why not just write down, Mrs. Norman Tyson?" And then she swept away. The elevator took her to the fourth floor and Claire stepped out, glancing at the numbers. She turned left, walked three doors down, and stopped in front of the door.

Did she really want to do this? If Norm found out, he might just be angry enough to quit being her manager. Did she want to do this badly enough to accept the consequences?

Weighing her answer, it took only a few seconds to reach it. She knocked lightly, waited, then inserted the key into the lock. It clicked, she twisted the knob and shoved open the door. She studied what she could see, called softly to Norm, but when there was no answer, she entered the room.

It was tidy, not like some men kept their personal space, but everything in its place. Clothes arranged in what seemed to be some kind of system. Pants, shirts, jackets were pressed and hung neatly. Ties hung on a rack by color. Shoes lined on their rack were polished. No worn out shoes in this room.

Claire had known Norm was rich. He had manners—to a certain degree. He was well-traveled and smart. And to most women, he'd have no problem being a great catch.

Whirling from inspecting his closet, she went straight to the polished desk set close to the large double windows. Only one drawer was locked, and Claire had no clue how to pick the lock. But she was good at skimming through papers to see what was important and what wasn't.

She went through each drawer, but it wasn't until she reached for the locked box stored beneath the desk that she hit pay dirt. The key was in the middle drawer—she was sure it was a match—and inserted the key. The lid lifted like a well-oiled machine, and Claire stared down at the contents of the box.

Letters. Dozens of letters. She didn't have time to read them all, and she certainly couldn't take them with her. Sighing, she lifted the box to the desktop and sat in the expansive, comfortable desk chair.

It took her fifteen minutes to sort the letters into possible piles. Some—only a handful—seemed to be notes without envelopes, and these she placed in a separate pile. She picked up the first letter in a pile she hoped would prove beneficial.

Exactly what she was looking for, she had no idea. But someone was terrorizing her, and she meant to find out who and why. Beyond that, she had no idea what to do—except confess to Wills what she'd found out—if she proved lucky.

She barely scanned the letters, most business ones, but none made any reference to her. She placed these in the box and turned to the next pile, which proved even less likely they were conspiratorial. Into the box they went.

The last pile was thinner, only three letters, and she sighed as she opened the first one. It appeared, at first, to be a legit business letter with initials as the signature.

A. M.

Why would someone sign a letter with just their initials for a signature? And who were they talking about when talking about *your cousin*?

She re-read the letter.

Dear Mr. Tyson:

We have a proposition to make to you. Your cousin referenced you as a talented and well-versed individual in politics and business. It would be a simple task, but important for the wellbeing of our country. If you would be willing to work with us, please send your answer via your cousin. We must have your reply by March 19 or we will assume you are not interested.

Yours for victory of our beloved country,
A.M.

The date stood out first to Claire. That was two months ago, right before they planned their trip to France. And just weeks before Norm began acting strangely. Did this letter have something to do with his actions? Was he working with the government in secret, much like Wills?

Claire pulled her large bag to her lap and reached in for her father's camera that she'd borrowed before leaving the house. Then adjusting the lens, she snapped a picture of the letter and refolded it, placing it back in the box. Time to move on to the next letter. It was even more troubling than the first one:

Tyson:

Per your questions: your duties would be simple. Through covert messages—using the method your cousin has relayed to you already—in such a way that will not be noticeable or detected, your cooperation in making this happen will ensure that our beloved country will be victorious. We urge you to do as we, and your cousin asks, in helping us achieve our goals.

Sincerely,
A.M.

It was all so confusing. What was he to do to convey these important messages?

Snapping a picture of this one, she wondered if she was doing good or muddling her own thoughts over what was happening.

Hesitating after replacing the second letter, she stared at the last letter. Why bother? She could make no sense of these. It sounded as if the government wanted Norm's help. But the terror she'd felt early this morning urged her to keep going. She had to have answers.

She pulled out the third letter and opened it. Her eyes widened. It not only had an entirely different tone, but sounded threatening. Was Norm being threatened by the government?

Tyson,

I hear you're getting cold feet. What you need to know is we cannot have anyone back out of our plans now. To do so will be detrimental to us and to you. Do you understand? We would hate to have to take drastic measures. People will get hurt.

Do you understand me or will we have to show you what happens to defectors?

A.M.

Claire stood and stared out the large windows. The sky had cleared and promised a warmer-than-usual day for May. The street was busy below, newspaper boys hawking their wares, people walking down the street in pairs or single, and quite a few cars rolled down the street, considering the gasoline rationing.

She was about to return to the desk when a figure across the street caught her attention. He was leaning against the side of a building, a homburg hat tilted to shield his face from the sun, but she was almost certain he was staring at her. She stared back, trying to discern if her imagination was playing with her emotions or if what she thought she was seeing was real.

Claire took two steps back, then three, until she was behind the curtain again. She touched the glass just a fraction to gaze out, but the man was gone. Her breath came out in a rush. Her hands shook, and she realized, she was once again afraid.

Paranoid was more like it.

She had to finish this. Jonah was to pick her up—she glanced at the wall clock—in fifteen minutes.

Carole Brown

Snapping a picture of the last letter, she hurriedly replaced it then eyed the last stack. Not many lay there. Four? Five? If she hurried...

Again, she snapped one picture after the other, replaced the letters and shoved the box under the desk again. Then making sure everything was just as she'd found it, she headed to the door, but the sound of a key being inserted into the lock stopped her from opening the door.

Norm was home.

Her gaze flashed around the room. Behind the curtains? No. In the closet? Definitely no. It'd be the first place the man would look if he suspected someone was in here. She headed for the coat closet anyway, and when it opened, she was thrilled to realize, the back wall was actually a door to the adjoining room. She pulled the door closed behind her just as the exterior door opened, and Claire leaned against the second room's door, twisting the lock behind her back.

She heard no sounds from the adjoining room, but she probably wouldn't. It was only then that she skimmed the room she was now in with her gaze. Someone was renting this room. Norm? She doubted it. Whoever it was just might return any time, and if she didn't want to get caught, she'd better leave now.

Gripping her bag, she headed to the door, twisted the knob, opened the door, and came face to face with a stranger. A handsome stranger. A well-dressed stranger who looked as if he knew his way around in the fashion world.

The stranger on the street who'd been staring up at her.

Chapter Twenty-Two

Wills stared up at the massive, impressive Ohio statehouse. If he'd been the type to be daunted by size and beauty, he'd have tucked tail and headed back home.

But he wasn't.

He'd confirmed the governor had a light schedule today before making the trip. Taking him by surprise, he hoped might give him an edge. Getting into the statehouse to see the governor when you had an invitation or appointment, was rough enough, but going in solo without that priceless piece of welcome was usually unheard of.

Wills had an edge, and he grinned even as he felt that piece of paper in his pocket. That, his best friend from basic training had assured him, would do the trick.

Sure enough, as he opened the stately door, a uniformed young man held up a hand. "State your business, Sir."

Wills didn't speak, only held out the open paper. The guard studied it for a minute then moved to a telephone and spoke softly in it, his eyes remaining on Wills. He nodded, hung up the phone and returned to the door. "Please go on up. The governor will see you."

Wills nodded, moved to the stairs, and began climbing.

~*~

"I hear you're a friend of my son." The governor was seated when Wills was ushered in, but he stood and came from around his monstrous desk. "Best friends if my guard was correct after reading the note you gave him."

"Yes, Sir. My best friend in basic training, Sir."

"So you're the one who always got my son in trouble." The words sounded critical, but the twinkle in the older man's eyes belied the sound.

218

"Oh, no, Governor. You've been misinformed. Logan was the mischief-maker, but I managed to keep him from any serious trouble."

"I can imagine." The governor threw back his head and laughed long and hard. "Sit, Sit. Tell me how I can help you. Came all the way from Cincinnati, I assume."

"Yes, I did. I'm sure you know by now I'm on a—uh, special assignment to find a spy in that area."

"I heard, although I don't know the details."

"In my investigation, I've come across the name of someone that is supposed to come highly recommended by you."

"Is that so? Who is this person?"

"Albert Miller."

"Albert Miller. I know him from back when. Had the privilege of meeting him several years ago. He was brilliant and going places. Won several accolades for his accomplishments in science."

"I see. Could you describe him to me?"

"Hmmm. It's been a few years. He's average height, thin and always decently dressed when not working, although that was seldom. His work consumed him. He was very smart and particular about work, more so than clothes and society."

Nothing in that description set the man apart enough to be able to identify him. "Was his nationality American?"

"Hmmm. I believe he has dual citizenship. United States and Germany. He immigrated to the U.S. quite a few years ago, but never relinquished his native citizenship."

"You wouldn't have a picture of him, would you?"

"No, I'm afraid not. There were some pictures taken years ago by the newspapers, but I never saved one. I've known him a long time, but we never kept in touch much. I'm afraid there's not much else I can tell you."

Wills stood. "Thank you, Sir, for your time. I know you're busy."

"I always make time for friends of my son. He's serving his country, although I could have gotten him out of the field duty. He wouldn't hear of it."

"That's Logan. He's a great patriot."

When Wills walked out of the capitol building, he stood at the top of the stairs and stared down into the busy street below. He'd not found out much, but he had learned two important things. This Albert Miller had citizenship in Germany—confirming Owens' thoughts on the German name—and more important, there were newspaper shots of the man somewhere. He'd have Owens hunt those down as soon as he got home. He should have asked where those pictures had been taken, but it was too late now.

Now it was time to get home.

~*~

It was late when Wills finally stepped out of the taxi at home. But he stopped abruptly and stared at the windows of the house. Almost all the windows were lit, and in the library, he could see movement, as if there were quite a few people walking about.

Fleeting thoughts sped through his head as he hurried to the front door. Had something happened to his parents? Had Captain Ossie taken ill? Or was Claire in trouble?

And why weren't the windows darkened with the shades?

His fingers fumbled with the key as he inserted it, and for once, he almost lost his cool. But when he finally flung open the door, he was greeted with exclamations and questions that were barely understandable, with all of them flying at him at once.

He held up a hand. "Wait. I can't understand. What's wrong?"

When the babble continued, he impatiently motioned for everyone to head back to the library.

"Sit. Pops, would you see that all the blinds are pulled in the house?" His heart swelled with happiness that everyone was present and accounted for except for Josie and her family and Claire, who was probably still out with her manager and band.

"Josie and Fina all right?"

Heads nodded.

"Claire?"

"We thought she was with you. Tyrell contacted Tyson, but he hasn't seen her. She left early this morning, and we've not heard a word from her." The worry in Emma Jaine's voice showed in her pale face.

"It's not like her. It's not like her." Captain Ossie's rambling words were distraught with worry.

"Captain Ossie."

"Yes, my son?"

"If Claire is missing, we'll find her. Tyrell and I, and even Jerry if we need him, will not stop looking till we have her safe and sound back home with you." Wills stared straight at the man who was like a second father to him. "Do you trust me, Sir?"

Captain Ossie ran a hand over his face then nodded. "I do, Wills, but she's my baby girl. Bring her back to me."

"I'll not stop until I do." Wills stood and turned to Tyrell. "I'd like you to check at the auditorium where she practices and see if she's there. After that, check the park where she walks all the time. I doubt if she's there, but you might find—"

Wills stopped talking and glanced at the rest of the family. But Tyrell had gotten the gist of what he wanted him to do. Find evidence that Claire had been there. Or not.

"And Jerry, if you'll contact the police to be on the lookout for anything suspicious in our area, around her entertainment building, I'd appreciate it."

As Wills was leaving again, his father stepped outside the door with him.

"Pops?"

"Son, I thought you ought to know this. I dropped Claire off at the apartment of that manager of hers early this morning, but when it was almost time for me to pick her up, she called me and said she wouldn't need me. She was busy with other things and wouldn't be home till later. She didn't give me any clues of where she was going or with whom. I tried to ask her questions, but she insisted she had to hang up, and then the phone clicked."

"Pops, what are you saying?"

221

"I got the feeling she wasn't alone. There was something in Claire's voice—a tremble? A warning? I don't know, but our Claire is always a straight-forward girl. I'm worried."

"Why didn't you tell the captain this? Someone could have looked for her earlier."

"I did mention it to Captain Ossie, but he sighed and said she was probably going out with friends to shop or on a secret date with someone. He said not to worry till later."

"And now we're all worried. You know how much I respect the captain, but he does indulge those girls of his."

"Now, Wills, no criticism of the captain."

"You're right, Pops, as always." Wills grinned at his father. "I've got to go now. You and Mother pray."

"You know we will, Son."

Wills walked away from the Rayner house with no grin on his face.

What had happened to Claire?

~*~

Wills headed to Tyson's apartment. He would have had no idea where the man lived if it hadn't been for his father pressing the note with the address in his hand at the last minute. Now, as the taxi zoomed toward downtown Cincinnati, Wills hoped with all his heart that he wouldn't find Claire there. The thought of Claire alone in Tyson's apartment...

"God, let it not be so."

When the taxi pulled up in front of the hotel, Wills hopped out. "Wait for me."

The doorman opened the door as Wills approached, but he ignored the open door and asked, "Have you seen this lady here today?"

The man studied Wills then glanced down at the photo of Claire from a few years earlier. He looked back at Wills. "Why do you need to know?"

"She's family, and we haven't heard from her. That's not like her." It was all Wills said, but it must have been enough.

"I believe so, late this morning. She wore a dusty red

skirt and sweater set. Good-looking young lady."

Wills thanked him and headed to the sign-in desk and asked the same question.

The man looked down at the register. "It looks like a woman came in around eleven this morning registered as Mrs. Norman Tyson. I haven't seen her leave, but then I was off from 10:30 until three."

"Right. Who's your fill-in?"

"Billie Yates usually fills in for me, but she left early feeling sick. As far as I know, no one's seen her."

"I see. I need a number for Norman Tyson's room."

He lifted a brow, but spoke the number anyway. Wills turned away then swung back around. "Key please."

"Let me call the room and see if Mr. Tyson's in."

"No. Definitely not. I just need the key."

"We're not supposed to—"

"I don't care. This is an urgent matter. Key now or I'll speak to your supervisor."

In slow motion, the man handed over the key, his mouth a scowl of disapproval. He murmured something as Wills walked away, but he ignored him. Claire was far more important than winning a battle with a cross clerk.

Wills took the elevator but wished he'd gone with the stairs when it stopped at every floor between ground and the fourth.

As he stepped out of the elevator, he saw someone—someone who looked vaguely familiar starting down the stairs at the other end of the hallway.

Odd. Wills shook his head. He hadn't time right now to follow the man, so he counted down the numbers until he came to 417. He checked the doorknob, and it was locked like he figured. He knocked with no answer then inserted the key.

It took only minutes to go through the apartment, checking under the bed, in closets and the bathroom. When he'd finally finished, he went to the window and looked out.

A man was walking down the street, and Wills was almost positive it was the same guy who'd started down the stairs earlier. He didn't look back, only hailed a taxi, climbed in and disappeared.

Wills started to turn away when something on the window caught his attention. He leaned close to study it.

Five fingerprints. As if someone had stood here and gazed out on the street as he had done. Carefully, he placed his hand to hover over the prints. His hand covered them without him being able to see the fingerprints. Wills' heart raced like a fast car. Claire had been in here, and not long ago, because if she hadn't been, the hotel maids would have already cleaned the window.

Where could she be?

Wills headed for the door and paused before opening it. Something eluded him. He listened and heard nothing unusual. He swept the place with his gaze again and nothing stood out. He shook his head. He was letting his imagination run away with him.

Unlocking the door, he stepped into the hallway and pulled the door closed behind him, making sure it was locked. It was then it hit him.

Claire's cologne. Not only had he seen a print he was sure was hers, but that smell in Tyson's apartment had been the brand of cologne Claire always wore.

Her signature cologne.

~*~

Wills did not want to go home. For one thing, Captain Ossie would be devastated that Wills had failed to find his daughter. Secondly, there was no way he could sleep or rest till he found Claire. But he needed to talk with Tyrell, and possibly Jerry, to detail what to do next.

When he walked up to his home front door, it opened without him doing so. His father stood there with a hopeful look that turned disappointed when he saw Wills' dejected expression.

"No good news, I take it?" His father spoke quietly, hoping, Wills knew, not to upset the household.

"A tiny bit, but not much, Pops. I'm going to talk to the men if you want to join us."

His father nodded, shut the door, and followed Wills into the library where Captain Ossie and his two sons-in-law stood waiting.

Wills spoke first, wanting to keep control of the

conversation. "Any luck, Tyrell?"

"Nothing definitive. I did find some disturbance in that spot of dirt—you know what I'm talking about—in the park. As if two people had a scuffle there, but nothing to identify that it was Claire."

Wills nodded and turned away. His heart felt as heavy as if it was weighted down with the largest rocks anyone could get in a large bag.

Don't give up yet. She is all right and you'll find her.

His thoughts of encouragement to himself didn't help much to bolster his emotions, but it did give him enough strength to face his family again.

"I didn't find Claire either." He studied their faces and could see they wanted more. "But I did find two clues that lead me to believe she was there."

"Where, Wills?" Captain Ossie's face must have aged in a few hours.

"In Norman Tyson's room, Sir, at the Grand Hotel downtown."

"That scoundrel! If he's hurt Claire—"

"I don't believe so."

"Why?" The captain's demand set Wills back a moment.

"Sir, I don't have any tangible reasons, but I know right here..." Wills placed a hand over his heart "...that she's alive."

The older man said not a word, only stared into Wills' eyes. Then he nodded and sat back in his chair, as if what he'd read there was convincing. Only someone who loved like Wills did could be so convinced.

"Here's what I did after entering Tyson's room. I searched it extensively for clues once I realized Claire was not there. Bathroom, under beds, his desk and..."

As if a hand had reached down from heaven and slapped him, the thought blasted into his brain. The closet, closet, closet.

"No. How could I not realize it?"

The other three men were on their feet, demanding to know what he was saying.

"I checked the closet, for sure, but what I didn't realize at the time was the connecting door. It was locked from inside the connecting room, so I didn't think anything of it, but..." Again, Wills hesitated. "...what if that's where Claire is?"

"You mean someone found her and locked her in there?" Captain's face was red as if he was ready to explode.

"Maybe. If someone interrupted her while she was in Tyson's room, maybe they did. Or maybe she escaped into there and locked the door herself. But, no, then she would have left when the danger passed. Or called for help." Wills paced from the fireplace to the window and back again. "Tyrell, where was Tyson when you called him?

"He didn't say, but the number was long distance. I could run it down if you want."

"No, don't bother. That's what I wanted to hear. He's out of town."

The three other men watched him pace and work out the problem.

"Are you thinking Tyson's done this?" Jerry inserted his question in between Wills' mutters.

"It couldn't have been Tyson who caught Claire in his apartment. But Claire—someone is obviously out to hurt her or get her for some reason. And I think I know why." He swung away from the others. "I've got to go back and check."

"Wouldn't it be better if Jerry and I went with you? It might go faster, and you don't know who or what you'll face." Tyrell stood as if ready to go into battle.

Wills hesitated. It'd be nice to have these two with him, but he might run into things they shouldn't see or know about. Colonel Waverly would be upset.

But then, Claire meant more to him than Colonel Waverly's regard.

"If you will, I'll accept your help." Wills turned to his father. "Do you mind driving us, Pops?"

"You know I will. Let me get the keys." Jonah left the room but returned in less than a minute.

"Captain Ossie, if you would, I'd like you to call Colonel Waverly and ask him to call the hotel and make sure we have access to any needed keys or to search the place. Please man the phone in case we call and need something or in case Claire calls. If she does, call the hotel and get that information to us."

"Will do, and Wills, God be with you. Bring her home safe."

"I'll do my best or die trying." Wills turned to Tyrell and Jerry. "We'll discuss plans in the car. Let's go."

Twenty seconds later they were on their way. Wills laid out his plan. "Tyrell, I want you to talk with the desk clerk, the doorman, and any of the staff to see if any of them saw Claire today and if she was alone or with someone. Jerry, if you'll get the key for the connecting room, number 419, I assume, then follow me, I'd like you to guard the doors while I check both rooms again, and help out if there's too many people for me to handle."

Both men nodded, and in fifteen minutes Jonah pulled up to the front of the hotel, and the three exited the car. As Tyrell swerved away to begin his questioning, Jerry hurried toward the clerk's desk to obtain the key for the room next to Tyson's then ran up the stairs to the fourth floor.

Wills had forgotten to return the key earlier. Good thing too, he figured. It just made everything go faster than taking time arguing for a key again with the desk clerk.

By the time Wills had walked through Tyson's room again, Jerry was there with the next-door key, and Wills wasted no time sprinting to the room. Again, he knocked, but when there was no answer, he inserted the key and shoved open the door gently.

The room was dark and no sounds reached his ears. He hesitated. Was that the sound of soft breathing? Was someone waiting to clobber him on the head, figuring him an intruder?

He wasn't going to wait around to find out. With a flip of the light switch on the nearby table, light spilled into the room, and Wills saw Claire.

Lying on the bed, eyes closed, she didn't move, and for a moment, Wills was sure she was dead.

But then he saw the slow but steady rise and fall of

her chest, and in four strides, he was at the bedside and bending over her, whispering, hoping he wouldn't scare her. "Claire, wake up, Gorgeous. Claire..."

He gripped her wrist and felt for a pulse then glanced at Jerry. "I think she's been drugged."

"Looks like it."

"We'd better get her home. Jerry, please get her purse and the camera then have Tyrell call the family doctor to have him meet us there. When she wakens, she'll feel much happier with the family."

"And the police?"

"Our men can call the police to check out these rooms after we move her. I doubt they find anything useful, after we have gone over it with a fine-toothed comb."

Jerry waited till Wills had gathered Claire in his arms, locked the door then sprinted ahead to get to Tyrell. Two minutes later they were headed home.

Jonah looked in the car's rearview mirror at Wills. "She's all right, Son?"

"She will be, Pops. She's been drugged, but I believe she'll be fine once it works out of her system."

"Yes, the captain will be happier too." Jonah smiled at his son, and Wills smiled back.

~*~

The doctor had arrived at the Rayner house a few minutes after Jonah pulled into the driveway. He'd confirmed that Claire was indeed drugged but should be fine in the morning. Let her rest and eat light foods tomorrow, and hopefully all would be well, he'd assured all of them.

When Wills rose the next morning, he planned on being home when Claire wakened, but an early morning call from Owens, who insisted she must see him, had him scurrying to meet her at the corner diner.

She was already seated at the table with two cups of coffee on the table. Owens looked up as he approached. "Sorry to bother you so early, but I knew you were anxious to get the results."

"Results from those fingerprints?"

"Yes. I asked them to put a rush on it, but they were

backed up, so it took a little longer than I wanted to get answers."

"I think they did a great job. Next day news is pretty fabulous." Wills lifted his cup and sipped. "Spill your beans, Owens."

"The fingerprints from the table that night when the unknown man and Hermie McCoy met, were the same as the man called Albert Miller."

"So we have two Albert Millers."

"How can that be?"

Wills gave her a skeptical look. "There's a simple answer, I'm sure. You know the picture you showed me of Albert Miller? The one that was faded and looked like something from the twenties?"

"I do."

"I believe we have two men sharing the same name."

"Meaning—you're thinking our modern forties mystery man is faking this look-alike from back in the early nineteen hundreds?"

Her tone raised his brows. "Do you have a better idea?"

"Not at the moment."

"Then let's run with it. You know I went to talk with the governor yesterday. When I returned, I found out Claire had been kidnapped and drugged after she went to Tyson's apartment-room at the Grand downtown."

"Is she all right?"

"I left before seeing how she was doing this morning, but the doctor said last night he thought she would be. I'm going to concentrate on finding out who did that to her. But here's what I want *you* to concentrate on next. When I spoke with the governor, he said he'd known this Albert Miller in the past. He also said there were newspaper clippings of him. I want you to run down those clippings. Find out all you can from them. Get pictures if you can. See if you can get in-depth information about this Miller from the past."

"I can do that. It might take me a few—no, I'll have it for you as soon as I can."

"Good. See if you can find out if he had a family, and in particular, family in the United States. Did he have children? Sons? Who was his allegiance to? Was he a loyal citizen or were there any rumors to the contrary? It's a big task, a lot of work."

"I'll pull in Freddie if I need to, Sir."

"Owens, we have only a few more days till the event. We've got to move fast."

"I understand that. I won't let you down."

"I may have additional information or requests for you. I'd like you to contact me morning and night until the event. Can you do that?"

"I can."

"Great. Then I'll expect your call this evening. I should be home, I'm hoping for dinner, so any time after six will work." Wills stood. "Thanks for the coffee."

When Wills left the diner, he knew where he was headed next. It was too early to check on Claire. Hopefully, she'd still be resting.

But him? He wanted to see if Tyson was home and question him. Then he'd make a stop at the Center for Arts in downtown Cincinnati, and see what he could find out about this upcoming event. After that, if all went well, he'd try to contact E.I. and see if he could come up with anything brewing in the shadows of the underworld about this event on the twenty-first.

If he managed to accomplish that much today, he'd be doing good and would feel free to take a few hours of relaxation with family tonight.

Wills lifted a hand for a taxi and climbed inside once one had slowed alongside him. "Center for the Arts."

The taxi took off, and Wills turned his gaze at the passing buildings. He knew this town like the back of his hand, so when fifteen minutes had passed and nothing like downtown came into his view, he switched his gaze to the driver...and met his steady gaze in the mirror.

Wills' alert antenna quivered.

Something was wrong.

Chapter Twenty-Three

Claire awoke the morning after with a headache. She stretched and tried to open her eyes, but the sunlight from the windows urged her to keep them closed. She pulled the covers over her head and tried to go back to sleep, but that was useless. Her mind was awake now, her thoughts beginning to force her to face the day.

She flung back the covers just as a knock on her door interrupted her groaning. Her croaking voice wasn't much of an invitation. "Come in."

Harriet opened the door, carrying a tray. She settled it on a bedside table even as she questioned in soft tones, "How are feeling? Better? I brought something light for you to sip and nibble at till we see how you do."

Claire propped her forehead on her fist and groaned again. "I have a massive headache, Harriet. I'm not sure I can eat or drink anything without vomiting."

"You poor child. You're in no shape to eat now. I'll tell you what, I have liniment that I use when I have an occasional headache. Let me fetch it for you. Lie down again, and I'll be right back. We'll try later with something to drink and eat."

"Thanks, Harriet. What would we do without you?

Claire managed a smile when Harriet murmured as she went out the door, "You wouldn't."

Harriet was a wonder. Claire could remember little about her own mother. But growing up with Harriet around had been second best.

Minutes later, Harriet was back with both the liniment and orders. "You roll over. I'm going to rub some of this on your shoulders and neck. Shut your eyes and relax."

Claire did as she was told, and in seconds she felt her body relax...her eyes closed.

When Claire wakened for the second time that day, she cautiously squinted through her eyelids at the clock on her stand. Twelve-thirty? Really?

But she felt better. A little lightheaded, but that was probably coming from the hunger pains her stomach was screaming at her.

This time when she opened her eyes, no nausea bothered her. She threw back the covers, gathered her things for a bath and headed to the bathroom. The long, luxurious soak did the trick. When she finally returned to her room, she dressed quickly.

Slipping into the kitchen moments later, she grinned at the look of surprise on Harriet's face. "I think I could eat all of that cake you're making for tonight. No one would know..."

"You're better, I see. Trying some of our Josie's tricks on me, I'm thinking."

"I am feeling carefree and happy." She whirled around the countertop and hugged the woman. "Your liniment did the trick, I do believe."

"I told you it was good. Sit, and I'll get you a slice of that homemade bread I made for tonight and some nice tea with a hint of mint in it. That should keep your stomach happy."

"It does sound good." Claire pulled out a chair. "What happened to me?"

Harriet gave her a sideways glance. "You don't remember?"

"No...I have these vague images floating through my brain, but I can't make sense of them."

"Hmmm. I see."

When Harriet didn't go on, Claire pushed her for answers. "Do you know? Tell me."

The cook set a cup of tea and the slice of bread with a thin coat of real butter spread on it in front of her. "Eat. Then we'll talk."

Claire knew better than to argue with her. She'd lost, along with her two sisters, more than one battle with this heroine of a woman. Taking on the Rayner family, then later the boarders, was a gigantic task, but Harriet had been up to it.

Claire ate and drank as she watched Harriet make a huge casserole for their dinner tonight. It looked yummy and with what salad greens the woman had managed to buy and find in her outside garden, it would be a home cooking delight. The boarders loved Harriet's cooking.

"I'm finished." Claire shoved away her plate and cup. "Now come sit with me and tell me what I did."

Harriet obeyed and spoke even as she sat. "You did nothing wrong. At least, that's what I heard."

"Then what happened?"

"None of us know why you were there, but when you didn't come home last night, we were really scared something had happened."

"But I don't always come home. Sometimes I grab a room in town or stay at our building..."

"I know, but you'd promised your father you'd be home last night, that you had no reason to stay in town."

"I see."

"Wills rescued you."

"He what?"

"Rescued you. He knew where to look."

"And that was where?"

"Your manager's apartment."

"Norm's apartment? I went there because—" Claire stopped talking as the vague memory of being upset, being afraid and determined to find out something. "I was looking for something, I think."

"You were? What was it, Dear?"

"It was, it was..." Claire frowned. "I remember being afraid. Of being determined to find out who—"

"Claire?"

"Someone tried to grab me at the park yesterday morning. Early, just at daybreak, I think. I remember that. I was terrified and angry. I think I kicked him."

"Claire Anne Rayner, I could give you a swat like I have Wills many times before. If you don't tell me right now what you were doing in the park that early when Wills already cautioned you about going out alone."

The stern tone Harriet was aiming at her had Claire laughing. "I'm afraid I'm too old for swattings now, Harriet, but I will tell you everything."

"Good. Then get going. I have work to do." The

woman huffed at her.

Claire knew Harriet was really worried or she'd never have been so upset, and she loved her the more for it. "After that almost-mugging, I came home, and by the time I had settled down, I wanted to see if I could discover who was out to hurt me. I knew Norm was gone for a few days, so I went to his room at the Grand, coerced a key from the clerk and let myself in."

"Clare Rayner." Harriet fanned herself with her apron. "Why would you think your manager would want to hurt you?"

"I know. After the fact, I realize what danger I was placing myself in, but he'd been acting so strangely and moody the last couple of months, I wondered. I had to find out."

"Go on then, as long as you've learned your lesson. Those kinds of things are better left to the men to do."

"Hmmm." Claire wasn't at all sure she agreed, although she had to agree dangerous situations weren't her forte. "Right. So I found nothing to prove he wanted to hurt me until I opened a box beneath his desk and found dozens of letters."

"Oh, my. I'm going to be needing some liniment tonight to help me sleep." Harriet shook her head.

"It wasn't scary, Harriet. No one was around then."

"Then?"

"Then. I found nothing in most of the letters, but there were three of them that seemed...interesting, so I snapped pictures of them. I figured I could have them developed on the way home last night—" Claire jumped up. "Harriet, I didn't get them developed, and I wanted to show them to, to..."

"To who?"

"Wills."

"Why Wills?"

"I don't know. There's something secret going on that has to do with his work, and he's been warning me—like you said—not to go out alone, so if he was telling me that, then it obviously had something to do with me, don't you think? And that must be why I thought those pictures might be important. I think. Maybe not, but..."

She was rambling, she knew it, and a glance at Wills' mother confirmed her suspicions. Harriet thought she'd lost her mind.

"Claire..."

"Don't tell me I'm losing my mind, Harriet, please."

Harriet laid a hand on Claire's trembling one. "I have no intention of telling you such nonsense. I think Wills had a very good reason to tell you that. He's smart, and if he thinks you're in danger, then he will do all he can to protect you. After all, he..."

It was Harriet's turn to falter.

"He what, Harriet?"

The woman looked at Claire. "I won't have you making fun of my boy, even if I do love you as a daughter."

"Harriet."

"I think you know what I was going to say."

"I think I do. Maybe we should change the subject for now."

"You think so?"

"I do. For now."

"Right. We'll let that subject lay to rest for now. Go ahead with your story. You forgot to get the pictures developed."

"I didn't get a chance to get them developed."

Harriet's eyes grew big, and she didn't have to ask the question that quivered on her lips.

"I started to leave then heard someone on the other side of the door. I was afraid Norm had returned early, but there was nowhere to hide. Nowhere. I panicked. So I unlocked the door to the connecting room, went in and locked the door behind me. Thankfully, no one was in there, so I waited."

"Claire, I'm warning you."

She laughed. "I'm teasing you. I figured I could leave and no one would be the wiser that I'd been in the room next door. I figured the coast was clear—"

"I hope you didn't go back in Norm's room."

"I did not. I opened the door of the room I was in."

"And?"

"A man was standing there. He shoved me back into

the room. He must have been pretty strong or knew how to handle a fighting woman, because he overpowered me quickly, tied my hands and ankles, muzzled me like a dog. When I wouldn't quit thrashing about, he pulled out a needle. I tried to scream but, of course, I couldn't. That's all I remember until I woke up in my room this morning."

"And Wills brought you home. Carried you out of that hotel and wouldn't let anyone help."

Claire propped her chin on her fist. "He was my hero then. I've never had one of those before. Always thought I could take care of myself."

"Which you can in most situations, Claire. But everyone needs help at times. That's when we thank God for friends and family."

"Wills as a hero. I want to laugh, but it's touching too. I've always disliked him so much" She saw the look on Harriet's face and hurried on. "He and Josie. She was just as bad, and you know it, Harriet. They both were wild and uncontrollable."

"They were, but I like to call it imaginative and adventurous."

"Softie." Claire scoffed at her but gave her hand a squeeze. "Anyhow, it's a new feeling to see him in a different light. I do believe Wills has grown up. I think I like it."

"I see."

That was all Harriet said, but it was enough to cause Claire to jump to her feet. She wasn't about to talk any further about Wills Mason. Especially not to his mother.

"I'm going to do something productive. I don't know what it is, but I'll find something."

"You do that," Harriet called after Claire as she hurried down the hall. "And while you're doing that, you think about—"

Claire clapped her hands over her ears.

Wills had rescued her? She could only imagine what she'd looked like, after fighting that strange man. Her hair had probably been a tangled mess, her clothes disheveled, maybe slobbering because she was unconscious. Ugh.

Claire felt her cheeks heating.

It was time to focus on something else.

~*~

"Stop this taxi right now." Wills reached up over the seat to grip the man's shoulder even as his gaze remained on the man's face in the mirror.

The taxi driver's gaze lifted to his again. "Take it easy, Man. Just taking a shortcut."

"Yeah, is that right?" Wills tightened his grip. "I said stop."

"Sorry, can't do that. E.—"

"What did you say?"

"Nothing. Here's your destination. Now get out." The driver slowed to a stop. "It's on me."

Wills looked at the desolate buildings. The few people hanging around looked as if they hadn't eaten in months. "This isn't the Grand, Man. And I'm not going anywhere until you tell me what's going on."

"That's what's going on." The driver pointed at a figure headed their way.

"Don't know—"

"Yeah, you do. He sent me to pick you up. You just conveniently wanted a taxi at the time."

"Who are you?"

The man gave him a sly grin and pointed at the man walking toward them. "I'm E.I.'s buddy."

Wills swiveled his gaze to take in the man almost on them. He wouldn't have recognized him if he'd met him face to face. This guy, the one almost stopping beside the taxi didn't look anything like the E.I. he was used to seeing.

E.I. didn't stop walking, but he slowed, and as he passed the taxi he tossed in a bit of paper. The driver picked it up and handed it back to Wills.

Wills read the words and looked up, studying the buildings within his vision. "I have no idea where Mickey's Fine Foods is."

"We passed it two buildings back. You'll have to go around back, but if you knock three times, E.I. will open it. He'll explain what's going on."

Wills nodded and tossed over a bill. As he exited, the

driver spoke again.

"I'll pick you up in twenty minutes one block over. Don't want to raise any suspicions. Not every character hanging around this part of town is exactly trustworthy."

He winked, and Wills climbed out of the car.

When Wills knocked at the back door of the building with its faded sign that still announced it'd once been Mickey's Fine Foods, he waited ten seconds before knocking again.

This time the door opened promptly, and E.I. stood there with a half-grin on his face. He reached for Wills and gave him a hearty hug, then pulled him inside. He must have cleaned up, because he looked better than he had outside on the street. More like the man he used to know.

He rambled on as he led Wills through the rooms. As they entered one of them, he gestured at the area. "My home away from home. Temporarily, of course."

Wills took in the dump, although it was as clean as could be under the circumstances. "Why do you do this? You could have a cushy job most anywhere."

"Why do you do what you do?"

"I didn't choose it. So I do what I believe is my duty."

"Same here, Wills. Same here. Sometimes you've got to do things others won't ever understand, but you don't stop because of their opinions."

"You're right." Wills took a seat on a stained cloth chair while E.I. settled on a mattress on the floor. "Why did you have me kidnapped?"

E.I. slapped his leg and laughed. "You always did have a serious look on life."

"I don't think my family would agree with that assessment."

"Then they haven't seen what I've seen in you. Anyway, I have news about some undercover things you might be interested in."

"Why the sudden extreme subterfuge?"

"I'm being watched, I think, and can't afford to risk exposing my cover."

"And who's the taxi driver?"

"We met here on the street when some guys were trying to rough him up a bit. I got him that taxi driver job."

"He's working for you?"

"Yep. And he's not as homeless as he looks."

"I saw that in the taxi."

"Good man, he is. I trust him fully."

"Nice to have people we can trust." Was E.I. rambling on for companionship or just avoiding the subject? "You said you have news?"

"I do, or at least, rumors I've heard."

"Then carry on. Some of us have to work, you know."

"Yeah, yeah."

"Here's what's being rumored. I don't have any idea who's behind it, so don't ask, but it's being said there's going to be trouble at the Thornton Center. Even less tenable are vague hintings of offing someone important. Have you checked the guest list for who will be there?"

"A cursory study, but my assistant is pretty thorough. If she'd sniffed something out, she'd have told me."

E.I. frowned. "Are you sure you can trust her? We live in dangerous times..."

Wills raised a hand. "As much as I trust you, I won't have a word spoken against her. She's gone above and beyond what I've asked of her."

"Right." E.I. looked a little embarrassed.

"You think you can get any confirmation on the person being targeted?"

"I don't know about that, but I'll do my best."

Wills stood. "Do you feel these rumors are reasonable enough to heed them?"

"I do. Most times when rumors of this sort are spoken of down here, they prove to be true. Sometimes things may vary a little, but I'd say ninety-five percent of times the rumors need to be taken seriously. I know some areas of the city aren't reliable, that is, the slums. But here? Yeah. I believe this one enough, I'd be taking precautions."

"Then I'd better get going. I've got a ton of things to do today." Wills headed toward the door but turned back.

"If you ever get done doing this undercover stuff, stop by at the house sometime. I'd like you to meet the family."

"I may do that. See ya around." E.I. lifted a hand and waved.

Wills shook his head at the crazy-looking tattoo on his friend's wrist. E.I. always had been a little insane when it came to being his own person. He grinned, sketched a wave at his friend and shook his head.

The taxi pulled up just as Wills turned the corner. The driver didn't say anything as he shuttled him downtown, but Wills was very much aware of the glances being given him in the mirror. What was that about? Sizing him up? Checking to see if Wills was angry over being escorted somewhere he'd not asked to go?

He wasn't angry. But he did wonder why E.I. thought it was of paramount importance to drag him down here when a simple telephone call would have done the trick. Especially since E.I had told him nothing set in stone. Vague hints were not much to go on. He'd check it out, all right. He wasn't about to let anything get by him.

But he had mentioned the Thornton Center which was a totally different venue than where he'd thought the event might take place.

Something about E.I. bothered him, but he couldn't put a finger on it. Maybe it was the way he'd looked so different on the street than when he'd seen him at his place. No one would have recognized him. Crazy guy. He had always had a thing for playing tricks.

Hopefully, E.I. would dig deeper until he got at the truth. The few days Wills had to discover the truth were dwindling fast.

Chapter Twenty-Four

Wills entered the Grand Hotel and went straight to the front desk. "Is Norman Tyson in?"

The young man who'd reluctantly given him a key before, looked up and gave him a half-snarl, half-smile. "No, he isn't. When he left, he said he wouldn't be back until tomorrow."

"Thanks." Wills whirled and started to leave when the clerk behind him spoke again.

"Sir. After you left, we found this on the floor under the bed." He was holding out a hat—a brand new-looking flat hat, a sporty checkered hat that looked as if it'd never been worn. It was the type of hat many of the privileged young people were wearing to show their independent spirit.

Wills walked back to the desk and took the hat. He looked over it, and inside a price tag still remained fastened to the brim. "Why are you showing this to me?"

"It was in the connecting room—419, the one next to Mr. Tyson's room. The room was messed, not destroyed and not over-the-top messy, but not like our maids leave the rooms, and certainly not how we keep our empty rooms."

"You're saying someone was in that room and misplaced their hat?" Wills looked at the man, watching his expression.

"I am. I have no clue why, but seeing as how you brought the lady down last evening who appeared to be—well, sick? Drugged? Hurt?—I wondered if the hat might be yours?"

"Did you now?" Ah, ha, the man didn't like him and was trying to place the blame of a messed-up room—or worse—on him. He studied the man. "I'm afraid I can't help you. For your information, the lady you're talking about had been drugged by someone in this hotel. I do hope we find she's fine, because, if for any reason, she's

241

not, then I would hate to say what could happen to this—this splendid place. Oh, yes, and of course, to you for interfering in a war investigation."

Wills did leave then and didn't look back to catch any expression of shock, hate or dismay the man might be shooting at his back. He was pretty sure he wouldn't be getting any parting looks of appreciation.

Next on his list was the Center for the Arts.

It was a gorgeous spring day. Wills decided to walk, seeing that the center was only a couple blocks away. Once there, he planned on walking through it, gauging where someone could set up bombs or hidden weapons. He wanted to make sure there were plenty of guards that could handle anything that came up. And he wanted them to go through the whole building before the event. Just to make sure nothing unexpected would happen.

Wills walked up the steps to the center and went inside. The magnificence of the place always impressed him the few times he'd visited. He walked up to the overhang balcony and went through it row by row. The balcony itself had two doors. There were no restrooms up here so anyone leaving during break would need to go to the first floor. Posting two guards up here should be sufficient.

At the front of the balcony Wills looked over the railing. It was a huge auditorium that packed out six to seven hundred people, including the balcony space. According to his information, there wouldn't be a packed auditorium. There were numerous doors, a stage with its own exit doors, and a secondary stage that held bands and other necessary crews.

Wills headed back to the ground floor, walked through the exhibit rooms—which were expansive—that held many paintings, statues and other items of worth and interest. He found nothing at the back of the center where crews used the storage spaces for miscellaneous items. There were no signs of explosive devises. Once finished examining them, he moved on to the basement, then stepped outside and walked around the building.

The place was massive. It'd take an army to guard it.

He grimaced. Colonel Waverly might not agree to the number of soldiers Wills felt were needed to secure the place. Then what?

He circled the building and stood on the steps, thinking.

The third item on his list of things to accomplish today was already taken care of when he'd been waylaid by E.I.'s friend in the taxi. It was still early. He hadn't heard from Owens yet today. Perhaps he ought to find a telephone booth and see if he could reach her.

At the corner of the street, he spotted one. When he'd dialed a number where he hoped to reach her, she answered after two rings.

"Sir, I've been trying to get ahold of you for hours."

"Oh, you have?"

"Yes, Sir. I wanted to report in to you."

"Let's not do it on the phone. Can you meet me at four at the diner?"

"I can."

He still had the Thornton Center to check out, but that could wait till tomorrow.

~*~

"Here's your coffee, Lieutenant. Just the way you like it." The sergeant set down the mug of coffee on his superior officer's desk. He felt a sneer coming. Why did she have to be addressed as Lieutenant anyhow?

"I hope it's better than the last few times. It keeps getting worse and worse every time. I think it's hurting my stomach."

"Surely it's not the coffee." the man protested, but since his superior wasn't looking at him, he managed a delighted grin. Just what he was hoping, and if all went well, he'd not have to be at the lieutenant's beck and call much longer. "Didn't you eat some spicy foods yesterday?"

"No, I did not. That was last week, Idiot."

The sergeant didn't care this time if his superior did see the smirk on his face. The sooner the lieutenant was out of his hair, the sooner he'd move up the ranks. He just knew it would happen.

~*~

"Look at this." Owens shoved a newspaper photo across the table at Wills.

Wills picked it up and studied it. "Who is this?"

"That, my dear boss, is the real Ulbrecht from Germany."

"Then who is the other man in this photo?" He picked up the first photo.

Owens shrugged. "I don't know. Yet. But whoever it is doesn't look anything like this second man."

"No, he doesn't. Have you found out if this man is still alive?"

"Dead. He was killed a little less than a year ago under suspicious circumstances, but the police never discovered who did it."

"Hmmm. Owens, I need to figure out how these two men are connected. There has to be a reason they're both going under the same name."

"We've got a bigger problem than that. This guy..." She pointed at the first picture. "...can't be our spy. I had a couple of people I know study the picture. They're positive it was taken in the late 1800s or very early 1900s."

"Which means he would be older. You think too old to be a spy?" Wills stared down at the first picture.

"No, no one ever gets too old for that role."

"True. But he would easily be in his late fifties or sixties. Usually people that age have younger men do the dirty work. Or get out of the business."

"You don't suppose they could be related?" Owens motioned for the waitress to refill her coffee cup. "They look nothing alike."

Wills shook his head, thinking. "This first guy looks familiar, but I can't think of who he reminds me of. I do think there could be a good possibility of some connection to a present-day person. But none of this helps know who is our spy."

"There's one thing I am sure about, Sir."

"What would that be, Owens?"

"That you will find out who the spy is. I believe we'll catch him and stop him before he hurts anyone."

Wills stood. "I hope you're right, Owens. I really do.

Good night. Call me in the morning with any news you have."

He felt like an old man when he heard Owens' vibrant, youthful voice behind him as he walked out.

"I will, Sir, and we will do what we set out to do. I know we will."

~*~

When Wills walked into the Rayner house three minutes later, he entered through the kitchen area. His mother, as usual, was there, finalizing the evening meal to be served in a few hours. She looked up as he let the door shut behind him.

"Wills, you're home. Do you need a snack before dinner?"

"I'm fine. Just wanted to let you know I'll be here for dinner tonight. I'm headed downstairs. I want to go over some things."

In the room he called his own, he pulled out his notebook where he'd scribbled some notes about his current investigation, and sat down in his comfortable desk chair.

He skipped over any notes about Claire. For now, he was not considering her a spy. If she was, then he'd have to have more proof than he had at the moment.

Next on his list were the names and notes on the people he suspected or had some kind of question about.

The Dame. She and Colonel Waverly seemed to be close. She and Hermie appeared to hang around together.

Hermie. Wills had heard him talking to that one man he and Owens had thought might be Albert Miller, the Mystery Man. Hermie was nosy.

Norm Tyson. Claire had said he'd been acting odd. Wills had seen him in conversation with a questionable man. He was also pretty sure it was Tyson who'd knocked him out that night on the street.

There was also the homeless guy and the taxi man, but it appeared the later worked for E.I. as an errand boy.

He, himself, had talked with the governor who

claimed to have known this Albert Miller. He'd also had contact with E.I., who said there were rumors of possible plans for a shooting at the Thornton on the twenty-first. And finally, there was the stranger who'd been in the concert hall that night Claire was singing, and again he'd spotted him from Tyson's hotel room window.

So, his suspects included The Dame, who he really hoped was the culprit. Hermie—Wills laughed. He seriously doubted the man was smart enough to pull off anything of this magnitude. Tyson? He seemed wily enough to try anything for gain, whether money, prestige or fame, but he wasn't at all confident he was the man he was looking for. And to add to the mixture was a mystery man. An unknown man that remained in Wills' head like a piece of putty that wouldn't be unstuck.

Wills was pretty sure that if he could identify the mystery man, he'd have gone a long ways to figuring out who else might be involved, where any destruction was planned, and who was the target.

Replacing his notebook in a desk drawer, Wills rose and went to his chair. He had fifteen minutes or so to relax before getting ready for dinner tonight. He wouldn't even close his eyes...

The next thing he knew, his father was shaking him awake.

"Son, are you planning on eating dinner with the family tonight?"

"What time is it?" He glanced at his clock. "Criminy. I didn't mean to go to sleep. I'll be up in a few minutes."

Twenty minutes later, he ran up the stairs.

His father met him. "You have a telephone call."

Wills nodded and headed to the stand where the house phone sat in the hallway. "This is Wills Mason."

"Wills, this is E.I. I've got that confirmation you wanted."

"Why are you whispering? Are you in danger?"

A soft chuckle was E.I.'s answer. "Only of getting caught talking to you. Listen. I know for a fact that the governor will be at the Thornton Center on the twenty-first. He's the target, and that's where it'll take place. I can't give you any more details. You'll have to find them another way."

"Are you sure about this? Your source is credible?"

"As credible as can be. Yeah, I trust him."

"Anything else you can tell me?

"No, only I suspect the perpetrator might be that mystery man, that Albert Miller you mentioned."

"Thanks, man. That's huge. I owe you."

"Again." Another chuckle. "Be seeing you."

"Sure, and remember—"

E.I. had hung up.

Wills set the receiver down slowly. He'd been given some news that might be just what he needed. He thought back on the conversation. When had he told E.I. about a mystery man?

He shook his head. No matter. If E.I.'s news proved true, he'd owe him one. Wills turned and almost bumped into Claire as she stopped abruptly in front of him.

"Where have you been? I need to talk with you."

"I've been working. Where have you been?"

"I doubt you want to know."

Wills eyed her. She did look a bit shamefaced. What had she been doing? He glanced into the neighboring library room then back at her. "Tell me."

"We don't have time right now. Are you too tired to wait up after everyone goes to bed? We could talk then."

"Sure, I can do that."

"Well, then, I'll talk with you later and fill you in. I hear Emma Jaine calling for me, and it's almost dinner time. Thank goodness we have no visitors tonight."

Wills stood at the doorway to the library and watched the residents and family mingle together for the last few minutes before dinnertime. Josie and Jerry had joined the family tonight with their baby Fina upstairs in the capable hands of the twins' nanny. He loved this bunch gathered here. He couldn't imagine life without them all.

Dinner was a simple one tonight, but good. The chatter was quiet with no elaborate conversations going on anywhere around the table. The atmosphere was pleasant and smiles were abundant. Wills sighed with contentment.

Once they'd adjourned back to the library, Claire and Emma Jaine headed to the piano. Shirley and Miss Gertie sat at a small table, putting a puzzle together. Jerry, Philip and Tom stood by the fireplace, talking occasionally, but seemingly contented to be together and relaxing. Papa had settled in a nearby chair, preparing to listen to Claire's songs.

Wills stood in a corner away from the rest, watching them and waiting on Claire to begin singing. In some ways he wished the evening was over so he and Claire could talk, but why wish his life away? There would be time later to talk with her.

Two songs later, Emma Jaine turned to Claire and spoke, laughter in her voice. "Sing us one of those new songs Norm has asked you to perform. Let your family judge whether it qualifies as one our Claire should be singing or not."

Claire's face flushed as she reluctantly agreed, which Wills had known she would do. She placed the music sheet from her file on the piano, Emma Jaine played a few notes, nodded, and Claire sang.

"Nine o'clock, ten o'clock, if you're not on time, then look out, Baby, you're gonna pay for the crime. I love you, Baby, but at 1840 Mossy Oak Street, You'd better be there, standing, on your feet. Wait for me, Baby, I'll be dressed in red, To you, tonight, I'm gonna wed."

Wills frowned, thoughts jelling in his head as if coming together to form a decent idea. She wasn't singing it right. Something was wrong.

She sang the stanza again, and Wills took three steps toward her. "Claire!"

Music stopped abruptly, and everyone in the room turned as if robots to stare at him. He paid no attention, only continued to stare at Claire as one thought whirled in his mind like a spinning top.

"Claire."

"What is it, Wills?" Claire's smooth forehead was

furrowed in a slight frown.

"That's not the way—I mean, that's not the way you first sang that song."

"It's not? Are you sure?" Her gaze didn't waver from his.

"What difference does it make, Wills? Let her sing. We're getting a laugh out of this jazzy song." Josie's face was a mask of laughter.

Wills paid no attention. "I'm very sure. That version is the way you sang it the second time. It's where your voice quavered."

"My voice quavered?"

"Yes. And you changed the words."

"I don't remember..."

"The first time you sang 'One o'clock, two o'clock, if you're not on time, then look out, Baby, you're gonna pay for the crime. I love you, Baby, but at 1620 Mossy Oak Street.'"

"You remember that?" Claire's face was a study, but he didn't have time to dwell on it.

"I do—"

"But, Son, why does it matter?" Captain Ossie was on his feet, a puzzled look on his face.

"I don't know for sure, Sir, but I feel it inside of me it's very important, and..." He turned to Claire. "...we need to talk. Now."

"But I thought we were going to—"

"Please, Claire, this can't wait. We have to figure this out."

"And you need my help?"

"I do." He turned to the captain, and Claire did the same. "Sir, will you excuse us? I think Claire may have the key to some very important things I'm dealing with."

"You'll be careful with her, Wills?"

"You know I will, Captain Ossie."

Captain Ossie waved a hand. "Then everyone out. Out now. Wills and Claire need this room."

"Sir, we can go outside in the garden or on the front porch."

"Claire?"

"I agree with Wills, Papa."

The captain waved a hand but the grin on his lips belied his gruffness of tone. "Then get on with you and let the rest of us enjoy our evening."

Wills asked as they went into the hall, "Do you need a sweater? It's pretty warm."

"I'll be fine." She shoved at the door. "Let's sit on the swing."

They settled there and sat for a few minutes, silent, studying the scene in front of them.

Claire stirred. "Tell me what's going on in that brain of yours."

"I'm not sure I know, but I'll try to explain the best I can."

"When I first heard you sing that song in France, I didn't realize then it was new to you. Later though, I heard you sing it again. And somewhere you mentioned how much you disliked it, that you hadn't wanted to sing it, but Tyson had insisted. Do you know why?"

"Why he insisted? He said some of the WAC ladies had written it."

"Some of the WACs, huh?"

"That's what he said."

"He didn't mention any names?"

"No. I didn't think to ask. Didn't care, really." When Wills didn't speak, Claire went on. "Does it matter? So the time and address changed. Why does that matter?"

Wills sat silent, thinking, as they swung slowly back and forth. Finally, he pulled in a deep breath. "Claire, I'm going to tell you something. Something that might be dangerous, but you cannot—I repeat—can not tell anyone. Can you do that? For me?"

She didn't hesitate. "I can."

"I'm looking for a very...very bad person. I think, but I'm not sure, that that song may be a message."

That soft frown was back on her forehead as she tried to make sense of his words. "A message for what?"

"That's what I don't know yet. But it seems to me to be a message to someone to meet at a certain place at a certain time." He glanced at her.

She nodded. "I guess it could be. But why me? Why would Norm want me to sing a song with a message in it?"

"I don't know. Could be he's a partner in crime, or someone is using him as a patsy, and he doesn't know it. I'm inclined to believe that is the case."

"Norm?" Claire chuckled. "He's so smart it's hard for me to see him being hoodwinked."

"Yeah."

The sharp glance she shot at him caused him to squirm a little. "I'm just saying if he knows what he's doing, then not only is he in serious trouble, but he could be dragging you into it too."

"I don't know, Wills. I just can't see that. He's been too good to me. He has plenty of cash, so he couldn't be doing anything for money."

"Not unless it's a substantial amount that would be hard to turn down."

"Maybe." She was shaking her head again, but slower as if wondering. "I'll tell you what. Let's go ask him."

"No. You will not do that. I mean it, Claire."

"Don't tell me what to do, Wills Mason."

"I'm not. What I mean is, I'm warning you it's too dangerous. I don't want you taking chances. Claire, this is serious business I'm in. I shouldn't even be talking with you."

"Does that brown-haired beauty you're always hanging around know about all this?"

"What?" He turned toward her, laughing, thinking she was joking.

She wasn't. "Why can she be involved, but I can't? Do you see me as some frivolous female who hasn't a serious thought in her weak little head?"

"Claire, of course not. I see you, not only as a talented and one of the best singers around, but a smart woman who knows her own mind and stands on her own feet. I feel honored that you're sitting here talking with me."

"Then tell me everything. I want to help."

"I can't. I'm—"

"Then good-night, Wills."

She'd stood and headed to the door before Wills jumped up and grabbed her arm.

"Please don't go. I'd like to sit here and talk with you some more."

She looked down at his hand gripping her arm then back into his face. "I really do think I could ask Norm who wrote the song without raising any questions. Please?"

Wills studied her face, seeing the desire to help, but wondering if he should allow her to get involved. It might go a long way to figuring out this case...

"Go ahead then, but Claire. Be careful. Word your question as innocently as you can. And make sure you don't make him think that's the reason you called."

"I can do this. Trust me?"

Her words weren't a statement but a question, and Wills answered with a nod.

She was only gone for about two minutes, and when she slipped back out, she was grinning. "Easy as pie. I told him I wanted to make sure he was all right and when he was returning. I asked him if there were to be any more new songs—and he said no—then casually asked who on earth had written them. I'm pretty sure his answer slipped out without him thinking."

Wills leaned forward. "Who?"

"You promise you won't cut me out—"

"Claire Rayner."

"Just kidding. It was that Nelson woman."

"The Dame?" Wills flopped back against the swing. As much as he disliked the woman, as much as he'd liked to have seen her as the culprit, he hadn't seriously considered her the one. Yet, with this information? What else was he to think?

"Good work, Claire."

"It was, wasn't it?" Her eyes widened. "Wills, I forgot."

"Forgot what?"

"To tell you what I did and what I have."

"I think I need to hear this."

"Wait. I've got to go get the evidence. I'll be right back."

Wills settled into the swing again and stared at the sky. Whatever Claire was getting ready to share with him, he knew he'd be able to handle it with God's help.

Two minutes later, she flung open the door and sat beside him again. In her hands was an envelope. She looked at him.

"Before I show you this, I want you to promise you won't be upset with me. Or I will regret showing you."

"I won't. I might get worried, but never angry at you, Claire." He held her gaze, wanting her to see his sincerity.

"All right. Here. I was upset at Norm for being so odd at times that I went to his room in the hotel and searched it while he was gone. I couldn't find any reason for it until I happened to find the letters. I took pictures of them—I was afraid to *take* the letters—and had your father get them developed for me this morning."

"That was a dangerous thing you did."

"I know it now. I didn't expect to get caught."

"It could have been much worse, you know." Wills spoke in as gentle a tone as he could, not wanting her to get upset.

"I realize that now, but I wasn't thinking then. I'd just had a frightening experience that morning and was irritated beyond irritation."

"What was that?"

She didn't say anything, only stared down at her hands. Finally, she sighed. "I went for an early morning walk in the park. I was on the way home and accosted by someone pretty strong. I only got away because I kicked him as hard as I could."

Wills' head spun with the thought of what could have happened to her. It took him several minutes before he could speak. "Did you get a look at the person? Anything at all you can tell me to identify him?"

"You don't want to know if I was hurt?"

"I know you weren't. The whole house would have been up in the air, the police would have been here, and you would have been under lock and key." He grinned at her, but his insides weren't smiling.

"You're right about all that. I wasn't hurt, just frightened terribly. I guess I knew I could have been hurt badly or killed even, and I fought like a mad woman. I do think I might have scratched his hand."

"Good. Anything else?"

"The only other thing I remember was his hands. They weren't rough like a worker's hands would be. Nor a homeless person. They were well taken care of."

"Really? That's surprising in a way."

"What do you mean by that?"

"I don't understand why a person, as you describe him—and well-groomed hands says a lot about a man—would be attacking you. Perhaps he didn't want to hurt you, just use you."'

"Wills, whatever do you mean?"

"As leverage. A bargaining tool to get something he wanted. If that's the case then he knows you or your family or something valuable that would be useful to him."

She sat silent a moment. "You could be right."

"I think I am. Do you think it was the same person who tied you up in the room next to Tyson's?"

"It never entered my mind. I don't know. Maybe. I didn't get a look at the person's face in the park. It could have been, I guess."

"Let's take a look at these pictures." Wills opened the envelope and slid out the three pictures. She'd done a good job of snapping the letters, and they were easily readable. Wills read the letters aloud.

"Dear Mr. Tyson:

We have a proposition to make to you. Your cousin referenced you as a talented and well-versed individual in politics and business. It would be a simple task, but important for the wellbeing of our country. If you would be willing to work with us, please send your answer via your cousin. We must have your reply by March 19 or we will assume you are not interested.

Yours for victory of our beloved country,
A.M."

Albert Miller? Wills picked up the second photo letter and read again.

"Tyson:

Per your questions: your duties would be simple. Through covert messages in such a way that will not be noticeable or detected, your cooperation in making this happen will ensure that our beloved country will be victorious. We urge you to do as we, and your cousin asks, in helping us achieve our goals.
Sincerely,
A.M."

"It has to be Albert Miller." He was talking to himself, but Claire heard.

"Who's Albert Miller?"

"Never—he's the man I'm looking for."

Claire laid a hand on his arm. "Wills, are you in danger?"

"I hope not." He grinned at her, hoping to get her off the subject.

"Be serious. You said a few minutes ago that I'm a strong woman. Let me be that kind of woman with you, Wills. I don't need sheltered all the time. Let me help."

If only he could. "That's the problem. We don't know who this Albert Miller is. He could be anyone, and I'm running out of time."

"What do you mean?"

"I've had information given to me that there will be trouble—we're thinking on the twenty-first."

"Applesauce."

Wills laughed. It sounded so much like what Josie would often say. He'd never heard Claire say such a thing.

"Why are you laughing?"

"Applesauce?"

"I know. But I'm frustrated. I want to *do* something."

"Claire, it's already midnight. I have a busy day tomorrow, and you have practice again, I think, don't you? Isn't Tyson supposed to be back in the morning?" When she nodded, he went on. "Can we pick this back up as soon as we both have more time?"

"I suppose so. If we stay out much later, your mother and my papa will be coming after us."

"As if we're still kids."

"You didn't tell me what you thought might happen on the twenty-first."

"No, but I'll share when I can. Agreed?"

She rose, gave him a half-smile and headed to the door. "Agreed. Good night, Wills."

"Goodnight, Gorgeous."

If she heard his last word, she gave no indication, and Wills wasn't sure if he was glad or sad about that.

Chapter Twenty-Five

The sergeant set the cup of coffee on his lieutenant's desk and waited. It was a ploy used all the time on him—making him wait—and he was used to it. But this time...this time he'd laced the coffee with enough of the poison to do the trick a bit quicker than he'd planned. He was tired of the lieutenant. He was tired of being an errand boy.

"Go ahead and drink it," The lieutenant offered, and didn't look up.

"I've already had two cups this morning." There was no way he was going to touch that cup to his lips.

The lieutenant's head rose, and piercing eyes in the pale face stared at him. "I said, drink it. Now."

"I can't. Sorry." The sergeant wanted to squirm but didn't dare. If the lieutenant had the least suspicion, he'd be dead.

The desk chair scooted back, slowly, and the lieutenant stood, a gun in hand. "Drink. The. Coffee."

Fear like rushing water from a broken dam ran through his very being. His legs wanted to give out, and he could barely control the trembling. "What are you doing? I can get rid of it."

"Oh, you will. By drinking every last drop." Steady, dark, amused eyes stared at him. "Is there some reason you don't want to drink this cup of coffee?"

"Why would you say that?" He could feel the sweat drops on his forehead quivering as if prepared to run down his face.

"You seem to be awfully nervous about this one cup of coffee. But then, it hasn't been one cup that you're deathly afraid of, has it been, Sergeant?"

He didn't say a word. How could the lieutenant know? Surely not. It was just a ruse to torture him in a new way.

There was a knock on the door.

Reprieved!

"Come in," The lieutenant bellowed.

The door opened and two men entered. They looked exactly what they probably were—scoundrels—but the sergeant didn't miss their toned muscles that bulged beneath shirt sleeves.

"Just in time, boys." She lifted the gun and again pointed it at him. "Good-bye, Sergeant. I'm not dumb. I know you've been poisoning me the last few weeks. At least, that's what my doctor told me. It didn't take a genius to figure out where it was coming from, especially after I had the remains in the last cup tested."

Had his body frozen in a block of ice? No, it was burning up. Surely this wasn't the end. Not after all he'd planned to do after getting in good with that guy who was leading this coup. Surely not—

"Don't. Please."

The lieutenant's finger tightened on the gun, a smile as wide as the Ohio River plastered itself on the hardened face, and the sound of a gunshot blasted into the room.

She placed the gun in the large bag beside her desk, picked it up and nodded to the two men. "I'm going out. Make sure everything is shipshape when I return."

Turning toward the door, the lieutenant kicked at the body. "And get rid of this sickening corpse."

~*~

Two days. Wills had two days to tidy up what he did know, make plans to protect the governor and make sure everything went smoothly that night without causing a ruckus.

Right now, he stood in front of Colonel Waverly's desk, waiting till the man finished talking on his telephone. When the colonel had finally finished, he pressed a button, gave instructions to his secretary then turned to Wills.

"I hope you have a good report, Mason."

"We do, Sir. I finally received confirmation from a contact with credibility of the truthfulness of it, that a coup was taking place at the Thornton Center. Although I heard this earlier, I had questions because of another place that seemed to be the more reasonable place."

"You have confidence this is the building?"

"As of right now I do. I will continue to work toward digging up any other useful information that may confirm or give me reasonable doubt that such is the case. Anyway, I would like to have ten well-trained soldiers in subterfuge and ability to work with unexpected situations."

"I'll issue the order today. Anything else?"

"Sir, we're going in blind, so everyone needs to be on the alert. Make sure the soldiers understand this. And if I find out there are any changes, and I can possibly do so, I will keep you updated."

"Do you need me there?"

"No, you go ahead to the Center for the Arts."

The colonel stood. "I don't suppose you know who the spy is? I take it you've ruled out Claire Rayner?"

"I have, Sir. And, no, I haven't totally figured out who is behind this scheme. I have ideas, some possibilities, but nothing certain." Should he mention The Dame's part? But was writing songs that seemed to have a message a crime? Maybe.

"You have two days, Mason. Do your best to be as informed as you can. I don't like blind spots when it comes to dealing with the enemy. You make sure you keep the governor safe."

"Right. I will." He turned away, hesitated and looked back at the colonel.

The man was watching him, eyes squinting, lips pursed as if he knew Wills wasn't sharing everything.

"Sir, there is one more thing."

"I thought so. Go ahead."

"I didn't want to mention it because, well, it has to do with you."

"With me? What are you talking about?"

"Or I should say, with a friend of yours."

"Matilda Nelson."

What? The colonel already knew she was a suspect? "How did you know that?"

The colonel gave a short, abrupt, unfunny chuckle. "Did you really think I would be seriously interested in a person like her? Why do you think I kept her close? For her entertaining conversation? Hardly. I had my doubts about her after I first met her, which wasn't orchestrated by me. Her nosiness in my business, her dislike of you, and not-so-casual efforts to get information from me put her high on my list of suspects. I hoped you felt the same."

The relief that flooded Wills' body was a release of the tension he'd felt since wondering whether the colonel was involved. "I certainly did. I couldn't understand how you, of all people, could be fooled by the likes of her."

"You can rest easy now that you know."

The glints of amusement in the man's eyes had Wills grinning. "Then I feel free to share that she is the one who's been writing songs that Norm Tyson has been urging Claire to sing. I believe, Sir, that is how messages are being relayed by the spy."

"And you think the spy is Nelson?"

"I'm not sure. She doesn't seem to have those qualities to run a spy game. But I could be misreading her."

"We'll soon know. I'll keep my eyes open at the Center of Arts on the twenty-first and have soldiers there for added help, while you keep track of what's happening at the Thornton."

"Sounds good. I'll let you know immediately if there are any new developments." Wills did leave then.

That evening, Wills sat on the porch again. By himself this time, thinking through all the tidbits of information he'd been given.

Two pictures of two different men. One from early in the century, and the other of a man who'd died over a year ago. Did they connect? And now a man who was going by the name of Albert Miller, which if their study was right, wasn't his real name.

A song with lyrics that had been altered naming time and place. Why? Had something happened to make The Dame change those two things? What would that something be? His intuition told him The Dame couldn't be the ringleader. As mean as she was, she didn't have the leadership ability it would take to corral the men to do her sub-work.

Then there were the letters that seemed to indicate Tyson was involved in something, which might be requiring Claire to sing those new message-songs.

And the confirmation on the planned shooting of the governor by a good friend of his—E.I.—since basic training.

Not enough. Not enough. When he'd worked undercover during Jerry's secret spying period, he'd known who was the bad guy. He'd known what to watch for, who to be on guard against. But this job? He felt like he was walking on hot ashes.

"Sir?"

Wills looked at the street where a car had pulled up, a window rolled down, and the voice that belonged to Owens, called to him. "Owens, what are you doing here?"

"I need to talk with you."

"Come on up then."

"I think you need to come with me, Sir."

For once in his life, he felt like arguing her, but another glance at her face had him standing. "I'll be right back."

Inside he spoke to Captain Ossie and his father. "I have to go. Urgent business."

"You haven't eaten," Captain Ossie protested.

"I have no choice."

His father nodded. "Go then, and come back to us safely."

"I will, Pops. Hopefully, I'll be home soon."

Wills walked out of the room and almost ran into Claire.

"Where are you going? Won't you be here for dinner? I wanted to talk with you again. Remember, we agreed to talk?"

"I've got to go, Claire, but we will talk. Soon. You can do this for me. Go over everything that's happened in the last few weeks. See if you can think of anything that seems odd or suspicious. Or pertinent. If I get home in time, we'll talk tonight. Otherwise, as soon as we can. Promise?"

"I promise, Wills. Be safe." She stood on tiptoe and kissed his cheek then whirled and went on into the library.

Wills stood, shocked with delight as he stared after her. Miracles did happen, it seemed.

But enough of the mushy stuff—at least for now. Grinning to himself, he hurried out to the waiting car and the best helper he'd ever had. He hoped he was about to hear some fantastic news.

But once he'd stepped inside the car, the look on Owens' face disavowed that thought.

"What is it?"

"Herman McCoy's body was just found in an off-beaten-path in the park."

"Hermie?" What on earth? "Do they know how he died, and why in the park?"

"I don't know. A young teen-aged couple found it—or their dog did—just minutes ago. I just heard and figured you should know."

"You're right. I think we need to find out what happened and if it pertains to our work."

"I agree. What can I do to help?"

"The local police will do a lot of the research for us. I'm primarily interested in who did this. We need to find out who Hermie was with last, and if that person is on our 'watch' list."

"Got it. Anything else?"

"That will do for now, I think." He stared out the windshield.

"What are you thinking, Sir?"

"Just wondering what ole Hermie got himself into. He didn't seem that bright, he was annoying beyond describing, and he always seemed to be on the lookout how to advance himself without too much work. Not a very admirable person, on the whole."

"I didn't really know him, but it seems you're right. Do you want to go to the park or talk to the police?"

"Let's take a drive down there. Has the body been moved yet?"

"I'm assuming not. We can probably be there in ten minutes or so."

"Let's go then."

Ten-and-a-half minutes later, Owens parked the car in the lot, and they both exited the vehicle and hurried toward the area.

There were a number of people there, and one person stood out to Wills. It was the detective who'd visited the Rayner house when Tyrell was working on a case a couple years ago. He motioned for Owens to talk with the coroner while he walked straight to the detective.

"Detective. I'm Wills Mason from the Rayner house. A friend of them. I'm working with Colonel Waverly on a different case that seems to tie into this man's death. Do you mind filling me in on what you know?"

"Mason. I remember. Your mother was the cook there and made some of the best cinnamon rolls ever. Don't know the man, but my associate informed me he's in the service. We haven't talked with anyone yet, but hope to speak with his senior boss tonight. Someone called The Dame?" The man looked up and grinned. "Sounds like a woman running a gang or a mob, don't you think?"

Wills gave him a chuckle, but inside his chest, his heart rate had picked up its pace. The Dame involved in this?

"Her real name is Matilda Nelson. She's an unofficial upper-class WAC and works closely with the troops here in Cincinnati. She's a self-appointed big wig."

"Why 'The Dame?'"

"She's a climber and ruthless at it, and when I say climber, I'm not talking about rock mountains. She's not overly friendly to anyone that I know of, and certainly not afraid to use someone to get what she wants."

"One of those hard boiled-broads, huh?"

"Afraid so." Wills nodded at the body. "How'd he die?"

"Gunshot wound to the heart. No defensive wounds and looks like a fairly close shot. We'll know more when the pathologist does his thing."

"Anything in the neighborhood that suggests a struggle?"

"No, looks like there might have been some footprints, but someone was wise enough to make sure they were erased before they left. It was too clean. I suspect the murder didn't take place here. Probably the person or persons hauled the body to the park thinking this remote spot might not be discovered for awhile."

"Leave it to a dog to sniff it out."

"Yeah. Good for us, though. It is out of the way. Hard to tell when it'd been discovered otherwise."

"True. Hermie wasn't a likeable person by any stretch of the truth, but I don't think he deserved to die like this. Sad."

"I'll let you know what we find out or you can contact us in the morning."

"Sure thing. Thanks for the information." Wills walked toward where Owens stood close to the car.

"Was he helpful, Sir?"

"Some. You?"

"He said he'll know more once he examines the body, but he's pretty sure the shot was point blank. Close."

"That's what the detective said too." Wills glanced down at his watch. "Late enough, you think The Dame would be gone from her office?"

"Maybe. What are you thinking, Sir?"

"I'm thinking I'd like to search her office for a gun. See if it's been used lately."

"But even if it has, she could have been at a range or used it for some other reason."

"Maybe. But I don't know of anyone else Hermie's been hanging around except for The Dame. At the least, it creates questions in my mind."

"True. Would you like me to tackle that job for you, Sir? I'm sure you have more things you need to do."

"Are you trying to get rid of me, Owens?" Wills grinned.

"Oh, no, Sir. Never. It's been a pleasure to work with you. An honor—"

"That's enough. You keep that up, and I'll have to tell Colonel Waverly I have no more need of you."

"Sorry."

"No need to apologize, Owens. I was teasing you."

She tossed him a grin with the glance that said she wondered if he was still teasing.

"Here's what I'd like you to do for me."

"Yes?"

"Stand guard while I search The Dame's office."

"That's simple enough." Owens stepped on the gas. "You've got it."

~*~

Wills walked around the office of The Dame. It wasn't a large room, but big enough. The two promotions The Dame had received were displayed on the walls behind her desk. He stood studying them, wondering if she'd manufactured them herself. Other than that, there was nothing to indicate a personal life. No pictures, nothing.

There was a small safe, but Will turned away from that. He wouldn't be breaking into that—at least, not yet, and he certainly didn't want to damage it to do so. Her desk was obsessively neat and clean, and Wills studied it before opening one drawer after another. The bottom one held a few letters—all of them copies of the ones sent to Tyson with the initials A. M.—the ones that he'd read when Claire had taken pictures.

Except one. This one was addressed directly to Matilda Nelson, and it was interesting, to say the least.

Tilly, my dear friend and fellow-patriot-sister,

I know things are not going as we planned with the hindrances from particular higher-ups, but we must stay steadfast in our duties. Do not allow certain parties to encroach their ideas of enemy countries in your mind. Pay no attention to those who are searching for us. We will win this war, and there is no one—no one, I assure you—who can stop us. We have resources beyond if needed. Not only that, but the end is near. If we can accomplish this one last act to atone for the past doings, then we will have succeeded, with me being able to join the greater group and you—hopefully—being able to achieve the advancement you have long sought for. I applaud you because once there, there is no stopping you. Think what good you can do to push our plan further.

By no means, feel guilty for what had to be done. He was getting too cocky. We have no use for that attitude and especially him.

The end is near. Be alert. Victory is ours.
Your fond brother in battle!
Albert

The Dame knew this Albert and seemed to be working with him. If it was referencing whatever was taking place tomorrow night—the twenty-first—then she had to be in on the scheme. If the latter part was referencing Hermie's demise, then she had to be in on that too, whether she pulled the trigger or had ordered it done.

Walking swiftly to the front door of the building, he motioned to Owens. "Do you have a camera with you?"

"I do. Did you find something?"

"I did. Hurry and grab that for me, will you?"

A minute later, Owens returned. "Here you go."

"Thanks. I'll be out in a minute."

Wills snapped pictures of the last letter, the envelope, then decided to do the same to the copies she'd received.

He was almost ready to go when a thought occurred to him. If The Dame was the one who'd killed Hermie, and she'd done it in here, wouldn't there be some kind of trace of blood? Or a gun that could be analyzed?

Wills squatted behind The Dame's desk, searching the floor, the bottom legs of the desk, then moved around to each side and finally the front. When he moved away from her desk, he spotted a minute spot at the very bottom of a filing cabinet. It was so small it could easily be looked over, no one ever thinking anything of it.

Snapping several pictures of it, both close-up and farther away, taking in the whole cabinet, he spanned the room with snaps from the camera. Then grabbing one of the available envelopes, he took his knife and barely scratched an edge of the dark red splotch, making sure it landed inside the envelope. He sealed it then gave the room a cursory study, gathered the camera and left.

He'd have Owens make sure the place was sealed off and a guard there in case The Dame, or anyone else, tried to enter.

It was time to get going. He had a sample to get

tested, some pictures to analyze and an event to get ready for, for tomorrow night.

It was going to be a busy next few hours.

~*~

"I know who it was." Claire's voice preceded her before she reached the porch swing.

Wills hadn't seen her for hours. She'd had her practice, and he'd been busy with checking out The Dame's office, coordinating the event coming up tomorrow night. Now, well, now it was almost midnight. He'd missed supper, but his mother had fixed a plate of leftovers stored in their refrigerator. He'd wolfed it down like he hadn't eaten for a week.

Come to think of it, he hadn't eaten much—just grabbing snacks where he could and on the run—for a couple days. A meal had been fantastic.

He smiled up at her and patted the space beside him. "I have no idea what you're talking about, but I'd love to hear it."

"Good, because it's good news. At least I think it is."

"I hope so. I need some good news."

She stretched a bit and shot him an I-told-you-so glance. "Do you remember when we checked out that room in my practice building?"

"So long ago?"

"Yes, it was quite awhile ago, but I don't forget. I should have recognized that cologne smell immediately."

"And why didn't you?"

"I don't know. Inexperienced in putting two and two together?"

"Although you weren't hurt, it could be because of the fear of associating it with what happened."

"Right. I might have been too afraid to accept what my mind was telling me."

"You? Afraid? No."

"You're teasing me, I know, but that's all right. I can take it."

"Are you sure?"

"I'm very sure."

"You've really changed."

Claire looked down at her lap. "I know. Not much. I'm

still pretty picky, but I'm trying."

"That's what counts, Claire. That's all that matters."

"Do you want to hear my news or do you want to talk more about me?"

"Definitely the first. Although the second is quite interesting."

Her laugh was like maple syrup.

"That smell was coming from a cologne I've smelled several times lately. I'm not sure if I'll ever like it again."

"And I take it you're talking about the tramp who stopped you at Josie's house?"

"That's the one person."

"Then there's when you realized the same smell was lingering in the room where you eavesdropped."

"For a good purpose."

Wills sat silent for a moment. "It seems strange to me that so many people around you have been wearing that brand of cologne."

"You're right. The homeless guy who confronted me, the person who left his cologne scent behind in the room in my building, and now the man who chased me." Her gaze was on the street in front of them. "I wanted to ask you, why would I be the target of some unknown-to-me man?"

Wills was slow to answer. "I don't know for sure, but I'm thinking it could be a way to get my focus off of the work I'm doing right now or, as I mentioned before, it could be a way to hold leverage over my head."

"Really? I don't like that."

"Me, either, Claire, because it would be a very effective way."

"I wouldn't want you to compromise your duty and work for our country for me."

Wills couldn't speak for a moment. If it came down to it, he hoped he'd do the right thing, but staring at her beautiful face gave him pause.

"Wills, there's one more thing. I've been thinking about that one song I've sung several times, the one you mentioned was changed. I'm not sure my thoughts will help, but I wanted to tell you what came to me."

"Go ahead."

Carole Brown

"We have a Mossy Oak Street here in Cincinnati. What if the number is the street address for a building? So I checked it out, and do you know what I found?"

"But neither of the buildings—the Center for the Arts or the Thornton Building—have those street numbers."

"No, but what if you reversed the numbers? Say the eighteen forty was really four eight one leaving the zero off."

"And the sixteen twenty is two six one? Claire Rayner, You are brilliant because—"

"Because both of those numbers are the numbers of the Center and the Thornton."

"Exactly. I could give you a hug. I think you've given me definite proof that something is going down at one or the other of those two places."

"I'm so glad I could help you."

"You definitely have. Claire, tomorrow will be overwhelmingly busy for me. I won't be able to be at both places. I have duties at a different building, but I want you to promise me you'll be careful. Very careful. Don't trust anyone, and keep your eyes open."

"I can do that. I promise." Claire stood and walked toward the door then turned back. "And, Wills, I wouldn't have minded at all a hug from you."

Chapter Twenty-Six

Claire sat in the porch swing the next morning, which seemed to be becoming a habit—a pleasant one, for sure. One that she supposed, she'd always now associate with Wills. She smiled, thinking of how pleasant he'd been lately. As for herself, it felt good to realize the dislike she'd held onto for so long had vanished. Her vow to Emma Jaine that he'd never be anything closer than a friend seemed a falsehood now.

She could imagine a lot of possibilities—

The door opening slammed shut the door of her dreaming. Jonah Mason stood there.

"Phone call, Claire, for you."

"Thanks, Jonah." She rose and went to the house phone in the hallway.

"Is this Claire Rayner?"

Colonel Waverly. She'd recognize his voice anywhere.

"It is. How can I help you?"

"I hear you'll be singing at the Center tonight before I give my speech."

"You've heard correctly."

"I wondered if you'd like me to swing by and pick you up? I'd enjoy escorting you."

Why not? He was a nice man and certainly entertaining. "I'd love that."

"Good. Then it's settled." His gruff laugh came through the receiver. "I want you to know, Miss Claire, that I was never happier than when Wills told me you weren't the spy."

"Why would he tell you that?" Claire smiled at his nonsense.

"Because I ordered him to get close to you. Rumors were, there was someone sending veiled messages, and it pointed to you. I figured since he knew you, he'd be the one to make sure you were on the up and up. And he did it. Last report, he cleared you..."

Colonel Waverly's voice went on and on, but Claire didn't hear another word.

As she hung up the receiver, the lightness and peace she'd experienced not five minutes ago had vanished. Inside her, where her heart usually resided, was a large stone. Big enough to weigh her down and destroy the pleasant thoughts she'd been enjoying about Wills and their possible future relationship.

She'd found out the truth.

Wills hadn't befriended her because of his attraction to her. His compliments and pretty nicknames for her meant nothing except as a method to get at the truth. He didn't love her. He wanted the truth. And he'd found it, she supposed.

She wasn't the spy he'd thought she was.

Everything else was a lie.

~*~

Wills counted the soldiers and men on duty as he strolled around the Thornton Center. The governor hadn't given his speech yet, but there were enough men who wanted to appear important taking their turns at long and boring speeches.

He'd seen The Dame once, standing with a man unfamiliar to Wills. He was an older gentleman, perhaps in his mid-forties. They didn't talk much, and when they finally left each other's company, the man gave her a nod and disappeared out of Wills' sight. The Dame proceeded to take a seat about mid-way down the auditorium, not speaking to anyone else.

Everything seemed normal.

Late last night, Wills had given Owens the sample of blood from The Dame's office, with instructions to have it analyzed. He'd not heard back from her yet, and after talking with the colonel, they'd decided to keep an eye on her before bringing The Dame in. They needed definite proof she'd killed Hermie or had it done, and they needed proof she was working with the spy. They couldn't tip their hat until they had both.

So he'd had a man following her all day today. And nothing had happened so far.

Wills headed to the hallway, hoping to catch another

glimpse of the man who'd stood with The Dame. Anyone she talked with was suspect, and he meant to keep tabs on them.

More important he wanted to make sure no other unknown people were here. Attendees had been screened, and no one without advance approval had been allowed to attend. That helped some.

As Wills returned from his inspection of the hallway, he passed the man who'd talked with The Dame and gave him a nod. The man touched his hat but kept walking. He disappeared in the restroom.

At the entrance to the auditorium, Wills stopped beside the guard and listened vaguely to the person speaking at the time.

Twenty-five feet down the hallway, the restroom door opened and a well-dressed young man exited. He glanced at Wills, smiled and nodded, and Wills returned the nod but didn't smile. He had no reason to smile tonight.

Instead of going into the auditorium though, the man headed for the exit doors. Wills paid little attention for a moment, but something nagged at him. What was it?

Wills ran over in his head the movements of the man. The restroom door opened, the man exited, walked smartly down the hall and nodded at him. Something...

It was the man's eyes. Light blue eyes. Very light.

Wills ran for the restroom, banged open the door and checked every area. Nothing. No older man who'd been with The Dame. But in the trash can, Wills found a stuffed sack filled with clothes, a cloth stained with makeup, and a false mustache. And below the sack lay a pair of dark brown shoes like the older man had been wearing.

The older man and the young one were one and the same. It'd been the perfect disguise, and one that he'd almost missed. A name was clanging in his mind, but it seemed so impossible he wanted to brush it to the side.

Wills hit the hallway running.

Who did he know who had the lightest blue eyes he'd ever seen? Only one person, and Wills knew the man very well.

Or, at least, he'd always assumed he did. That's what he got for going on assumptions.

He thrust his head in the auditorium and checked to see if The Dame was still in her seat.

Gone.

"Stop the governor from going on the platform. Lock him in the secure room," he yelled at the guard. "Stay with him and by no means, allow him to go on stage. Got that?"

He didn't wait for an answer.

Wills wanted to bang his fist into a wall somewhere, but he hadn't time for theatrical actions. He turned and ran for the exit door just as the door flung open and Owens entered, barely missing running into him.

She grabbed his arm. "Sir. I've got news."

"Can't stop. Come ride with me." Wills threw the remarks at her even as he scoured the street in both directions. Neither The Dame nor the man were in sight.

Lifting a hand, he hailed a taxi. Tossing the largest bill he had over the seat, he instructed the driver to head to the Center for the Arts and get there in double time.

The driver slammed his foot on the gas pedal and made tracks.

It was then that he turned to Owens who'd pushed herself into the taxi beside him. "Your news. Hurry and give it to me. We'll be at the Center for the Arts in minutes."

"The military picked up two men who've confessed that the Dame shot Hermie. Also her gun is missing. But we did find some shells at her residence that matched Hermie's chest wound."

"So we have her."

"Looks like it. And the picture of the letter you took matched the ones that were sent to Tyson."

Wills nodded. "And now, I know who our spy is."

The taxi swerved into the parking lot of the center and stopped in front of the door. Wills took no time in running inside the building, Owens following, and he didn't stop running till he reached the auditorium. He fastened his gaze on the people sitting there. His gaze searched and found the person he was looking for. At the back of the auditorium stood a young, well-dressed man. There was no sign of a gun, but Wills couldn't take the chance. Running, he headed toward him, and the spy saw him coming.

Claire was on stage, talking, laughing as she spoke the words of introduction to Colonel Waverly. The guests were beginning to clap, and Wills saw the spy lift his gun aiming it at him, then switching his aim toward the stage.

The gun blast crowded out the warm welcome the colonel was receiving from the people-filled auditorium. A scream interrupted the words from the stage, the attendees stirred, and more screams filled the air.

People began running, screaming, but Wills paid no attention as he threaded—and as gently as he could—moved terrified people out of the way.

Ten more steps, and Wills plowed straight into the back of the man who had turned, preparing to flee. They tumbled to the floor, but surprisingly, the man didn't fight. Instead, he turned his head, his unbelievable blue eyes fastened on Wills, and he grinned even as Wills motioned for a guard to slap handcuffs on the man.

"I never dreamed when I began my duty here that you'd be my nemesis. I'd salute you if my hands weren't handcuffed."

"And I never dreamed I would have ever associated with a murdering spy." Wills jerked him from the floor. "Why, E.I., why?"

The man shrugged. "You know better than to ask that. I was doing my duty. My grandfather taught me well, and if it hadn't been for my father insisting I enter the United States military, I would have defected a long time ago. After Colonel Waverly forced me into that dangerous assignment, and I came back home half the man I was before, I knew I would pay him back and while doing that, do my duty to my beloved homeland, Germany."

"Really, E.I., if that's your real name—"

"It's Ubrecht Muller, after my grandfather. Of course, my father carried the name too, but he was useless to our cause. I got rid of him as soon as I came back. It was the least I could do to honor my beloved grandfather."

Wills stared at the man he'd thought was a friend, a trusted contact. Had it all been a lie?

"So was all the information you fed me a lie? To steer me off track of finding you?"

"You always were too good for this world. Of course, it wasn't all lies. I fed you enough truth to keep you around. I was the tramp who approached Claire, the same one who talked with you late that one night in your home garden and begged for food. I was everywhere, Wills, and you didn't know, although if you'd been smart enough, you'd figured it out a long time ago. I was always one step ahead of you."

What the man was saying was the truth, but Wills wasn't done yet.

"That all might be true, E.I. or Ubrecht, whatever you want to call yourself, but in the end, I'm the one who won the battle, and I'm pretty sure that's all that matters." And then, he nodded to the two servicemen guards and turned his one-time friend/traitor over to them. "Double watch. Don't trust him for one second. He's a slippery fish, and this one we don't want getting away."

Wills turned his back and studied the auditorium. It had thinned out, and only a few stragglers, a few other soldiers, the colonel, Claire and her people stood about. Wills walked to them.

As he approached, Wills called out. "Colonel Waverly, let's get you out of here."

The colonel roared his disapproval. "Mason, have you lost your mind? I'm perfectly able to get home by myself."

"I can't let you do that, Sir. *You* were the target."

For the first time ever, Wills saw shock on the elderly man's face. "Me?"

"You, Sir. As soon as I realized who the spy was, I figured you were his target."

"Tell me quickly what happened."

"There was a young man you sent on a dangerous

275

mission five years ago. He was very talented, but unwilling to go. I believe, Sir, he begged you not to send him. Am I right?"

Colonel Waverly's eyes widened with understanding. "Are you talking about—"

"I am. He is of German descent. Owens is on the phone now, digging into the Millers' background, now that we know who the spy is. I think we're going to find out that our spy today is worse than we ever dreamed."

"Then it's my fault this spy is operating."

Was that sadness in the man's voice?

"No, Sir. Everyone makes their own choices in life."

"Shouldn't you see that he is taken to the cells and not getting loose someway?"

"I have Owens overseeing that, and two trustworthy guards who I know can handle the man. I won't leave you until I know you're safe."

"Are you saying I can't take care of myself?"

"No, Sir, I know you can, but you assigned me to this job, and I have an obligation to carry it through."

"I recognized that stubborn streak in you the first time I saw you, Mason."

"I prefer to call it determination, Sir." Wills motioned to two of the nearby guards. "I want you to stay with the colonel. Do not let him out of your sight, and I want no one—no one—to come near him for any reason, but me. Understood?"

The colonel huffed, but Wills ignored him.

The men nodded, and Wills turned away. Next on his list was to make sure Claire—

The first notes of her musicians' instruments carried to him, and he heard her beautiful voice speaking from the microphone...

"Colonel Waverly, the crowd is dispersed. There are only a handful of us still here, but we'd love to hear you say a few words tonight to *us*. We've so looked forward to it. But before you do that, I want to sing a new song I wrote myself for a certain person. Listen."

Wills, standing with the colonel just at the edge of the curtains, stared at Claire, the love of his life. Would she sing to him?

Carole Brown

It was so unexpected, the love I felt for you. It was so unexpected I was caught unaware. How much you suddenly...unbelievingly...unexpectedly meant to me. Your eyes filled with warmth and love, your lips whispered words that made my heart sing. It was unexpected to know you loved me so, to know...I loved you back.

Minutes later, her song ended with a warm and enthusiastic applause from the few still on the stage. She turned and held out her hand to the colonel, who was strolling toward her.

But then, she moved. At the opposite end of the stage, emerging from behind the curtains, The Dame stepped into view.

Wills stared at her, but before he could do more than register that it was really The Dame, she began speaking. "Heil, Hitler! Our mission will be accomplished with or without our leader."

Her gun lifted, and Wills knew who her target was.

The colonel was halfway across the floor.

Claire whirled and ran, straight toward the colonel, screaming for him to hit the floor. The gun blasted, the colonel flinched, but didn't fall, and Wills saw the gun shift toward Claire.

Wills ran then, and had never raced faster than at that moment. He passed the colonel and plowed straight into Claire, clasping her to him as they tumbled to the floor the exact time the second blast filled their ears.

From the corner of his eyes, Wills saw the soldiers close in on the woman as she managed a third shot. The Colonel dove for the floor, but his body wasn't the only one to fall.

The colonel had managed to pull his own gun and trained it on The Dame. Wills was sure she never realized what had hit her.

The ones still on the stage erupted into a volcano of voices while the colonel, unhurt, rose and bellowed his commands to the guards. Wills didn't see the action, but he could hear the commotion and the words from the colonel when he realized The Dame was dead.

Wills was too busy staring down at Claire, who'd rolled over and was staring up at him.

"Wills?" Her voice was as soft as a whisper, but he heard her plainly.

"Yes, Gorgeous?"

"Do you still think I'm a spy?"

Wills was taken aback for a moment. "Indeed, I do not. Whoever put that thought in your head?"

She tilted her head in the direction of the still-bellowing colonel. "He did. I was hurt at first, then I realized we live in a dangerous world. You have to do what you do even when you don't want to. You're too loyal to do otherwise. And that made me..."

"Made you what?"

She didn't answer his question. "You do know I've changed my mind about you, don't you?"

"I'm not sure I know that. You might have to explain to me what you mean." His mouth twitched as he tried to hold back a smile.

Her eyes twinkled at him. "I've never been able to resist a hero, and now, twice, twice, mind you, you've saved my life."

"I love being *your* hero, Gorgeous."

"There's no one else I'd rather rescue me, Wills Mason."

"I'm amazed and over the moon at your words. But are you sure about that, Claire Anne? There are no doubts, no hesitation, no reservation? Have you prayed about it?"

"Yes, I'm sure, and there are no doubts, hesitations or reservations in me. And no, I haven't prayed—yet. But I plan to be in church Sunday morning, where I will speak to our pastor, who I'm sure you know—Tyrell Walker—and let him know, I'm turning my life over to God."

"Really, Claire?"

"Really, Wills. And if you don't kiss me right away, I do think Colonel Waverly will be over here, whisking you away to some duty he thinks only you can fulfill."

"Are you sure, my love?"

Carole Brown

"More sure than I've ever been about anything." And then she sang a phrase of her last song to him. *"It was so unexpected, the love I felt for you..."*

Wills' kiss put an end to her beautiful singing, and neither man nor woman paid any attention to Colonel Waverly's bellowing voice that demanded Wills' attention.

Chapter Twenty-Seven

Colonel Waverly reread the letter he held in his hands.

Dear Sir,

As you know I requested and you granted me a leave of absence to spend some much needed time with my family. Coming as a surprise to you, I'm sure, will be the notice that Claire Anne Rayner and I were married last night. We talked it over with our family, and they were all for it. It was a simple affair, and both of us want, later, when the war has ended, a lovely dinner and banquet with a select group of friends—including you, and our family.

I wanted to explain a little more about our spy. Albert Miller, the third, was the grandson of the man in that first picture I left with you. He and his grandfather were so much alike, both in greed, lack of compassion toward their fellowman and desire for achievement. The spy's father, the only one of the three who was decent, was the true patriot of America. He immigrated here, and worked hard as a well-known scientist until his death, which we now are confident was done by his own son.

As you know, the man who was one of my best contacts for so long, E.I., was a master of disguise. That's why he was able to work uncover for so long in revealing secrets to the Germans. He used whoever he could to achieve his goals, including Norman Tyson, a person who really didn't know what he was getting into, and Tyson's cousin, Matilda Nelson. Herman McCoy, of course, was her flunky, who unfortunately pushed forward his demise by dreaming of loftier dreams than he could achieve.

Those blue eyes of E.I.'s, at the last, gave him away. And, afterwards, I remembered that tattoo on the underside of his wrist. I should have caught that much sooner.

All of the pertinent information is in the report I wrote

up for you, but I wanted you to know my own thoughts about it all.

It has been a privilege to work with and under you. I appreciate all that you've done in training me to be the best in whatever I do. I accept the promotion to Sergeant Major given to me, and Claire and I have agreed I should continue my work with you for the time being.

One thing though: if you ever tell my gorgeous wife what I'm doing again (like making sure she wasn't a spy) I will have to have a serious talk with you. She's been holding that over my head, and that, my fine colonel, is, as she insists, payback for all those growing-up years when I teased her sorely.

Of course, then, there is the making up part...

I am, as always, your respectful and humble sergeant,
William Mason

The colonel laid down the letter and removed his glasses. Then staring out his window, he chuckled. That boy would never grow up.

The End.

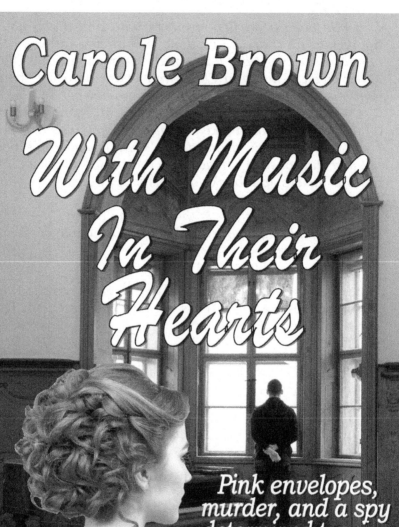

Carole Brown

With Music In Their Hearts

Pink envelopes,
murder, and a spy
determined to win.

The Spies of World War II

Chapter One

December, 1941, Pennsylvania

Rejected.

Tyrell Walker stared down at the evaluation form, up at the government issued photo of President Roosevelt mounted on the wall and back down at the paper in his hand. The single word blazed up at him, sneering and final.

Blood pounded in his head and swirled in his mind along with the patriotic band music blaring from a nearby radio. What was going on? How could this be? He'd been healthy his whole life without a day's sickness other than the usual childhood illnesses. Why all of a sudden was he classified as physically unfit?

And rejected because of it?

"I don't want this." He looked across the steel-gray, military issued desk to the man seated behind it, and tapped the papers in his hand. "This isn't in my plans. I want to serve my country."

Sympathy flickered, then as quickly vanished in the eyes surveying him. The sergeant's shoulders reared back as if to ready himself for an argument. "Those are your orders. Go home."

Sorry? *Sorry?* Tyrell couldn't remember the last time he'd lost his temper. It was all he could do to force back the angry words threatening to spill from his mouth.

But before he could speak, he caught a movement from the corner of his eye. A tall, gray-haired man stood near the door. What was a *two* star general doing here? Close behind him, a red-haired woman hovered, her padded shoulders broad and fashionable, her waist tucked in tightly, a large feathered concoction of a hat

1

settled on her head at an angle. A short, checkered-suited older man slouched...he'd seen him, but where? Was he a prominent businessman the newspapers featured often? Had he seen him at a luncheon? Both men were gazing at him as if he were a specimen from a scientist's lab.

Better keep his mouth shut. Chewing out a low-level sergeant wouldn't do any good.

Giving the sergeant a curt nod, he whirled and exited the building. What now?

He had his preaching ministry, thank God. But he'd had his heart set on enlisting. The nation's declaration of war had spurred him to get a head start on the flood of enlistments. Wasn't this what God wanted or had he missed the plan? Nothing for it but to go ahead and contact the bishop. Still...

A payphone booth stood across the street, and he headed toward it and flung the door open. Inserting the change, he dialed the bishop's number from memory. After the fourth ring, Bishop Victor's secretary picked up and put Tyrell straight through. The man of God's low-key, but confident, voice came across the line.

Tyrell explained what happened, fighting to keep the disgust from his voice. The Bishop might be a gentle man, but he held strict policies for his ministers. Tyrell didn't need him questioning his motives. "Looks like I'll need the appointment we talked about."

A pregnant pause filled with nonverbal questions had him wondering if the bishop had hung up.

"Good choice." Bishop Victor cleared his throat. "We'll find a post for you."

What did he mean? Not the one they'd talked about? Had the post been given to a different ministerial candidate? "What do you—"

"Lots of choices to serve your country." Warmth filled the old man's voice. "God's plans for you, my son—"

"What are you saying?"

"I have next Monday open. Come by, and I'll give you the details." Bishop Victor hung up.

Knuckles tingling, Tyrell squeezed the receiver in his clenched fist and narrowed his eyes. The man had been too chipper. As if he'd known Tyrell would call. The bishop's former concern whether Tyrell should enlist had been replaced with—satisfaction.

For the life of him, he had no idea what he'd done to deserve two slaps in the face in one day. Tyrell stepped out of the booth and glanced at the cloudy sky. No sign of the sun, and no sign of God's face smiling down ready to do battle for him.

The building he'd left stood dark and brooding, not at all inviting or even encouraging to those who might wish a little before signing away several years of duty. It was suspicious, if you asked him. Why the rejection when he was healthier than a athlete? Who were the two men staring at him in the draft station? And why was the bishop playing tiddly-winks with the truth? If he was.

Odd. Very odd.

Flagging a taxi, he crawled into the back seat and gave directions to a hotel. As the driver pulled away from the curb, Tyrell cast another look at the building.

A long, black Oldsmobile Special pulled from the driveway, and for a moment, suspicion chewed at his nerves. Ridiculous. The driver could be a chauffeur going after a military dignitary or delivering one. He slouched in his seat, the better to study the car. But instead of falling way behind the speeding taxi, the car kept pace twenty feet or so behind them.

The familiar tingle tickled his neck. The one that had clued him in right before every trick his best pal had tried on him.

Ten minutes later, the taxi driver's guttural voice broke into his thoughts. "Say, mister. What you done anyway?"`

"What?"

"I figure you're either in big time crime or an important man."

Neither of those described him. "Why is that?"

The coffee-colored eyes of the taxi driver met Tyrell's gaze in his rearview mirror. "Cause the way a certain big black car is staying on our tail. Tried to lose them, but..."

His driver's brows wagged, admiration edging his

voice. "Whoever's driving knows what he's doing."

No wonder this ride seemed to take forever. Tyrell glanced out the back window. The car from the government building was following *him*? He doubted that.

"Don't want to get involved in any shooting, man."

Shooting? Tyrell motioned for the guy to stop. He flipped a bill across the seat, exited, and slammed the door. He'd see what would happen now. The driver's fear seemed groundless, but was it?

Resting his palms on the top of the taxi, he glanced back at the idling car. Not good. Slapping the taxi top, he moved back as it sped away, then headed the opposite direction.

The car came to a crawl behind him.

The street ahead was deserted except for the two old men lounging against a brick wall, alone and still, except for the occasional puffs on the cigarettes dangling from the sides of their mouths.

On a quick whim, he crossed, took the next house's sidewalk, circled around the porch, and sprinted around the place onto a graveled alley. Two blocks away, to the left, stood the flashing sign of his hotel. Tyrell turned left.

A vehicle's tires spinning gravel behind him warned him he'd not lost the black car. Slowing. Creeping. Engine purring. Only a few feet separated him from the car and making a sudden decision, he jogged around the corner and hugged the building trying to put distance between them. The car's tires squealed as the car sped up. The driver took the corner, gravel crunching and spinning into the air.

They must have spotted him for the driver braked, throwing the passenger forward. Tyrell flung himself at the car and grabbed for the door handle.

The window slid down.

Something tugged at his arm.

And the handle tore from his grasp as the car accelerated.

The seemingly belated, reverberating crack of a gun vibrated the air around him.

The car spun around a far corner, and Tyrell reached up to rub his stinging arm. The sticky wetness drew his attention.

Blood. He saw the tear in his coat sleeve, the minute traces of blood oozing.

He'd been shot?

Why would they—whoever they were—want to shoot at him? It was a scratch, and they'd been close enough to kill him if they'd wanted to.

They didn't want to. What *were* they after? A scare tactic? To warn him away? From what? Perhaps all this was a coincidence, a figment of his active imagination.

No sign of the car. Satisfied he was rid of them, he entered the hotel. At the reception desk, he filled out the necessary papers, climbed the stairs, and headed down the hallway.

At the far end, a red-haired woman inserted a key into the lock.

Was she the same woman who'd been in the recruitment office? That hat. ..He called out, "Hey, lady."

Her glance peeked from beneath her luxurious hat, tilted at just the right angle to hide one side of her face. With a flip of her plaid skirt, she shoved open her door and disappeared inside.

Tyrell hesitated at his own door, next to her's, but inserted his key and entered. Inside, he switched on a light then as quickly flicked it off. He stepped to the window.

And drew in a breath as if he'd been sucker-punched.

Down below, across from the hotel, the streetlight reflected off a long, black Oldsmobile Standing beside the car staring up at the hotel, stood Ben Hardy.

His cousin and best friend.

Chapter Two

"I've got the person." The smallish man smoothed a mustache too big for his face. His conspiratorial grin was aimed at the man seated opposite him. He crossed his legs and adjusted the crease in his checkered pants.

The other man didn't smile. His immaculate dress and stiff spine shouted, don't mess with me! His stiff, starchy attitude demanded respect. "He's got to have nerves of steel to penetrate the plant's security."

A chuckle, as if the two were the best of friends. "Oh, you won't have to worry about this one. She's up for anything."

"She?"

"Sure. Won't find a better candidate."

Blue Eyes stroked his chin, his cold, cold eyes measuring the other. "She proficient in secretarial work?"

"Let me say, you won't be sorry she's on your side. She's sharp, can keep quiet, and likes money. And the best secretary I've seen."

For the first time, Blue Eyes smiled. "Excellent. We're going to need rooms—"

"Done. Rayner Boarding House on Mulberry is perfect for what we need."

"You know these people?"

"The father owes me. My efforts in the senate have been instrumental in several jobs landing in his lap." Small man recrossed his legs.

"I see. You've already contacted him?"

Small Man nodded. "He'll cooperate. Sent a note to him with a list of those needing rooms.

"What? That's a cock-eyed action."

"Ease up He has no idea why."

"This infernal noise is driving me crazy." Blue Eyes

stomped across the room and flicked off the radio. The jazz music stopped abruptly, the silence ominous.

The small man shoved a piece of paper across the desk, and Blue Eyes studied it. "Who are these people?"

"A list of tenants and prospective ones at the boarding house. The first two are a husband and wife. A very important couple."

"I see. And this last name?"

"I happened to be at the right place at the right time. I went to see General Bridges on an entirely different matter and overheard a vital piece of information."

"What does that have to do with us?" Blue Eyes snarled. Disdain couldn't have been any thicker.

"Orders from above were to reject this guy's enlistment and send him on to Cincinnati to check out a certain spy." Small Man rubbed his hands together in glee. "Being the outstanding citizen I am, I recommended the Rayner Boarding House. If there's snooping, we need to keep our eyes open, wouldn't you say?"

For the first time, approval shone in Blue Eyes' voice. "Well done. And which name is our secretary?"

A stubby finger pointed at a name on the list.

Blue eyes met Small Man's smirk with a jerky nod.

The small man sat back in his seat. "Going to need any more flunkies?"

"Got it covered." He strolled to the window and peered down at the street. "I don't want any hitches."

"Trust me."

Blue eyes whirled, the fanatical intelligence blazing. "I trust no one. Not even you."

Small Man didn't hesitate. "I didn't get where I am today by any pussyfooting. I want my share of the money." His words were hard, his voice brisk.

"You'll get it. I want no mistakes on your part. I'll not tolerate any slip-ups."

Small Man met the other man's gaze and held it for a long moment. When he dropped his, he realized he'd failed a test. If push came to shove, he wouldn't be the one to come out on top.

Chapter Three

January, 1942, Cincinnati, Ohio

Claire's red lips parted, and her sigh ripped through Emma Jaine Rayner's heart, sending a wave of remorse through her body.

Her head throbbed from the tension of pushing a foot-dragging sister to do her best. That, and the worry over certain tenants had her nerves stretched as tight as piano string. "Let's try that hymn one more time."

"Leslie and I planned on going shopping this afternoon. Can't I for once have fun?" The plaintive whine melted her will. Petulant blue eyes flared at her a hair short of rebellion.

"You still don't have that measure in the third line correct and insist on holding the second note when you need to go up. Both are quarter notes."

Her younger sister brushed at a strawberry blond curl falling against her cheek.

"Your lessons with the new professor begin next week. You insisted you wanted to study under him and need to be in top form before you begin."

The tense lips relaxed. "Of course, I do, but I don't see why I can't have more time for fun. All I do is work, work, work."

"You've already spent most of the afternoon listening to 'The Shadow' on Papa's radio." Emma Jaine drew in a deep breath. "You love to sing, dear."

Sinking into the nearby wingback chair, Claire's shoulders drooped, her boxy, sailor top showing off her slenderness. "Not for eight hours a day. And not to sing a song for Sunday morning worship."

"You're exaggerating. That's..." Claire had given subtle hints that her interest in music was waning. Why hadn't she taken notice before now?

Her sister took her stance beside the piano again, and Emma Jaine let her fingers beguile the music from the piano keys. The words of the majestic hymn, "A Mighty Fortress is our God" flowed from her sister's throat, tightening her own.

She steeled her wavering will. She wouldn't give in to Claire's pleadings for less practice and more fun. Her sister had outstanding talent, and keeping her from becoming sidetracked was Emma Jaine's duty. She owed her that even if her social-conscious sister didn't appreciate the encouragement right now.

At the same difficult measure, a deep, rich voice rang out, guided, led, and lifted Claire's where it should go. Emma Jaine's fingers fumbled on the keys and then scrambled for the right ones to accompany Claire and the powerful voice.

The two singers reached the finale, the blending voices so exquisite Emma Jaine caught her breath. She swiveled on the piano bench.

In the entryway, a man leaned against the doorway. The briefest hint of a smile touched his lips. His arms folded across his chest, a Homburg dangling from his fingers. Black hair shone in the sunlight beaming through the narrow window nearby and cast blue tinted jewels of color through the strands. Lively, intense eyes blazed with life. The scent of spice wafted toward her.

Had her secret dream come true or was he a vision? Maybe her eyes were playing traitor and conjuring up a man or was she plain starved for male fellowship?

Who was he?

Emma Jaine shivered and caught herself from leaning forward. His eyes shone the deepest moss green she'd ever seen.

The corners of those eyes crinkled.

She'd been staring straight into a gaze locked on her own. With her heart beating like African drums, she tilted her head. "You've got a magnificent voice." Embarrassment iced her tone.

"I spent four years at the Yale Conservatory of Music." His speaking voice coaxed pure music from his inner being. "Sorry to walk in, but I knocked several times,

9

and no one answered. Wanted a closer listen to this talented young lady and couldn't resist chiming in."

Four years at Yale? Impressive. She glanced at Claire and frowned at the starry-eyed gaze the girl bestowed upon the man. Best to take matters into her own hands.

"I'm Emma Jaine Rayner and this is my younger sister, Claire."

The stranger inclined his head. "I'm interested in renting a room, and your place was recommended."

Her sister sashayed across the room, her pleated skirt swinging provocatively. Emma Jaine repressed the urge to swat her. At sixteen, the girl radiated the promise of a beautiful woman and practiced her womanly wiles with come-hither glances on any attractive man in her vicinity.

Emma Jaine cleared her throat, but Claire paid no attention. Her smile outshone a thousand-watt bulb when she gushed her admiration. "I love your voice. You wouldn't want to sing a duet with me Sunday morning at our church, would you? It's so-o-o boring singing by myself."

The man hadn't moved from his place at the doorway. Emma Jaine hurried to interrupt. "I'm sure he's too busy to cater to your wishes. He won't have time to bother."

Ignoring her, Claire smiled up at him, her eyes pleading for her own way.

"On the contrary, I'll be at your church Sunday." His gaze softened. "If your sister doesn't mind, I'd love to sing with you."

Claire reddened. Emma Jaine's heart ached for the girl's obvious pleasure. She wished she could scoop her up and assure her exaggerated actions weren't needed. Claire's naturally sweet nature defied any artificial or forward means of winning admiration from future admirers.

The girl's gaze dropped to the floor and swept back up to the man in a deliberate flirt. His response was another brotherly smile, and she sauntered out of the room, the scent of her flowery cologne lingering long after her footsteps echoed down the hallway.

Frowning, Emma Jaine turned her attention back to him.

He strolled about the room, stopped to study the portrait of her mother over the mantel and pulled a book off a shelf.

Emma Jaine thrust her chin higher. How could he be nonchalant after invading her home and allowing a sixteen-year-old child to flirt with him? "You're certainly good with young people, but please, don't encourage her to flaunt herself."

The man glanced at her and the corners of his mouth inched upward. "With me? Never even occurred to me. I like young people. They're open with their emotions and refreshingly honest." He replaced the book. "I've been appointed to temporarily serve as the new minister at Grace Community."

"Our church?" A tsunami wave of shock spread through her. This man was their new minister? This man she was prepared to...dislike?

Dislike because he was handsome and confident? Arrogant was more like it. Because Claire wanted to flirt with him? Claire didn't mean anything.

"What do you say? Do you have any rooms available for rent?" He stood twirling his hat, not a hair out of place, not a wrinkle in his immaculate pin-striped suit, his shoes as shiny as the day they'd been bought.

Ugh. Her own everyday dress had seen much more wear; was, in fact, a hand-me-down from her own mother's never ending supply of dresses. True, she'd revamped it to a more modern style, but still...Emma Jaine pulled herself back from the blankness. "Why won't you be staying in the rectory provided by the church?"

"Since I probably won't be here long, I've decided not to bring any furnishings with me. The church board agrees the best solution would be to secure a small furnished place close to the church."

A fishy explanation that was overly long. "We only have a second floor apartment available. I'm sure it would never be—"

"Perfect."

11

His exuberance irritated Emma Jaine. He was too...too perfect. Much too tempting for her sisters. Especially Claire. And his presence would disturb the pleasant placidity of their home.

Who was she kidding? With the problems in her own home threatening to break out, *she* was anything but placid.

But more to the point, how could she refuse a minister? *Their* new minister.

"Meals are provided?"

"What?" She shook her head, trying to rid her brain from the errant thoughts. "We offer two regular meals a day. A buffet breakfast from six thirty to ten a.m. and supper promptly at seven thirty p.m. A light lunch is extra, but can be arranged."

"Two meals will be fine. Is the apartment ready for me to move into now?"

"It is. Why is the position temporary?"

"We live in troublesome times. With many young fellows enlisting there's a shortage of pastors." His eyes darkened to an evergreen. "Just following orders."

"That's ridiculous." Traveling ministers did serve many of the country churches that could not afford hire a fulltime minister. But her church? In 1942? As one of the largest and richest in the state, they could easily afford a minister with no duties but ministering to the congregation.

His lips curved in a teasing smile. "You do what you have to do and learn to live with your decisions."

Emma Jaine shrugged. "I don't like haphazardness, and I still think such a thing is ridiculous."

His head inclined toward her. "Thanks for your observation."

Anger at his teasing sent heat to her face, but she bit back her retort. He was to be their pastor, he said. "Would you like to see the rooms?"

"I would."

Emma Jaine stood and closed the book of music on the piano. She moved toward the hallway, and the charisma that radiated from him bombarded her back. She shivered again.

A rambunctious shout echoed from the top of the staircase. Emma Jaine jerked her head up in time to see Josie, dressed in pants, sliding down the banister with Wills Mason right behind her. Both jumped and landed in a heap on the floor, their gasps of laughter filling the hallway.

"How could you, Josie May Rayner?" Emma Jaine propped her hands on her hips. "Couldn't you be more reserved now that we have boarders?"

Josie's vibrant cinnamon-brown eyes glinted with glee, daring her older sister to object. She reached up a hand to smooth back the chestnut curls tumbling across her forehead. "Wills dared me. I haven't ridden those stair rails in years."

Wills stretched full length on the flowered carpet rug, ankles crossed and hands propped behind his head. "Most fun I've had in weeks. Want another go, Jos?"

"Your mother called for you a half hour ago." Emma Jaine's affection for the lad kept her tone lighthearted.

The tall young man jumped up and saluted Emma Jaine. The mischief in his eyes caused them to shine like polished mahogany. His teen-aged, sardonic tone pushed his luck. "Yes, ma'am. I finished my chores, and I'm off till four. Ma'am."

The rascal. She didn't care about Wills's chores. But for Wills to act like he was eight was one thing. A different matter for her sister. "Get out of here before I find work for you myself. And, Wills, I'm not your ma'am."

"Yes, ma'am." Wills agreed and ducked as if expecting a punch. Winking at Josie, eyes twinkling with the promise of more mischief at a later date, he swaggered down the hall, his chuckles drifting back to the threesome.

Emma Jaine sighed at Josie's studied attitude of ignoring her.

The man stepped forward, extended a hand and helped the girl to her feet.

Josie smoothed her wrinkled blouse and tried again to brush back rumpled hair. She drew the ribbon from her hair, shrugged and stuffed it into a pocket.

"Don't be such a fuddy-duddy." Her words, if not exactly scornful, were filled with daring.

"I'm going to be old before my time trying to make a lady out of you. Are you ever going to grow up?"

"Don't scold, Emma Jaine."

The man beside her piped up. "Am I meeting Cincinnati's most famous ice skater?"

"I hope to be.' Josie dimpled at the stranger's comment. Her eyes met the man's with openness and speculation. "And I'm Josie. Emma Jaine didn't care to introduce us."

"Never mind, Josie." Emma Jaine interrupted. "Did you get your flute practice in today?"

"Horsefeathers, no."

"Don't use slang. Papa hates it. And please make sure to change for supper tonight. Last night I thought a ragamuffin had visited." She grinned to take the sting from her words. "My favorite ragamuffin."

Josie ran down the hall and shot a retort over her shoulder. "I like my clothes."

Emma Jaine watched her go, aware that the new pastor stood beside her, studying them both.

His low voice spoke next to her ear. "You've got your hands full."

She jumped and realized his face hovered inches from hers. Her gaze dropped to his lips, and she sucked in a breath. Shakily, she stepped back. "I don't mind. I love the responsibility and count caring for them a privilege."

"Circumstances are a heavy load on small shoulders." His gaze locked on her, the barest hint of a smile tipping his lips. "Too much makes for a wrinkled face if you're not careful."

"You don't need to concern yourself about me or my wrinkles."

"Right. It's not any of my business."

Was he laughing? "Are you ready to check out the rooms?"

She led the way up the worn, but intricately-carved dark oak stairs, and a tingle of pleasure rippled through her as she slid her hand over the smooth wood of the banister.

"Who is Wills?"

"Wills is our live-in helps' seventeen-year-old son. He's grown up with us and is like a brother."

"You're fond of him."

"I am. He tries to associate with Claire, but he's too rambunctious for her. He and Josie get into mischief together."

"He seems like a decent young man."

"Baseball, swimming, and his schooling keeps him occupied. Thank God."

"He goes to public school?"

"Papa's talked with Jonah about sending him to college if he continues to do well." The apartment door creaked. She made a mental note to oil the hinges, flicked on the light and moved aside so he could view the room.

It was a comfortable room, and one of Emma Jaine's favorites. The warm browns and cool blues were an even contrast with just the right amount of rugs to soften the difference. The filmy curtains at the windows lent elegance to the space but not too much, while the modern striped spread begged for a man's presence. Overall, a satisfying living area.

Striding to the bed, the prospective renter bounced once and shot her a grin like a mischievous boy. He stared at a wall painting—a vivid aqua sky surrounding the silver plane—above the bureau before pulling out a drawer. Stepping to the window, he pulled aside the curtain. In a swift motion he touched his forehead and let the curtain drop back into place.

Her senses went on alert. Had he *signaled* someone?

"I'll go after my luggage and return..." he glanced at his watch, "...around six fifteen in time for supper."

"Fine. I'll inform Harriet. We usually meet in the front room about fifteen to twenty minutes prior to supper for socializing. Anything else you'll need?"

"How many sets of keys do you keep?"

"Jonah keeps an extra set, but they're locked up. Why?"

"Hmmm." Tyrell rubbed his chin. "Who are the other tenants?"

"We have three other apartments on this floor. Yours is the front one overlooking the street. The other three-room apartment is directly behind yours. Hamilton Blake rents it."

"Who is he?"

"The Vice President of Prescott Bank. He's been here three months." How pompous. As if she was proud of his achievements.

"Is he close to your family?"

"Not at all." Why did she want to squirm like a child in trouble?

"Sounded—"

"It sounded like nothing." She'd firmly squash any surmising on his part.

He swiveled away. "Right."

Emma Jaine caught his knowing smirk. He had baited her to get a rise out of her and had succeeded. Would she ever learn to control her temper?

She gritted her teeth. This man—*this minister*—was going to be one aggravating tenant. The discordant note in their usual peaceful atmosphere.

"Ministers are usually calm, dignified, and nice." Emma Jaine prodded. *Not men with breath-taking eyes.*

He grinned. "I'm not *your* usual minister."

"You're not *my* minister in any way." That retort ought to put him in his place.

"Don't you attend—"

"Yes, but—." The broad grin spreading across his tanned face sent her spinning around. No need to linger long enough for him to turn her little victory into his.

With long strides, he headed down the long stairwell. "I'd like to get a detailed list of everyone living here. Would you have time to write it up before this evening?"

"A detailed list?" Emma Jaine paused at the top of the stairs. "Whatever for?"

His green eyes glinted. "Might be a robber in the house."

"There are no robbers in this house."

"You never can tell. Anyhow, I'd like to invite them to church." He sketched a small salute and was gone.

Emma Jaine stared out the hall window. A movement

from across the street caught her attention. A figure moved away from the tree and paused as if studying the house.

She pulled back from the window.

The front door opened, closed, and her new renter hurried onto the sidewalk. The other guy had gone, but her renter dawdled at the gate, then turned left as if... Was he following the guy?

Maybe he was an impostor and not a minister.

Nonsense. She'd been listening to way too many Orson Wells programs. Her fingers gripped the banister. Who was he? Did he think he could enter her boarding home, give orders, and pry into her business? And those teasing eyes of his...She swallowed.

Starting down the stairs, her mind whirled in confusion. She'd always been a fair hostess, never speaking harshly to anyone living here. And in the past half hour she had done so to this man any number of times.

But worst of all—Emma Jaine moaned to herself as she sat down on the bottom step—she'd rented an apartment to that scalawag of a minister. He'd signaled while standing at the window. And he obviously loved to torment.

Dear Lord, what have I done?

She'd not even gotten his name.

Emma Jaine dropped her head in her hands. She was losing it. How could she have forgotten to do such a minute task?

She had a sneaking suspicion he could cause her to lose what sense she had left.

Other Books by Carole Brown

Denton and Alex Davies Mysteries:
Hog Insane
Bat Crazy

Spies of World War II
With Music In Their Hearts
A Flute in the Willows
Sing Until You Die

The Appleton WV Mysteries
Sabotaged Christmas
Knight in Shining Apron
Undiscovered Treasures
Toby's Troubles

Troubles in the West
Caleb's Destiny

Women's Fiction:
The Redemption of Caralynne Haymen

Misc
West Virginia Scrapbook
Christmas Angels (WW II short story in the Anthology *From the Lake to the River*)

Carole Brown has spent time as a newspaper reporter, as well as a journal and newsletter editor. When not penning her own novels, she mentors beginning writers and serves as Coordinator of the Ohio Chapter of the American Christian Fiction Writers.

Carole and Dan, her pastor husband, reside in SE Ohio and have ministered and counseled across the country. Together, they enjoy their grandsons, traveling, gardening, good food, and the simple life.

An award winning author, Carole Brown loves to weave suspense and tough topics into her books, along with a touch of romance and whimsy.

Carole loves to connect with her readers. You can find her at her blog: unnebnkwrtr.blogspot.com/

And on facebook:

www.facebook.com/CaroleBrown.author

If you enjoyed reading this book, let others know...and bless Carole Brown with an honest review.